$\mathcal{H}$e stood there studying her, not smiling. Then his eyes drifted down over her body. No one had ever looked at her that way before, the heat tangible, making her feel both panicked and excited.

Then everything changed.

It happened so fast that she didn't have time to think. One minute she was holding on to being sensible Chloe, smart, sane, safe, her life as it had always been. Then the next she whispered, "Kiss me."

One long beat of silence passed before a tremor raced through him. "With your innocent blue eyes and mouth meant for sin, you look like you could easily steal something I've never been willing to give," he stated cryptically.

But before she could question him, he groaned and cursed. Then this stranger pulled her into his arms. . . .

Also by Linda Francis Lee
Published by Ivy Books:

DOVE'S WAY
SWAN'S GRACE
NIGHTINGALE'S GATE
THE WAYS OF GRACE
LOOKING FOR LACEY
THE WEDDING DIARIES
SUDDENLY SEXY

Sinfully Sexy

A Novel

Linda Francis Lee

IVY BOOKS • NEW YORK

An Ivy Book
Published by The Random House Publishing Group

Copyright © 2004 by Linda Francis Lee

All rights reserved under International and Pan-American Copyright Conventions. Published in the United States by The Random House Publishing Group, a division of Random House, Inc., New York, and simultaneously in Canada by Random House of Canada Limited, Toronto.

This book contains an excerpt from the forthcoming book *Simply Sexy* by Linda Francis Lee. This excerpt has been set for this edition only and may not reflect the final content of the forthcoming edition.

Ivy Books and colophon are trademarks of Random House, Inc.

www.ballantinebooks.com

ISBN 0-345-46272-6

Manufactured in the United States of America

First Edition: October 2004

OPM 9 8 7 6 5 4 3 2 1

Cover by Sally Cato, Design Management, NYC

Sinfully Sexy

PHOTO COPY

From the desk of Julia Boudreaux

Chloe, here's a copy of the quiz I was telling you about that I found in <u>Sexy!</u> magazine. Answer and return. Kate has already taken the copy I sent her and passed with flying colors.   xoxo, j

Julia, I can't believe you were serious about taking one of those <u>Sexy!</u> quizzes. They're a cliché. But fine, here are my answers. —Chloe

Sexy! Sex Appeal Quiz
How Sexy Are You?

MULTIPLE CHOICE

1. If a man doesn't touch you on a first date, you automatically assume he:
    a. Is not attracted to you
    b. Must be gay
    c. Is nervous or shy

    Touching? On a first date?

2. If you were reincarnated as an animal, which would you be?
    a. A sleek, prowling tiger
    b. An elegantly aloof panther
    c. A beautifully regal Persian cat

Why can't they be more original with their choices? How about something like a llama? A versatile, trustworthy animal that can be counted on. Am I allowed to write in answers?

d. A uniquely lovely llama—I choose d.

3. If you were flirting with a man at a party, he'd be most likely to say:
   a. You know how to have fun, wild thing.
   b. You could use a drink, babe.
   c. You look like Trouble with a capital T.

   d. Given my habit of attracting the completely wrong sorts of men, a man might as well be wearing a sign on his chest that says: Hey babe, I'm Trouble with a capital T, and I promise I'll break your heart.

WORD ASSOCIATION

1. Hottest Hunk = *Jalapeño Jack Cheese*
2. Sweetest Sensation = *Triple-layer velvet cake with whipped cream icing*
3. Perfect Position = *Curled up on the sofa, reading a good book*

To: Chloe Sinclair <chloe@ktextv.com>
Katherine Bloom <katherine@ktextv.com>
From: Julia Boudreaux <julia@ktextv.com>
Subject: Stunned

Chloe, sugar, how is it possible that you failed a *Sexy!* quiz?

xo, j

To: Julia Boudreaux <julia@ktextv.com>
Chloe Sinclair <chloe@ktextv.com>
From: Katherine Bloom <katherine@ktextv.com>
Subject: No offense but . . .

. . . is it *possible* to fail a *Sexy!* quiz?

Just wondering,
Kate

Katherine C. Bloom
News Anchor, KTEX TV West Texas

To: Katherine Bloom <katherine@ktextv.com>
Chloe Sinclair <chloe@ktextv.com>
From: Julia Boudreaux <julia@ktextv.com>
Subject: Chloe's *Sexy!* Quiz—DOWNLOAD NOW

Kate, for animal, she wrote in *llama*. Need I say more? However, I've scanned her answers and attached. All you have to do is download and judge for yourself.

xo, j

<<attachment>>

To: Julia Boudreaux <julia@ktextv.com>
Katherine Bloom <katherine@ktextv.com>
From: Chloe Sinclair <chloe@ktextv.com>
Subject: Maligned

Hey, a llama is a perfectly respectable lifestyle reincarnation choice—a fine animal that is not given due credit.

And Julia, you might own this station, but I'm the manager. So both of you GET TO WORK!

Chloe Sinclair
Station Manager
Award-winning KTEX TV

To: Chloe Sinclair <chloe@ktextv.com>
Katherine Bloom <katherine@ktextv.com>
From: Julia Boudreaux <julia@ktextv.com>
Subject: Fine

Whatever. And speaking of work, I can't make the party tonight at
the Hilton Hotel. Kate already has wildly romantic plans with Jesse
of the unable-to-change sort, so that leaves you, Chloe. You have to
go in my stead. Please wear something partyish . . . and try to think
more like a feline than a llama. I'll send something over to your
house for you to wear.

xo, j

p.s. I've hired a man named Trey Tanner to give us a comprehensive
analysis of the station. Short-range prospects, long-term viability,
and such. We're meeting with him tomorrow morning in the
conference room. 10 a.m. Don't be late.

o n e

It never would have happened if she hadn't taken that quiz.

At least it never would have happened if she hadn't taken it and failed.

Failed.

Her.

Chloe Sinclair, who had never failed a test in her life.

Granted, she hadn't been particularly serious when she took the *Sexy!* quiz, writing in her responses instead of choosing one of the multiple choice answers. Deep down she knew it was ridiculous to be upset, since she hadn't taken it seriously. More than that, what did an idiotic quiz like that really mean? Nothing. She knew it. But what had started out as a joke had touched a nerve that she hadn't realized was raw.

Failing—or perhaps the fact that she hadn't even tried to pass—spoke to the reality of something deeper. She had given up on any sort of love life and devoted every ounce of energy to her job as station manager of KTEX TV. But as far as she was concerned, the cutthroat world of television programming and advertising revenue was a piece of cake compared to the convoluted labyrinth that was the male mind.

She was mature; men were not.

She wanted inspiring, intellectual dialogue; men wanted sex.

But she had promised herself that she wouldn't have sex again with any man until she knew it was right, until she knew that he was the man she was meant to be with. Which meant one, and only one, thing.

She hadn't had a lot of sex recently.

Given her answers on the *Sexy!* magazine quiz, she had to wonder if she'd ever have sex again.

Had she really filled in the second question with *llama*? She suppressed an embarrassed cringe. Sure, llamas were an industrious animal, but she had also heard they spit.

As if *that* was the problem with her answer.

Earlier that evening, while getting ready for the cocktail reception for the Heart Association that was being held at the Hilton Hotel, Chloe had dressed in her usual, simple black cocktail dress that she wore to just that sort of business/social obligation. But when she had looked at herself in the entry hall mirror, taking in her straight shoulder-length dark hair cut in a sensible bob, her oversized glasses, and the bangs that made her look twelve instead of twenty-seven, she was reminded of her grandmother's constant refrain.

"Thank your lucky stars you were born plain-looking, Chloe love. Your gift is being smart and sensible. Don't ever let that desert you."

Her grandmother had died a year ago, and still, even missing her every day, Chloe had to wonder how being plain could possibly be a plus on anyone's list of Great Things to Be.

That's when she realized why an idiotic magazine quiz could upset her so much. Lucky or not, she *was* plain. She wasn't sexy. Or perhaps more accurately, she had never even tried to be sexy.

That's when everything changed. One minute she was headed to the kitchen for the decadent comfort of a slice of triple-layer velvet cake with whipped cream icing, then the next, something she hadn't recognized flared inside her. She wanted to feel beautiful. She wanted to feel sexy. She wanted to forget the carefully mapped out rules for acceptable and respectable female behavior that her grandmother had instilled in her.

She should have had the cake.

Instead, her heart had pounded when she hurried back to her bedroom. With quick strokes, her hands practically shaking with a mix of trepidation and excitement, she put makeup and blush on over her pale white skin and dusting of freckles, lipstick over her lips, and mascara on her rarely mascaraed eyelashes. She even curled her straight hair, swept back her bangs, and pulled it all up in an elaborate twist. She even wore the dress Julia had sent over.

Thirty minutes later, standing in front of the mirror a second time, Chloe hadn't recognized herself.

No one would call her a llama tonight.

There was just one tiny little problem now that she sat in the hotel parking lot, wearing the dress and even the silky gloves that had sex appeal written all over them.

She couldn't bring herself to get out of the car.

She sat there having sheer, unadulterated second thoughts about how she was dressed. The determination and bravado that had gotten her this far was swept off like a hat in the late September wind that had decided to pick up the second she drove into the parking lot—like some sort of sign that she had no business going inside dressed as she was. But she had promised Julia she would attend, and it was too late to drive all the way home and change. She was the designated KTEX TV representative for the evening, and as the station's general manager, she knew she had to show up.

Without a parking valet or doorman in sight at the small hotel, Chloe turned off the ignition, then gathered the impractical purse that didn't have room in it for anything more than blush, a brush, and some breath mints. Not her usual priorities. But tonight, Chloe felt like anything but her usual self.

The second she stepped out of the car, a gust of wind kicked up, the sort that rushed across the city, gathering speed until it hit the towering peaks of Mount Franklin. The car door slammed shut and she was carried along in a rush of wind that pushed her through the parking lot on heels so high that she felt like she was teetering on her toes. She could hardly see where she was going, and for half a second she tried to cover her hair with her hands. But fancy hairstyles were forgotten when every ounce of her concentration was consumed by staying on her feet.

"Ahhh!" she cried out into the wind, the sound carried off.

She plunged across the tarmac, the bite of sand stinging her skin as she headed the short distance to the hotel. She could barely see for the churning wind, her hair pulling free, whipping against her face. She thought she was alone. But without warning, she ran into another body. Hard. Jarring them both.

The impact sent her lurching forward, arms extended like she was flying. It happened so fast that she couldn't regain her balance. Her gloved hands hit the pavement first, the tiny chain on the purse like a vise around her wrist.

Next, her knees crashed into the ground and pain shot through her. She lay there stunned.

"Are you all right?"

A man's voice, deep and commanding, came at her in a disjointed muffle through the wind. She tried to pick herself up, but before she could manage, strong hands came around her, and he swept her up with ease. She tried to make out who he was, but he was much taller than she, and she couldn't see more than his shirt when he pulled her close, his body blocking the wind.

Huddled together, he propelled them the remaining few steps to the hotel entrance. Despite the pain, she was very aware of the man's touch, of the way his arm was secure around her, the way he controlled her body easily. She had the altogether foreign thought that she was safe.

The hotel's sliding doors whooshed open, then closed behind them. The sudden calm after the storm felt like a deafening echo against her ears. Her eyes stung from the sand, and her knees burned. She could hear the low murmur of voices from the reception in the distance. There were several people in the lobby in varying states of dishevelment from the wind.

"Are you okay?" the man asked again, his hands clasped around her arms to keep her steady.

Her curls fell in tangles from her once-elegant twist. She could feel that her dress was askew and her gloves were ripped to shreds. All the effort she had gone to to get ready was ruined.

She was a mess, making it impossible to attend the party now. "Fine, fine," she stated bleakly.

She felt him tense, felt the heat of him in the simple touch of his hand. "You aren't so fine," he stated with calm insistence.

"What?"

He took her elbow and guided her away from the lobby. He swept her along again, but when they came to a set of double doors leading to the hotel guests' rooms, she stiffened.

"Where are you taking me?"

"I'm staying here."

"You're taking me here, as in to your . . . your . . ."

"Room?"

"Exactly," she stated primly. "I can't go to your room."

He made some kind of grumbling noise deep in his chest, but instead of guiding her through the doors, he tugged her away and soon had her inside an elegant ladies' room decorated in marble and brass. Thankfully, it was empty. Though not as thankfully, he slid the lock home.

"Now what are you doing?"

"You're bleeding."

"Bleeding?"

He pointed.

"Oh," was all she managed to say when she glanced down at herself and got a really good look. Her once-shimmering thigh-high stockings were ripped beyond repair, blood and grit marking both of her knees like a six-year-old's after a playground fall.

On top of that, she had never been all that great with blood.

"Oh," she repeated, this time sort of wobbly.

"Don't go weak willed on me now."

"I am not weak willed," she stated, her spine straightening.

"That's what I like to hear."

Next thing she knew, he had her up on the marble counter as if she didn't weigh anything at all, her skirt riding high. That was when she looked up and saw his face.

Her first real look. She wasn't sure if she sucked in her breath or if she sighed. She only knew that her world went still.

They stared at each other, she on the sink with her chin tilted slightly, he standing so close that his thighs touched her knees. He looked as surprised as she felt.

It seemed like an eternity that their gazes locked, but it probably wasn't more than a second.

He looked as commanding as he had acted. He was tall, his dark hair brushed back, his dark eyes filled with intelligence, knowing and confident. His autocratic control of the situation was apparent in the hard line of his square jaw. This was a man used to getting what he wanted.

He wore a finely made shirt that molded to broad shoulders and narrowed into a lean waist and long legs. Standing there, he appeared to be in charge of his surroundings, not giving a second thought to being in a ladies' bathroom with the door locked and a woman he didn't know. He didn't smile or say a word, though his gaze seemed to draw her to him. But after another second, his eyes narrowed fractionally and he gave a barely perceptible shake of his head before he focused on her scrapes.

"Let me look at your hands."

He didn't wait for her to agree. He took each wrist, peeling the shredded gloves away finger by finger. This time she knew she sucked in her breath when his hands, large and tanned, cradled hers, pale in comparison.

Fortunately, the gloves had protected her palms. Her forearms hadn't been as lucky.

"These have got to hurt," he said, studying them.

Once he said it, she was reminded that they did.

He took one of the fancy paper towels, soaking it with warm water, the hotel monogram going dark as it got wet. Despite his commanding size, his touch was gentle as he cleaned the blood and grit away. The sting was blocked out by the sizzle of sensation this hard-chiseled man caused. She watched him as he concentrated on the job—the way his head tilted so he could get a better view.

She was aware of every breath he took, the sound like a caress against her ear. He cradled her arm as he cleaned her wounds. She couldn't remember the last time she had been touched—by anyone. She grew light-headed and she swayed.

He glanced up. "How are you doing?"

"Fine," she whispered.

Better than fine. She felt strange, hot tears of yearning burning in her eyes as he nodded his head in approval and moved on to her knees.

But the torn stockings were in the way. Without hesitation, he reached under her dress. She gasped. Like a lover's, his strong hands brushed against her legs. Her breath shuddered through her body, feelings that had nothing to do with wounds or healing settling low until she felt the need to press her knees together. But she couldn't because his forearm and hand was in the way. Her head swam at the feel of his fingers finding the tops of her ruined thigh-highs—first one, his hands so close to the juncture between her legs, then the other, as he whisked them down and tossed them in the trash.

The act wasn't intended to be sexual, but when the only physical attention she had received in ages had happened when she got a manicure, this man's touch made her world tilt even more. It was the sort of feeling, she realized, she had waited a lifetime for. Intense. Like a dream you don't want to wake up from.

She had hammered her life into the contours she deemed acceptable. But the reality of whom she had become made her wonder at the price she had paid.

Feeling this man's hands on her thighs, even innocently, made something flare.

Rebellion against everything she believed to be proper? Imprudence?

No, she realized. Nothing so complicated. It was hot, simple, and unrestrained desire.

But she wasn't about to give in to something like that, least of all with a stranger. She was smart. She was sensible.

"I could have done that," she stated over the rapid dance in her chest, her eyes shifting nervously as she tried to find someplace to look besides the silky waves of his hair.

"No need now."

He concentrated on her knee. She tried to find the old Chloe, the one she knew, the one who would demand that he take his hands off her.

"I was trying to sound intimidating," she said.

He glanced up at her, one dark brow rising. "I guess it was the squeak in your voice that threw me."

"I did not squeak!"

"You did."

Her mouth fell open. "This really isn't going as it should."

"I didn't realize there was a certain way to do this."

"There is."

"I must have missed that day at school."

"Funny."

He smiled then—for the first time, she realized—and her breath caught a little more. It was amazing, like the sun coming through a dark, stormy sky. Then he straightened. "There. One knee done."

Sure enough, one side was cleaned. It still looked horrible, but the grit was gone.

"Are you a doctor?"

"No."

"A paramedic?"

"Not that either."

"Then you just go around saving damsels in distress?"

For reasons she couldn't fathom, that wiped every trace of humor off of his face, the clouds returning.

"You've been reading too many fairy tales," he said sharply. Then his features settled back into hard-chiseled command. "Would you rather I left you in the hotel driveway and continued on to find a cab as I intended? Is that another rule I missed?"

He looked at her, his dark eyes direct, as if he could see into her mind, her heart. She looked away, then couldn't help herself. She glanced back.

Her voice caught in her throat. "You're making fun of me."

After a second, that half smile of his reappeared, reluctantly, his head tilted ever so slightly. "Never."

Then he refocused on his project. Her knees.

"This one's a real mess," he said, pressing a new paper towel to the ragged skin.

"Ouch!"

He leaned closer, and she looked down at him, his hair thick and dark. He didn't wear cologne, but he smelled clean and strong. She had a startling image of him leaning close to kiss her. Sensation flashed through her. Hot, sweet, and intense. She thought of touching him. Reaching out. Of being a feline instead of a llama.

This was the sort of man who made a woman feel sexy. Dark and dangerous, commanding the world around him with nothing more than a look and a few words.

A stillness descended over her, fine and crystalline, and she had never been so aware . . . of a man's hand on her knee. Of the way his strong fingers splayed against her inner thigh. And when he looked up, she was sure he felt it, too.

Their gazes locked, their bodies close. He glanced at her lips, and a teasing sweetness made her yearn even more.

But he was a gentleman.

After one last glance at her mouth, he returned his attention to her knee. The outside world was forgotten. She felt cocooned by awareness. She felt every time his thigh brushed against hers.

Everything that wasn't her, everything that wasn't Chloe Sinclair, surged up. Suddenly she wasn't embarrassed at the thought of being sensual. She wasn't afraid of being rejected.

And wasn't that really why she had been afraid to be sexy? The fear of rejection?

Sitting there now, with this man touching her, this stranger with his hands on her body, she felt every bit of embarrassment melt away beneath the terror of what she wanted to do. Give in. Touch him back. Good girl Chloe Sinclair wanted to be sinfully sexy.

She felt dizzy at the thought, her heart beating hard as she clutched her hands together to keep herself from doing what she knew she'd regret. She thought of splashing cold water on her face. She counted to ten, then twenty. She concentrated on all she had to do over the next few weeks. She had to approve payroll. Find new advertising dollars. Brainstorm new programming options. But when he finished with her knee, he straightened again, his competence and composure disarming.

He stood there studying her, not smiling. Then his eyes drifted down over her body, his eyes flaring with something hot. No one had ever looked at her that way before, the heat tangible, making her feel both panicked and excited.

Then everything changed.

It happened so fast that she didn't have time to think. One minute she was holding on to being sensible Chloe, smart, sane, safe, her life as it always had been. Then the next she whispered, "Kiss me."

One long beat of silence passed before a tremor raced through him.

She was being forward and inexcusably loose. But as if a dam of restraint had finally broken apart, water rushing through, crashing at her defenses, she didn't care. Just this once she wanted to lose herself in the arms of this stranger who would disappear from her life when it was over.

Tonight, just tonight, she didn't want to be sensible or even smart. She wanted to be free and wild and filled with unchecked desire.

Frustration kicked inside her when he didn't kiss her. He only looked at her, didn't reach out. He took her in, and she cringed at the sudden thought that even made up and not looking anything like her usual boring self, he wasn't attracted to her.

What an idiot to think that a man this strong and handsome and clearly powerful would want her—even with no names mentioned or strings attached.

"Oh, God, I've completely made a fool of myself. I'm sorry." She tried to get down off the counter, the movement reminding her of the scrapes on her knees.

"You haven't made a fool of yourself," he said, his voice ruggedly insistent, his body blocking her way. "You are beautiful and desirable—"

Her snort was a knee-jerk reaction, the old Chloe surging back ruthlessly.

"—but you don't know the first thing about me."

That stopped her. She cocked her head and studied him. Was he testing her?

"You don't know me either," she whispered. She met his

eyes, and she bit her lip for a trembling second. "That's the point."

She startled him, and from the look of him she guessed he was rarely surprised.

His brows slammed together. "I could be a . . ."

"What? A murderer?"

"I am not a murderer." He sounded put out.

"Okay, then a Mexican bandit?" She tried to smile.

"Are we living in the same century?"

He looked at her lips again, despite his better intentions, and she could see something that her inexpert eyes swore was desire. Hope surged, and she felt an impatient anticipation.

"Would it help," she asked breathlessly, "if I promised that *I'm* not a bandit?"

She expected him to laugh, or at the very least smile. Instead his gaze darkened. "I'm not so sure about that. With your innocent blue eyes and mouth meant for sin, you look like you could easily steal something I've never been willing to give," he stated cryptically.

But before she could question him, he groaned and cursed. Then this stranger pulled her into his arms.

They clung together, the warmth of his body surrounding her. Their kiss grew instantly hot, their mouths slanting together as if neither of them could get close enough. His hands ran down her spine, and she knew with a heady sense of certainty that whatever his reasons for kissing her, this wasn't about pity.

She wrapped her arms around his shoulders. She didn't admit how many times she had imagined something like this. In her dreams, in her fantasies. Giving in to a forbidden passion.

He ran his tongue along her lips, opening her more. Their

tongues tasted and probed as she tugged his shirttails from his pants, wanting to feel skin.

"Who are you?" he whispered hoarsely against her ear.

She hesitated for a second, then said, "Does it matter?"

She didn't wait for an answer. She ran her hands up his chest, material gathering against her wrists, and after another second he gave in again.

"Wrap your legs around me," he commanded in a gruff voice.

A sharp thrill ran through her, centering deep and low. She did as he asked, then felt a shiver of excitement as he unzipped the back of her dress, the beaded skirt riding higher until it came up around her hips, the top sliding lower until it revealed the curve of her breasts. And no bra.

He picked her up and wheeled her around, pressing her back against the finely papered wall. Then he dipped his head, that dark hair brushing against her cheek as he trailed his lips along her skin.

"God, you're soft."

Lower and lower until he took one nipple in his mouth. He had exuded raw sensuality just tending to her wounds. Now, with his intent purely sexual, there was an animal fierceness to him that scared her as much as it thrilled her.

White-hot electricity pulsed along every nerve ending. Struggling, she tugged her arms from the restraint of her dress, the beads bunching in cool heaviness against her hips. When she was finally free his thumbs found her nipples. She felt hungry and needy in a purely physical way.

She groaned without an ounce of inhibition when his thumb and forefinger closed on one taut peak. She trembled inside and her head fell back against the wall. Then he ripped off his shirt, lowering her just a bit, and it was in a moment of gasping surprise that she felt the hard contours of his naked chest against her breasts. She felt alive and

captive at the same time, pleasure heightened by the illicit-
ness of what they were doing.

Reaching up, she tangled her fingers in his hair, instinctively arching to him as he seared his mouth across her
body. When he gently sucked one breast, her hands knot-
ted, and she had to force herself to let go.

Neither of them said a word. They came together in a
dance of silence. Slowly, he let her down until she stood,
her dress falling to her ankles. His mouth nipped at her
skin. He cupped her bottom, the thin edges of a thong she
had secretly purchased doing little to separate their bodies.
Palms to flesh, his fingertips curled low until she felt him
touch the juncture between her spread thighs.

The contact surprised her. At first she felt self-conscious.
She started to break free. But that was the old Chloe, the
one she'd find again once she walked out the door and
never saw this man again. But right now she wanted to let
go. While she had the chance. No one ever had to know.

Drawing a breath, she widened her legs. His deep, guttural moan brought an answering cry welling up in her. She
felt desperate, like this was her only chance. She wanted
more of him, wanted to be closer. He must have sensed it in
her. He pressed their bodies together. He kissed her again,
his hands coming up to frame her face as his mouth re-
claimed hers.

He sucked at her lower lip, before teasing her mouth
open, allowing him in to taste her more intimately. She
didn't realize she had moaned until the sound rumbled in
her ears. She felt small and cherished, even beautiful. Her
hair was wild, but the way he held her made her feel as if
he could hold her forever and he'd be lucky.

His hands slid down her neck to her shoulders. The heels
of his hands grazed the tops of her breasts, but not lower
this time. The tips of his fingers brushed back and forth

over her collarbones as he kissed her. She thought she would cry out in frustration before he finally cupped her breasts in his palms.

He pressed them high, his fingers teasing the peaks, circling. She felt his breath against her ear when he ran his tongue along the delicate shell. Then his thumb and forefinger closed with gentle insistence over her nipple. Pulsing once, twice, his tongue dancing the same rhythm in her mouth. She felt everything in the core between her legs. Hot and needy.

When she groaned, he secured her spread-eagle against the wall, his hands touching her, worshipping her . . . wanting her. Cupping her hips, he pulled her to his hardness, again and again, ever so slightly, in that rhythm prescribed by his tongue.

She trembled, stunned by the strength of her need. His breath on her nape was like wind to a fire.

He cupped her jaw, tilting her face to him. "I want you," he whispered. His voice was laced with the sound of raw hunger.

"I want you, too," she answered.

And when he started to undo his belt, she reached down to help, their fingers tangling together.

Frantic, they tugged at the buckle and leather, and the sound of the door banging against the lock didn't reach her at first. Her world consisted of this stranger and his hands on her bare skin. But something must have registered with him because he cursed and tore away from her.

With a sudden flash, she realized people must be gathered just outside the door. She could hear them talking, some woman complaining that the hotel shouldn't lock the only bathroom they had in the main lobby. Then someone else who told them to step back, followed by a jangle of keys against the lock.

"Oh, my gosh!" she gasped.

Thankfully her stranger wasn't paralyzed. He immediately whipped up her shimmery dress, whirled her around, and had her zipped back up with the proficiency of a dresser at a Broadway play. Just as the keys turned in the lock, he had his own clothes back in place.

"Let me handle this," he stated, stepping in front of her to block her from view.

He stood like a warrior, his stance wide, his features dark, his frame massive and forbidding. If anyone could protect her from embarrassment, this man could.

But Chloe was hardly paying attention. With her heart in her throat, she lowered her head, tucking in her chin. Her heart beat like a drum, pulsing through her, and the second the door opened, she flew into action. She wheeled out from behind him, startling the small crowd who had gathered, and dashed for the door.

She felt badly for leaving the stranger to deal with the mess, though not badly enough to stay. Not even the realization that she had left her tiny purse made her hesitate. But just when she got through the crowd, for one quick second, she looked back. He was looking at her, his hard-chiseled face quickly shifting from surprise to anger when he understood what she had done. A shiver of regret raced through her. He didn't look like the type of man any sane person should anger. She prayed she never saw him again.

She flew out of the hotel, into the wind that hadn't died down. She felt as if she was falling farther into a kaleidoscope of scenes in her head. Of him. Of her. Blending together in passion, then separating. Distinct, but different. Changed.

Anxious to get away, she found her car, thankful for the ever-practical Hide-A-Key box under the wheel well. She had to get home, back to her world, to put her life back into the order she had worked so hard to achieve. But when she slipped into the front seat, then finally managed to get the key in the ignition, she had the fleeting thought that her perfectly ordered world had just changed for good, and that she would never be the same again.

Everyone at _____ busted waited for him to answer the ___ barraging questions the both ___ firing ___ answered ___ ___ and the ___ had the inspiration to ___ for publicity, and it worked. But the station had ___ its ___ or find itself on the shortlist again.

To: Julia Boudreaux <julia@ktextv.com>
Katherine Bloom <katherine@ktextv.com>
From: Chloe Sinclair <chloe@ktextv.com>
Subject: Emergency

I've tried to call you both but your lines are going directly to voice mail. Which means you're online. When are you going to get second lines or DSL?!!! But first things first! Can we meet at Danny's Cuppa Joe for a breakfast confab before our 10 o'clock appointment? It's an emergency, plus I'm starving.

Chloe Sinclair
Station Manager
Award-winning KTEX TV

To: Chloe Sinclair <chloe@ktextv.com>
Katherine Bloom <katherine@ktextv.com>
From: Julia Boudreaux <julia@ktextv.com>
Subject: You?

Chloe, darling, I've never heard of you calling an emergency confab. I've just gotten out of the shower. I can be there in an hour. Can you give us a hint?

Also, before I forget: At our meeting with Trey Tanner, let me do the talking.

xo, j

p.s. Hopefully you'll fill us in about last night's party. It's all the buzz that some man was caught in a compromising position in the women's bathroom. How is it possible that the one party I miss turns out to be the party of the year?

To: Julia Boudreaux <julia@ktextv.com>
Katherine Bloom <katherine@ktextv.com>
From: Chloe Sinclair <chloe@ktextv.com>
Subject: Oh dear

Let's just say I'm aware of the man in the bathroom. I'll see you in an hour. Kate, can you be there?

Chloe

To: Chloe Sinclair <chloe@ktextv.com>
Julia Boudreaux <julia@ktextv.com>
From: Katherine Bloom <katherine@ktextv.com>
Subject: Will do

And what is this about ladies' rooms with men in them? And Julia, who exactly is this Trey Tanner? Why haven't you mentioned any of this before yesterday's e-mail?

K

Katherine C. Bloom
News Anchor, KTEX TV West Texas

To: Julia Boudreaux <julia@ktextv.com>
Katherine Bloom <katherine@ktextv.com>
From: Chloe Sinclair <chloe@ktextv.com>
Subject: Ditto

I'm wondering the same thing. You've never mentioned getting an outside analysis done of the station. Though thankfully you didn't go to someone like that cutthroat, prehistoric warrior-type Sterling Prescott from Prescott Media, who is notorious for gobbling up small stations at outrageously low prices. You didn't, did you, Julia?

Chloe

To: Chloe Sinclair <chloe@ktextv.com>
Katherine Bloom <katherine@ktextv.com>
From: Julia Boudreaux <julia@ktextv.com>
Subject: Dash

If I'm going to be at Danny's in an hour, I've got to dash. Just rest assured that in all my phone calls and e-mails with Trey Tanner, he was nothing but kind and helpful.

xo, j

p.s. And what is this about warriors? You've been watching Mel Gibson again, haven't you?

To: Julia Boudreaux <julia@ktextv.com>
Katherine Bloom <katherine@ktextv.com>
From: Chloe Sinclair <chloe@ktextv.com>
Subject: Bad feeling

Why do I get the feeling that you are hiding something, Julia? You're the one with the thing for Mel Gibson, not me.

Chloe

two

*T*here were warriors, and then there were warriors.

Sterling Prescott had never held a sword in his life, but there was no question that there wasn't a person who had dealt with the man who didn't regard him with respect and even a little fear. He went after what he wanted, and he got it. The only bloodshed involved, however, was the red ink on the accounting ledgers of other men who couldn't make their businesses work. Sterling was known for going in, buying them out, then handing the enterprise over to his team of experts to turn it around. Or sell it off in pieces.

Soon all that red ink turned to black. Or, as some had said, the red turned to gold. Sterling Prescott was a corporate raider par excellence.

Sterling paced the confines of his suite at the Hilton Hotel. He couldn't believe he was in El Paso, Texas. But he was, all because he had fired Trey Tanner.

Hell.

Though that was the least of his concerns just then. He couldn't believe he'd nearly had sex in a hotel bathroom with a woman he had never laid eyes on before like he was no better than a sex-crazed adolescent.

He was many things, but not that. He was the oldest son of the St. Louis–based Prescott family, was CEO to Prescott Media, and had single-handedly brought the company back from near ruin after his father had done his best to run it into the ground.

Trey Tanner, apparently, had wanted to do the same sort of thing.

"Sterling, really," Trey had pleaded, *"if we help these women save their station, it will go a long way toward changing your . . . I mean, our reputation."*

Sterling swore an oath. He was not some knight in shining armor. And he wasn't in the business of doling out charity to every needy Tom, Dick, or even Mary. Hell, in order to save the family business, he'd had to look at the world around him with a detached, business eye. No emotion. No sentimentality. He'd had to get the job done. And he had.

Prescott Media was the fastest growing family-owned media conglomerate in the country. Sterling had every intention of continuing that growth. KTEX TV was the next jewel in his crown. The jewel would already be in place if Trey Tanner hadn't gotten emotional about the situation. Now it was Sterling's job to clean up the mess and close the deal. And it would be a deal. For Prescott Media. KTEX TV was deep in debt and without a viable plan to put it back in the black anytime soon.

Just Sterling's sort of station.

Picking up his cell phone, he dialed. A receptionist came on the line.

"Prescott Media. How may I direct your call?"

"Connect me to Betty Taylor."

"One moment, please."

Over the years, he had made a point of retaining a polite distance from everyone at Prescott Media. He didn't give parties, he didn't stand around and chat, just as he didn't give interviews to newspapers or magazines. He kept to himself, working behind the scenes. He liked the anonymity that it carried. Not that beautiful women and powerful men didn't seek him out. They did. He dated often. Many women over the years. He enjoyed them all. Gave them pleasure, took his own. Then moved on. His focus was on rebuilding the family business.

More than once his grandmother had said that he needed to slow down, to start living. Even he knew that rebuilding was no longer an accurate term in reference to the work being done at Prescott Media. They had rebuilt. He and his family had more money than they could ever spend. But work was his life. Finding a new prey made his heart pound. Closing deals made his blood hum through his veins. Or it had.

"Mr. Prescott's office."

Betty Taylor was a fifty-five-year-old, neatly kept woman who ran his office with the efficiency of a military sergeant. Everyone at Prescott Media was afraid of her. She wasn't shy about speaking her mind to anyone and everyone— except Sterling. She showed her employer nothing but the utmost respect.

"Miss Taylor, it's Sterling."

"Mr. Prescott, good morning. How are you?"

"Fine."

"How's the weather?"

"Haven't a clue."

"Good, we've gotten that out of the way. I have several messages for you."

Sterling amended his assessment. Betty Taylor treated him with the utmost respect, though she was not above goading him now and again when it came to his dealings with several members of the Prescott family. Once she had overheard his grandmother state, as only Serena Prescott could, that he had no life beyond his job. Betty hadn't said a word, but her sniff was confirmation enough.

"You've had three calls from Senator Dickson's office. He clearly wants you to speak at his fund-raiser."

"I don't speak at fund-raisers."

"I told him that. He wants you anyway."

Sterling shrugged indifferently. "What else?"

The woman went through a list of important executives and politicians who wanted something from him or Prescott Media. "And Mel Burton from PR called, wanting to know when he can announce the acquisition of KTEX."

Damn. He had instructed the man to put together a press release. The minute the deal was done, he wanted to move quickly to let the media world know. Because when he finally acquired the El Paso station, Prescott would have three significant markets in the Southwest. He already had Albuquerque and Tucson. When he had El Paso in the bag, he planned to connect all three to increase coverage—or more important, to increase ad revenue by appealing to national advertisers who wanted package rates on regional advertising spots.

He had no doubt that wrapping up the deal would be child's play. The station's founder and owner, Philippe Boudreaux, had recently died, leaving his only child in charge. The extensive notes Sterling had put together regarding the station had described Julia Boudreaux as a wild, pampered, rich girl who no doubt would be thrilled at washing her hands of the headache.

Beyond the Boudreaux woman, there were only two other players that mattered. Kate Bloom had just married golf star Jesse Chapman, and from everything he had learned, the couple was wildly in love and preoccupied. Sterling didn't think she'd be a problem either.

The only unknown was the station manager. Chloe Sinclair. By all accounts, she was smart and savvy, and she might put up a fight. But he had no doubt that he could handle her. He'd have her begging for a buyout in no time.

"Betty, tell Mel to hold on to the press release until he hears from me. I should have everything completed by lunchtime. This afternoon, at the latest."

"Will do."

"Anything else?"

"Your mother called."

Which brought to mind the other reason he had traveled to the westernmost portion of Texas.

His brother. Ben Prescott. The black sheep of the family.

He could hear his secretary hesitate, and well she should, since the youngest Prescott had given him nothing but headaches. Wild parties. Assorted women of dubious backgrounds. But the worst of Ben's sins, as far as their mother was concerned, had to do with his choice of careers. Law enforcement. His mother hated that her youngest child could get himself killed at any time.

"She asked if you had seen your brother yet," Betty explained.

"What she really wants to know is if he's agreed to come home."

"That would be my guess, sir."

Sterling tamped down the flare of frustration. "Tell her that I am seeing him this morning."

"Shouldn't *you* call and tell her that?"

Only Betty Taylor could get away with saying such a thing.

"No, I shouldn't. If anything comes up, you can reach me on my cell phone."

He disconnected the call and felt a surprising weariness at the thought of his brother. Ben had always marched to a different drummer, as they said—and generally it was to any drummer that was sure to make his family crazy.

Their mother had wept for weeks when Ben announced he was moving to Texas and was going into law enforcement. Then she'd nearly gone into seclusion when a few years later he had taken an assignment with an undercover vice unit in El Paso.

There were times Sterling felt that Ben was doing everything he could to erase who he was. He had made it clear he wanted nothing to do with Prescott Media.

But now something had gone bad with an undercover operation. Ben wouldn't talk to anyone about what had happened, or about having taken a leave of absence from the force.

The family was worried. And it was Sterling's job to bring the younger son back into the fold. As far as Sterling was concerned, the timing couldn't be better. Ben was having doubts or maybe concerns at the same time Sterling had a deal to close. Coming to El Paso had been the perfect opportunity to kill two birds with one stone. Secure the station, and show Ben the greatness of Prescott Media in action.

He had no doubt he could have a contract in hand and Ben heading home in a day, if not two.

If only he could get that woman out of his mind.

A knock on his door saved him from his thoughts.

The minute his brother entered, Sterling felt a smile pull at his lips. The younger man looked just like him, though while Sterling knew he was a large man and in good shape, Ben wore danger like a second skin.

He had the same dark hair, the same dark eyes, but one of his brows was sliced by a thin scar. It was amazing he hadn't lost an eye. The first time their mother had seen it, she had just about passed out. Their sister, and the only other child in the family, had smiled knowingly and finished their mother off by stating that women's panties must melt away at the mere sight of that scar.

Their father had grumbled and returned his attention to the miniature military figures he built. Their grandmother had hid a smile.

But Ben wouldn't have made anyone smile this morning. He looked mean and spent. Sterling felt true concern as he shook his brother's hand.

"Ben," he greeted.

"Sterling." Ben shoved his hands in his jeans pockets. "What brings you to town?" He asked the question with a hard edge, as if he didn't want to hear the answer. "I told Mother that I'm not coming home."

"Ah, you think she sent me here."

"Didn't she?"

Sterling avoided the question. "I'm here because I have a deal to close."

"I thought Trey Tanner was your henchman."

"Trey went soft on me. But we don't need to go into that. I'm meeting with the station personnel in an hour, at ten. Why don't you come with me?"

"Sterling, how many times do I have to tell you I'm not interested in the business?"

"I know you're not. But I thought we could go to lunch after the meeting is over."

"I'll meet you wherever you want."

"Unfortunately, I don't have a car."

"What, no limos available?"

"Funny. But I really did want to see you. Besides, humor me. I thought that if you came to the meeting, I could impress you with how great Prescott Media really is."

* * *

"I'd like two eggs, scrambled, bacon, hash browns, and a large orange juice."

"What kind of toast?"

"White. No, make that wheat." Chloe hesitated, trying to decide one last thing, then plunged ahead. "And a side order of pancakes. Please."

"What?" she demanded when she noticed Kate and Julia smirking at her.

"You must have some serious emergency to need all of that," Kate offered.

"I'm hungry."

"And you ordered to prove it," Julia quipped.

True, but since she had sworn off even so much as speaking to another man again after the debacle last night, what did fat thighs matter anyway?

This morning there wasn't a trace left of the woman from last night. Sensible Chloe had returned with her demure clothes and straight hair, the brush of freckles no longer covered up by makeup. If only she could wipe away her indiscretion in the hotel bathroom as easily. Well, she conceded, maybe not wipe away everything. Her body still tingled when she remembered the way the stranger had touched her. His hands on her body. But she remembered as well the sheer embarrassed horror she had felt when the hotel's maintenance man and several women crowded through the door. Women definitely didn't like being kept from the ladies' room.

She shook her head.

The waitress took Chloe's plastic menu, secured it in the crook of her arm, then smiled, pad in one hand, her miniature pencil posed to print the next order.

Julia ordered toast and coffee, her gold charm bracelet jangling against the Formica tabletop, her nearly waist-length black hair pulled back into a stylishly sleek ponytail.

Of the three best friends, Julia was the true beauty. Kate was cute with her froth of curls and hazel eyes. Chloe knew that she was plain in a respectable, squeaky-clean way.

Kate glanced at her menu. "I'll have the heart-shaped pancakes, with strawberry syrup."

"Off the kids' menu?" the waitress asked, surprised.

Julia laughed. "No, off the sappy She's in Love menu."

"So sue me," Kate shot back with a very-much-in-love smile as the waitress left.

Julia laughed. "No need. You're allowed to be sappy in love."

"Encouraged to be, actually," Chloe added.

Kate sighed dreamily. "But enough about me. We have an emergency to discuss. Chloe, spill."

Chloe drew a deep breath, wondering for half a heart-beat if this was the sort of thing she shouldn't tell anyone, including her best friends. But then she chided herself and launched into a detailed, monotone, reporterlike explanation and thorough analysis of how she felt after she failed the quiz. She recounted the feeling that she couldn't spell *sex appeal* much less have any.

"You're saying," Julia asked, trying to understand, "that after you failed the *Sexy!* quiz, you decided you were going to be sexy?"

Chloe hung her head. "Yes."

"And that's the emergency?"

"Yes. No. Well, not exactly."

"This should be good."

Chloe hesitated. Could she really say the words out loud? "It's *not* good. It's horrible. It's . . . I . . . I nearlyhad-sexwithastranger."

Kate blinked, her coffee cup clattering in the saucer when she nearly dropped it.

Julia's mouth dropped open. "Did you say what I think you said?"

Chloe leaned forward, wrinkled her nose, and made a drawn out, melodramatic sound of dismay. "Yes," she moaned.

"When?" Kate demanded.

"Last night."

"Last night? Where?" Julia was confused. "I thought you were going to the Hilton for the Heart Association reception."

"I was."

"Was? So you didn't go?"

"Not exactly." She winced. "But I got close."

Julia sat back. "Good Lord, what are you talking about?"

Pressing her eyes closed, Chloe gathered her thoughts, then plunged ahead with her story. She told her friends about the unfamiliar need to be sexy. Explained about getting dressed, driving to the hotel, sitting in the car. She mentioned the wind, running into the man, falling. Then she added the last part about how she ended up in the hotel bathroom. On a sink. With a stranger.

Julia went very still. "In a bathroom? Was it the same bathroom they found some man in?"

"That would be my guess."

"Chloe!" Julia and Kate chimed together, leaning close with wildly wicked gleams in their eyes.

"You were the woman in the bathroom with some man?" Kate gasped.

"It's a pretty nice bathroom," Chloe said with an apologetic shrug.

"Can you believe it?" Julia stated, impressed. "Our little Chloe has done something that has all the tongues in town wagging."

"Thank God they don't know it's her," Kate added.

"Always Miss Practicality," Julia announced.

"Someone has to be. And you know why this happened, don't you? She finally rebelled."

Julia and Kate exchanged a glance, then said in unison, " 'Thank your lucky stars you were born plain-looking, Chloe love. Your gift is being smart and sensible. Don't ever let that desert you.' "

Kate shook her head and smiled with a deep, caring love for her friend of more than two decades. "Sounds to me our little Chloe finally proved her grandmother wrong."

Julia scoffed. "If the woman weren't already dead—"

All three made the sign of the cross.

"—then she should be shot."

"Stop, stop. Grandmother loved me. She kept me after my mother died—"

Julia and Kate sighed, then Julia continued the story they all knew so well. "She raised you, supported you, loved you after your father disappeared. Which reminds me, now that your father has found you again all these years later, is he ever going to move out of your house?"

"Julia, my father is no trouble. I'm glad he's staying with me."

"Fine, fine, not a word against Regina Sinclair or Richard Maybry. Besides, your grandmother also said that men 'lie, cheat, and leave.' I happen to agree with her on that."

"Julia!" Chloe and Kate exclaimed.

Julia didn't pay them any mind. She smiled and leaned forward. "Tell us every little detail about last night. What's his name? What does he look like? Are you going to see him again?"

Chloe winced again, then answered the questions in the order they were presented. "I don't know. Dark hair, dark eyes. When I was dashing out the door, I didn't say good-bye, much less ask for another date. In fact, I left so fast that I forgot my purse—or rather your purse, Julia. I'll get you a new one."

"I'm not worried about the purse." Julia smoothed her already smooth hair with her delicate hand, her perfect nails glittering like bright pink jewels. "I'm just trying to understand. Are you telling us you nearly had sex with a stranger for no other reason than you wanted to have sex?"

Chloe knew she couldn't lie, no matter how distasteful it was. "Yes. I mean, it just hit me. I wanted to have sex. Though not with just any man. With that man. Something about the way he looked at me, or maybe it was the way his body protected mine from the wind. Or maybe because he cleaned sand and grit out of my arms and knees." She pulled back her long sleeves and held up her arms as proof, exhibiting the angry scrapes.

Kate and Julia *eww*ed appropriately.

"It was like I let go and didn't have to think because I didn't know his name and he didn't know mine and I'd never see him again." Chloe hung her head. "There it is."

Julia banged her jeweled hand on the table. "Brava!"

Chloe's head came up. "What?"

"Good job. Though I hope you were on the verge of pulling out a condom for the main event."

"I don't carry condoms!"

"Then you better start if this is going to become a habit. It's a big mistake if you don't. Oh, and maybe you should borrow some of those sexy sex products that Kate used on that segment of *Getting Real* the day she decided to go crazy herself and be sexy." Julia tilted her head in thought. "There must be something in the air."

Kate blushed, though she looked more than a little pleased with herself—or perhaps she was just pleased with the outcome of that disastrous show. As well she should be. She ended up with the love of her life.

"This is not going to become a habit!" Chloe blurted. "In fact it will never, I repeat never, happen again. There will be no sex products, and there certainly will be no big mistake!"

Julia's gaze danced wickedly. "Speaking of big . . . did you get far enough along to find out if he was, you know, big?"

Kate bit her lip to keep from laughing. Chloe blinked, her mouth opening and closing, unable to find words to respond.

Julia and Kate glanced at each other, then laughed out loud. "She's back," they stated in unison.

"What's that supposed to mean?"

Julia patted her hand. "Just that our sweet Goody Two-shoes has returned, every trace of wild woman gone."

"Exactly," Chloe stated. "Every trace is gone."

And it was true. Her well-ordered world had returned to its normal orbit. She liked order. She liked lists. She liked knowing she had her world under control. And she wasn't about to throw all that away for a few minutes of fleeting sexual satisfaction with a man who had rugged good looks and strong hands that had drifted over her skin as if he had touched her many times before.

A shimmer of longing ran through her at the memory. Maybe if she saw him just one more time . . . Absolutely not.

She nodded firmly, making her feel in more control already.

It was always that way when she was with the girls. It had been Kate and Julia who had taken her under their wings after her mother died. The state had sent her to live with her grandmother, a wonderful but exacting woman who had loved her with a rigid discipline. After Regina Sinclair died, she had left Chloe her house, a sense of self-worth, and a strict code of ethics.

That was a year ago, her vivacious grandmother's sudden death leaving her saddened and surprised to be without her. But Chloe hadn't been alone for long when the father she had never really known had had a heart attack. The hospital had called her at her father's request, and as soon as he was discharged, he had moved in with her.

As he had recovered his health during the past six months, they had lurched along, trying to find common ground. He was a charming man, wonderful and happy. But she didn't know how to bridge the polite distance that stood between them. She worried about him, and while she didn't know him that well, she felt a deep yearning to have him in her life.

"Well," Julia said, breaking the silence. "Chloe has confessed her delicious sins, we have cheered her on, but now we have no choice but to get to the office. Trey Tanner should be there anytime now."

They paid the bill, then hurried across the street to the low brick building that housed KTEX TV. Oversized satellite dishes that had yet to be replaced by smaller, newer ones beckoned in the parking lot like concave moons. A billboard with Kate's likeness ran along the side of the building. *Getting Real with Kate* had become a success. Ratings had been good. They were on their way back to regaining their standing. Or so Chloe had thought. She wondered if there was something Julia wasn't telling her.

"Julia, you didn't answer my e-mail regarding this Trey Tanner," Chloe said. "He's only here to analyze the station, right? He's not like someone from that horrible Prescott Media who takes obscene pleasure in gobbling up stations that have hit rough spots?"

Security buzzed them into the building. Because the station was small, they had to enter directly into the warehouselike space that housed the main set. Julia pressed her finger to her lips unnecessarily. Which made Chloe's heart step up its beat.

What was going on?

By the time they had made it through another doorway and they could talk again, Chloe felt a low bead of panic start to build.

Julia turned to Chloe and Kate, her expression professional and businesslike. "I need this to go well."

The seriousness of her tone instantly got their attention.

"Is something wrong, Jules?" Kate asked. "Is the station okay?"

Julia scoffed, but the lightness was forced. Chloe's panic grew.

"Of course everything is okay," Julia added with a strained smile. "I just felt it necessary to bring in an outside opinion. And I've heard great things about Trey Tanner."

"I've never heard of him," Kate said.

"Well"—Julia shifted her weight—"not many people have. But he comes highly recommended. I would appreciate it if both of you would sit in on the meeting. With my father gone, you're the only two people I trust. I'll meet you in the conference room."

Abruptly Julia turned and headed toward her office, her stiletto heels clicking against the tile.

Kate and Chloe exchanged a glance.

"I thought things around here were getting better," Kate said.

"They are." Or were they? The Boudreaux family let her run the station, but they had always kept the books themselves. "I guess we should go in and meet this Trey Tanner."

"I'll meet you there," Kate said.

Chloe headed down the hall, stopping briefly in her own office to store her purse and retrieve a pen and a pad of paper. Then she made her way to the conference room. But when she turned the handle and glanced through the top portion of the door that was made of glass, her heart went still, her blood froze in her veins, and she thought maybe, just maybe, she was going to pass out on the floor.

"Oh, my God," she whispered.

three

Chloe couldn't breathe.

"Surely not," she said. "It can't be."

Two men stood in the conference room, talking, their backs to her. They both had dark hair and large builds. But one of them made her think of the man from the Hilton bathroom.

"Please, please, please no," she pleaded softly.

"Please no what?" Julia asked, coming up behind her.

Kate arrived next, glancing at her watch. "I like a man who believes in being on time. Trey Tanner gets points from me. Who's with him?"

The two men turned around, and Chloe's knees nearly buckled. The stranger she had nearly had sex with stood there with a quiet ease.

"Yum," Julia stated. "They're cute if you like rugged, manly alpha males."

Chloe looked on with her heart pounding and a strange traitorous tingle fizzing through her body like champagne bubbles. He appeared every bit as commanding as he had last night. Handsome in a way that was all about self-assurance and power. And he was here!

Oh, my God, he's here!

Panic mixed with a heady rush of awareness. She wanted to throw her arms around him, but at the same time she wanted to melt away into the terra-cotta tile floor.

With a nearly silent groan, Chloe started to turn away, intent on sending a message in with Lucy, the receptionist, that she was suddenly, unavoidably, detained. But her groan wasn't silent enough. Julia cocked her head and grabbed her arm. "Showtime," she whispered.

Great, great, great.

Okay, she told herself, don't panic. She could do this. Besides, today her hair was straight, her bangs were down, the freckles across the bridge of her nose were blazing with not a speck of makeup in sight. What were the chances that he'd even recognize her?

With a sound that was a cross between a growl and a whimper, Chloe rummaged around in her jacket pocket for her oversized glasses, pushed them on to be on the safe side, tucked her chin close, and entered the room behind Julia and Kate. She clutched her notepad protectively to her chest and felt her hair swing against her cheeks like curtains in a way that she hoped hid her face.

Julia walked to the head of the table. "I'm Julia Boudreaux, and this is Kate Bloom Chapman from our hugely successful *Getting Real with Kate*. And this is Chloe Sinclair, our station manager."

The other man, not the one from last night, reached out and shook Julia's hand. "I'm Ben," he said simply.

Julia tugged away with a start, her lips parting as if his touch had surprised her. She blinked, then blinked again, and shook her head. But then the odd moment passed and Julia was back to her normal self. Chloe's best friend looked the man up and down, then said, "I figured you weren't Trey Tanner. From my e-mails with him, I didn't think that he would show up wearing jeans to an important meeting."

Ben raised a brow and actually laughed, completely unperturbed by Julia's surprisingly biting remark.

Chloe sat down quickly, and she would have sworn she felt the other man's eyes on her. She realized with a sinking heart that he was probably remembering her that very second. Just as she remembered him. Trey Tanner. What were the chances that the man Julia had hired to help them would turn out to be the man from the bathroom?

Chloe mumbled her greetings.

"Is something wrong with your voice?"

This from Kate, whom Chloe saw out of the corner of her downcast eyes looking at her oddly.

"I think I'm getting a cold." Chloe sniffed for effect.

Kate cocked her head. "In the last five minutes?"

Chloe stared at the pad and pretended to write.

Julia turned to the other man. "You must be Trey Tanner."

He was still staring at Chloe, and his brow furrowed in confusion. Chloe braced herself for what he would say next.

"It's you!"

"I never thought I'd see you again!"

"I was crushed when you ran out on me like that!"

"You are the most stunningly beautiful woman I have ever met and I can't live another second without you."

"I'm sorry, but there seems to be a mistake," he stated, that same deep, rumbling voice washing over her senses. "I am from Prescott Media, but I'm—"

Chloe's head jerked up. "What?" she blurted.

Every eye in the room turned to her. She tossed her pen down on the pad. "Did I hear you correctly? You're from Prescott Media?"

He hardly looked at her. In fact, it hit her then that he hadn't been staring at her. And he wasn't all that happy about having been interrupted. Not only had he not been on the verge of exclaiming his admiration and love, but as it turned out, he hadn't even recognized her!

Chloe realized with a rush of relief that she was safe.

He didn't recognize her!

Followed quickly by a disgruntled, *He didn't recognize her!*

Her brows slammed together. She couldn't believe it. Was she so pathetically ugly without makeup that he didn't even notice a resemblance?

A part of her brain realized that she was being irrational. She should be rejoicing at her luck. But that other part, the one that had obviously sent her to the party dressed up in the first place, was insulted.

She lifted her chin a notch. Surely he just hadn't seen her well enough. How could he not recognize her? She might look a bit different this morning, but they had shared a passion that she was sure was the sort that people wrote about in songs, in books, in movies. A passion that meant he should recognize her soul.

Okay, so she'd been reading too much lately. But really, he should at least think she looked familiar.

"I'm sorry for the interruption," Julia said, glaring at Chloe. "I know that your time is valuable."

Chloe barely listened as Julia rushed on with ridiculous platitudes and gushing appreciation for him coming all the way to El Paso to meet with them.

Raising her chin another notch, Chloe pushed the paper and pen away from her with a noisy swish. But still Trey Tanner didn't notice her. She even pushed back her hair, drummed her fingers on the table, then in a fit of completely and utterly immature foolishness, she whipped off her glasses. All that was missing was a *Ta da!*

To no avail.

In fact the only person in the room who seemed aware of her at all was Kate, who kept glancing at her as if at any minute she might sprout a second head. Which might not be a bad idea since then maybe one of them would ring a bell in this Trey Tanner.

Trey Tanner. From Prescott Media!

Her frustration turned to anger. How could Julia have done this?

"As I was saying," he stated firmly, cutting Julia off.

Chloe snorted. "You were saying that you're from Prescott Media, home of that corporate cutthroat and modern day robber baron Sterling Prescott."

That got his attention. It got the other man's attention as well. Ben actually chuckled.

Julia whirled around to face him. "Who exactly are you? Ben, you said. Just Ben. Like Cher, I suppose."

Ben whistled appreciatively, not in the least cowed by Julia. He simply smiled and made a big production of saying, "Yep, it's Ben. I'm *Trey's* younger brother, Ben Tanner. Yes, Ben Tanner, here to be inspired by his big brother's greatness. Though, Trey"—he turned to the other man— "next time you talk to your boss—Sterling, isn't it?—you might want to mention that he has one bad reputation here in El Paso."

Chloe watched as Trey looked like he would strangle the younger man. Then she turned to Julia. "How could you?" she asked plaintively. "How could you have invited Prescott Media into our station? It's like inviting a fox into the hen-house."

"Chloe, please," Julia implored. She laughed uncomfortably. "I'm sure that you're wrong about Prescott Media."

"Wrong? Haven't you read the articles? Trey Tanner works for a hard, cold butcher of a man who is as notorious for snatching up stations for a fraction of their worth as he is for being reclusive. Can you imagine how awful and hated Sterling Prescott must be that he can't even show his face?!"

Ben seemed to choke on his amusement.

Trey got defensive. "The last I heard, it was legal to make a profit in the United States."

"Great, justify lowball offers and hostile takeovers with the American flag. Though why am I not surprised that you'd defend your boss. What's the saying? *An underling doesn't fall far from the tree.*"

The man's jaw worked.

Chloe turned to Julia. "Kick him out now while you still can. I bet you money he is here with a lowball offer in that fancy briefcase of his. He'll leave you with nothing. And forget the fact that the rest of us won't have a job." The reality made her heart go still. But she couldn't think about that now. "Can you deny that is what you're here to do?" she demanded of the man.

He looked murderous, his hands flattened on the fine wood tabletop, throwing frustrated glares at Ben each time he chuckled gleefully.

"I assure you that you are mistaken about Prescott Media," Trey Tanner stated. "But take Prescott out of the equation for the moment."

He leaned forward, every inch of him rippling with that commanding power as he launched into a discussion about media trends, local versus national programming, ad rates, and the decline in advertising revenue in all media. Yada, yada. Chloe barely heard over the anger, frustration, and yes, fear that she felt.

She, Chloe Sinclair, who was notorious for her copious

note taking and list making, only stared at her pad of paper. But she couldn't help the situation if she didn't concentrate.

For the next fifteen minutes, she forgot last night. She became absorbed in the information he spilled out with the ease of an expert.

Mr. Expert. *Yeah, right,* she thought ungraciously, not to mention unfairly.

Everyone stopped and stared at her.

She cringed. "Did I say that out loud?"

Julia looked at her with an astounded glare. "Yes, Chloe. You did."

"Sorry."

"Yes, she's terribly sorry," Julia gushed uncharacteristically.

"No need to apologize." He turned to Chloe. "Ms. Sinclair, isn't it?"

"Yes."

"If you have something to share," he said, a warrior's calm settling through him, "I'd like to hear it. I'm always open to alternate interpretations of what is going on in the media today."

He sat back and studied her with a bone deep detachment. He really didn't recognize her.

"Well, it's just that you are talking about KTEX as if we are in terrible shape."

He didn't respond.

"But we aren't."

He still didn't say anything, which made her feel the need to defend her stance even though he hadn't contradicted her. She had seen other people fall into this trap, start talking and talking as if they couldn't stop themselves.

"KTEX has turned a corner after the success of *Getting Real with Kate.* And with a few more well-thought-out programs, we can turn around completely. I resent you speaking of the station as if it's already in the grave."

"Fair enough."

He reached down into his briefcase, pulled out a file, opened it, then extended a set of papers.

Chloe glanced over them and sniffed again. He had spelled out clearly what she already knew but hadn't wanted to face. The reality of television was that they were dependent on advertising revenue. Not only were ad dollars down across the board for all venues, but television had been hit especially hard. For an independent station like KTEX, it was even more disheartening.

But Chloe wasn't about to concede defeat. Instead she felt the need to push hard to discredit him. "This might be true, but we have already begun our turnaround. We increased our revenue by eighty-three percent during *Getting Real.*"

"True. But that was only during the single episode where you showcased a mini-golf tournament," he clarified. "That's finite programming. Nothing that solves your larger issues."

"Meaning?" Kate said, worry in her voice.

The man looked directly at Kate. "Meaning that El Paso is cut off from most other cities. You don't have much in the way of bleed factor. El Paso is a good 250 to 300 miles away from any other city of significant size. Tucson, 316 miles to the west. Albuquerque, 267 miles to the north. And going east, Dallas–Fort Worth is twice that distance, with more cactus than people between here and there."

"Cacti," Chloe said glumly.

He looked at her hard. "I stand corrected."

But on the bigger picture, she knew he was right. Texas wasn't like many states that were built with towns running together, making it hard to tell where one ended and another began. In Texas, the minute you left the El Paso city limits, you didn't see much more than those cacti and the occasional small town, like some sort of holdback from the days of the wild wild west. Unless they bought another station in another city of significant size, KTEX's audience was here, and that was pretty much it.

"But a population of nearly eight hundred thousand is nothing to sneeze at," she countered.

"No question. But given the geography, it's finite."

"Las Cruces isn't so far away. And we have Juárez right across the border."

"Las Cruces is a small market. As to Juárez, do you plan to start broadcasting and advertising in Spanish?"

She hated that he was right.

He looked at some of his notes. "Based on the information I have here, you have to turn things around quickly, or you'll be too far in the red to realistically pull out."

"Many companies operate in the red at one time or another," Chloe added defensively. "We will pull out of this. We have time. Don't we, Julia?"

All eyes turned to Julia, but she didn't respond.

Lucy knocked on the door. "I'm sorry to interrupt, but the conference room has been reserved for eleven o'clock, and they're here."

Kate turned to Julia. "Reservations for the conference room?"

Julia stood up from her place at the head of the table, the men following suit. She smiled tightly. "I think we are done here for now. Mr. Tanner, Lucy will show you to my office. I'll meet you there momentarily."

With that she was gone.

In apparent shock, Kate stood, then extended her hand. "It was nice to meet you." Then she disappeared as well.

Ben said he needed to use the phone and headed out.

Chloe blinked, trying to quell the sudden uneasiness she

felt. But that uneasiness no longer had anything to do with what had happened between the two of them last night. She was pushed off balance by the sudden fear that she didn't understand all the forces that had been set into motion by his arrival. Julia had gone to Prescott Media without a word to her.

Chloe hardly realized that the man had picked up his briefcase and headed for the door. When she did, she was so relieved that he was leaving that it barely registered that he had turned back at the last second.

"Ah, I forgot," he said.

She was jarred from any sort of relief when she looked up. For the first time since their misguided interlude at the hotel, their gazes truly met. He smiled in a way that turned her insides to putty and made her knees go weak. The kaleidoscope began to churn again. Images. Yearning. The memory of his mouth closing over her breast. His hands sliding up her thighs.

She could only be thankful that he hadn't recognized her when she walked into this room. She had wanted to forget her moment of indiscretion since the second it happened. Now, in addition to that, she knew that she couldn't afford to feel anything for him if she had any chance of saving the station from Prescott Media.

But then he reached into his briefcase, before extending his hand to her, and the world ground to a halt when she saw the tiny, glittery evening purse sitting in his large, chiseled palm.

He smiled then, leaning close, and said, "You left this behind when you disappeared on me last night."

To: Chloe Sinclair <chloe@ktextv.com>
From: Katherine Bloom <katherine@ktextv.com>
Subject: No!

I can't believe it! Trey Tanner is the man from last night?!!! Julia is going to flip. Have you told her yet?

Kate

Katherine C. Bloom
News Anchor, KTEX TV West Texas

To: Katherine Bloom <katherine@ktextv.com>
From: Chloe Sinclair <chloe@ktextv.com>
Subject: Not yet

I haven't had a chance. She's talking to whoever it is she rented out conference room time to. How do you think she'll take it? Julia's always Ms. Modern until it comes to issues involving the station.

Chloe Sinclair
Station Manager
Award-winning KTEX TV

To: Chloe Sinclair <chloe@ktextv.com>
From: Katherine Bloom <katherine@ktextv.com>
Subject: Warning

I think you need to warn her, at the very least, so that she's aware of the situation as she's dealing with the man.

Kate

To: Katherine Bloom <katherine@ktextv.com>
From: Chloe Sinclair <chloe@ktextv.com>
Subject: How?

The man is waiting in her office right now!

Chloe

To: Chloe Sinclair <chloe@ktextv.com>
From: Katherine Bloom <katherine@ktextv.com>
Subject: re: How?

As soon as he leaves, tell her then. I think this has to be done in person. Keep me posted.

Kate

four

Sterling stood in Julia Boudreaux's office and watched the receptionist leave. Ben found him a second later. The minute the door shut, the younger Prescott laughed with great relish.

"So, *Trey,*" Ben said with emphasis, "did I mention how impressed I am by how highly thought of you are?"

"Ben," Sterling warned.

"Not to worry, big brother," Ben answered, momentarily distracted as he studied the ultrafeminine, leopard print sofa with purple trim in Julia's office. "With the things that Sinclair woman was saying, I didn't want to admit I was a Prescott either." With a laugh and a shake of his head, he sat down like a king on a throne.

Sterling narrowed his gaze at his brother. "I have no problem admitting who I am."

"Then why didn't you?"

Sterling raked his hands through his hair. He, Sterling Prescott, known for his cold control, felt a low bead of frustration over this ridiculous situation. He would have straightened out the mess with his identity if the woman from last night hadn't arrived.

Chloe Sinclair.

He had been so consumed by the sight of her he hadn't even realized that the Boudreaux woman had assumed he was Trey Tanner.

He wasn't one to be taken by surprise. One of his strengths in business was thinking of every eventuality ahead of time so he would be prepared no matter what he came up against. But he had never dreamed that he would see the woman again, at least not in the form of the station manager for KTEX TV.

He nearly smiled at the unexpected shock of her reappearance in his life. Hell, his smile had more to do with the unexpected shock of their encounter in the bathroom. He had been with many women before, but something about Chloe Sinclair was different. She had been sultry and filled with an unleashed passion like nothing he had ever experienced.

But he wasn't the type to make love to strangers. In this day and age it was dangerous, though that hadn't crossed his mind when his mouth had come down on hers.

All he had felt was sensation, heady and intense. But that didn't explain how he had felt when she—Chloe—had walked into the conference room hours later.

His body had recognized her before his mind had. The sizzle of comprehension racing along his skin had been like an adrenaline rush, followed by the gears in his brain finding purchase when he saw through the bangs and big glasses. The difference between the woman last night and the woman this morning was that without the makeup and extravagant hair, she was even more intriguing. He never would have believed so much wildness could hide behind such a prim exterior. He had nearly said something, an unfamiliar lightness flaring inside him.

But he had realized in the next second that she was praying he didn't recognize her. Standing there, he could hardly get his head around the idea that a woman didn't *want* him to recognize her. This after a lifetime of women throwing themselves at him.

Which had thrown him, and too late he had realized they had mistaken his identity.

He had no interest in sharing that with Ben, however, whose amusement was equally as grating as Chloe's reaction to him. God, what a mess.

To think he had brought Ben here to impress him, make him see that life with Prescott Media could be exciting. That a job in the media business could serve as a replacement for the life he had been living here in El Paso that had somehow gone awry.

He glanced at Ben and wondered not for the first time if the youngest Prescott would ever tell him what had happened.

"Damn," Ben said with a chuckle, "you've gotta love the whole mistaken identity thing for a man whose power is derived from his name."

Every thought about his brother's past hardened into a knot of growing frustration. "My power is not derived from my name."

Ben looked at him in wry disbelief. "Are we talking the same language here?" He glanced at his watch and shot him a teasing grin. "Though you better hurry up and fess up to who you are, make your lowball offer, and ruin these women's lives so we can make it to lunch on time."

Sterling's jaw worked. "What are you implying?"

Ben only shrugged, crossing his ankle over his knee as he leaned back with his arm lining the ridge of the small sofa that looked even smaller with him sitting on it. "I'm not implying anything. I'm stating the facts, just like they were stated earlier. You buy and ruin." He shook his head. "Did she really call you a modern day robber baron?" He laughed.

Sterling glowered.

"Look," Ben said, "I get that you have a responsibility to our family. Hell, I know Mother and Diana expect to be kept in the style they are accustomed. And God forbid Dad runs out of money to buy those damn toy soldiers. But the thing is, you don't even do the turning around part yourself. You come in, and whether it's intentional or not, you ruin people's lives. Then you bring someone else in to run things."

Sterling felt a vein drum in his head. He also noticed that the humor in Ben's face wasn't more than skin-deep. The youngest Prescott might tease, but he really was angry about the way Sterling did business.

Sterling felt both off balance and oddly defensive to be seen in such a poor light by his younger brother.

"Face it, Sterling. Women flock to you and you succeed in business because of your name and your money."

The words were put out there like a line drawn between them.

"That is not true. I succeed because of my skill. And I won't even dignify the issue of women with any response at all."

Ben laughed out loud. "You might have succeeded because of skill years ago, I'll give you that, but not anymore. Now you're everything that woman said you are. Hell, you couldn't charm Chloe Sinclair and win her approval if your life depended on it."

Sterling stood still, every muscle strung like a tight wire until he felt as if he vibrated with tension. Because the truth was, he had come to a crossroads in his life. He was successful, had made more money for the family than they could ever spend. But he no longer felt the challenge and excitement that he had felt when he first stepped up and took over the helm of Prescott Media.

He felt uncomfortable now, remembering his father's embarrassment when Sterling had stepped in and made it clear the elder Prescott wasn't needed. But Sterling had been too focused and consumed to care. He'd been too pissed off about the state of the company to feel anything but determination to fix what his father had broken.

But he'd done that, and more. Then why did he feel this emptiness? Why did he feel that if he were cut, he wouldn't bleed? Why had he nearly made love to a stranger in a hotel bathroom? Could it be because of the fact that she hadn't known who he was? That she was drawn to him, not to Sterling Prescott?

As much as he hated to think about it, how long had it been since a woman had cared solely for him, not about the money and status he brought to the equation? And how long had it been since he'd faced a challenge of the sort that he couldn't easily fix with his name and money?

He had the sudden urge to roll up his sleeves and feel the charge of his twenties and early thirties. But his time was too valuable for that. His job now was to find the properties, buy them for cheap, then hire someone else to turn them into moneymaking machines.

Just as Ben had said.

Just as he intended to do with KTEX TV.

Just as Chloe Sinclair had predicted.

Sterling stared through the glass enclosure in the office wall, looking out into the world he was on the verge of . . . disrupting. And then he saw the woman.

Chloe.

She walked down the hall, her dark hair brushing her

shoulders, her bangs framing the largest blue eyes he had ever seen. Her skin was pale and white, with a dash of freckles across the bridge of her nose, making him think of the elegant china dolls his sister had collected as a child.

But there had been nothing childlike in the woman last night.

The memory hit him hard. *"Kiss me."*

She had wanted him, had wanted him to be a stranger. She hadn't cared about his name.

Chloe Sinclair had been drawn to him without any clue as to who he was. She had wanted him, just him, not because he was a Prescott, not because he was a man of wealth and power—as she had made abundantly clear this morning.

But now she wanted nothing to do with him, and that was brought about, at least in part, because she thought he was merely *associated* with Sterling Prescott. He refused to admit the shudder he felt thinking about what she would have said if she had known that he actually was that man.

He was alternately intrigued and angry at the woman.

But more than that, now that he had found her again, he couldn't imagine going the rest of his life without finishing what he had started in a hotel bathroom less than twenty-four hours ago.

Chloe disappeared into an office, and Sterling turned back to his brother, who studied him with an expression he didn't like.

"What?" Sterling demanded.

"If I'm so wrong about you, then prove it."

"What are you talking about?" He shifted his weight uncomfortably.

"A challenge, big brother. Fix KTEX TV without the use of your name or your money. Turn the station around and win Chloe Sinclair's approval. And do it all as Trey Tanner."

"This is ridiculous."

"If you don't think you can do it . . ."

The words hung between them as a challenge.

Sterling's jaw clenched. "You're talking about a childish game."

"I'm talking about proving that you aren't who Chloe says you are. Prove that you aren't everything I'm afraid you've become. Turn this station around, save those women's careers, and prove that you aren't as cutthroat and callous as you're accused of being."

Sterling's heart began to pound, his temples throbbing as he stared at Ben.

The younger man looked away, glancing at the wall, though Sterling was certain he saw something entirely different from the bright pink walls.

"If you succeed," Ben said, this time quietly, "I'll make the family happy. I'll leave the police force for good and I'll hire on at Prescott Media."

Sterling never showed emotion, but he had a hard time covering the surprise he felt now. "You're kidding."

Ben glanced back. "I've never been more serious." He seemed to search for a smile but in the end couldn't find it. "Truth is, I might be in the market for a new line of work. I just never thought it'd be with Prescott." He shrugged, a glint returning to his dark eyes. "Not that I think for a second that you can pull it off. I have a feeling KTEX TV is in a world of hurt. Why else would that Boudreaux woman risk contacting Trey Tanner? As to getting Chloe to do something that would show her approval, I can't imagine that happening even if you did turn the station around. She hates your guts."

"The Sinclair woman does not hate my guts—"

Ben raised a dark brow, amusement flickering in his eyes.

"—and there isn't a television station around that is so broken that I couldn't fix it."

"So you accept?"

Sterling stared at him hard. "Did the undercover job really go that wrong?"

Every ounce of forced humor evaporated. "Don't change the subject." The two men faced each other, then Ben added, "Are you up for the challenge?"

Sterling couldn't let it go so easily. "What happened, Ben?"

Ben's jaw ticked this time. "I don't want to talk about it."

They stared at each other, both men strong-willed, until Ben relented. "Maybe another time. Okay?"

Sterling hesitated, then nodded. "Whenever you're ready."

Ben's grin returned. "So, does that mean you accept the challenge? Turn KTEX TV around and win Chloe's approval, all without telling anyone that you're Sterling Prescott and without Prescott funds. For a month, you'll be Trey Tanner—a man here to help."

Thankfully Sterling didn't have to answer the absurd idea because the door rattled opened. Out of habit, Ben rose to his feet.

Julia Boudreaux entered the office. Instantly Sterling felt the shift in his brother. Sterling had made an art form of reading other people's body language. It gave him an edge when negotiating a deal. In this office, he sensed in Ben part awareness of and part determined detachment from the woman who had just entered.

Sterling glanced at Julia. She was a piece of work, no doubt. A true beauty who must have had everything handed to her on a platter. The leopard print and purple couch spoke to that. But it wasn't Julia who intrigued Sterling.

As if to tease his senses, Chloe filed into the office next. But even her sensible knee-length skirt couldn't hide the fact that she had great legs. But great legs or not, she didn't look happy to be there.

Julia said something to Ben, who said something back, but Sterling didn't hear. His gaze was focused on Chloe as she walked across the room without so much as a glance in his direction. But when she came up next to him, she surreptitiously shoved that damned purse into his hands.

"You clearly have me mistaken for someone else. That isn't my purse. And until my misfortune today, I've never seen you before in my life."

Chloe watched as the man raised a brow in sardonic amusement. But she held firm. After she had left the conference room, she had come up with a three-part plan. Deny. Deny. Deny.

"Excuse me," Julia interjected. "I'd like to get started. I also would like to state my apologies for the earlier meeting." She eyed Chloe. "We aren't usually so unladylike in our treatment of people who are interested in *helping* us. And I think Chloe would like to say something."

Chloe stared at Julia as if she had lost her mind. "Me? You want me to say something?"

"An apology," Julia said pointedly.

Oh right. That. She rolled her eyes. "I'm sorry you work for a man like Sterling Prescott."

That granite jaw of his went tight and Julia groaned.

"That's your apology?" he asked.

"Do you like it?"

His jaw really started working then. Good.

Crossing her arms over her chest, she forged ahead. "A more pressing issue, however, is what is Prescott Media's decision? Are you going to ruin us or help us?"

She actually scoffed, since she was so certain of his answer.

"I'm going to help."

Chloe blinked, then sat down with a thunk on the ridiculous leopard sofa. "You're going to help?"

She felt many things. Surprise, sure. Then a second of relief, no question. Followed closely by suspicion. "Why? How? What's in it for Prescott?"

The man sat in a side chair, leaning back as he studied her. He looked intense, totally hot, and completely unfazed by her pointed questions.

He tugged his cuffs, looked at his brother for one long second, then returned his gaze to hers. "Sterling Prescott is really nicer than anyone appears to believe."

Ben chuckled.

She couldn't help it when she snorted. "You've probably never even met him."

"Chloe, please," Julia implored.

And rightfully so. Chloe had never acted so childishly in her life. But the combination of the bathroom incident and this man who could ruin them left her out of sorts and fighting mad. And she would fight if she had to. Growing up with an unbending grandmother and no other family to speak of forced a girl to give in or fight. Chloe had always fought.

Today was no different. They couldn't lose KTEX. Even if it meant accepting this man's assistance.

"Sorry," she stated.

"Ah, another of your heartfelt apologies."

This time Chloe raised a brow. Mr. Tanner had a snippy streak in him, too.

"So what's the deal?" she persisted.

He glanced one last time at his brother, sighed, then said, "The deal is I spend a month of my time, graciously donated by none other than Sterling Prescott, and turn this station around."

"And again, what's in it for Mr. Gracious?"

The man muttered something she knew wasn't nice, then he considered her. "I'll work on a contingency basis. Prescott Media earns a percent of the increased ad revenue that I bring in."

"That's it?" Julia breathed.

Chloe glared at her for caving so easily.

The Tanner guy looked amused. "Yes, that's it."

But Chloe knew they weren't out of the woods yet. This was sounding too good to be true. "What kind of a percentage are you looking for?"

She watched him shift into a purely business mode with ease. She hated that she was impressed—and not just a little turned on.

He glanced at Julia. "A sixty-forty split."

"Sixty for us?" Julia asked hopefully.

"Julia! No way," Chloe stated. "Ninety-ten in our favor."

"That's absurd," he barked, then visibly reined his temper back in. "The best I can do is seventy-thirty in your favor."

"In your dreams. Eighty-twenty."

"Chloe," Julia implored.

The man studied Chloe over steepled fingers, then said, "Seventy-five–twenty-five."

Chloe opened her mouth to counter.

He cut her off. "And that's final."

This time Chloe studied him. She knew she had reached his limit. Besides, it was a fair deal. "Seventy-five–twenty-five sounds all right. Julia?"

"Agreed," the owner stated in a rush of relief.

It was done. It was happening, and suddenly every ounce of bravado faded away and Chloe was left with the horror that now she was going to have to see this man again. And again. For a month.

"I suggest we waste no time and get started," Julia said.

"Mr. Tanner"—Chloe would have sworn he grimaced—"why don't you give us your initial assessment of KTEX?"

"There's no secret here. You need more revenue to offset your mounting debt and accruing interest. And to do that, you need to bring in more advertising."

"As I mentioned earlier," Chloe said, "we are planning more programs like the golf episode of *Getting Real*."

"That will help, but that's too little, too late." He looked at Julia. "Isn't that correct, Ms. Boudreaux?"

Chloe felt a chill run down her spine, and she glanced over at Julia to see if this was true. The woman's blood-drained face spoke louder than words.

But Chloe's concern was tempered by the sheer concentration that came over Trey Tanner's face. She could practically see the wheels in his head spinning as he assimilated this situation.

"As a result," he said, "what you need is something that can be easily and quickly produced, for little money."

His dark eyes flared with an intense excitement that made her think of a warrior who was ready to do battle and was certain that he would win.

"A reality show," he stated. "You need a locally produced reality show."

"A reality show?" Chloe asked.

"Exactly. We need to produce a reality show like MTV's *The Real World*. Or Fox's *Joe Millionaire*. You have one basic setup that runs for as long as you want. Recurring show, recurring audience. Recurring revenue. We can do it, and we can do it in a month."

We.

Chloe leaped up and started pacing back and forth across Julia's office. Not that she had far to pace, since the room wasn't that big, and every time she got close to Trey Tanner's chair, her mind flared an imaginary, flashing red warning sign, causing her to jerk around and head in the opposite direction.

"What kind of a crazy idea is that?" Chloe demanded. "Reality shows are a dime a dozen."

"But not locally based reality shows," Trey interjected. "We're talking about pioneering into new territory."

"That's crazy."

"You run it in place of your local evening news."

"You want to produce trash in place of news?"

"As I said, I'm talking about producing something that will earn a recurring stream of revenue—unlike your news."

Insulted, Chloe defended their evening newscast, going on about how twenty-four-hour cable news had saturated the airwaves. Which only served to make Trey's point. They weren't making money in news. But a reality TV show could.

"If you air the show while everyone else is airing news, you'll provide an advertising outlet advertisers can't get anywhere else. You'll have businesses flocking to pay you whatever you want to secure thirty- and even sixty-second spots. Plus, you don't have to forget the news forever. Just for a while. Just until you get the balance sheet balanced."

She hated that she saw the logic. She felt oddly disconcerted and angry, though she knew deep down this was about more than his suggestion. She didn't know how to manage this situation. How would she be able to concentrate, much less get anything done, if the man was working in the building? What would she say if she ran into him at the watercooler? How could she ignore him in the staff meetings Julia had recently started having?

Chloe had given him the upper hand the minute she let him pull her into the bathroom.

She mentally rolled her eyes. She had given him the upper hand the minute she *launched* herself at him like a grenade.

Geez, Chloe.

And she wasn't sure how effectively her pretend-she-had-never-seen-him-before plan would work. Though thankfully she'd had the inspiration to shove the purse back in his hands and tell him he was mistaken.

Maybe it would succeed if she just kept up with the theme.

With that thought in mind, she looked him straight in the eye. "I realize I don't know you at all, and have never seen you before in my life—"

His lips crooked at one corner. Not a good sign.

"—but I think I can safely say that you aren't as familiar with the El Paso television market as I am."

He responded by reeling off a whole slew of facts about her hometown and its television viewing habits. He knew the market, which didn't bother her because her only real goal had been to continue to hammer home the I've-never-seen-you-in-my-life theme.

Julia leaned forward. "How exactly would this work?"

Trey reached into his briefcase and pulled out a pen and a pad of paper. He made a few notes. When he finished, he set the pad down. "The station could put on a bachelor type show—"

"A bachelor show?!" Chloe barked.

Ben sat back and got comfortable. "This should be good."

"Watch and learn, little brother." Trey was obviously warming up to his subject. "On our bachelor show we—"

There was that *we* word again.

"—will have a fresh twist. To start out, we'll tape each segment like any other reality show. We'll have six episodes total, each edited down to forty-four minutes, leaving sixteen minutes for advertising. What will make us stand apart is that instead of waiting until we have an entire season in the can, we'll air each show the same night we tape it. It's how they do the *Late Show with David Letterman,* and it's the next best thing to live television."

Trey started to pace, excitement and plans rushing through him in a way that was almost palpable. "As I mentioned before, we can do the whole thing in a month."

"You want to air the entire program in a single month?" Chloe asked.

"No." He smiled. "A single month to plan, produce, and run the program." He glanced around the room. "Then at the end, KTEX will be in a position to pay off the debt." He glanced at Ben. "Saving the station." He looked at Chloe. "I'm sure that should please you."

Was this guy for real?

"Two weeks to plan, then we'll air six episodes over two weeks," he added. "Let's say we air each Monday, Friday, and Saturday night."

Chloe was stunned by the sheer amount of work that would have to be done. She couldn't think of anything to say. But the truth was, it wasn't such a horrible idea.

"We'd have a show that was part *The Bachelor,*" he explained, "part *The Real World.* We could call it *The Catch.*"

"Interesting," Julia mused, her voice rising with excitement. "If I have this right, it would be a series of segments that will be cheap to make and will bring in tons of ad revenue."

"Exactly," he confirmed.

Could these two be any more sickeningly cheerful about a prospect that would send her over the edge? Chloe thought dismally.

Trey Tanner's dark eyes glittered with a predator's success. "We'll be combining the strongest elements of two already successful shows, giving us something new in a genre of television that is exceedingly popular, but crowded."

"The more I hear about this, the more I like it," Julia enthused. "We just need to find a bachelor and some women. How many were you thinking?"

"Ten or so. We'll have to sit down and make a plan."

"How about *The Catch and His Dozen Texas Roses*?"

Chloe was as surprised by her interjection as everyone else. But she couldn't seem to help herself. The producer in her was always at work.

"I like it," Trey stated with an approving nod.

His cell phone rang. After glancing at the readout, he said, "Excuse me, I need to take this."

Ben stood, tipped his imaginary hat, then said he needed to stretch his legs. Julia watched him go.

When Chloe would have followed, Julia stopped her. "Please go along with this," she pleaded in a whisper. "We really need it."

Chloe's concern resurfaced. "What is going on?"

"Nothing I can talk about now. But I need you to help, not antagonize, the man."

"Fine." She headed for the door just as Trey flipped his cell phone closed.

"I'm going to need you to work with me on this, Ms. Sinclair."

"Me?" Chloe asked, looking around the room as if he were speaking to someone else. "Me, as in *me* work with you?" Being civil to him at the watercooler would have been a stretch. Actually working together on a project would be impossible.

Julia implored her with her nearly violet eyes.

"Is that a problem, Chloe?" he asked.

"Yes!"

All eyes focused on her, and she realized she was acting like a completely unprofessional lunatic—sort of like last night. She nearly dropped her head into her hands. Not to mention that Julia was speaking with a seriousness that few people would have believed possible for the woman who had always taken pride in never having a deeper concern than if Raspberry Shocker nail enamel was passé.

"I mean, yes, there is a problem, Julia. Unfortunately my schedule is full."

"Then clear it," Julia said. "*The Catch and His Dozen Texas Roses* is what KTEX TV needs. We are going to move into the new millennium." The station owner stood. "I'll leave you two kids to talk. Get back to me when you have a solid plan."

"Julia—" But Chloe cut herself off. What was there to say?

"What?"

"Nothing."

Julia studied her for a second. "Is there anything wrong, Chloe?"

"With me?" She laughed, the sound jarring. "Absolutely not. I'm great. Better than great."

Julia nodded, then left the room.

All too quickly, Trey and Chloe were left alone.

"You appear to be caught off guard about this," he said, not unkindly. "It wouldn't be because of last night."

"There was no last night!"

"I beg to differ."

"Beg all you like—"

There went that brow again.

"—but how many times do I have to tell you that you've mistaken me for someone else?"

"Fine, have it your way. For now."

"For now?"

He started putting his pen and paper back into his briefcase. "I won't push. But I would like to know why you're so upset about the show."

Chloe blinked and looked at him and said the only truly honest thing she had said since she saw him in the conference room. "I thought you were coming in to study the station. I had no idea you knew so much already."

"Julia sent most of the information beforehand."

Chloe hated that Julia hadn't told her about it, and from the look on Kate's face earlier, she had been just as surprised.

"Oh," she managed.

"KTEX needs a hit, Chloe. Badly."

But what really bothered her was that any sort of smash hit involved this man.

"Since the station needs a hit fast," he added, "I have to work quickly to get this show on the air. As proficient as I am"—he actually smiled at her in a way that made her knees go weak—"I can't do it by myself. I need a coproducer."

"And that would be me."

"You got it," he confirmed.

"I'm really not so sure that I'll be able to do this."

"Why not?"

"My schedule really is full. Budgets to work on, shows to schedule, payroll to meet."

Her mind spun with too many things. This man, last night, right now, this new turn of events.

"That's fine. I'm happy to work with anyone on this project. If you'll assign someone else, I'll get started."

Chloe groaned. "There is no one else."

"No assistants?"

"Nope."

"No in-house producer?"

She sighed. "I've been serving as in-house producer since we had to let our last one go."

"So what do you propose?"

Chloe flopped down into the matching chair across from Julia's desk, pushing her glasses up with one finger pressed to the bridge. "I guess I have no choice but to work with you on this."

"You make it sound so horrible."

"It is."

"Come on," he teased. "Was I really that bad last night?"

They both knew he wasn't. But she still wasn't willing to surrender her I've-never-met-you stance.

"You really aren't going to give up, are you?" he asked.

"I've been called tenacious."

"A better word might be *stubborn*."

"Thank you."

"Fine. Have it your way. But we'll need to get to work right away."

He stood. Unfortunately he stopped just in front of her, planting his hands on the arms of her chair. His dark eyes sparked with humor, and his incredibly sensual mouth tilted up at one corner. "If you want," he said, "we can start in the bathroom."

He pushed away and was gone before she could chuck her notepad at his head.

Julia, I hope you know what you're doing by giving Prescott Media a toehold in KTEX. It hardly seems possible that we can create and air a program all within a month. What happens if it doesn't work? Will we be deeper in debt? Is this creating an even greater opportunity for Prescott to swoop in and offer you a price that is even lower but impossible not to accept because we are in worse straits than before?

Chloe

Chloe Sinclair
Station Manager
Award-winning KTEX TV

From: Julia Boudreaux <julia@ktextv.com>
Subject: Worry

You're giving me heart palpitations, Chloe. Me, Miss Never Have a
Care. I really don't like this new life. But now with my father gone,
I don't have any choice. Do you have a better idea that will save
the station?

As to the month, you produced Kate's big golf show in two weeks.
I don't see a problem.

Julia

To: Chloe Sinclair <chloe@ktextv.com>
From: Katherine Bloom <katherine@ktextv.com>
Subject: Status

Have you told Julia about your nocturnal encounter with Trey Tanner
yet?

Kate

Katherine C. Bloom
News Anchor, KTEX TV West Texas

To: Katherine Bloom <katherine@ktextv.com>
From: Chloe Sinclair <chloe@ktextv.com>
Subject: Not yet

I haven't had a chance. But I will. Just as soon as I can get her alone.

C

To: Julia Boudreaux <julia@ktextv.com>
Katherine Bloom <katherine@ktextv.com>
From: Chloe Sinclair <chloe@ktextv.com>
Subject: Will do

All right. I'll do everything I can to ensure the success of the new show. I've already scheduled short promos to run announcing the cattle call for talent. <g> We'll announce it on the news. Kate, I'd like you to say something on *Getting Real*. We'll certainly get the word out. I just can't imagine any woman in her right mind would want to do this.

Chloe

five

So she was wrong.

The line of men and women vying to be on KTEX TV's new reality show, *The Catch and His Dozen Texas Roses,* snaked around the building and down the street. From all appearances, West Texas's entire eighteen-to-thirty-four-year-old demographic had turned out, and not a few fifty and older were mixed into the line.

Did these people have no pride? Chloe wondered as she sat at the long folding table in what had been, until an hour ago, the lunchroom at KTEX. Now it was the interview room, hastily set up to accommodate the hundreds of men and women who had turned out to vie for their fifteen minutes—or two weeks—of fame.

Trey Tanner sat next to her.

She had a stack of photos and résumés sitting in front of her. She could feel him studying her as she made a great production of going over—or pretending to go over, given how uncomfortable she felt—the résumés of each applicant.

"I don't think we'll have trouble getting our bachelor or

our twelve Roses," he remarked, his dark eyes glittering with humor.

Sitting next to him was bad enough. Having him smile at her made her want to scream. Scream in frustration over the way her heart sped up. She was not allowed to feel anything for the man. She was supposed to be doing mental penance for her complete and utter lack of good sense last week. But whenever her gaze happened on him, she couldn't help herself from glancing at his mouth. The only thing that saved her was that every time he opened that very same orifice, something completely arrogant and autocratic came out that made her think CEO instead of underling. This man didn't act like he knew the first thing about taking orders from anyone.

"What?" he asked, breaking into her thoughts.

"Nothing." She shook her head and refocused on the stack in front of her. "We'd best get started if we plan to interview everyone out there. We will have to go fast, and even then it will take hours."

"If you had let me go through the photos, I could have narrowed the search down quite a bit. I would have weeded out the undesirables."

"What are you talking about?"

"The dogs, dirtbags, and do-gooders."

"That's completely unfair! And mean."

"Have it your way. If you're willing to take the time, so am I. I aim to please." He smiled, though it looked really forced and really suspicious. Chloe studied him closely.

"Let's get started," he said. "Where's our first hopeful?" he called out.

KTEX's twenty-three-year-old receptionist appeared in the doorway faster than she had done anything since coming to work at the station. She was dressed in a way that

Chloe had never seen. She either wanted a job on *The Catch* or she was interested in Trey Tanner.

Chloe glanced down at her own sensible skirt and low heels. It was as if she had not only lost every trace of sexy, but had headed even farther in the opposite direction.

"Bring in the first candidate," Trey instructed.

"Yes, sir." The woman turned to go.

"Lucy! You report to me." Trey glanced over at her as she ridiculously added, "You can bring in the first applicant."

Trey chuckled and Lucy rolled her eyes. Chloe decided she could learn a thing or two about commanding people.

The first candidate happened to be a man. He introduced himself as Leonard Parsimmons.

"Thank you for coming in, Leonard," Chloe said kindly.

He wore a short-sleeved button-down shirt tucked into neatly pressed khaki pants. He couldn't have been taller than five-five, though his résumé stated five-seven-and-three-quarters. He had sandy blond hair that fell forward onto his forehead, and another glance at the résumé put his weight at 139 pounds. He was a slight man with a shy smile.

"Next," Trey said, startling them.

"What?" Chloe demanded. "We haven't even asked any questions."

"As you said, we have to go fast or we'll be here all day."

"But we have to ask questions."

Trey gave a weary sigh and sat back.

Chloe looked at Leonard. "Mr. Parsimmons, what is your favorite color?"

For the next few minutes, they talked and laughed. The man was a delight, kind and sweet, and Chloe loved him. By the time she finished, she actually walked him to the door.

"I think he could work," she said, returning.

An expression of disbelief spread over Trey's face. "You've got to be kidding. We're supposed to make people want to watch the show, not make them change the channel as fast as they can."

"He's great!"

"He's horrible."

"Give me one good reason why."

"Would you date him?"

"Sure."

"Really? He's going to make you hot and wet? Can you even imagine sleeping with him?"

Chloe choked. "You're awful."

"I'm not awful. I'm just trying to get at the truth."

"The truth? Oh, sure. I recognize your type."

"What are you going to do, compare me to Leonard? Stereotype us both by saying he's kind and gentle and I'm a Neanderthal who thinks sex is a game and my only goal is to score?"

"Exactly!"

"You're wrong. I enjoy women and I enjoy them in bed. I admit it. But women rarely admit what they really want."

"Aaawwwk!" She was so appalled her head felt like it did an *Exorcist* spin.

"Women say they want Ashley," he continued with bold assurance, "when they really want Rhett."

Her mouth fell open.

"They say they want sweet and sensitive, but they really want a strong man who's confident enough to protect them."

She could feel her lips flapping as she tried to find words to express her disgust. "You . . . are . . . the . . . most arrogantly atrocious man I have ever had the misfortune to meet."

The next Catch candidate entered, an overmuscled body-builder who didn't appear to have a neck.

"Oh, look," she hissed quietly with a saccharine-sweet smile. "A man whose knuckles scrape the ground. Your hero."

"I'm not talking about Tarzan—"

She snorted.

"I'm talking about someone like"—he considered, then continued—"John Wayne. The sort of man who doesn't take no for an answer and saves the town at the end of the day."

"Male Behavior 101 learned on the Turner Classic Movie station. I'm impressed."

He wiggled his brows.

This time she was the one to hurry the candidate along. "Next!"

A woman entered. The minute Trey smiled at the voluptuous blonde, Chloe knew that this was going to be the longest few weeks of her life.

"Tammi with an i" smiled and cooed at Trey, leaning over whenever she had a chance to show off her Pamela Anderson breasts. Like that would get her the job.

"I think she's a perfect choice," Trey said once Tammi left the room. "Just the sort of woman who will keep viewers away from the remote."

"Could you be a little less predictable?" she countered. "Besides, this is supposed to be a family show, not Wet Dream TV."

He laughed out loud.

They interviewed three more women in a row. And Chloe had the idea to ask the questions from the *Sexy!* quiz.

"If you were reincarnated as an animal, what would you be?"

Trey's lips spread in amusement, and then he asked her what her response would be. She refused to answer, though not one of the women said llama.

Chloe decided to leave out that question after a woman named Jazzy Jamison, wearing heavy black eyeliner and long red nails, looked Trey up and down and said, "I'd come back as a fierce, man-eating lion who roared."

When she exited, even Trey agreed she was a little scary. At least they could scratch another off the list.

It took them hours, but by five that evening, they had narrowed the 347 interviewees down to five men and twenty-five women.

By late afternoon the following day, it was time to make the final decisions. "I really think Sherry Webb would be a good Rose," she said.

"Miss Brains?"

"Do you have to give them all names?"

"You're the one who started it by referring to 'Tammi with an i' as Ms. Boobs."

She cringed. "It was wrong and mean, and I never should have said that."

"Too late."

"How about a deal? I'll let you choose Tammi if you let me choose Sherry."

"We're going to make decisions based on bargaining?" he asked.

"You'd rather pull names out of a hat?"

"I was thinking we should consider attributes that would make them appealing to a television audience."

"You're obsessed with channel changing."

"You should be, too, since you manage the station."

Now that was a little embarrassing, since he was ab-solutely right.

"I'm starved. We never had lunch," she said, her head throbbing from the process.

"Then let's eat." He looked around as if he expected a waiter to materialize, then appeared surprised by the sparsely furnished lunchroom.

"You looked confused," she said.

"No, not at all. We'll go out."

"We don't have time. We can order something."

"You do that?"

"Don't you?"

"Actually, no, I never have."

"What planet did you say you're from?"

He blinked. "A regular planet. Let's order."

"What do you want?"

"What do *you* want?"

"Why are you avoiding the question?"

"I'm being the polite, kind, sensitive man you say you desire."

"Then pizza."

He made a face.

"You don't like pizza?!"

"I love pizza. Order any kind you like."

She went to the phone and called Pepe's Pizzeria. Trey was on his cell phone, sounding all commanding, when she turned back. She left him in private, thankful to get away from his unnerving presence.

Twenty minutes later their meal arrived. Trey had come to look for her, and when she pulled money out to pay, he stopped her.

"Let me get that."

Such a gentleman.

But suddenly the gentleman jerked to a halt as he stared at his wallet. He didn't have any cash. He started to pull out a credit card, then quickly pushed it back as if he didn't want her to see it, and flipped his wallet shut. "I'll have to owe you on the pizza." He didn't look happy about it.

She could tell he made a mental note, and she felt certain he was the sort of man who always paid for a woman's meal.

In the lunchroom, they had to tackle the final decisions regarding the cast of *The Catch*. But the task was made bearable by the large, thin-crust pepperoni pizza.

Chloe picked up a piece and stopped just before biting when she noticed Trey was looking at her.

"What?" she asked.

He shrugged, then dove in. He picked up a slice and took a bite. "This is good." He sounded surprised.

"If I believed in aliens, I'd swear you were from some other world. Are you sure you're from St. Louis?"

"Positive. Born and raised. Family still there."

"Are you from a big family?"

"Not big. Just my parents and brother who you met, and I have a sister. I also have a grandmother who is a whirlwind. In fact she's originally from El Paso. She met my grandfather when he was stationed at Fort Bliss."

"Tanner. What kind of a name is that?"

He went very still, then he muttered a curse. She swore he was on the verge of saying something, then seemed to think better of it.

"I don't have any idea what kind of name Tanner is."

"Why do you look like the type who'd know everything about your family and where they came from?"

Because he was, Sterling wanted to tell her. He did know everything about his heritage. The Prescott heritage.

It was all he could do not to tell her who he really was. But it was too late now, and the truth was, not only did he want to prove to his brother that he could do this, but Sterling felt a deeper need to prove something to himself.

He also wanted to know more about this woman.

She intrigued him. And she certainly wasn't intimidated by him. A rare combination in his world. As rare as him having pizza at a folding table in El Paso, Texas.

Even when Prescott Media was foundering, his family had lived in the same grand manner as it always had. It wasn't until his grandmother had come out of her widow's grief that she had realized what was happening. That's when she came to Sterling.

Shaking the thought away, he watched as Chloe tipped her head back, the slice tilted up as she tried to guide a long string of cheese into her mouth. She was enchanting, innocent, and completely unconcerned with what he thought of her. No posturing or posing.

"Tell me about you," he said without thinking.

She nearly dropped the pizza. "What do you want to know?" she asked after a long second.

"Anything."

"There's nothing interesting to tell."

"How old are you?"

"None of your business."

"Do you really prefer men like Leonard?"

"Leonard was nice."

"Leonard was a bore."

"Next question."

"Fine. Tell me about your family. Your mother, your father. Do they live here in town?"

He would have sworn she grew flustered.

"No personal questions," she said.

"Why not?"

"Because it's none of your business."

"You've been asking all the same sorts of questions of these candidates."

"Maybe, but they're interviewing to be a Texas Rose. I'm not."

"Fair enough. Then tell me what animal you'd be reincarnated as."

Red seared her cheeks.

"That embarrasses you?"

"A little."

"Then why did you ask the women?"

"If you must know, I took a quiz and I answered with llama. Don't laugh."

"I won't. I'm impressed. The llama is a hardworking, trustworthy animal that is underrated."

"Exactly!"

"The only downside is they spit."

She stared at him, amazed, and for the first time since she had walked into the conference room, her defenses wavered.

"They do spit! Not many people know that."

"I think a llama is a perfectly respectable reincarnation choice."

She gasped. "I said the same thing!"

With an amazed and surprised smile, Chloe took another bite of pizza, a stringy piece of cheese popping off to curl on her lip. Sterling watched as she chewed, her lips moving, and he wanted to kiss her.

Instead he reached out and wiped the cheese away, restraining himself from pulling her onto the table and satisfying his urge. But the piece of cheese didn't go away.

He wiped again and it finally came off, only to stick on his finger. He shook it, then shook again, then before he knew it Chloe was laughing. Laughing at him. Sterling Prescott, notorious ladies' man. And she laughed until she had tears streaming down her cheeks.

But every trace of humor fled from her expression when

his gaze drifted to her mouth. Laughter broke off. Her lips rounded in a silent *Oh*.

Automatically she touched her mouth as if hoping to find more cheese. But nothing was there.

When he looked back into her eyes he laughed softly, heat drumming through him. The hard ruthlessness he normally felt was amazingly gone, but something far more dangerous took its place. Desire that made him feel unhinged and reckless.

He leaned close, the fluorescent lights casting shadows on her face. "Why is it," he whispered, "that I'm drawn to you?"

"You make it sound so bad." Then she blinked. "And it is bad," she added, summoning up indignation.

She opened her mouth to add more, probably a detailed explanation as to why they shouldn't pursue this crazy path. But he pressed his finger to her mouth.

"Shhh. Don't say anything else."

He saw the tremor run along her body, saw her pulse in her neck. With slow determination, he ran his finger down her cheek, then under her chin. He tilted her ever so slightly. He knew that she understood that he would kiss her. He could see how her irises flared, the blues of her eyes going dark with desire.

"God, who the hell are you?" he demanded raggedly.

Chloe didn't answer. Couldn't. She tried to think about the fact that she was supposed to be doing penance, not giving in to the very thing that had got her into trouble in the first place. She tried to wrestle her thoughts back into order. Instead she sucked in her breath, then touched him. Just a touch. Just on his cheek, the skin just barely rough despite a close shave. She loved the feel of him, the scent of him, spicy and clean, like wild grasses.

"You make me crazy." He said the words like an accusation. "You talk back and question me at every turn."

"And that's a bad thing?" she whispered, not moving away.

He laughed grimly, a sweet vibration of sound. "You undo me."

Then she felt the last of his resistance melt away as his hands reached up, his palms lining her jaw, his fingers trailing back into her hair. "I want you," he whispered raggedly, a hairbreadth away from her ear. "Here, right now."

It was crazy. She had promised herself that such behavior was a one-time thing. But she could hear his need whispering in her head like a rush of air, causing the feelings to shift and change. Desperate need turned to willing desire, sought after like a brass ring. Right then she couldn't think of anything more than losing herself in his arms.

Expertly, he tilted her head a little more and he leaned forward. She started to close her eyes. She wanted to feel his mouth against hers one more time, feel the same sensations she had felt the other night . . . when she had gone crazy. Gone wild. *Had been sinfully forward,* she could all but hear her grandmother say.

Thoughts rushed through her head as he bent his head to hers. Grandmother. Propriety. Smart girls don't kiss strangers. Prescott Media's hired henchman could be nothing less than dangerous.

"No!"

She blurted the word as sense finally returned. With a squeak and a jerk, she leaped away, nearly knocking him out of his chair.

"Chloe?" His eyes narrowed.

"I can't. We can't."

He reached for her, and she leaped farther away.

"Why not?"

"Because. Besides, your cell phone is ringing," she added hastily. And it was.

He ignored the phone and they stood facing each other. He cocked his head. "Does this mean you're going to disappear on me again?"

She stared at him forever. "Yes, that's what it means."

He surprised her by looking pleased. "At least you've stopped trying to pretend that night didn't happen."

Damn. "Well, it won't happen again."

"Why? Because you're not that sort of woman? Is that what you're going to say?"

"No. I was going to say that you aren't my type."

"What type is that?"

"Arrogant, brash, used to getting what you want."

"I do get what I want," he stated arrogantly, brashly. "And I want you."

"*That's* when I'd say I'm not that sort of woman. You were a fling, a diversion. A stupid mistake."

His brows slammed together.

"All brought on by the fact that when I answered that reincarnation question we talked about, I wrote in *llama*."

She could tell she wasn't making him feel any better, and he already didn't like the fact that she had called him a mistake.

She backed up even farther. "It's getting late, and I've got to go."

He studied her with menacing dark eyes. Then he pulled his phone out of its holder and glanced at the readout.

"Since you aren't going to kiss me yet—"

"Yet!"

"—I'm going to return the call. But I shouldn't be more than forty-five minutes." He headed for the door. "I'll meet you back here at six-thirty."

"I have plans at six-thirty," she called after him.

"Change them."

Then he was gone, leaving her staring at the closed door in sheer, utter disbelief.

Who did he think he was?

To: Sterling Prescott <sterling@prescottmedia.com>
From: Betty Taylor <betty@prescottmedia.com>
Subject: Direction

Mr. Prescott:

I have fielded several calls from your family members. Your sister has called three times—she is less than pleased that you left town without approving the money she needs to close on her condominium. Your mother has called twice, and your grandmother just told me that if I didn't tell her where you were, she'd have me fired.

Please advise.

Best regards,
Betty Taylor

Executive Assistant to Sterling Prescott

To: Sterling Prescott <sterling@prescottmedia.com>
From: Diana Prescott <diana@prescottmedia.com>
Subject: Where are you?

Why aren't you back yet? And why didn't you approve my request regarding the money? If I don't close on that condo, they will sell it to someone else. It isn't fair that I have to come to you for everything. I'm a Prescott, too. Not some underling who earns a salary!

Diana

p.s. Ben's all right, isn't he?

To: Sterling Prescott <sterling@prescottmedia.com>
From: Vendela Prescott <vendela@prescottmedia.com>
Subject: Not amused

Dear Sterling:

Why haven't I heard a word regarding Ben? Your father and I are sick with worry. Last night at the Manards' soiree (five hundred guests, and I was astounded how so many of my friends are aging), I could hardly have fun for thinking about the two of you off in Texas doing who knows what.

Please call. Getting information out of your secretary is impossible.

With love,
Your mother

To: Sterling Prescott <sterling@prescottmedia.com>
From: Serena Prescott <serena@prescottmedia.com>
Subject: E-mail

Dearest Sterling,

You have forced an old woman to use this god-awful e-mail
contraption since despite my threats to that abysmal Cyclops who
guards your whereabouts, I haven't received a bit of information
regarding the success of your mission. I liked it better when I was
still on the board of Prescott. Then I could have fired her. Alas, I'm
forced to resort to this. Why haven't you returned with young Ben in
hand?

Sincerely,
Grandmère

To: Serena Prescott <serena@prescottmedia.com>
Vendela Prescott <vendela@prescottmedia.com>
Diana Prescott <diana@prescottmedia.com>
From: Sterling Prescott <sterling@prescottmedia.com>
Subject: Update

I am here with Ben. He is doing well. I will be spending the month in
El Paso, as a business deal has come up that requires my full
attention. I will keep you posted.

SHP

p.s. Diana, the property will still be there when I get back. I will not
sign off on a purchase until I've seen for myself that it is a good
investment.

Sterling Prescott
Chairman and CEO, Prescott Media

To: Sterling Prescott <sterling@prescottmedia.com>
From: Serena Prescott <serena@prescottmedia.com>
Subject: Trip

Dearest Sterling,

A month in El Paso, you say. Perhaps I should come down. I haven't been to El Paso in ages. What I'd give for some Mexican food like my father used to make. I think a trip could be just the ticket.

Yours,
Grandmère

p.s. I'd be careful with Diana, if I were you. You know how she can stir up trouble when she doesn't get her way.

To: Serena Prescott <serena@prescottmedia.com>
From: Sterling Prescott <sterling@prescottmedia.com>
Subject: Absolutely not

Grandmère, this is not a good time for you to visit. As to Diana, rest assured, I can handle my sister.

I will be in touch.

SHP

Sterling signed off of the remote access to the Prescott Media e-mail system. He had known running Prescott from Texas would require a delicate balancing act, but he hadn't anticipated his family causing him the most aggravation.

Not that he should be surprised that Diana would act up. She was spoiled, had never worked a day in her life, and believed that spending money was the only way to find true happiness. But he knew how to deal with that. Keep her on a tight rein. In the end, she always came back in line. She wouldn't dare risk gaining his displeasure so thoroughly that he would completely cut her off.

The middle Prescott heir went about planning parties with the precision of a military general. But no one could deny that Diana had a smile that could light up a room. Though as the saying went, when she was good, she was very, very good. When she was bad, she was horrid.

As aggravating as Diana was, however, he cared for his sister and would never let anything happen to her.

But Diana wasn't the family member who concerned him.

What he hadn't expected was trouble in the form of his grandmother. The last person he needed to show up in El Paso was the family matriarch, all around busybody, and the only person he knew who wasn't the least bit afraid of him.

That is, she had been the only person until he met Chloe. He had a feeling that his grandmother would like Chloe a great deal.

Serena Cervantes Prescott was an eighty-three-year-old whirlwind of energy who insisted on being called Grand-mère, as if only the French version of grandmother was grand enough for her. Sharp as a tack and just as pointed in her opinions regarding everything from the way the country was being run to Prescott Media's future plans.

Her husband, Sterling's grandfather, had started Prescott after he was honorably discharged from the army. Preston Prescott had brought his bride back to St. Louis, and the two of them had put Prescott Inc., as it was called back then, on the map. They had built the business from the ground up. But after all their hard work, their only child, Sterling's father, had taken over and nearly ruined everything.

The minute Sterling graduated from Harvard Business School with an MBA in finance, he had returned home to take over the reins, fighting to save the foundering business.

Rupert Prescott had actually been relieved to step aside once he had gotten over the embarrassment of being forced out. Grandmère had lamented more than once that she had babied her son and had no one but herself to blame for Rupert's lack of drive.

As a result, she had ridden her grandsons hard over the years. No question, Sterling was driven to succeed. Ben was driven as well, though much to the family's dismay, he was driven to be anything but an employee of Prescott Media.

Sterling packed his laptop into his briefcase, then headed down the hall for Chloe's office so they could finish up their planning session. He registered in some recess of his mind that the place had an empty feel to it. Employees had already departed for the day with the exception of a skeletal evening on-air staff. But it never occurred to him that Chloe would have left.

He stopped at the threshold to her office and was genuinely surprised when she wasn't sitting at her desk. When he scheduled a meeting with someone, that person was always there.

He glanced around, saw no one, then pulled his cuff back and looked at his watch. He noted that it was only 6:27. He sat down to wait.

At 6:30 he grew impatient. At 6:35 he stood and began to pace. He walked around her office, took in the neatly organized desk, the AT-A-GLANCE calendar, her small, neat print noting meetings and events occurring over the course of the month.

He picked up a framed photograph of three young girls. He could tell they were Chloe, Julia, and Kate. Then another of them when they were older. And a single photo of Chloe with an older woman. A grandmother, probably; but no one else.

He thought of his own family. There was no avoiding them. Not that he wanted to. As the head of Prescott Media, he was the unnamed patriarch of the family. His father left all decisions up to him. Which is why Sterling had traveled to El Paso to take care of the wayward son rather than one of their parents.

Like thoughts of him could make him appear, Ben knocked on the door and leaned in.

"Hey, *Trey,*" he greeted with a smug smile. "That has a certain ring to it."

Sterling wasn't amused—by his brother's delight or by the constant reminder that he was using someone else's name. But now that he was committed, he didn't know how to untangle the situation without making things worse. Besides, as much as he didn't want to admit it, he hadn't felt this alive in years.

He glanced at the clock: 6:45, and still no Chloe. "Where the hell is everyone around here?"

Ben laughed. "Looks like they're gone. Which is good, since the sooner we leave and head over to the car rental place, the better."

"I've got to meet with someone first." Scowling, the elder Prescott glanced at his watch again. "Where is she?"

Ben craned his neck back and looked around the empty building. "Who?"

"Chloe."

"Really?" He glanced around her office. "Where is she?"

Irritated, Sterling tugged at his cuffs. "That's what I'd like to know."

A lone office light flicked off down the hall. Julia emerged, pulling the door shut behind her.

Ben instantly grew alert, a smooth coolness sliding through him, making Sterling see for the first time the man who had become an undercover agent. But this coolness wasn't the sort of reaction that a man on the hunt would exhibit. Ben looked like he didn't know what to make of the wild beauty.

Julia came toward them, her leopard print purse swinging on her shoulder, her heels so high that it was a wonder she could walk. But no question Ben was looking her over.

Julia looked Ben directly in the eye, and Sterling would have sworn that the beauty was self-conscious. But then she preened for the younger Prescott, as if she knew he was studying her and she was enjoying every minute of it. But Sterling was too concerned about other matters to give it much thought.

"Julia," he said, breaking into whatever was going on between those two. "I'm supposed to meet Chloe at six-thirty. She's not here."

"True, she isn't," she responded, though she smiled wickedly at Ben.

"Where is she?"

Without ever looking at him, she said, "It's Tuesday, which means she's at World's Gym. We all go on Tuesdays. Though I'm running late. There's a new, incredibly cute instructor for the six-thirty and seven-thirty kickboxing classes." Julia shifted her gaze to Sterling. "Chloe has a crush on him. She wouldn't miss Tuesday Kick for anything. Gotta run if I'm going to make it to the next session."

Julia walked past the men and headed out of the building.

Both men watched her go, though it wasn't Julia who Sterling saw in his mind's eye.

"Come on, let's go," he commanded, already grabbing his briefcase and heading out the door.

"Where are we going?"

"To the damned gym."

Sterling ignored his brother's lamenting groan.

The men drove up Mesa Street from downtown in Ben's black Range Rover.

"I take it you've got it bad," Ben said, breaking into the tense silence.

"What are you talking about?"

"You, for Chloe."

"There is nothing going on between me and Chloe Sinclair, and I certainly don't have anything bad—unless it's a bad case of irritation over a woman who isn't doing her job."

"Ah, so that's why you're hunting her down after hours for some meeting?"

"We have a show to produce," Sterling bit out tightly.

"And I guess I'm supposed to be impressed by your dedication to the job. Workaholic, no life outside the office. The sort of life you want me to lead?"

"I guess that puts me between a rock and a hard place for an answer."

Ben grinned. "You bet, big brother."

They raced up Mesa Street. No matter how many times Sterling drove through town, the geography surprised him. Even though it was October, the trees were still green. The massive mountain range, with its dangerous cliffs and rocky ledges rising up from a city that was nestled at its base, looked red in the setting sun. The mountains flowed down into the Rio Grande river basin, then rose up again on the other side in what he had learned was Mexico. But today, none of that made a bit of difference in his mood. By the time the two men pulled up to the building on Mesa Street, Sterling was jaw-ticking mad.

Out of habit, Sterling took his briefcase with him as he strode into the gym. Ben followed and made some sort of an explanation when Sterling didn't stop at the front desk, a perky receptionist calling out for him to sign in.

Ben shook his head and wondered what the hell was going on with his brother. Ben knew without having to be told that Sterling had come to El Paso to force him to return to the family. And for the first time since Ben had left St. Louis, he wondered if returning wasn't what he needed to do.

That was the only reason he could come up with for having said he would return to St. Louis if Sterling saved the station. At the time, saving the station in a month hardly seemed possible. But he had forgotten Sterling's drive—a drive that was exhibited now as he hunted down someone who had stood him up for a meeting.

But would that get the job done?

And if Sterling did succeed, could Ben really give up life in law enforcement?

He didn't know the answers. In his second week on leave from the force, he still couldn't think about, much less talk about, his partner being killed in an undercover drug deal gone wrong.

A commotion to his left cut into his thoughts. Thankfully. Though not so thankfully he realized that Julia Boudreaux was at the center of the tumult.

Why wasn't he surprised?

Hell, the woman was a piece of work. Her long, black-lacquer hair was pulled back, her violet eyes flashing. She said what she felt, when she felt like it. He had enough strong women in his family. He wanted a woman who knew how to be soft, sweet, and kind. A woman who knew how to fill his mind and his body with the sort of heady desire that tasted like bourbon warmed between two hands.

Leaning back against the wall, he watched her work the crowd, all men, all circling around her, trying to get a morsel of her interest. She doled out and withheld attention in a way that he couldn't believe drew any man. She flirted, she toyed, she even waggled her finger at one massively muscled man like he was nothing more than a naughty little boy when he tried to steal a kiss.

Ben thought about exiting the building. He would have turned away and left Sterling to his own devices, but then one of the slew of Julia's admirers wouldn't leave her alone. The muscle-bound bodybuilder grabbed her close. Julia's face went very still, and Ben saw panic flare in her deep twilight eyes.

With a curse, Ben strode across the distance in a few determined strides. Blood pounded through him, driving him forward—though it was something more than habit that pushed him on. Something he couldn't name.

One minute he was detached and calm, the next he tore the muscleman away from Julia and pinned him against a bulletin board loaded with announcements. Roommates wanted. Maid services. Diet supplements. Thumbtacks popping from the cork, flyers fluttering to the floor.

"Hey, man, what the fuck are you doing?" the man stammered, puffing up.

But he was no match for Ben's strength and skill in subduing others.

"Keep your hands off the lady."

Muscleman started to protest, but Ben banged him against the corkboard once again.

"You're fucking crazy, man."

"Maybe," Ben conceded, blood ticking through him like fire. "Do you want to find out how crazy?"

Ben loosened his grip, and the minute he did, the man hurried away.

It took a second for the insane feeling to pass. Finally he turned to face Julia, uncomfortable with the realization that this possibly could change things between them. He had seen before how women grew attached to the men they thought had saved them.

Julia looked him up and down like a feline on the prowl, her gaze like fingernails raking down his torso during hot sex.

"Mmm," she cooed, "you big strong man. Did that make you feel manly? Do you like banging people around?"

Clearly she wasn't on the verge of throwing herself in his arms and thanking him. It pissed him off that he cared.

Raking his hair back with his hand, he said, "I was just trying to help."

She stepped closer, every trace of panic gone so completely that he wondered if he had imagined it.

"I don't need your help, Mr. Boy Scout. I've been fending off men since you were a kid trying to play doctor with the silly girl next door."

He studied her closely, not sure what he felt. But finally he felt a knowing smile pull at his lips. "I didn't have to try hard. I was pretty good at playing doctor. Do you want to relive a little bit of childhood and play now?" He planted his hand on the wall above her head. "Since you're so strong and anything but helpless, I'll even let you give the exam."

The deep violet of her eyes darkened and she bit her white teeth into her lower lip. Heat flared, and Ben felt a fiery need to pull her close. Press her body to his. Leaving him ill-prepared when she smiled wickedly and said, "Really, I get to be the doctor?" Then she reached down and grabbed him by the balls.

His thoughts cemented.

Her gaze was hot, sultry, and amused. "Cough, big boy."

He wasn't sure, but he thought he might have choked instead as she laughed, the sound rising up into the exposed metal rafters.

The minute she let go, she purred, "I'll send you the bill in the mail." Then with a flip of her hair, she turned on her heel and walked away.

Sterling saw Chloe almost immediately on the opposite side of the gym. As predicted, she was in a glass-walled workout room filled with rows of mainly women following the lead of a single man on a small platform in front.

His jaw ticked with impatience.

Chloe stood out from the line of other kickboxers. That dark hair was pulled up in a short ponytail that bounced with every kick and punch. She wore warm-up pants, even though every other female in the room had on tights that made them look naked. But it was Chloe who made his pulse beat faster.

Irritation and frustration combined with physical need, only serving to make the flame of his anger burn brighter. Damn her sexy hide.

He had understood when he took her into the hotel bathroom and pulled up her skirt that her body was meant for sin, all sleek skin and curves that she now kept hidden underneath demure clothes and warm-up pants.

But he hadn't seen her body that night. He had felt her, catching fleeting glimpses of skin and curves in the hazy mirrors. Images, memories, that haunted his dreams. Now, watching her through the glass like she was a china doll in a curio cabinet, he felt an unwelcome hardness between his thighs at the sight of her. He wanted to touch her again, brush his hands along her body. And he would. He would complete this damn show. Fulfill the bargain that he had made with Ben. Then he would make love to Chloe and finish what they had started days ago in a hotel bathroom. And he wouldn't feel an ounce of regret.

But that would happen later. Not now.

A woman in little more than a tank top and thong bumped into him and smiled suggestively as she continued on toward a line of weight machines. Looking around, he could hardly believe that he was standing in a gym as the kickboxing class came to an end. He told himself to find Ben and get the hell out of there. He would deal with Chloe later. And he would have, but when Chloe walked up to the instructor with a shy smile, he forgot about leaving.

His eyes narrowed, irritation kicking up again like his new best friend when the instructor tucked a strand of hair behind her ear. Sterling's mouth pressed into a hard line when she blushed. Chloe Sinclair, Miss Hot and Heavy in the bathroom, pink with innocence now.

Then she saw him. At first she looked surprised. Next he expected her to look guilty because she had missed their meeting. But Chloe never did what he expected. Her mouth fell open in exasperation.

Even though Sterling couldn't hear a word they said, he could tell through the glass that the instructor asked, "Who's that?"

She crossed her arms on her chest, and Sterling could read her lips. "Don't worry. He's nobody." She turned away.

Him, Sterling Hayden Prescott, a nobody.

When Chloe glanced back at him, probably hoping he had disappeared, he crooked his finger at her. She rolled her eyes in response, then said good-bye to the instructor. Picking up her gym bag, she headed out of the workout room. Sterling waited for her to come over to him. Several sharp things he planned to say to her rushed through his head. But the minute she walked through the door, she turned left and headed for the stationary bikes.

It was ridiculous, this anger or whatever it was he felt. But anger was something he could deal with. So be it.

He strode over to the bike where she now pedaled furiously, leaning low over the handlebars.

"We had a meeting scheduled," he stated without preamble, setting his briefcase down.

"I told you I was busy."

"And I told you that we had to meet."

She glanced over at him, her eyes bright, her cheeks red with exertion. "Do people always jump through hoops to accommodate your every whim?"

"Of course."

"Of course!" she scoffed, put her head down, and pumped at the bike so hard he expected the two-wheeler to take off.

"Let me amend that," he stated. "Everyone accommodates me with the exception of you. You never do anything I say."

She actually preened like he had given her an award. "Mindless submission is overrated," she said with a smirk.

"I think you're being stubborn simply for the sake of being stubborn."

"I am not," she blurted, her chin thrust out stubbornly.

"Then why didn't you wait for me?"

"Because I always go to Tuesday Kick."

"To see the instructor?"

Her feet actually came off the pedals in her surprise. After a second, she said, "No, not *solely* to see the instructor." She waggled her brows. "Not that he isn't reason enough to come to Tuesday Kick."

He swore.

"I'm here to exercise. It keeps me sane and helps me work better. Surely you do more than work. Don't you have a personal life?"

Personal life?

Sterling's world revolved around the job. The hunt. Closing the deal. He couldn't remember ever thinking in terms of a life beyond work. He dated. He attended the social functions that he had to as both the family representative and as the chairman and CEO of Prescott Media. But standing around making small talk, in his opinion, was an utter waste of time.

Mostly he worked. And he enjoyed it.

At least he had until this tiny woman said two fateful words. *"Kiss me."*

"My personal life isn't the issue," he stated, his jaw ticking. "We have to finalize the locations for where the Roses and the Catch will stay if we are going to have the paperwork completed in time for taping. Moreover, I have better things to do with my time than follow you around in order to get something so important done. I don't appreciate your unprofessional irresponsibility when it comes to making this show a success."

Her eyes went wide and her mouth fell open. Her feet came off the pedals for good this time, and he swore she would have launched herself at him if he hadn't reached out and lifted her off the bike. She still hadn't found her voice by the time he plunked her down on a small, narrow, black, padded workout bench. When he straddled the opposite end, he had to catch her hands when she tried to push him off.

"Enough," he bit out. "We have a job to do, and it's next to impossible to carry on a conversation with you huffing and puffing on a bike that is going nowhere. Which means there's no time for playing around or moon-eyeing a kickboxing instructor when you should be doing everything in your power to save KTEX TV."

Her open mouth snapped shut until her lips pursed hard. "You self-righteous, know-it-all bast—" She cut herself off, then leaned over, yanked up her gym bag, and pulled out a manila folder. "Here."

His thoughts hardened. "What is that?"

"Look inside," she shot back.

He did. "Houses?"

"Yes." She drew the word out with impatience of her

own. "I used a Polaroid camera and took the photos this morning."

"This morning?"

"Around five or so, when I was being *unprofessionally irresponsible.*"

He didn't feel a moment of remorse. He was impressed. And he told her so.

That took the words right out of her mouth. He could tell she tried not to care. With jerky movements, she started pulling out photos from the file he held.

"I spoke to a real estate agent," she explained, "who sent over a description of possible properties, but several that sounded interesting didn't have photos, or if they did, they were too small to make out."

"So you drove around and took pictures at five in the morning."

"Yeah, well . . ." Her tone was belligerent.

"Let's see what you have."

As he leafed through the photographs, she spoke. "I gave some thought to doing the whole thing in a hotel. But there isn't enough room for all the equipment we're going to need. So I ruled that out and stuck with single-family dwellings."

He held up a pair of photographs. She said, "Those are two homes in an area called Mission Hills. There's a little map attached to the back of each photo that shows where the house is in relation to KTEX."

"They're nice, and they're close to the station, but there's nothing that says fantasy about them."

Chloe nodded. "You're right. The hardest part is finding two properties that are close to each other so that we can use one crew and not have to hire another."

He studied the second set. "Too small."

Then another. "Too sterile."

By the time he got to the bottom, there wasn't a single pair of houses they could use. But he wasn't surprised. He'd done some work on the housing situation himself and had seen what they were up against.

"I'm meeting with the Realtor again after I work out," she said, impressing him even more. "But at this point I'm stumped, given our price range."

He reached over and retrieved his briefcase. "I found something."

"You did?" She didn't sound in the least put out that he might have succeeded when she had not. She sounded excited.

He pulled out his own set of photos and held them up without any description.

She sat up straight on the bench. "Wow! They're great. I recognize that one. It's in the Coronado Country Club, isn't it?"

"It is. Apparently the owner has been trying to get it used in a movie. He'll settle for TV. I've gotten the price down."

"You're a genius!" she said excitedly, or even graciously, he conceded, after how he had treated her. "How much?" she asked.

"A thousand per week—"

"What?!"

"—on the big house. Seven-fifty per week for the smaller bachelor house."

She shook her head in disbelief. "It doesn't matter how good a price they are, we can't afford them."

Sterling glanced at the photos. He knew she was right, had been debating that fact since the second he knew he was close to pushing the owner just as far as he was going to be pushed. Every man had his limit. Sterling was a master at knowing just when he was about to hit it. The man who owned the set of properties in the country club area had gotten there.

The setting for *The Catch and His Dozen Texas Roses* would be like a character—a minor character, but a character nonetheless. For his plan to succeed, ratings for the show had to be through the roof. For that to happen, viewers needed to love the bachelor, and either love or hate the Roses. But on top of that they needed to love the houses, to dream of living there themselves.

Which meant Sterling had a decision to make.

"What if I got . . . Prescott Media to pay?" he suggested carefully.

Chloe thrust out her chin. "Why would that ratty old Prescott pay for the houses?" Whatever ease had surfaced in her disappeared. "Are you sure that you and that Prescott aren't trying to pull something here?"

Sterling leaned forward. "You've got it wrong about my intentions . . . and about Prescott."

She was close enough to kiss. He could see how her pulse flared, not in passion this time, but in a sort of warrior's determination that he recognized. He realized with a start of surprise that he couldn't underestimate her, that she would fight harder than he had imagined she would. He wondered what it would feel like if she ever fought for him.

Which was ridiculous.

"That remains to be seen about you and your intentions," she stated. "As to Prescott," she added, "I don't believe for a second that he has any redeeming qualities. I've heard too many stories about what he has done to other stations."

"You know the problem with you, Chloe Sinclair?"

"I don't have a problem."

"I beg to differ."

"Beg all you like."

He smiled. "I don't beg."

"That's right, men like you and Prescott *take*. Pillage, conquer."

"I think you're obsessed with Prescott."

"I am not!"

"Aren't you? You talk about him every chance you get."

"I'm not interested in talking about Sterling Prescott. And you shouldn't be either. Though I'll give you points for being loyal."

Sterling felt a twist of frustration, and not a little outrage that she could talk so dismissively of . . . well, Sterling Prescott. Part of him relished the thought of that moment when she finally found out who he was. He imagined she would squirm and dangle with contrition.

Though part of him thought that she just might make *him* squirm and dangle in contrition.

He mentally cursed. He had never squirmed in his life.

"You're too thin-skinned," he said. "That's your problem. Life isn't for the meek. Life is about finding what you want and taking it. Otherwise you'll never achieve anything, and you'll get walked all over."

"Is that what you tell yourself to justify working for a corporate raider?"

"Am I raiding anything now? Is he? Is anyone trying to steal anything from you? Or am I trying to save your station?"

She looked at him forever. "I wish I knew. I wish I could figure out why you're here, and what it is about you that makes me think you aren't telling me everything."

Even though she had been off of the bike for several minutes, when the electronic timer beeped, her body visibly heaved a sigh of relief, and she stood.

"Let me think about the house issue," she said, wiping

her face and neck with a white terry cloth towel. "I have an idea that I want to mull over."

"What kind of an idea?"

"Mull first, discuss later."

The fact was, he didn't have much choice. He hadn't found anything viable, and the challenge was to succeed without his name or his money. He couldn't, in good faith, pay for the damn houses himself.

Ben stood off to the side, that amused grin spread on his face. "Hey, Chloe." He focused on his brother, his smile broadening. "Hey Trey, I'll wait for you out at the truck."

Chloe looked from Ben, as he left the building, to Sterling. "It's amazing the resemblance."

"I've heard people say that, but I don't see it," Sterling said.

"Yeah, you probably won't. Despite the fact that both of you look like *Mr. Danger*"—she laughed and rolled her eyes—"Ben actually looks friendly every once in a while, unlike you."

He shot her a scowl. "I'm friendly."

"Sure you are," she scoffed. "But that's okay. I can tell you care for Ben, and I'll give you points for that, too."

"Of course I care for him. We're family."

"Family."

The word seemed to surprise her and a change came over her.

"You never did tell me anything about yours," he said. "You like to play your hand close to your chest."

"There's nothing to tell," she stated defensively.

He considered her for a second, then asked the question that had been on his mind. "Do you have one?"

"What?"

"A family."

"Of course I do! I have a father." She hesitated, worrying her lip. "He's great. Really, a wonderful man. We're close, just like you and Ben. He loves me a lot."

He wasn't sure whom she was trying to convince, him or herself. "Congratulations," he said. "I'd like to meet him."

She stared at him in surprise, then said, "We aren't dating, Trey. We don't even know each other. So stop nosing around and asking questions. We are working together on a single project. That's it. And I intend to keep it that way."

He could read people easily, and Sterling knew that she didn't want to talk about her family, while at the same time she looked at the bond he shared with his brother with something he could only call yearning.

She turned, her ponytail bouncing, but he wasn't about to let her get away that easily. He caught her arm, stopping her.

"Chloe?"

She eyed him cautiously.

"I really am impressed with the effort you've put into *The Catch*," he said.

Then, as if he could do nothing else, he leaned down and kissed her.

She didn't pull away, and after a second she seemed to melt just a bit, leaning into him as the kiss grew deeper.

He cupped her face, tilting her to him. What he had intended to be a simple kiss left him wanting to take. *"Pillage and conquer,"* she had said. And he wanted that. He wanted her to press against him in a long, slow burn.

A second later, realizing where they were, he pulled back. Her eyes were hooded with desire, molten and blue, until finally she blinked.

"Well," she managed on a shaky breath. "I wonder what you do when someone not only impresses you, but actually comes up with a solution to a problem. You must have some kind of Awards Night there at Prescott Media."

Surprise made him laugh out loud, and several people turned to look at them. Chloe took the advantage to break free, then hurry away, yet again disappearing, this time into the ladies' locker room.

To: Julia Boudreaux <julia@ktextv.com>
Katherine Bloom <katherine@ktextv.com>
From: Chloe Sinclair <chloe@ktextv.com>
Subject: Final stretch

Everything is coming together better than I could have hoped. The only remaining problem is the matter of housing for our bachelor and contestants.

We really can't afford to rent anything that will make a viable "set" for the show. Though I wondered if there isn't something we could do with our own homes that would solve the problem. I hate to ask, but can either of you volunteer? Since all three of us are neighbors, using our houses would be cheap *and* convenient.

Chloe

Chloe Sinclair
Station Manager
Award-winning KTEX TV

To: Chloe Sinclair <chloe@ktextv.com>
Katherine Bloom <katherine@ktextv.com>

From: Julia Boudreaux <julia@ktextv.com>
Subject: Volunteer

What do you have in mind, Chloe? House the Roses in one, and the Catch in one of the others? Are you sure we don't have the money to rent something else?

xo, j

To: Julia Boudreaux <julia@ktextv.com>
Katherine Bloom <katherine@ktextv.com>
From: Chloe Sinclair <chloe@ktextv.com>
Subject: I'm sure

We really don't. You wouldn't believe the prices of any place worth using. But I was thinking that we could use your house for the Roses. Kate's house really isn't an option for the Catch, though perhaps the guest cottage in her backyard could work.

Chloe

To: Chloe Sinclair <chloe@ktextv.com>
Julia Boudreaux <julia@ktextv.com>
From: Katherine Bloom <katherine@ktextv.com>
Subject: Housing

I hate to do this, but I really don't want the cameras around my house. With Jesse working so hard on his game, I don't want the distraction. Sorry!! But what about your house for the Catch, Chloe? You could stay with me and Jesse, and your father could stay in the guest cottage.

Katherine C. Bloom
News Anchor, KTEX TV West Texas

To: Julia Boudreaux <julia@ktextv.com>
Katherine Bloom <katherine@ktextv.com>
From: Chloe Sinclair <chloe@ktextv.com>
Subject: Father

That is really great of you, Kate, but I hate to uproot my father so soon after his heart attack.

Chloe

To: Chloe Sinclair <chloe@ktextv.com>
Katherine Bloom <katherine@ktextv.com>
From: Julia Boudreaux <julia@ktextv.com>
Subject: Reality check

Your father had a heart attack six months ago, sugar. And it was a mild episode, to boot. He's perfectly fine now. I say we use your house. And if your father feels awkward staying in Kate's guest cottage, then he can stay at my mountain house in Ruidoso during the taping. I'd love to see someone staying up there. Plus, you don't have to worry that he'll be alone. I pay the Normans a fortune to take care of the place. They'll be there to take care of him.

Now, you can tell him, or I can. We need your house for the Catch if any of us are going to have jobs when this is over.

xo, Julia

Chloe felt a thrill of pleasure when she pushed in through the back door of her house. Though it was still hard to think of the place as hers even after her grandmother had willed it to her. Chloe still missed her grandmother every day. She missed the woman's wisdom and kindness, even if that kindness was wrapped up in strict, unrelenting dictates.

When Chloe was growing up, her grandmother had told her to be happy and not to think about her own mother dying so young. Oddly, being happy was a habit now. It was easy to be happy, easier than letting life get to her. At least that had been the case until she ran into Trey Tanner.

"Dad! I'm home."

She didn't get a response, not that she really expected one. Despite the six months he had been living with her, he still wasn't used to being called Dad. Though it was harder to call her father Richard.

She realized that most grown women who hadn't known their father until they were twenty-seven probably wouldn't dream of calling the man Dad. But that was just it. For as long as Chloe could remember, she had done just that. Dreamed of finding her father again, dreamed of coming home and calling out *Dad!*

But this wasn't a dream. The fact was, more than twenty years ago he had left her and her beautifully vibrant mother, changing everything. After he left, Chloe had relentlessly questioned her mother about where he was. She had never answered until finally one day, in a fit of loving frustration, she said, *"Sweetie, he's gone. That's all there is to it."* Her mother died shortly after that.

It had been the state who came to get her, putting her with a foster family until they found the grandmother she hadn't known existed. Regina Sinclair might not have spoken to her daughter in years, but she had taken her granddaughter in without reservation, and loved her and guided her from the second she walked through the door.

Chloe had never seen her father again—until six months ago. Not until he'd had a heart attack and hadn't had any other family to help him. It was the hospital who called, surprising her when they said, *"Your father has had a heart attack."*

She had never understood why he had left or why the state hadn't taken her to her father. Because he hadn't wanted her? Had the state asked and he said no? When she had asked her grandmother, the only response Chloe had gotten was *"Who knows the mind of a man? All that matters is that he left. But it's his loss, Chloe love. Remember that. He's the one who missed out on watching you grow up to be a lovely, sensible girl."*

Chloe set her purse on the small kitchen desk. The house was on a beautiful stretch of Meadowlark Drive, right across the street from the seventeenth fairway of the El Paso Country Club. Decades ago, when her grandmother moved to the area, it had been a mix of farmland and small adobes used to house laborers. Time had gentrified this part of town, until her grandmother's neighbors were people like Julia's parents, who built sprawling mansions. Even Kate's house, on the other side of Julia's but not as large, had a guest cottage, a swimming pool, and lots of land. Regina Sinclair's property had been a tiny gem surrounded by much larger jewels.

The first thing Chloe had done after she inherited the property was to spend every penny she could drum up to update the place. The kitchen was her favorite. The warm terra-cotta color she had painted the walls. The Mexican tiles she had used as trim. And the stenciling she had added herself to accent the curved Spanish archways leading into the den and dining room.

She savored the space for a moment before she forced herself to go in search of her father to talk to him about *The Catch* and the need for the house.

She found him in the den. At fifty-eight, Richard Maybry was still a handsome man. When she came home in the evenings, he always smiled and asked about her day. She loved how they talked, and she knew he was truly interested in what she had to say. He was no trouble at all, and while she was an adult and didn't need to be living with a parent, she enjoyed having him there. She could tell he enjoyed being there with her. But she still hadn't figured out how to break through the polite distance that stood between them. They both were kind, caring, but always polite, as if they didn't know how to begin to be a real family after so much time had passed.

He never failed to ask what he could do to help. Paint the house. Fix the plumbing. *"Something, anything to help,"* he once said with exasperation showing through. But how could she let him after he'd had a heart attack? What kind of a daughter would she be if she loaded him up with chores, letting him do work, when what he needed to do was make sure he regained his health?

Surely he understood that. They were family. She was all he had. Or was she?

He called some woman every night and smiled and cooed like a schoolboy. Did he have a girlfriend? Some gray-haired matron? If he did, he wasn't telling Chloe about it.

"Hi, Dad," she said.

He sat in an overstuffed chair in front of the television. He craned his neck to look at her, smiled, and stood. "Hi, princess."

Princess. Despite her age, the endearment made her smile.

"How was your day?" he asked.

"Great. Really busy. Remember the new project I was telling you about?"

"Remind me."

He followed her back into the kitchen, listening to her tell him about *The Catch and His Dozen Texas Roses*. She made a pot of tea, and she felt an amazing love burst in her as they sat at the table together after so many years of being apart.

In time, as they truly got to know each other, she was sure they would forge a bond and be just as close as she had told Trey Tanner they already were.

Before she had a chance to tell him more about *The Catch*, he said, "I thought I'd try out that mower of yours."

There he went again.

"Dad, you don't need to do that."

"That's debatable. But that's not the point. I want to do it." He stood and took his cup to the sink, this time looking more determined to get outside and work.

"Dad, no, you're a guest," she blurted out as the only excuse she could think of. She had read that men frequently felt vulnerable after a heart attack. The last thing she wanted to do was add to any underlying fears by saying that she thought him fragile.

He stopped in his tracks, then turned back. Suddenly he looked older.

"Dad," she gasped. "Are you all right?"

"Yes, yes. I'm perfectly fine." He sighed. "I think I'll go lie down for a bit."

"Should I call your doctor?"

"No. I'm just tired." He headed in the opposite direction, then stopped again. "By the way, I'm going out later tonight—"

"But—"

"Chloe, really. I'm fine. I've promised a friend that I'd take her out to dinner."

"A friend?"

"Yes."

"Oh. Well, um, where are you going?" Her brain scrambled to find an opening. To start finding out about him, about his friends . . . about where he had been for the last twenty years.

"I'm taking her to the Central."

"Lucky woman."

He smiled then, a glitter lightening his gray eyes. "No, lucky me."

Chloe blinked, then blushed. Was he implying he was going out to get lucky? Should a man who'd had a heart attack be thinking about sex, much less having it?

She started to say something, then snapped her mouth shut. How could she possibly broach something like that with a man she didn't know all that well?

When she didn't respond, he said he was going to rest, then get ready.

Reminding herself that her dad had said friend, not sex kitten, she told herself she couldn't worry about it. It wasn't until she was changing in her room that she remembered she hadn't told him about needing the house. But she could do that before he left.

She pulled off her skirt and blouse, kicked off her sensible shoes. She pulled on shorts and a plain blue T-shirt. There really were chores that needed to be done, and she threw herself into doing them with the relish of a woman who loved hard work. She needed to vacuum and dust. She polished and waxed, each movement more determined. In the kitchen, she scrubbed and straightened. Next she would move on to the lawn and bushes. After that, once everything was done, she'd work in her garden. A treat. Her favorite part of the day.

But first . . .

She pushed up the metal door on the garage. A small smile pulled at her lips when she saw the new mower she had purchased. While other women were getting excited about high heels and pearls, Chloe loved the shiny red, self-propelled mower. It had taken her a few tries before she got the hang of the machine. She'd even run over a plant or two before mastering the clutch. But once she had, the mower made yard work a million times easier.

An hour later, as the bright West Texas sun finally gave out, she closed the garage door. She returned inside with a feeling of accomplishment. She also felt that she couldn't put off any longer asking her father if he would move out for a couple of weeks while they shot *The Catch*.

At the kitchen sink, she splashed her face with cool water, then pressed a damp cloth to her neck. By the time she returned to the den, he had showered and dressed in nice slacks and a crisply ironed shirt.

"How does your old man look?" he asked.

The easy camaraderie had returned and she smiled. "You'll be the most handsome fellow there."

He kissed her on the forehead, and tears of happiness pricked at the backs of her eyes.

But when he pulled away, she remembered what she had to do.

"Dad, I have a favor to ask."

"Is something wrong?"

"No, just an issue with our bachelor show. We need two houses close together—one for the bachelor, and another for the contestants."

His head cocked. "And you need this house."

"Just for a couple of weeks," she added hurriedly.

"Princess, don't worry about me—"

"You don't have to go far. Kate has offered you her guest cottage."

He got an uncomfortable look on his face. "She's your friend who's married to the golfer, right?"

"Yes, but—"

"Chloe, it's hard enough infringing on you. I couldn't do it to someone I'm not related to at all."

"It won't be any infringement."

"Chloe, really—"

"Okay, if that doesn't work, then Julia said you could stay at her house in Ruidoso. There's no one there, except for the couple who lives in the small cottage behind the house. They take care of everything there, and Julia always has guests staying there. That's what it's for. It's no imposition at all!"

"Ruidoso?"

He hadn't ruled it out. Good. "You said just the other day how hot it was despite the fact that it was already October."

"I guess I could do that. It's nice of her to offer. But really, I shouldn't—"

"Dad, please. Don't say anything about moving out. I

want you here. And just as soon as the show is over, I want you to come back."

He looked at her with something she was sure was love.

"Thank you, Chloe. You've given me more than I deserve."

He turned to leave, heading to the door.

She didn't know what happened to her, didn't know why after six months of wanting to ask and holding it back, this time she couldn't stop herself. "Dad? Why didn't you ever find me before now?"

He got really uncomfortable. "Ah, princess. I don't have an easy answer for that. But I am sorry that I waited so long." He walked over to her, kissed her on the forehead. "Can you forgive me?"

"Oh, Dad, of course I do."

"Good." He gave her a hug, then departed.

She realized he hadn't answered the question. But he had apologized. It was a start. He might be leaving for the next two weeks, but he'd come back. Surely. They would talk more then.

It amazed her to think that her life just might be on the verge of falling into place. She was developing a relationship with her father. And the last piece of *The Catch and His Dozen Texas Roses* was fitting together. For now, that was all that mattered.

To: Julia Boudreaux <julia@ktextv.com>
Katherine Bloom <katherine@ktextv.com>
From: Chloe Sinclair <chloe@ktextv.com>
Subject: We're on

_____

Dad is going to Ruidoso. He leaves in the morning.

Chloe

Chloe Sinclair
Station Manager
Award-winning KTEX TV

_____

To: Chloe Sinclair <chloe@ktextv.com>
Katherine Bloom <katherine@ktextv.com>
From: Julia Boudreaux <julia@ktextv.com>
Subject: Ticktock

_____

And not a second too soon. I'll bring over the keys and instructions
about how to get there.

Anyway, how did the rest of it go? Are you okay, sugar? There's only one person in your life who has the ability to undo our strong Chloe. And that's Richard Maybry.

xo, j

To: Chloe Sinclair <chloe@ktextv.com>
Julia Boudreaux <julia@ktextv.com>
From: Katherine Bloom <katherine@ktextv.com>
Subject: Agree

Chloe, you're all right, yes? I worry about you when it comes to your father. Do you want to come over for a glass of wine?

K

Katherine C. Bloom
News Anchor, KTEX TV West Texas

To: Chloe Sinclair <chloe@ktextv.com>
Katherine Bloom <katherine@ktextv.com>
From: Julia Boudreaux <julia@ktextv.com>
Subject: Better idea

Let's go to Bobby's Place for a little celebration. We'll have cosmos and maybe something to eat. It's been weeks since the Girls went to Bobby's. Though oops, sorry, I forgot. I can't. I have a date with a delicious bad boy who is sure to make me purr.

xo, j

p.s. Brava on getting the house secured! We're on our way!

To: Julia Boudreaux <julia@ktextv.com>
Katherine Bloom <katherine@ktextv.com>
From: Chloe Sinclair <chloe@ktextv.com>
Subject: Date?

What is it with you and bad boys, Julia?

To: Chloe Sinclair <chloe@ktextv.com>
Katherine Bloom <katherine@ktextv.com>
From: Julia Boudreaux <julia@ktextv.com>
Subject: Don't make me laugh

As if the two of you don't know!

xo, j

eight

Everything was set.

Sterling sat back in his makeshift office and felt an arrogant satisfaction at how things were going. The show was scheduled to start taping the following day. Eight a.m. sharp.

Julia had just informed him that the fifteen- and thirty-second spots promoting the show had been running successfully for the last five days, and the response was more than encouraging. They'd had phone calls to the main switchboard and e-mail to the new address he had set up, all showing excitement about the coming presentation of the program they were teasing as *The Catch and His Dozen Texas Roses*. No video of the bachelor or the girls. Just alluring clips of the back of an unknown man in a tuxedo and an assortment of faceless women wearing long, beaded gowns.

At this point, El Paso was intrigued. In a matter of twenty-four hours they were about to be tied to their televisions without a thought for the remote. He felt the rush of impending success in his veins. The challenge and the taste of imminent victory were sweet on his tongue. At least success in turning KTEX around.

The only piece of all this that frustrated the hell out of him was Chloe. He hadn't been able to get the memory of her in the bathroom out of his head. Or get her to soften toward him at all.

She still drove him crazy. Him, known for his ironclad control. He who never showed emotion. And she still made it clear she wanted nothing to do with him.

Which made him all the more determined to win her over.

Not that he planned to get involved with her on a serious level. He wasn't interested in getting involved with any woman at this point in his life. He'd made a rule of that. Primarily in self-defense. He couldn't think of anyone in the last ten years who hadn't made it clear she wanted to be Mrs. Sterling Prescott. Women had been trying to gain his attention for as long as he could remember. He was used to it. But there were moments when he wondered if any of them wanted more than the prestige of his name and the money that came with being part of the Prescott clan.

It had never bothered him before. However, he had never thought about children. He'd been too busy rebuilding to think of beginning a family of his own. But he was older now, thirty-five, old enough to start thinking of a family of his own.

Wedding any of the wealthy socialites he usually dated seemed about as appealing as marrying a porcelain doll. He didn't want to think about being stuck in a marriage like his parents had. He knew they loved each other in their own way, but the truth was, each was more concerned about his or her own world. His father and his life of little pressure and ease. His mother and her grand parties and days filled with social functions. Each of them had come from that world and saw no reason to live any differently now. The women Sterling met were varying versions of his mother.

Which was what made Chloe unique.

She had zero interest in the rich Sterling Prescott. And while she wanted nothing to do with him as Trey Tanner either, that was because of her distaste for his association with a man like Sterling Prescott.

But when she hadn't known he was from Prescott Media, when she had simply reacted to him as a man, she had wanted him.

"Kiss me."

Heat raced along his skin at the thought. He wanted her. He wanted to take her in his arms and finish what they had started. And he would.

She intrigued him. He wanted to know more about her. Where did she come from? What was it that made her seem so different from other women he had met? Why was she even more closed off about personal issues than he was?

A fist banged on his office door. "Knock, knock."

Ben stood in the doorway, looking rugged and disreputable in a plain black T-shirt, faded jeans, and some chunky black boots that looked like they belonged on a construction worker.

Sterling hadn't seen him in over a week, not since they had gone and finally rented a car. The minute Sterling had keys in his hand, Ben had slapped him on his back and said, "You're on your own. Good luck. Though if you need me, just call."

Sterling had called him this morning to ask him to come by the office.

"Hello, Ben. Come in. I'm glad you could stop by."

"What's up?" Ben asked, sitting down in the metal folding chair across from him with a smile that Sterling had noticed never came easily anymore.

"Two things." Sterling picked up a sheet of paper.

"You made a list for two things?"

He shot him a look. "No, it's an address. I wondered if you could take a few remaining items over to the houses we're using as sets for *The Catch*. We start taping tomorrow, and the ever faithful Taurus we rented is full."

"No problem." Ben reached out and took the address. "What else?"

Steepling his fingers, Sterling considered his brother. "I want you to find out everything you can about Chloe."

Ben eyed him. "You've got to be kidding."

"Have you ever known me to kid?"

"No," he conceded. "But I've also never known you to do anything stupid either."

"I don't see any harm in learning a bit about a woman who is working for me."

"Last I heard, you hadn't bought the station yet."

"Do it anyway. And don't give me the Trey-wouldn't-do-it excuse. When he was working for me, I paid him enough to afford to do a background check on someone."

"Are you sure you want to do this?"

"Probably not. But do it anyway. Check around. She has a father. She told me that he loves her, that they're close. I heard he's traveling so that we can use her house for the bachelor. But where's the mother? Or any other family? What kind of family is she from?"

"I didn't realize social standing made a difference in how a person performed her job," Ben stated with a raised brow.

"Never hurts to know what you're up against. As we both know, a family has a great deal to do with the kind of adults we become." Sterling stood and came around the desk. "You can use my computer. I've got a few things to finish up with Chloe before we head over to the houses."

Sterling didn't wait for an answer. He headed down the hall toward Chloe's office.

Ben watched him go, shaking his head. How could anyone related to him be so clueless? And Sterling was definitely clueless when it came to anything other than business.

There was no denying the man was a gifted deal maker. But Ben often thought that his older brother had lost touch with the real world—the world that most everyone else lived in. The world Ben lived in, breathed in, existed in.

The question was, Could Sterling ever find his way back? Did he want to?

"Look who's here."

Ben swiveled in his chair. Julia stood in the doorway. Her skirt was short, tight, and undoubtedly showed off her great ass. He still remembered walking behind her down the hall the other day.

He forced himself to look away from the rest of her body that cried out for a long, hard, hot night of sex.

"If it isn't G.I. Joe," she purred.

Ben smiled and stood. "If it isn't Barbie."

"Cute," she said, clicking into the office. "I'm looking for your brother. Have you seen him?"

"He's meeting with Chloe."

She turned to go.

"Hey, cupcake," he called out.

She raised a perfect brow and mouthed *Cupcake*.

"How long have you, Kate, and Chloe been friends?" As long as he had a job to do, he would start by questioning Julia.

"Who wants to know?"

"Just curious. You don't often find three women working together who seem to be the sort of friends you are."

"We've been friends for as long as I can remember, or at least for as long as it matters."

"You grew up together?"

"Next door to one another." Then she shifted the focus. "What about you and Trey? Where were you raised? He was so chatty in e-mail before he showed up. I never would have guessed he was the strong, silent type based on his e-mails."

Ben knew when not to push. "Amazing what e-mail can hide." He pulled his keys from his pocket. He would use his own computer at his apartment to start his search on Chloe. "I'm making a trip over to the set. I'd best get going since I don't have much time."

"What, do you have a hot date tonight?"

She seemed surprised by her question.

He leaned close and smiled at her. "Would you care?"

Julia laughed with disdain. "Are you on drugs?"

"You're a drug, cupcake. Mind altering and equally as lethal."

Then he turned and disappeared before he could do the crazy-ass thing he wanted to do. Kiss the hell out of her.

Sterling walked into Chloe's office without knocking. She leaned over her desk, her fingers flying over a calculator, tallying and retallying, a pencil clamped between her teeth.

"Hello," he said.

Her head jerked up, and he was surprised by the way her blue eyes lit up like Christmas ornaments, her happiness and enthusiasm blazing, her expression unguarded.

She opened her mouth and held out her hand to catch

the pencil when it dropped. "Have you seen this?" she demanded excitedly. She waved a piece of paper at him.

He peered closer.

"It's the numbers for the show. Good numbers. Great numbers. Amazing numbers. I've run and rerun everything, and based on the ad revenue we're pulling in, this has to come close to meeting the station's debt! With one show! It's amazing!"

It was the first time he had seen her truly let her guard down around him. The sight sent a jolt of surprising pleasure through him—pleasure that he had put a smile on her face, even if it was simply with numbers.

She leaped up and did a little victory dance. Her hair swung out, and her arms extended up in the air like Rocky's. So unplanned, so very real. Not practiced and measured, or determined to please.

"Your plan is genius!" She stopped and looked at him, then smiled even more broadly. "I apologize. I was completely wrong about the show. The advertisers have gone crazy. I can't tell you how many times I've heard everyone from Cost's Dairy to Home Ford tell me how local news isn't drawing big enough numbers. And just as many don't want to pay for spots on national programming."

"So you approve?"

"Approve? I'm thrilled! We've hit the jackpot!" She raised her chin and looked him straight, unflinchingly in the eye. "And it's all because of you."

Success.

It shouldn't prove hard to get her to say something to Ben to make her approval known. He should have been happy that another piece of his plan had fallen into place. But somehow this threw him. One minute he was lamenting the fact that she continued to be headstrong against him. Then the next, when she openly told him she approved, he felt an angry dissatisfaction. Which was ridiculous.

He had the disconcerting thought that he wished like hell she had been pleased with Sterling Prescott, not Trey Tanner.

"It's what I'm here for," he said curtly. "We just have a few things left, then we can head over to the house to make sure everything is set."

If she noticed his tension, she didn't let on. "Great!" she said, then sat down and planted her elbows on the desk.

Clearly she wasn't one to hold on to grudges, he thought as he sat across from her. She saw the success they were about to have, and she was nothing if not thrilled and grateful. He had seen his share of people who, when proven wrong, stubbornly refused to admit it. Not Chloe.

"What's left?" she asked. "I'll do anything."

He stopped in the middle of handing over a sheet of paper. He felt his brow rise, heat rushing through him. "Anything?"

He saw the minute she blushed. "Well, um—"

He laughed out loud. That was the other thing about her. No matter how ticked off he might be, she had the ability to make him laugh. "Just joking."

"You?"

"I can joke with the best of them," he stated defensively.

"Then tell me a joke."

That stumped him. He couldn't think of the last time he had heard a joke, now that he thought of it. Not since he was a kid and they did that orange banana thing.

"And not some knock-knock, orange you glad I didn't say banana thing," she added.

"You're scary," he said before he could think.

"Me? Why?"

Because it seemed like she understood him, could read his mind, and the childish orange banana joke was merely an example. He didn't like it at all.

"We have a long night ahead of us," he said by way of answering. "Is there any coffee around here?"

"Great idea. I'd love a cup. Can you bring me one, too?"

Sterling stared at her for half a second as the gears in his brain tried to assimilate her request. "Coffee? You want me to bring you some coffee?"

"With a little milk and two cubes of sugar would be great." She laughed, sliding her silky dark hair back behind the perfect shell of her ear. "If the caffeine doesn't work, hopefully the sugar will. Thanks, Trey."

For a second he was confused, then he winced. He was Trey. Damn.

"Well, sure," he said out loud, nodding as he stood. He'd never gotten coffee for anyone in his life. Someone always brought it to him. But Trey Tanner would bring coffee.

"Yes, I'll get coffee," he said with determination.

He stopped at the door when he realized he had no idea where he was going to get it.

"In the lunchroom," she said. "Where we set up our interview station."

"I knew that."

Sterling walked down the hall. He had pulled together the show in the requisite two weeks, saw no reason that the show would not run without a hitch during the following two weeks. Plus, not minutes earlier he had gotten Chloe to admit she approved. He was on the fast track to proving he was more than his name and his money. He felt ready to take on the next challenge.

He never would have guessed it waited for him in the lunchroom.

Inside the small room, he found the coffeepot, but there wasn't a drop of brew to be had. Now what?

He went to a row of cabinets, went through each until he found a tin of Folgers with a stack of paper sleeves on top. Though there weren't any sort of instructions about how to make it. So he guessed. He shoveled grounds into a paper sleeve, added water, then hoped for the best.

He was admittedly ridiculously proud when Chloe poked her head in just as the last of the trickle dribbled to a halt.

"I thought you might have gotten lost," she said.

"No, I had to make a pot."

"Oooo, Trey, I'm impressed. You come up with great ideas and can brew coffee, too."

Chloe watched as he searched for two cups. He really was handsome in a rugged way. And making coffee for her made him seem even more rugged. So confident in his masculinity that he could serve her without feeling threatened. Living on the border of Mexico, she dealt with more than her fair share of men who still thought they were back at the turn of the century—the twentieth century.

She curled up on a straight-backed chair and rubbed her hands together as he poured her a cup. She felt oddly comfortable sitting there with him now that she was forced to concede there was more to him than she had believed. He hadn't been trying to fool them. He was saving the station. And now he had made her coffee.

"About those numbers," he said, sitting on the edge of the table after he served them both.

"Wait," she interrupted, "cheers!"

She clinked her cup with his. The first clue that all was not right was the smell. But she only got a whiff on the way past her nose, not enough for the warning sign to go off in her head. Too late, she took a sip.

"Ahhgh," she managed over a choke.

"What?" He jerked his cup away so fast that coffee sloshed over the side. "What happened?"

She cleared her throat.

"The coffee? Is something wrong?"

She had never seen such a wounded expression. You'd think it was the first cup he'd ever made, it meant so much to him.

"Wrong?" she equivocated, hating to hurt his feelings. "No, nothing's wrong."

He took a sip, and she swore she could see his straight dark hair start to curl.

"Haven't you ever made coffee before?" she asked carefully.

His shoulders came back and he took another sip, this time with determination. "I love a good, strong cup."

"Then you succeeded." She stood and took her cup to the sink. "It's really kind of late for coffee anyway."

It was endearing how he had tried, then blustered through. She smiled as she emptied the mug, then rinsed it.

But when she turned back from the sink, her breath caught. He was there, close, standing in front of her. She felt her pulse leap. He reached out, but he didn't touch her. He set his coffee down on the counter beside her.

Their gazes met and held. Suddenly all traces of teasing were gone. Stepping closer, he never looked away. She pressed back, the counter against her spine. Then he touched her. Just barely, the backs of his fingers brushing along her cheek.

"I've wanted to do that for days," he said, his voice a gruff whisper of sound.

She didn't reply, didn't know how. Her skin tingled where he touched her, her body beginning a slow, deep, steady throb.

"I can't get you out of my head. I think of you, I dream

of you." He caught her off guard when he tugged off her glasses.

She grabbed at them, but it was too late.

He held them up and looked through them. "As I suspected. Clear, nonprescription glass."

"That's not true!" She tried to get them back.

"Isn't it?"

Biting her lip, she wrinkled her nose in guilt.

"Why?" he asked.

She shrugged. "A habit, I guess. First I wanted to look older. Then smarter."

"And you thought glasses did that?"

"They did."

"I think you look plenty smart without them."

He tossed the glasses onto the counter next to their cups. The plastic frames clattered on the Formica. Then he braced his hands on either side of her, bringing them face-to-face.

"I'm going to kiss you."

"I'm not sure that's such a good idea."

"Why?"

"We hardly know each other."

"That didn't stop us at the hotel."

"Thanks for the reminder."

"Of what? Of how sexy you were? Of how much you made me want you?"

"Did you?"

"Yes."

She looked at his lips, wanted to lean into him. But doing it would be crazy. He worked for Sterling Prescott. He was an employee of a company whose entire raison d'être seemed to be gobbling up weaker entities and spitting out anyone and anything that didn't suit it. She didn't understand how again and again she found herself drawn to a man that she couldn't like or respect.

But that was the thing, she thought suddenly, her breath drawing in sharply. He wasn't like that horrible Sterling Prescott. Trey Tanner was filled with kindness and honor. Trey Tanner understood that a llama was a perfectly respectable reincarnation choice.

She thought about this man, thought about how she had worked hard to keep him at arm's length. But now, with everything on the verge of falling into place, she was forced to reassess.

The truth was, she had been keeping him at arm's length first because she had been embarrassed by her behavior at the hotel. Then she really did hate Prescott Media and all they stood for. But Trey Tanner had proved he was a different sort of man.

Startled and amazed and perhaps more relieved than she wanted to admit, she blurted out, "I owe you an even bigger apology."

"What for?"

"I've misjudged you," she added with bone-deep sincerity.

He smiled then, just barely. "So you're saying you were wrong about me?"

Her eyes narrowed with emotion. "Yes."

She expected him to gloat. But the single syllable caused a flicker of surprise in his dark eyes, hardly seen, the flash of emotion covered up so quickly she wouldn't have seen it had she not been staring right at him.

He didn't gloat, didn't say anything at all. He cupped her face with his hands, so large and strong. Then he tilted her just a little more as he leaned closer. The brush of his lips sent a thrill through her body, and her breath exhaled softly.

"Better than I remembered," he whispered against her mouth.

He kissed her again, slowly, like an expert gentling a skittish mare. She wanted to run away. She wanted to throw her arms around him and demand more. With a sigh, she gave in.

When he ran his thumb across her lower lip, she opened to him just as he kissed her again. His tongue retraced the path of his thumb along her mouth until he dipped slightly to taste her. Just a taste.

She breathed in, inhaling his scent. Slowly he pulled her to him, her eyes going wide before drifting to his mouth. They stood facing each other as he reached out and ran the backs of his fingers along her jaw.

She felt the wild flutter of her pulse.

"You're so soft," he said.

"You're so hard."

Then red singed her cheeks. He grinned, seeming pleased, as his hand ran up her arm, the sensible material of her blouse so thin that she could feel the heat of him.

"I am hard," he answered, "painfully so. All you have to do is walk into the room and I want you."

Her body melted against him as his hand slid around her back, his other cupping her face to tilt her to him. He touched her with his lips then, barely, softly, his teeth nipping at her mouth. The feel of him made everything fade away—sense, reality, the world beyond the lunchroom door—making it impossible to pull away.

He groaned into her mouth, and she tasted him, the hint of peppermint mixed with the dusky taste of coffee.

"You do something to me," he said, the words a gruff accusation as he trailed his lips back to her ear.

Her head fell back, exposing the long column of her neck, and he sucked gently as her fingernails curled into his shirt. He stroked the line of her jaw with the backs of his hands, then lower and lower, until he came to the V of her blouse. Holding her, he traced her lips with his tongue and undid one button after the next.

Her heart raced. Her mind whirled with anticipation and alarm. When his hand slid inside and he cupped her breast, she gasped. For one long second she tensed, but when he ran his thumb over the thin lace of her bra, her mouth opened on a silent sigh.

Her resistance faded away and he slipped his palm into the cup. In an explosion of passion, they couldn't get close enough. Their mouths slanted together, their hands exploring. Never letting her go, he turned them around until he could lean back against the edge of the counter, pulling her between the hard brace of his thighs. The gentle curve of her abdomen cradled his hardness, and when she moved just so, she could tell that sensation shot through him. He wanted her. Here, now. And she wanted him. Badly. Which was why it was so difficult to stop things.

With her body screaming in protest, she dropped her head until her forehead pressed against his chest.

"Chloe, what is it?" he asked over a ragged breath.

The truth was, admitting that she had misjudged him and starting something up with him now were two very different things. Maybe something could work out between them, but not yet, not until they finished this show. If he was still interested after they were done, then maybe . . .

Looking up, she touched her tender lips. "The night at the hotel was crazy, but this, you and me, right now, would be crazier. We're working together. This"—she waved between them—"would cause problems on set and with the others. This would make things . . . weird."

His dark eyes narrowed. "Weird?"

"See, I really do need those glasses. Already my vocabulary has gone downhill."

She watched as the clouds on his face began to clear. He

drew a deep breath, then chuckled, his smile revealing straight white teeth and a surprising kindness.

"It would make things awkward," she restated quickly.

"Only if you let it."

He tried to pull her back.

"No, really." She pressed her hand against his broad chest. "I'm sorry I've been so rude these last couple of weeks. I'm sorry that I equated you to your employer."

He went stiff.

"Prescott Media is a horrible place—"

Something flickered in his eyes, like candle flames catching for a second in a slight breeze.

"—but I see now that you're not anything like that company. You have helped us. And I thank you for that."

She touched his cheek. "You are honest, and straight-forward, and kind. I admit that now."

He seemed to debate something, or maybe he was counting. Either way, his features were dark with some kind of emotion she couldn't place.

"But we still can't be together," she continued. "At least not in the middle of this hugely important project. The station is depending on you and me to make this work. We can't afford any distractions."

She took the opportunity to step away. Clearing her throat, trying to breathe normally despite her racing heart, she smoothed her clothes. "Are you heading over to the house with the final load of things?"

"Yes, but, Chloe—"

"Trey, I'm not going to change my mind. I've got to run. It's getting late, and I've got to make one last call before I leave here." She smiled at him with heartfelt kindness. "Then I'll meet you at the house."

He debated. "Fine. But we need to talk. Challenge or not, there's something I need to tell you."

"Challenge? Sure, this is a challenge, but it's nothing we can't face together and make work. I've got to dash, then we can talk later at the house."

He studied her for a long second, then he nodded. She would have sworn he looked grim. But he wouldn't look grim for long. After being so mean for the last two weeks, she decided to put together a thank-you surprise for him. But what kind of things did he like?

She hurried back to her office and closed the door. Quickly she dialed directory assistance and asked for the number of Prescott Media in St. Louis.

When she was sure that Trey was gone, she dialed the number. A receptionist answered on the first ring.

"Prescott Media."

"Yes, this is Chloe Sinclair at KTEX TV in El Paso. Could you connect me to Trey Tanner's secretary, please."

To: Jason Hughes <jhughes@HughesSecurity.com>
From: Ben Prescott <sc123@fastmail.com>
Subject: Question

Jagger: I need you to do a search for me. A woman named Chloe Sinclair. Works at KTEX TV.

Thanks,
Ben

To: Ben Prescott <sc123@fastmail.com>
From: Jason Hughes <jhughes@HughesSecurity.com>
Subject: re: Question

Ben, my man. Where the hell have you been? I've called. Left messages. No response. Is that any way to treat an old academy buddy? Didn't think so. Let's meet for a beer. Shoot some pool. Let me know that you're doing all right. You're going back to the PD, right? I keep telling everyone you'll be back. Don't make a fool of me, buddy. But hey, if you decide not to, I can always use you here at Hughes. You'd be great at security.

Now, what's this about the Sinclair broad? What do you want to know? I ran her through the system, and she doesn't have so much as a traffic ticket.

Jag

To: Jason Hughes <jhughes@HughesSecurity.com>
From: Ben Prescott <sc123@fastmail.com>
Subject: re: Question

Sorry I haven't gotten back to you sooner. I've been busy. You know how it is. But we'll get together soon.

As to the woman, I have someone who wants to know things like the sort of family she's from, what her parents do.

Thanks,
Ben

To: Ben Prescott <sc123@fastmail.com>
From: Jason Hughes <jhughes@HughesSecurity.com>
Subject: re: Question

Will do. I'll get back to you when I find something.

Also, heads up. I told Susie that I heard from you. She wants you to come to dinner. You know how women are. She's not going to take no for an answer. She forced your e-mail out of me.

Jag

To: Ben Prescott <sc123@fastmail.com>
From: SusieQ@nixpit.com
Subject: Dinner Invite

Dear, dear Ben,

My feelings are hurt. You haven't called or come by. Little Jason is wondering where his godfather has gotten himself to. Come to dinner. Any night you want. I'll make your favorite meal. What was it again? See, now you have to call to tell me. <g>

Jagger's worried about you. Call.

Lots of love,
Susie

To: Ben Prescott <sc123@fastmail.com>
From: Diana Prescott <diana@prescottmedia.com>
Subject: What's this?

Dear Benjamin:

Not a single word from you. Mother's in a fit. What is she supposed to tell everyone after she promised that you were coming home? And now Sterling. First you go AWOL in Texas, now Sterling is proving equally elusive. What is it about that town that appears to be the black hole for our family? What is going on? And when are you coming home?

Your sister,
Diana

p.s. Has Sterling mentioned my condo?

To: Diana Prescott <diana@prescottmedia.com>
From: Ben Prescott <sc123@fastmail.com>
Subject: re: What's this?

Sorry, brat, I've been busy. I'll probably come home for a visit during Christmas. As to Sterling, let's just say he's got his hands full.

Love to you and Mom,
B

p.s. Haven't heard a word about a condo.

nine

"Yes, I'm holding for Trey Tanner's secretary."

"Who is calling, please?"

"This is Chloe Sinclair. I'm the station manager of KTEX TV in El Paso, Texas."

"Ms. Sinclair, I'm Bert Parsons in personnel. You were transferred to me because Trey Tanner's secretary, well, ah, she quit three weeks ago. Could I help you?"

"Oh," she stammered, her brain trying to understand. "But then Mr. Tanner must have a *new* secretary. Maybe she's called a personal assistant. Whatever her title is, I'm certain he talks to her all the time."

"Ms. Sinclair. I'm sorry, but Mr. Tanner is no longer employed by Prescott Media."

Chloe sat very still at her desk, the pencil she had been doodling with halting midcurl around one of a slew of *y*s attached to a whole slew of *Trey*s she had written over and over again like she was a silly seventh grader in junior high.

"No longer employed there?" she asked, the words sticking in her throat. "I don't understand."

"Trey Tanner was . . . His employment was terminated."

"As in fired?" *Fired!* Her mind raced. "Oh, my God!"

She realized in a startling jab to her ribs that he must have been fired for helping them. That horrid rat Prescott must have been furious when he learned Trey had offered to help rather than swallow up KTEX like some gluttonous killer whale. Then Sterling Prescott had fired him. Trey was here doing this on his own. That had to be it! He had stayed in El Paso like some knight in shining armor. And the reason he was in such a hurry to succeed must have been to insure Prescott couldn't regroup, then come down here and swallow them up after all.

A few minutes earlier, when Trey had mentioned the challenge he faced, he must have been referring to the challenge of going up against Sterling Prescott.

Her stomach roiled with panic and amazement. She could hardly quantify the myriad ways she had misjudged Trey. She felt guilt and the need to defend the man at the same time.

"He was fired because he came to El Paso to help us here at the station, wasn't he?" she accused.

"Miss, I assure you I can't tell you why he was let go. But if you would like to get in touch with him, let me give you his phone number." He read off a series of digits. "It's for his home in Clayton."

"Clayton?" she asked, confused.

"Yes, it's just outside of St. Louis. I spoke to him a few minutes ago. I'm sure you can reach him there now."

The gears in her brain jarred as she took in this new piece of information. The number he had given her wasn't in El Paso. She tried to understand.

"Good-bye, Ms. Sinclair."

"Wait!"

The man on the other end sighed. "I'm really busy, and I can't help you further."

"Betty."

"What?"

Her heart started pounding so hard she thought she would be sick. More than once she had heard Trey refer to his secretary as Betty.

"Whose secretary is Betty?"

"The only Betty in our employ is Betty Taylor. Mr. Prescott's secretary."

Her head swam. "Mr. Sterling Prescott?"

"Yes. Would you like me to transfer you to her?"

"No. No! I mean, no," she said, fighting for calm. "I've got a meeting. I can call back later. Thank you."

She slammed the receiver down in a panic and stared at the phone like it had burned her. Trey Tanner wasn't Trey Tanner at all.

She felt hot and cold and sick to her stomach. She felt like a washcloth being twisted at the end of a long bath.

Sweet, kind Trey Tanner was a figment of her imagination. He was Sterling Prescott. Cutthroat, callously indifferent corporate raider of the worst kind.

And a liar.

The words sank in.

They had let the fox into the henhouse.

Chloe sat back in her chair, light-headed with despair. The man she was drawn to wasn't who she had believed he was. Tears of disappointment burned in her eyes.

"Why?" she whispered, hating the feeling of betrayal. But wasn't that how men were? Isn't that why she didn't date anymore, because eventually they broke your heart? Hadn't that been the real reason she hadn't taken the *Sexy!* quiz seriously?

But following closely on the heels of despair came something else. Something hot and burning that she finally recognized as blazing fury. As always, it was easier to be mad than hurt.

"Liar," she bit out, yanking up her purse and heading for the door. "Liar, liar, liar," she added in time with her footsteps as she headed out of the building.

She got on I-10 instead of taking Mesa. She drove with her hands clutching the steering wheel. She was going to show up at the houses, the sets, and expose the bastard for who he really was.

Then another thought hit her, sending a chill down her spine. What was he doing here? Why was he pretending to be a man whom he had fired? Was this some elaborate ploy to gain the station after all? Had he known that they would resist his lowball offer?

None of it made any sense.

When she pulled up to Julia's house, which would serve as the main set, she saw Trey's—no, damn it—Sterling Prescott's rented Taurus parked in the drive like he owned the place.

Slamming out of the car, Chloe marched up to the front door with furious anger pushing her on. She didn't ring the bell. She entered and was hit by a crush of voices. Women were everywhere, most of them the Roses who had made the final cut.

They talked excitedly, looking over racks of clothes that had been brought over from various boutiques in exchange for free advertising. Already Chloe could see how the women gravitated into smaller groups. Cliques.

Heat ran down her spine as it made her think of junior high and high school. Girls circling together, excluding others. Thank God for Kate and Julia, since she had never felt all that comfortable around others. The few times she had gotten friendly with other girls, she never was able to bring them home or reciprocate with birthday parties and sleep-overs. Her grandmother didn't believe in them. Kate and Julia had known all about her family, or lack thereof. They provided her with a safe place.

One of the Roses sat apart from the rest of the group. The smart one. Chloe wondered if she had made a mistake in insisting that Sherry be one of the contestants.

But then she shook the thought away. They needed a variety of interesting contestants, plus the woman was smart enough to figure out how to make this work for her. Besides, Chloe had bigger problems to worry about just then.

She started toward the kitchen, but stopped dead in her tracks when she saw Trey—no, Sterling—deep in conversation with one of the cameramen. Sterling was tall, taller than anyone there. Dark and handsome. She remembered their kiss—what, had it really been only an hour ago? She remembered the hope she had felt that he was kind and good after all.

She pressed her eyes closed, railing at herself for being so gullible.

Clenching her fists, she opened her eyes. And found that he was looking at her. Really looking, as if he was trying to understand what he saw—or what he felt.

Then he smiled, that chiseled face of his lighting up.

Hello, he mouthed.

Liar.

She turned away, sensed his sudden confusion, but she didn't care. She ducked and sidestepped her way through the crowd to find Julia.

Her dearest friend stood in the kitchen, laughing at something one of the television grips said to her. Julia had made an art form out of flirting and teasing.

"Chloe, sugar, there you are! I was beginning to wonder

if our illustrious coproducer of *The Catch and His Dozen Texas Roses* had disappeared." But then her smile faltered.

Chloe knew that Julia instantly sensed that something was wrong. That was the way with Julia, all fun and games and wildness until one of her little chicks needed her. No one else ever realized that about the pampered only child of the wealthiest man in El Paso.

"Chloe, sugar, what is it?"

Sterling Prescott started making his way toward them, his gaze hard and determined.

"We've got to talk," Chloe whispered. She took Julia's arm.

"Of course." Julia glanced around. "We'll go to my bedroom to get away from this crush of people."

They started forward, but Sterling blocked their path. Chloe tried to veer around him, and the man's controlled features furrowed even more.

"Chloe." One word, but everyone there sensed the command in his tone.

She ducked her head, held on tighter to Julia's arm, and kept going.

"Chloe!"

But this time it wasn't the man who called out to her.

"Kate?"

Chloe and Julia stopped and found an out-of-breath Kate racing into the house. "We've got a problem." Kate took in her surroundings, noticed the crowd. She pushed the kitchen door shut, secluding them from the rest of the crew and contestants, though she pulled Sterling inside with the three of them. "You need to hear this, too."

"I don't think he does," Chloe snapped.

More confusion on his face. But Kate didn't notice. She plunged ahead. "Our bachelor and one of the Roses ran off to Mexico to get married."

Then silence. Dumbfounded quiet as every one of them absorbed the news.

"You're joking," Julia choked out.

"I wish I were. But I'm not. I had a note on my desk from both of them. They thought that since I'm newly married, I would understand how they fell in love and couldn't go through with a show that is all about finding love after they had already found it. Can you believe this?"

Kate, always calm Kate, screeched.

Julia said a few things that they definitely didn't teach in etiquette classes.

Chloe started to pace.

"We'll have to postpone the show," Sterling said.

Chloe whipped her head up. Had this been the plan all along? Was this his creative way of ruining them? Had he paid the Catch and the Rose to run off so he could claim they needed to hold up the program?

"We can't postpone," Kate interjected when Chloe couldn't get a word out of her mouth. "We'll be ruined. We've banked everything on this. Isn't that right, Chloe?"

Everyone looked at her. "That's true. We can't afford not to start taping. We've already finalized our schedule. Six episodes over two weeks. We have advertising booked. And everyone here knows that if we don't run the show, we don't get the ad revenue."

"If we don't get the ad revenue," Julia added, her voice hollow, "we can't pay the bills."

"And that isn't acceptable," Chloe finished. "We'd go under. You know that . . . Trey? Don't you?"

He appeared decidedly uncomfortable. His brother, Ben, if he really was his brother, had walked in and stood off to the side, his arms crossed on his chest, one dark brow raised.

"If we don't air *The Catch* tomorrow night at six o'clock

as scheduled, we will be a prime target for a hostile take-over. Isn't that right, Trey?" Chloe continued pointedly.

She and the man who had come into their lives stared at each other.

Kate threw her hands up. "There's only one solution. We have to find another bachelor. We never showed the guy's face in the promos. We just have to find someone else."

All at once, Julia, Chloe, and Kate pivoted toward Ben. It took a second before he realized what they were thinking.

He stood away from the wall and put his hands out. "Sorry, no can do."

"Why? You'd be perfect," Kate said.

"I can't." He looked at his brother. "I'm on leave," he said, the words hesitant, "from a job that . . . wouldn't allow me to be on a television show."

Julia studied him. "What are you, a thief? Not interested in having your mug on the screen for fear that someone visiting the post office might recognize you on one of those posters?"

Chloe couldn't tell if Julia was trying to be funny or if she was really trying to be a bitch. She was only succeeding in the latter. Though it hardly registered because Chloe had another idea.

She turned to Trey, Sterling, whomever. An unfamiliar but deliciously wonderful feeling of revenge slid through her. "I have a better idea. Trey should do it."

"What?" he blurted.

"Yes, the more I think about it, the more I like it. Bachelor Trey. It has a nice ring to it, don't you think?"

"Oh, no. Not me."

"Why not, Trey?" she asked slyly. "This is your brilliant brainchild, insisting we had to have a bachelor show called *The Catch*. Remember how you told us that if we went for it with this, it would save us? Well, surprise! It's not. In fact, you and I both know that if we don't start taping and airing the first show tomorrow as planned, KTEX TV will be ruined." She let the words sink in. "Or was that your plan all along, Trey? Maybe you really are as horrible as the despicable Sterling Prescott, after all."

Kate gasped. Julia cursed.

"That wasn't my intent," the man said through clenched teeth. "When I came up with this plan, my intent was to save the station." He scowled, then started to pace, raking his hand through his hair. "There's got to be someone else who can step in."

"Who?" Chloe demanded. "We don't have time to do more interviews. And we sure as Hades can't bring in some stranger off the street. He could be any sort of stalker and we'd end up with the same sort of debacle that Fox had over that *Who Wants to Marry a Millionaire* guy who'd had a restraining order slapped against him." She smiled without an ounce of humor. "We can't afford to put our lovely Roses in danger like that."

He stopped and skewered her with a gaze. Then all of a sudden, he changed. She could feel it like a storm blowing through on a gust, and he surprised her. "Fine," he said. "I'll do it."

Julia and Kate cheered. Ben choked. Chloe couldn't believe it. And she really couldn't believe it a second later when he actually smiled.

"However, there's one condition," he added.

Chloe didn't like the look on his face.

"We also need to find a replacement for our missing Rose," he explained, his gaze incisive.

"Replacement?" Chloe repeated.

"That's right," Kate said with a weary sigh. "We've got only eleven women now."

"Eleven, twelve," Chloe reasoned, "what does it matter?

It's the bachelor that's the issue. Trey as the bachelor solves that. So you have to do it." She turned away.

"Not so fast," he said ominously. "Last I heard, eleven doesn't make a dozen. I'll be the bachelor on the condition that you fill in as the missing Rose."

She gaped at him. "Me? I'm not going to be a Rose! And who's going to notice a single missing Rose anyway?"

"The viewers," Kate stated.

The man's smile widened. "Exactly. And whose idea was it that we advertise *The Catch and His* Dozen *Texas Roses*? Not *His Eleven Texas Roses*. Or even just *His Texas Roses*."

Julia and Kate turned their eyes on her.

"Okay, so it was my idea. But—"

"Chloe, he's right," Kate said. "Viewers will notice. We need another Rose. I'd do it, but I'm married. And Julia can't do it because everyone in West Texas knows who she is. Which leaves you."

"I can't do it!"

"Why not?"

"Why not?!" she blurted. "I'm shy, remember! Me, Miss Sensible and Boring. Me, Miss Completely Unsex—" She snapped her mouth closed. "Me, Miss Can't Do This!"

"I think you'd be perfect," Julia cooed. Her eyes went from Chloe to Trey, then back again. "Besides, I've noticed recently that your shy streak has been on vacation."

"Julia," she hissed.

"Enough, you two," Kate said. "This is the only solution. Trey is from St. Louis and won't be recognized in this market. Chloe, shy or not, you've made such a point of being behind the scenes over the years that no one knows you. And as you said, we have to get started. We don't have time to look for anybody else."

"But what about work? I have a station to run."

Julia jumped in with a response. "Kate and I will do it

for you. We'll divide the load and get it done. Besides, it's only for two weeks, and almost all your attention was going to have to be devoted to *The Catch* anyway. So it will work out fine."

Chloe couldn't believe it. She also couldn't believe the man's smile. He had sowed the seed, then let her best friends bring the plan to fruition. The guy was really shrewd.

This time she was the one who started to pace. There had to be another solution. But what?

They really didn't have time to find someone else.

"Lucy!" she yelped. "We can get Lucy to do it."

"I don't want Lucy," Trey stated ominously. "I want you."

Chloe ignored the shiver of feeling that raced down her spine and settled with a traitorous tingle between her thighs.

"Whether you want her or not doesn't matter," Julia replied. "Lucy's not an option. She might be the biggest flirt in town, but she's got a boyfriend."

Great, just great. But then Chloe had yet another idea.

Why *not* do the show? It would get them on the air in time to start bringing in the much-needed revenue. Which meant that they would save the station . . . *and* it put Trey Tanner, aka the reclusive Sterling Prescott, in the television spotlight.

Yep, it wasn't such a bad plan after all.

"I've reconsidered. I think it's a great idea. I'll do it," she announced.

Kate clapped in relief; Julia hugged her. But Mr. Game Player himself did what he did so well. He raised a dark brow.

Chloe smiled at him—a big, fake, sweet taste of Texas smile that spread from here to Houston.

Two could play games, Mr. Prescott. And she had no intention of losing.

Chloe, sugar, you changed your mind awfully quick. Kate, didn't you sense it, too? One minute she was adamantly against doing it, then suddenly she said yes.

At first I was simply relieved. Now I'm not so sure I should be. Tell me what's going on in that pretty head of yours.

xo, j

Really, nothing's going on in my head. I am doing what is right for the station. I am contributing. I will do my part.

Chloe Sinclair
Station Manager
Award-winning KTEX TV

To: Chloe Sinclair <chloe@ktextv.com>
Julia Boudreaux <julia@ktextv.com>
From: Katherine Bloom <katherine@ktextv.com>
Subject: Agree

I agree. Chloe, what gives? I know how stubborn you can be. Spill.

Katherine C. Bloom
News Anchor, KTEX TV West Texas

To: Chloe Sinclair <chloe@ktextv.com>
Katherine Bloom <katherine@ktextv.com>
From: Julia Boudreaux <julia@ktextv.com>
Subject: Red, white, and missing

Kate, she sounds like a bad patriotic song. And Chloe, where are you? Why aren't you answering your e-mail?

Life used to be so simple before Daddy died. Now I have to worry. Life is giving me gray hairs!

xo, j

To: Julia Boudreaux <julia@ktextv.com>
Katherine Bloom <katherine@ktextv.com>
From: Chloe Sinclair <chloe@ktextv.com>
Subject: Pshaw

Girls, girls, girls, stop panicking. I had to dash back to the office now
that I'm going to be spending even *more* time on Meadowlark Drive.
As to my intent, I have nothing up my sleeve. But no one can blame
me if I don't last very long on the show.

C

p.s. I love patriotic songs, and Jules, you don't have a single gray
hair on that head of yours. Stop being dramatic. xoxoxoxoxoxo

To: Chloe Sinclair <chloe@ktextv.com>
Julia Boudreaux <julia@ktextv.com>
From: Katherine Bloom <katherine@ktextv.com>
Subject: Trouble

Chloe! What are you up to? What do you mean you can't be blamed
if you don't last very long on the show?

Chloe?!!!!!!

Kate

By eight o'clock the following morning, taping for *The Catch* was ready to begin. Giant lights illuminated the rooms that they were using as sets in Julia's sprawling mansion. Anything that could be seen as clutter was removed. They turned the Boudreaux's grand living room into a ballroom by removing most of the furniture and the fine Oriental rug from the gleaming hardwood floor. They would use that space for the opening show to introduce the entire cast to the television audience. In the days to come, the station would use the stunning dining room set for romantic dinners—that is, if dinners with more than one Rose could be considered romantic. Then finally, they would use the main, smaller living room for that place where their bachelor would dole out the roses at the end of each episode. A place of joy and pain.

The rest of the time, the cameraman would follow the contestants with his camera, along with a sound and lighting man. It was an easy setup, low cost, but gave the show a modern and hip look.

By six that evening they had to have forty-four minutes

of programming in the can and sixteen minutes of commercials so they could wow audiences across the city.

"Can you say pressure?" Chloe whispered to herself as she went over the last details on one of her many lists. Though even she couldn't deny a bud of excitement over the challenge and potential of what they were doing.

Pete, Kate's director from *Getting Real with Kate*, had been enlisted to direct *The Catch*. And now, after a fitful first night of little sleep in Julia's home turned dormitory and stage set, Chloe was as ready as she would ever be.

"Okay, does everyone understand the plan?" she asked, quieting the Roses who circled Julia's dining room table.

Julia stood to the side, her body surprisingly tense. Now that Chloe was sleeping in the same room with Julia—the other Roses strewn throughout the rest of the bedrooms, living dormitory-style—Chloe knew Julia hadn't slept well. For the first time in her life, Julia looked stressed.

Last night after things had calmed down, Chloe had started to tell Julia who Trey Tanner really was. But in the end, after they had put the new Catch and his dozen Roses together, she hadn't been able to say the words. Chloe knew that in ways Julia wasn't willing to show anyone, she had been barely holding on since her father's death, which had left his only child alone and devastated by the loss. But Julia had never been one to show her feelings. So she smiled and worked and did what she had to. But Chloe knew that she was barely holding on.

Chloe had to make this work—and it could. But Julia finally snapping and getting hysterical over Trey Tanner turning out not to be Trey Tanner at all wouldn't help matters. Chloe needed everyone calm and working at their best levels. Julia might be the owner, but Chloe was the station manager. And she had every intention of managing this situation back into success. Which meant she had no choice but to be one of the dozen Texas Roses.

Chloe pulled on a determined smile. "Ladies, let's review what we are going to do one last time."

The Roses sighed. They had already spent a good thirty minutes going over the show, then another twenty discussing Chloe suddenly joining the cast. It had become clear early on that the girls didn't think she had more than a snowball's chance in hell of winning, so they hadn't protested the odd arrangement too vigorously. Besides, not one of the Roses wanted the show to be cancelled at this late date.

Chloe launched into her spiel. "We will tape all twelve Roses being introduced to the Catch. This will be your chance to make a good first impression. Then we will tape each Rose engaging the Catch's attention. I've allotted thirty minutes for each of you, with a short lunch break at noon."

Shuddering at what these women had to do—engaging a man's attention, trying to win his approval—Chloe reminded herself that it was all for a good cause. They were saving the station.

"I know we've been over this," Mindy, the nurse, said, "but let me make sure I'm clear. We each introduce ourselves to the guy—"

"The Catch."

"I can't call a man the Catch."

"Fine. Then call him Trey."

Or traitor, liar, schmuck would do. But Chloe held that back.

"Good, I can do Trey—"

Nina, the bitch, grinned. "Did you see him last night? I could do him, too."

A few of the women tittered nervously. Others burst out laughing. Nina preened, pleased with her wit.

"So," Mindy said, moving on, "we introduce ourselves to Trey. After that we have to come up with some way to make him want to keep us on the show."

Chloe couldn't help mentally cringing at the sheer disgustingness of the idea. Men should be begging each and every one of these women for a few seconds of her attention. Women should not have to beg to be given a rose. It was degrading. It was embarrassing. She couldn't believe she had agreed to this. But that was the show. Women trying to snag a single man's interest.

You're saving the station.

She shut her eyes and silently repeated the words to herself three times, all but clicking her heels together like Dorothy— with the deep-down thought that when she opened her eyes, she'd be back in Kansas. That, or she wouldn't be on the set for *The Catch and His Dozen Texas Roses.*

She opened her eyes and looked around. No such luck.

Leticia, the voluptuous vamp, as Julia was fond of calling her, smiled wickedly and made a purring sound. "I know how to make a man want to keep me around."

"I'm sure you do," Chloe said, "but remember, this is a G rated show. Any lewd behavior won't make the cut. If you want to get airtime on TV, keep it clean."

"Whatever," Leticia said, studying her nails as if she was suddenly bored.

Mindy was getting frustrated and a little jumpy from nerves. "Okay, just bear with me," she continued. "I'm trying to understand. What kind of things are you talking about?"

Julia strode up and interjected. "Realistically, each of you has only twenty minutes to *catch* the Catch's attention since it will take a few minutes to stop taping, switch to the next Rose, then start taping again. So think about some sort of quick attention grabber. Hasn't there been something you've done in the past that gained a man's attention—as Chloe said, of the G rated sort? Though I would add that a little PG 13 wouldn't hurt."

Mindy cringed.

Leticia cooed.

Chloe was glad to see Julia was back to her old self.

"Listen, Mindy," Janice, the sweet one, said, reaching out and placing her hand on hers. "Just be yourself. You're great and wonderful and smart and he's going to love you."

The other Roses groaned.

"I'm serious," Janice persisted. "Just smile and talk to him, and he'll love you."

"You realize," vampy Leticia said to bitchy Nina, "this is sweet Janice's way of getting Mindy off the show pronto."

"It is not!"

Nina laughed.

Leticia held up her hands in mock surrender. "Whatever you say, girls. But Mindy," she said, focusing on the nurse, "just talking isn't going to do a thing. You've got to dazzle him."

"Me? Dazzle?"

"You bet. Tell him he's the best-looking stud you've ever seen in your life."

Mindy's eyes got wide and worried.

"You're going to be fine," Chloe assured her. "I'm sure there are lots of things you can do."

"Think of this as a mini–Miss America contest," Julia cooed.

Eleven Roses gasped. Chloe looked at her best friend like she had lost her mind. "Miss America?"

"Like the talent portion. Sing. Dance. Do something that

will catch the judge's eye. And in this case, the judge is the Catch."

The back door slammed, and Trey walked into the house with a suitcase in hand. Every woman there froze at the sight of him. For the first few seconds, Chloe forgot that he was a liar.

Her pulse kicked up, and she involuntarily sucked in her breath at how beautiful he was. He had dressed in a tuxedo that fit him like a glove; his white shirt was simple, no ruffles, with black onyx shirt studs that disappeared beneath a dark gray vest. Conservative but sexy at the same time. The formal evening clothes accentuated the dark fierceness of him.

He was breathtaking, like a prince at a rogues ball.

Which reminded her of just who he was. Sterling Prescott. Cutthroat media mogul. CEO of Prescott Media. Corporate raider extraordinaire. Though she still thought of him as Trey.

"Sorry I'm late."

He smiled at her, that slight grin that was given out so rarely that it seemed like a treasured gift. Not that *she* felt that way, but more than one of the Roses sighed. *Geez.*

"I've been on the phone all morning," he said to Chloe, "clearing my plate so I'll have all day to deal with this. I brought my suitcase. I guess I'm the one staying at your house now."

She studied her clipboard, trying to ignore him, since she couldn't take looking at him much longer. Because the truth was she had the urge to launch herself at him again, and not because she was angry. How was it possible that she was still attracted to the man when she knew him to be a horrible conniving person? It was unfair. Unheard of for her.

On top of that, she wasn't happy about having him stay

in her home. It felt intimate and knowing, as if she was giving him a peek into her soul. Had he been a stranger, it wouldn't have mattered. But this man wasn't a stranger. Not anymore.

"Yes, you're staying at my house," she stated with her best in-charge voice. "I'll take you over during the lunch break."

"That works."

Ever since he had become the Catch, he had taken this new job seriously. In fact he had taken it so seriously that he had stopped teasing and flirting with her altogether. Suddenly he was Mr. Professional in every aspect of his dealings with her. He was treating her as nothing more than one of the dozen Roses.

Good!

Good!

"For now," she added, "you can leave your suitcase in the kitchen, then we can get started."

For the first time she realized how quiet it had gotten. Every one of the Roses sat in rapt attention. They might have joked about winning the Catch's eye earlier. But now, seeing the man in the light of day, dressed like an elegant warrior king, each of them was truly trying to figure out a way to stand out. Even their shy nurse had a glitter in her gaze that was all but predatory.

Chloe had to tamp down a surge of desire that she told herself was nothing more than perfectly normal competitiveness.

"Let's go to the ballroom," she instructed.

That was one of the more amazing aspects of Julia's childhood home. Not only was it huge and lovely, but the grand living room, as they called it, could be turned into a stunning ballroom.

The Roses filed in, their heels sounding hollow against

the hardwood floor. Each of them was already dressed in her formal gown donated by Henri's Formal Wear. Even the camera equipment and lighting shades couldn't detract from the shimmering beauty of the crystal and mirrored space.

As a child, Chloe used to sneak in and pretend to dance. She was Cinderella, and she would dance with her imaginary prince, who always arrived just in time to rescue her.

Shaking the thought away, she directed the girls to the chairs and sofas that had been left in the room. When she had everyone seated, she directed Trey to stand in a lattice archway covered with roses and ivy that she and the director had set up earlier.

"Okay, Pete, it's all yours," Chloe said.

"But what about you?" Julia asked.

Everyone looked Chloe over. Chloe glanced at herself in the wall of mirrors and had to swallow back a gasp. After finalizing the set, she hadn't had a second to get ready.

"I'm one of the six who we'll tape after lunch."

Trey interrupted. "We want to have a wide sweep of all twelve Roses. Which includes you."

"I haven't had a chance to get ready. Plus I don't have a dress yet. Henri is bringing something over. Our AWOL Rose's gown didn't fit me. And the vendor already took the extras away."

For the first time since he arrived that morning, he looked at her with that sensual knowing. "I can think of a dress you have that would work well."

Her heart leaped into her throat, and she was certain red seared into her cheeks. She started to protest.

Pete agreed. "I'd rather do the wide shots this morning. That way we can get started editing that tape for the show's opening."

"Go change," Trey commanded. "We'll start with the individual intros. Then once you get back, we'll do the wide sweep."

Knowing they were right, she left. Julia followed. "What dress is he talking about?"

"There's something that I forgot to mention," Chloe began with a cringe, "in all the excitement about the show and the plans and whatnot—"

"Whenever you use *whatnot,* I know something's up."

"Nothing is up. It's just that I sort of forgot to mention that"—she drew a deep breath—"the night I nearly had sex in the hotel bathroom—remember that night?"

"Yes," Julia said very carefully.

"Remember how I said it was a stranger?"

"I do."

"Well, that stranger would be Trey."

"What? Our Trey? Bachelor Trey?"

"That's the one."

"Why didn't you tell me?"

"I was going to. But I found out that Trey was from Prescott Media, and then Kate and I thought I should tell you in person. . . ."

"You told Kate?"

"Yes, that first day, but I wanted to tell you in person and you were busy and then things got kind of out of control and I hated to mention that on top of finding out that you were having such issues with the station. Anyway, then I forgot I hadn't mentioned it. Until now."

Julia started to pace, her kitten heels clicking on the floor. "Great. So why the news flash now?"

"Remember the dress that I borrowed from you that night?"

"That's the dress he referred to?"

"You got it."

Finally Julia stopped and smiled. "See, I told you that dress would make you stand out in a crowd."

"Unfortunately, I never got to the crowd part."

Julia laughed out loud, took Chloe's hand, then pulled her along to her bedroom. In a matter of thirty minutes, with Julia's help, Chloe dressed and fixed her hair. They worked on her makeup, and Julia even insisted on a dab of perfume. When finally they returned to the ballroom, Chloe hardly recognized herself.

When she walked in, Pete was taping one of the Roses as she introduced herself to Trey. Several heads turned. Trey concentrated on the moment like a pro. But the minute Pete called cut, Trey looked over at her as if he had sensed she was there all along.

His dark eyes heated with a sensuality that she recognized. She felt as if he undressed her with his gaze.

"Next!" Pete barked.

Leticia stood from her chair, her red dress glittering like a jewel under the intense lights. "I'm ready."

Trey refocused.

"Roll tape."

Leticia strode forward, staring directly at Trey. Chloe could feel the intensity that the woman exuded. Her body looked like every man's wet dream.

"The camera adds twenty pounds," Julia whispered. "She's going to look fat."

Chloe told herself that she wasn't happy about it. In fact, she forcefully reminded herself of her plan.

"Hello, Trey," the woman purred in an I-want-to-have-wild-passionate-sex-with-you voice. "I look forward to spending time with you. I look forward to getting to know you. And I hope you look forward to me."

She emphasized the word *me*. Not *seeing me*, or even *getting to know me*.

No one under the age of thirteen would understand the double meaning, but everyone older would. Trey smiled, then kissed the back of her hand.

Next came Mindy. If the nurse had been worried before, she had packed the worry up along with her white stockings and crepe-soled shoes. Chloe would have sworn that the royal blue organza blouse she had chosen was unbuttoned a few buttons lower than when everyone had first gathered in the ballroom.

"Hi, Trey," she stated, sounding more like a high school cheerleader than a medical professional. "I'm hoping that we have some time to spend together. I thought that you might want to practice a little CPR."

Chloe choked. Julia swallowed back a laugh. Trey, if he was surprised, didn't show it. He chuckled appreciatively, and Chloe knew that when they showed his hint of a roguish smile on television tonight, every woman in El Paso between the ages of eight and eighty would fall madly in love with him.

"He's good," Julia commented.

If she only knew how good.

The first six introductions were completed with a few minutes left before noon. Pete thought it was a good idea if they got Chloe's intro out of the way, since, as a professional, she should be quick and efficient. Then they'd only have five to do that afternoon.

Pulling back her shoulders, Chloe walked forward. Professional or not, her knees were shaking with both fear and excitement. She was going to be on TV!

Even though she had worked at KTEX since she graduated from college, she had never been in front of the camera.

But the second Pete called action she froze.

Chloe stared in horror at the dark, opalescent lens of the

camera. She squeaked when Trey reached out and touched her chin.

"Hello," he said kindly.

"Ah, hello," she managed, still staring into the lens. *Think, Chloe, think.*

"Ah, hello," she repeated.

"Cut! What the hell is going on with you, Chloe?" Pete bleated.

Sense returned the minute the red recording light blinked off.

"See, I told you I was shy! I shouldn't be doing this. I'm not cut out for this."

"Pull yourself together while we do the sweeping shots of the entire group of women instead."

The wide-angle shots of all the Roses went quickly. When they were done, Pete added, "Chloe, we'll do your intro after lunch with the remaining girls." He turned to the group. "We'll start back at twelve-thirty. Don't be late."

The Roses were herded out to the kitchen, where Julia's housekeeper Zelda had laid out a spread of sandwiches, salads, and sodas. But no one was hungry.

Trey came up to Chloe. "You said you'd take me to your house."

"Oh," she groaned, still embarrassed at having failed at something so simple. Stage fright! Her! "Of course."

She headed out the back door. Trey grabbed his suitcase and followed. She didn't slow down, despite her high heels, as she took the path she had taken a thousand times before between Julia's mansion and her own house.

When they stepped through the archway that connected the side yards, Trey tilted his head. "So this is where you live."

"Yes," she replied, trying not to feel defensive.

Her home was tiny compared to Julia's. But she loved it,

and she was proud even though no doubt it was probably microscopic compared to anything this man would live in.

"I find it fascinating that you work with Julia and live next door to her, too."

"Kate lives on the other side of Julia."

"Did you move here at the same time?"

"No. We all lived here as kids."

"You moved here with your family? Do you still live with them?" he asked.

Her jaw felt tight. "It was my grandmother's house before she died a year ago."

"I'm sorry."

She relaxed, but just a bit. "She left it to me."

"So you live alone."

"Actually, no. My father moved in six months ago."

He glanced around. "I guess you really are close to your father if he lives with you."

"Absolutely." She looked around as well. "Though I wish I could spend more time with him."

"What?"

"Nothing. Tell me about your friends and family."

That distracted him. Suddenly he was lost in some kind of thought that she couldn't fathom.

"There's nothing to tell."

"Sure there is. Tell me about your friends from when you were a kid, guys you went to school with."

He stared out into the yard, at the flowers and trees, without responding. After a second, he walked around her on the narrow path, not touching her, and headed for the house. She would have sworn he said that he didn't have *any* friends.

"No way."

"What?" he asked.

"You don't have any friends?"

"I didn't say that."

"Sure you did."

"You're mistaken." He walked to the back porch like he owned the place, pulled open the screen door that was at the top of two cement steps, and gestured for her to enter. "The clock is ticking until we have to return."

"Fine. If you don't want to talk about not having any friends, who am I to push?"

He muttered an oath under his breath, and used his head to gesture for her to get inside.

The minute they entered, she felt at once relaxed and nervous. This house invoked such a mixed bag of feelings in her. Her home for so long, and now she even owned it. But it still felt more like her grandmother's house, however much Chloe had added her own touches.

Trey looked around. But it wasn't the tiles or the stenciling he noticed.

"Who's this?" he asked with a smile. "Though I think I can guess." He peered closer at the framed color photo. "That's Julia; that's Kate." He straightened. "And that's you." He turned to look at her. "You were cute."

"Cute?"

Uncomfortable, she strode past him, praying he couldn't hear the pounding of her heart at the unfamiliar compliment. "I was never cute. Come on, I'll show you around and fill you in about the rules."

"Rules?" he queried, setting the photo down. "You expect me to live by rules?"

That's when it hit her.

"Instructions," she clarified, her mind suddenly racing.

If he wanted to pretend to be Trey Tanner, regular working stiff like the rest of them, who was I not to let him live like an average, ordinary, not filthy-rich guy?

"Helpful hints, is more like it," she added. "I'll just show you around so you'll know where everything is when you need to clean the house." Inspired, she gestured to a closet, opening the doors like she was on a game show.

"Clean the house?" he asked incredulously. "You expect me to clean?"

She batted her eyes innocently. "I would have done it myself for the other Catch, but since I have my hands full now with both producing and being *on* the show, it seems like you can clean for yourself."

He made a noise that she pretended was agreement.

"Over here we have the dishwasher. Detergent is under the sink along with anything else you will need. Windex, 409—"

"What is 409?"

"Tsk, tsk." She wagged her finger at him. "Don't tell me we are going to have another coffee episode."

"My coffee was great."

She snorted. "Whatever. It's never too late to learn," she told him, then turned and headed for the refrigerator. "I didn't know what a bachelor would want. But I bought pork chops for the grill. Lettuce and tomatoes for salads. Cold cuts for sandwiches. There's plenty of things in here that you can whip up for lunches and dinners."

"Whip up?"

"You know, cooking. Or is that something else you don't know about? Good Lord, Trey, where were you raised?"

She looked at him with devilish seriousness.

"I know about cooking," he grumbled, his humor evaporating.

At least he didn't out-and-out lie and say he knew *how* to cook. She didn't believe for a second he had cooked himself a meal in his life. But she only smiled.

"I knew we had to feed our bachelor, so I worked meals into the budget."

"But not a cleaning service."

"Oops, no." She giggled with relish and closed the refrigerator door as the last piece to her plan fell into place. "The only other thing you'll have to do is mow the lawn."

Genius. Pure genius.

"I am not going to mow the lawn."

"You don't know how, Trey?" she asked with a sweet pout. "Is that beyond your talents?"

He glared. "It is not beyond my talents."

"Good!" She turned on her heel and marched out to the garage, where her brand-new, wonderful mower sat. "Ta da! What do you think?"

"I think you're intentionally trying to make me crazy."

"Would I do that?" She tried to look hurt.

"Yes."

She laughed out loud. "Let me explain how it works."

She told him about the self-propelling mechanism, the pull cord for starting, and the ever-important clutch. "Do you want me to demonstrate?"

"I can use a mower," he stated arrogantly.

She raised a brow, then shrugged. "Watch out for my flowers."

When he growled and looked like he might do something they would both regret—kill her or kiss her—she swept out of the garage. "That's about it. Now I'll show you where you'll sleep."

Which meant bedroom, and bed, and her body started another slow rise to awareness.

He followed her back into the house. She saw the irritation in his eyes, but good manners compelled him to hold the doors for her as they returned inside. Every time their bodies got close, she could feel the heat of him, like sun breaking through a cold cloudy day.

At the back of the house, she bypassed her own bedroom, proceeding to the guest room. But he stopped at her door and looked inside.

"You can't go in there!"

He did anyway.

Crossing her arms over her sequined-and-beaded chest, she was put out by the way he constantly did as he pleased. She tried not to be affected by the sight of this tall, strong man in a tux who looked so out of place in her tiny bedroom. One of these days she would have the money to replace her twin bed and simple furniture that she'd had since she moved to El Paso. In junior high, Julia had marched into the house and told Chloe's grandmother that her granddaughter's room was an embarrassment. She had then proceeded to dole out instructions to Chloe and Kate as to how to paint all that furniture.

The paint had remained, faded but well cared for. Her grandmother had watched silently, only nodding her head in approval when they were done.

Now, decades later, with a sophisticated man taking it all in, she felt vulnerable and very young.

"Amazing room," he said.

She wrinkled her nose in surprise. "You like it?"

He turned around and met her gaze. "I like *you*."

"You don't like me. And I certainly don't like you," she sputtered indignantly.

But that didn't stop him from smiling confidently. "Did I tell you how great you look?"

She snorted with effort because in reality a little thrill raced down her spine at the compliment. "First I'm cute, and now you say I look great? What's gotten into you?"

"I had a hell of a time concentrating on all the other women today because I was thinking of you."

"You can't play favorites."

"I never said you were my favorite."

She punched him in the chest.

He laughed out loud. "Ouch."

"That didn't hurt."

"True."

Then he reached out. But she was too fast for him. She leaped away and tried not to look like she was hurrying to safety. "We have to be back on the set in fifteen minutes. Can't afford to dawdle when the clock is ticking."

eleven

Everyone took their places back on the set at Julia's house. Trey was the last to return, and Chloe would have sworn he looked at her with a strange grimace as if he didn't get who she was. Or maybe it was that he didn't quite get what had happened between them in her bedroom. She suspected there weren't many women who walked out on him.

Good. One more example for him of what the real world was like. Though this afternoon she planned to give him a lesson he wouldn't soon forget.

"Let's get started, people," Pete called out. "We need to finish up and pronto."

The next five Roses were taped doling out the sort of sugary Trey-you-are-so-amazing sorts of lines that made Chloe feel like she was going into a diabetic fit. Though she knew just how to cure the sweetness, and ultimately succeed in her plan to get kicked off the show.

"Chloe, you're up," Pete called out.

She still wore the sexy dress, and she was feeling a little feisty, which helped matters. The minute the camera started to roll, she had just the sort of out of body experience that she knew she'd need to get through this—especially after she'd gone stock-still in front of the camera that morning.

She strolled up to him, thinking feline—Persian, roaring lion, sultry tiger—every step of the way. He stood there with his hands clasped in front of him, his feet apart. He looked commanding and powerful, his shoulders wide and strong beneath the perfect cut of his tuxedo.

"Hey there," she cooed with a sexy softness.

Suspicion narrowed his dark eyes faster than if he had bit into a lemon. It pleased her that she had scratched his polished surface. With effort, she held back a giddy smile.

She took the remaining steps, working her hips, and stopped barely a hand's length in front of him. Tilting her head back so she could look him in the eye, she thought bold, sexy, bad girl thoughts, then reached out and walked her fingers up his chest. "Oooo, you're such a big strong manly man."

Suspicion turned to wry disbelief—or maybe it was leery disbelief. Either way, she could tell from his expression that he knew something was up.

"I just love big strong manly men. Those types of guys I heard you mention."

That really got his attention.

"What was it you said?" She thought she might have purred. "As I recall, you said you're a Neanderthal who thinks sex is a game and your only goal is to score." She pretended to shiver with pleasure, though in truth the pleasure she felt had everything to do with the strange choking sound he was making. "You did say that, didn't you, Trey?" she asked with an innocent smile at the camera. "Oops, did I make you mad?"

She didn't wait for him to answer. She started to turn away, having every intention of beating a sexy, albeit hasty, retreat. But he startled her when he caught her arm. His grip was like steel, but surprisingly gentle.

"I think you must have me mistaken with someone else. I certainly have never thought of sex as a game. Sex is about two people sharing a connection."

The awareness that sizzled through the room was tangible, and every one of the Roses swooned.

She was supposed to have left him standing there speechless, dumbfounded. Instead he had regained the upper hand in a matter of seconds. Damn, damn, damn.

She turned her back on the camera and leaned close. "You just made that up," she hissed. "You don't believe it."

He gave her an aggravatingly knowing smile.

Things weren't going as she planned.

Okay. She rolled her shoulders. Think. Regroup.

"Fine, but I do know what you said," she said for the audience to hear. "Think back," she persisted. "Are you sure you never said something like that? About men and women, and perceptions? Perhaps when you were in the 'interviewing' process?"

She saw the minute he remembered what she was talking about. The day when they were questioning potential candidates for *The Catch*.

This time he leaned close so no one could hear, his jaw muscles starting to tick. "I was talking about what *you* thought I must think."

The camera might not have picked up the actual words, but it surely made out his defensive stance—like a guilty man who had been caught, and wasn't happy about it.

Relief!

"A technicality," she whispered with a laugh. But the

truth was, she felt anything but triumphant. At the look on his face, all she felt was guilty and mean.

She steeled herself against her conscience. The fact was, he started this. She shouldn't feel guilty. She was adding a little spice to the show and she was getting herself the boot in the process. It was perfect.

She forced a carefree laugh for the camera, then tugged her arm away and headed off the set, but not before she finally got herself back in order and remembered to slap him on the butt and wink.

If he could have, she was sure he would have murdered her right then and there.

Perfect! She had just regained the upper hand.

Yep, she practically gloated. It was just a matter of time before she was sitting on the sidelines, producing full-time, with Trey mad as Hades and leaving her the hell alone.

Kate was truly shocked. Julia was trying hard not to laugh out loud.

"Did he really say that?" Julia wanted to know.

"He did," Chloe said with a superior shake of her head. "Or sort of," she amended.

"Sort of? Chloe, what did he say?"

"That. But he was just saying what he thought I thought about the sort of man he was. Or *is*. He is." She cringed. "But he did say it. Just for different reasons, perhaps, than I let on."

"And you think that's going to get you kicked off?"

"Wouldn't you kick me off if you were in his shoes?"

"No question."

Julia laughed, Kate shook her head, and Chloe was feeling relieved. But her relief was short-lived.

"What do you mean, you're offering me a rose?" she yelped an hour later when he called her name as the camera taped the first rose ceremony.

With the camera light glowing green, he pruned the list down to eight. She was the eighth and final Rose he called. Some of the girls preened and gushed. Others sat quietly, clearly thankful to still be in contention. While others, including sweet Janice, sat on the sofa, holding back tears of disappointment that they hadn't been chosen. Chloe, on the other hand, was furious. Pete and his cameraman caught it all.

"You can't offer me a rose," Chloe stated. "You're supposed to cut me. I was horrible, mean, a total witch!"

It was Trey who turned to the director with barely held patience, and called, "Cut."

"Great, cut the camera, cut four other women, but you won't cut me! Well, too bad, I don't accept your rose."

The Roses and the stagehands gasped.

"You can't not accept," he said through gritted teeth.

"Says who?"

"Says me."

"And that matters why?"

"Because I'm the boss!"

He visibly tried to rein in control. This was more of the man that she expected him to be. This was a man she could hate and ignore. Not the fun, playful guy from earlier. Not the guy who actually looked a little hurt by what she had falsely accused him of.

"No, you are not the boss," she stated. "You're the co-boss. And I say a Rose can say no. It will be great. Viewers will love it. Isn't that right, Julia?"

The owner of KTEX TV grimaced. "Actually, I think he's right. We can't make our bachelor look any more unappealing than he already looks."

"Unappealing?" Trey demanded.

"Sorry," Julia responded without looking the least bit

contrite. "I'm not sure where you learned to woo a woman, but it might very well have been in Neanderthal 101. That said, we don't need you looking any worse, since it's too late for us to find someone else." She turned to Chloe. "Accept the damn rose and let's get this done. We only have an hour until airtime, and we still have to edit the footage. Tick, tick, tick, everyone."

Chloe glared, but she knew Julia was right. She hadn't thought about the ramifications of making their bachelor look so pathetic that a Rose would cut him.

Their Catch needed to look like a rugged alpha male. She might not like that, really, she told herself firmly, but tons of women loved that kind of guy. And while they would scream at the screen and throw verbal tomatoes at him, they would swoon just a little since they didn't have to deal with him in real life. For this show to succeed, first thing tomorrow morning, every secretary and soccer mom in the city limits needed to be talking about the Catch over coffee.

She just *had* to get him to cut her. Which led her to Plan B.

At the end of the next episode, he would cut the field down from eight to six. She had every intention of being one of the two he sent packing.

To: TheCatch@ktextv.com
From: MD20/20@sploto.com
Subject: Hottie

Wow, man, the Catch is cool. Love the hot bod babe, Leticia. But Chloe is the best. She's a trip and a half. I wouldn't mind getting into her pants.

Mad Dog

To: TheCatch@ktextv.com
From: theman@qakoo.com
Subject: Dinner

Dear Chloe:

I write to you as an ardent admirer. The minute the camera took in your lovely face, I was mesmerized. You are a breath of fresh air in an otherwise sterile world of stale and stagnant television. I would be honored if you would allow me to take you to dinner.

Yours sincerely,
Albert Cummings

To: TheCatch@ktextv.com
From: Praying4U@nixpit.com
Subject: Sin

To Whom It May Concern:

I am writing to tell you that I find your new show, *The Catch and His Dozen Texas Roses,* to be a despicable excuse for television. Do you really think that programs such as *The Catch* will open the pearly gates to heaven for you? I think not.

Please reconsider airing what surely has been a temporary loss of judgment.

Sincerely,
Pastor Hartwell Lerner

To: TheCatch@ktextv.com
From: jbean@jbean.org (Jennie Bean)
Subject: Love Chloe

Chloe is awesome! I teach three sections of women's lit at the University of Texas, and Chloe is just the sort of role model I like to present to my students. She tells it like it is, and a stuffed shirt like Trey would be the luckiest guy in the world if he ended up with her.

You go, Chloe!

Best,
Professor Jennie Bean

To: TheCatch@ktextv.com
From: BHawkings@spotmail.com
Subject: Wow

Dear KTEX TV:

Love your new show, *The Catch.* Really love the wow factor of
Leticia. She is one fine hottie. And Mindy, well, she could charm the
socks off a cat. Keep the shows coming.

B. Hawkings

To: TheCatch@ktextv.com
From: Rocketman@nip.mail.com
Subject: A fan

Dear Chloe, Just a short note to tell you that you're hot and great
and you have an instant fan in me. Keep up the good work.

Love ya,
Rocket

To: TheCatch@ktextv.com
From: theman@qakoo.com
Subject: Surprise

I'm sending you a surprise. I hope you'll think of me fondly.

Albert Cummings

To: Ben Prescott <sc123@fastmail.com>
From: Sterling Prescott <sterling@prescottmedia.com>
Subject: E-mail Attachments

Ben, I've attached some of the e-mails we are getting about the show. A lot of guys are taking an interest in Chloe. Does this look like anything we should be concerned about?

SHP

<<attachment>>

To: Sterling Prescott <sterling@prescottmedia.com>
From: Ben Prescott <sc123@fastmail.com>
Subject: re: E-mail Attachments

Meet me for a beer at a place called El Pescado, on Doniphan. Can't miss it. The blue building with the fish on it. We'll discuss the e-mails.

twelve

Sterling felt raw.

He wanted Chloe with a driving need that pulsed through his body. And she eluded him at every turn.

It had been three days since they had taped and then aired the first segment of *The Catch,* and he still could no more believe that he was obsessed with a woman who wanted nothing to do with him than he could believe he actually was a bachelor on a dating show. Hell, he couldn't believe he was on a reality show at all. He was a highly respected corporate CEO, not some pathetic guy desperate for television exposure and a date.

He hated the situation, hated having to be someone else, hated every single time Chloe looked at him with those innocent blue eyes and called him Trey.

He wanted out. But he was caught in his own trap.

After he had made coffee in the lunchroom that day, he nearly told Chloe everything. He still couldn't believe the way she made him do things he shouldn't. Thankfully the whole missing bachelor and Rose debacle had gotten in the way. Not that he was at all thankful that becoming the Catch had saved him from ruining the deal he had made with his brother. But he had promised his family he would bring Ben home—his brother whose dark eyes now darkened with something more than color. Ben Prescott was haunted by something he didn't want to talk about.

Sterling swore and knew that he would do whatever it took to help his brother—and if a reality show was what he had to do to accomplish the feat, so be it.

But hell, he couldn't believe he was wasting his time having to deal with other women when all he wanted was one.

He saw now that despite Chloe's wildness in the hotel bathroom, she was far from experienced. She had wanted him, but it was a desire that had burst out like a dam giving way. She had given in to something beyond her control and reason.

Chloe wasn't easy—in more ways than one, he conceded with a wry smile.

But that wasn't what surprised him. He was surprised by the fact that every time he was near her, he, Sterling Prescott—always in control, always reserved—felt a nearly foreign need to tease, play, and have fun.

Fun, him.

It had taken him days to even understand what he was feeling.

Desire? No question.

Intrigue? Without a doubt.

But there had been more than desire and intrigue since the day she pretended not to know him when she walked into the conference room looking like a squeaky-clean librarian. He couldn't imagine why she would go to such effort to hide such sultry sexiness beneath a determined plainness.

He had never known a woman who exerted so much effort *not* to be sexy. He wanted to uncover her secrets . . . and he wanted to laugh and play and have fun.

He wanted to kiss her, make love to her . . . and damn if he didn't want to chase her around the room, swing her over his shoulder, and tickle her until she cried uncle.

What was he thinking?

Running his hand over his face with a frustrated groan, he didn't understand it. And quite frankly, he didn't like it. Sterling Prescott didn't do things like that. He didn't chase women in any fashion. Not in sexual pursuit, and certainly not in play.

It was past midnight when Sterling pulled up to the small, squat bar brightened by multiple lights in the dark. A multicolored fish was painted across the Easter egg blue front, a wooden door placed in just a way that made it seem like you were walking into the guts of the fish when you entered. Not the sort of establishment that Sterling Prescott generally frequented, reminding him of something else he wasn't used to feeling toward any woman not a part of his family. A need to protect.

If Chloe was in any danger, he wasn't going to sit back and let something happen. All of a sudden having a cop in the family wasn't so bad.

Sterling entered the bar wearing the only kind of clothes he had with him here in the westernmost reaches of Texas. None of which were appropriate for a fish hangout, he decided when he looked around. The men wore jeans, boots, and simple shirts—western shirts, T-shirts, even short sleeve shirts despite the fifty degree temperature. No one wore a tie.

The women wore jeans as well, for the most part, though some had on short skirts and lots of makeup. Though he decided that had nothing to do with Texas and everything to do with being in a bar and looking over every man who walked through the door.

Through the dim haze, Sterling saw Ben sitting at the bar, wearing his usual T-shirt, jeans, and black boots. He had a nearly full glass of beer in front of him.

"Nice place," Sterling commented as he sat down next to his brother.

Ben grinned. "The El Paso Country Club was already closed. Besides, I don't think 'Trey' could have gotten a membership."

"You're not going to let up, are you?"

Ben took a pull on his glass, then he smiled as he set it down. "Not if I can help it. I love seeing you twist in the wind every time Chloe calls you Trey. It's priceless."

Something inside him did twist every time she called him Trey. He hated it. But it was about more than the lie—which was bad enough. It was that after a lifetime of being private, he wanted to share with her who he really was.

When she had asked about having friends, he had wanted to tell her about growing up in the Prescott house, where they were never allowed to do normal kid-type things—no ordinary fun. No digging in dirt, no blasting off rockets. He had thrown himself into studying. Diana had thrived on the petted world of frilly dresses and society teas. Ben had been the one who strained against it.

But Sterling couldn't tell Chloe about any of that since it didn't mesh with the man he was pretending to be.

The irony of the situation wasn't lost on him. For the first time in his life, he felt like he could let his defenses down around a woman—only he couldn't because he was living a lie.

A bartender came forward. "What'll you have?"

Sterling glanced over at what Ben was drinking. "I'll have a beer."

"What kind?" the man asked.

"Whatever he's having."

"One Coors on tap coming up."

The brothers didn't say another word until Sterling's tall, frosted glass sat in front of him and the bartender was busy with another customer.

"So what do you think of the e-mails?" Sterling asked without preamble.

Ben considered a moment before he answered. "Hard to say. But they seem pretty harmless. A Holy Roller, a man hater, and a bunch of guys who have it bad for Chloe." He looked over at Sterling. "Are you Albert Cummings?"

"Funny."

"Just asking." He went back to his beer with a wry grin. "I'll see if I can find anything on the e-mail addresses. They're probably nothing. But better safe than sorry."

"Good," Sterling said in his autocratic way.

The men stared at the bar backsplash for a while in silence.

"So," Ben began, "how's it going other than the e-mails? Are the numbers working out so the station will survive?" He swiveled his head and grinned. "Am I on the verge of having to go to work for Prescott Media?"

Sterling glanced over at him. "Would that really be such a bad thing?"

The grin disappeared, replaced by that haunted darkness that was never far away. "Sometimes I think it might even be the best thing I could do. Then other times I can't imagine dealing with the world you live in."

"What's wrong with that world? It's your world, too."

"No, it's not. It never has been. You know that. Not everyone is meant to be a part of the world he is born into. That's why I became a cop. I'm good at it, and I like it." He took a long swallow of his draft. "At least I did." Ben stopped abruptly and cursed.

"Ben, tell me—"

Ben cut him off. "I can't," he stated forcefully.

Sterling didn't know what else to say. In business, in his world, he had so much control. But he had virtually no control over his brother.

After a second, Ben called out for another beer.

The bartender took the empty glass and napkin, wiping down the space with an expert swipe. Then he set the new beer down.

"Thanks."

The bartender merely nodded, then went on to the next customer.

"Look, Sterling—"

Sterling realized that this was the first time Ben had called him by his real name since that first day.

"—I'm fine," Ben continued. "I just need some space. We can talk about all of this after *The Catch* is over. We'll both know where we stand then."

Having a drink of his own beer, Sterling studied Ben in the mirrored backsplash and decided that he wouldn't press.

"So tell me about the show," Ben said finally. "You never did answer my question. Is it working?"

Sterling shrugged. "At this point," he confessed, "I'd like nothing more than to toss in the towel to be done with the farce."

"Are you saying you want to call the deal off?"

Sterling set his beer down with a thud. "Will you come home to St. Louis?"

"No," Ben said shortly. Then he grimaced. "Hell, I appreciate that you care, Sterling. I really do. And I get that you've had to make some hard choices over the years. But your back's not against the wall anymore. So I can't figure out why you can't stop."

This time it was Sterling who didn't want to talk, and the awkward silence flared.

"Hey, sorry." Ben looked at him like he really meant it. "You're not going to throw in the towel. You never have. That's something I've always admired about you. Regardless of how difficult something gets, you never give up." Ben placed his hand on his brother's shoulder for a second before he dropped it away. "Tell me what it is about the show that's making you crazy."

Sterling grumbled, awkward when the conversation turned to him. As the head of his family, he didn't share his problems or concerns. His job was to solve everyone else's. Talking about the specifics of the show, however, was another matter.

"The Roses and their tactics are enough to put a man off dating for a lifetime, and Chloe—"

He cut himself off, having no idea what he wanted to say.

"What about Chloe?"

"Let's just say I've never met a more difficult woman in all my life."

Ben laughed out loud. "She's not difficult, Sterling. She's as normal as most every red-blooded American woman I've met."

"She's not acting like the other red-blooded women on the show. They have no idea who I really am. They think I'm 'Trey,' some guy crazy enough to actually consent to finding a wife or girlfriend on a television show. And they are acting like every other woman I've ever encountered."

"It's the competitive spirit. What woman wants to get tossed off TV?"

"Chloe," they said at the same time.

They laughed out loud, then each took another long drink of beer.

"She really wants me to kick her off," Sterling said after the laughter had trailed off. "I mean, really."

"Can you blame her? I'm not sure what's up between the two of you, but she hasn't liked you since she first set eyes on you during that meeting in the KTEX conference room."

Sterling had to clamp his mouth shut over the near admission that it hadn't been their first meeting. But he was not a man to kiss and tell.

"If you're trying to win her heart—"

"I am not trying to win her heart, Ben. I just have to get her approval, remember? And frankly, for about five minutes, I had it."

The younger Prescott held his hands up in surrender, though the knowing smile that curved on his face was far from agreement. "I find that hard to believe. Regardless, I should rephrase. If you want to get her to stop making a fool of you on television—"

Sterling groaned.

"—then you better start doing things different."

"Like what?"

Ben made a face as if the answer was obvious. "Seduce her with your charm."

Sterling felt uncomfortable underneath his brother's amused gaze.

"You understand what I'm talking about, don't you?" Ben persisted.

He didn't. "Charm?"

Ben rolled his eyes heavenward. "Hell, Sterling."

Truth to tell, Sterling wasn't altogether sure what charm entailed. He'd never consciously thought about winning a woman in his life. It just happened.

One of the women in El Pescado's came up to Ben, leaning close, rubbing up against him, making him laugh. Clearly he knew her, since he slapped her butt and said he'd see her later.

"You call that charm?" Sterling asked as he raised an ominous brow. "I'm not sure that taking charm advice from you is going to get me anywhere. A bit like the blind leading the blind."

"Hey," Ben said with a laugh, "she wants me, doesn't she?"

"I suppose, but I really don't think a slap on the butt is going to get me far with Chloe Sinclair."

"You're probably right."

A long swallow of beer by both men ensued, each of them lost in thought.

"Okay," Ben announced, "go with that sensitive crap."

"What?"

"Women are always saying they want a sensitive guy. Maybe you should cry."

Sterling almost choked on his beer. "I am not going to cry."

Ben conceded defeat with an expression that said clearer than words that Sterling shouldn't come whining to him when he failed. "Then just look sad," Ben instructed. "Tell her some sad sack story about losing your teddy bear when you were five."

"I never had a teddy bear in my life."

"That's not the point."

"You're advocating that I lie."

Ben looked at him. "I'm not sure you should get all righteous over lying just now, given your situation. But that isn't what I was suggesting. Just think about something sensitive, then tell her about it. Women love that shit."

"I take it you've used this ploy?"

"Never." He smiled devilishly. "But I hear it works like a charm."

Sterling swore.

"Sorry, just trying to be helpful." Then Ben grimaced. "Did you really say that sex was a game and the goal was to score?"

"I didn't say that," Sterling bit out, then he sighed. "Okay, maybe I did, but I was making a point that that was what *she* thought I thought, not what I really thought. I was—"

"Look, just be nice to her. Smile, look at her like you really see her, not her body. Rather, that you see her, see inside her. Don't act like you want to get her into bed. She doesn't strike me as someone who would be after your money. And I'd swear she's someone you could trust."

Sterling stared at his not-so-little brother. "What's this? Are you trying to help me win?"

Ben turned back to his beer. "I guess as much as I hate the thought of going back to St. Louis, deep down I really don't like seeing you twist in the wind."

Silence descended between them.

"Thanks," Sterling said quietly.

"Nothing you don't feel about me."

The moment was interrupted by another conversation that jarred into their minds.

"You know it, man. That Chloe babe would be one hot fuck. Did you hear what she said to that corncob-up-the-butt twerp Trey?"

Sterling wasn't sure which pissed him off more. The Chloe remark or the Trey comment. Either way, he stood up from his bar stool.

"Sterling," Ben demanded. "Sit the fuck down."

But it was too late for that. Sterling had never been in a fight in his life, but that wasn't because he had backed down. Growing up, he had always been big. The minute he stood up, his size had intimidated anyone who got in his face. As an adult, he hadn't been in a situation that called for physical intimidation.

The two other men saw him and stopped talking. Sterling could feel what he was certain was intimidation. But after a second they started to laugh. Laugh. At him.

"Hey, it's corncob butt before our very eyes. Doesn't look like you're going to get a chance to screw that cool piece of butter. Mmmm, mmmm, Chloe is mighty fine."

They weren't laughing for long. Sterling did something he had never done in his entire life. He wheeled back, then followed through with a right hook to the first man's jaw.

"Fuck," Ben muttered.

But when the second man leaped forward, Ben flew into action. The four men started to brawl, fists flying, skin smacked. Sterling felt something hit his body. One of the men vaulted onto Sterling's back, only to get tossed when Sterling jackknifed, flipping the man over his shoulders. The guy's breath came out in a grunt when he hit the floor.

In a matter of minutes the two men realized they weren't going to win and they fled. When the door pushed open, the brothers heard the sirens.

"Great," Ben stated, wiping blood from his broken lip. "Stay here. I'll take care of this. The last thing we need is to have you arrested for disorderly conduct."

Ben went out into the parking lot to speak to the officers. Sterling pulled out a stack of bills from his pocket. Ever since the pizza debacle, when he'd had to let Chloe pay, he had made a point of carrying cash at all times.

He set the money on the bar, grimaced at the pain the movement caused, then went out to face his fate.

By the time he got there, Ben and the officers were laughing.

"Hey, it's Trey," a patrolman called out. "Benny here was just telling us that some twerp was giving you a rough time. Called you a corncob, did he?" The policemen laughed. "No doubt it was brutal. Hard on a man to hear how a woman is making a fool of him. I feel your pain, man."

"I can't believe you told them that," Sterling stated.

Ben shrugged. "They already knew about the show. I just added a detail or two. I wasn't looking forward to having to bail your ass out of jail."

An hour later, when Sterling walked into the little house on Meadowlark Drive, he had never been so exhausted. Plus, his whole body hurt like hell. Stripping as he walked to the bedroom, he went to the shower and stood under the hot water. When he was too tried to stand any longer, he dried off, then fell buck naked into bed at three-thirty a.m. He was asleep before he hit the sheets.

Chloe woke at four-thirty in the morning. She couldn't sleep. Julia slept in the bed beside her like they were back in junior high, having a sleepover. But better in bed with Julia than in one of the other rooms with the other girls. Or as Julia had started calling them, the Roses Who Fight.

Chloe might have set out to be the Thorn in the Catch's Rose Garden, but who knew that throwing adult women together in a competition for a single man could become all-out warfare? It was hard to know whom to be more leery of. The really nice ones, or the ones who said to your face that they were going to kick your butt.

Not wanting to disturb Julia, Chloe pulled on a robe over her thin nightgown. She knew everything was in order, ready to tape the next segment of *The Catch*. But still she couldn't calm a bead of anxiety that welled inside her.

She went down the hall checking on the girls. Seven of the remaining Roses were divided among three bedrooms, with Chloe bunking with Julia in the fourth. Julia hadn't been able to bring herself to put anyone in her father's vacant bedroom.

Peeking into the first room, Chloe saw Mindy and Leticia were sound asleep. In the second room, Jo Beth, Marnie, and Nina were sleeping as well. But in the third room, only one bed was occupied. Jessica was missing.

Chloe tried to decide if she needed to panic.

Kacey, Jessica's roommate, woke. Groggy, she said, "Is it already time to get up?"

"Jessica's missing."

Kacey glanced at the other bed, then she blushed guiltily.

"Kacey, tell me where she is."

"I can't. Really," she replied apologetically.

"If you don't tell me, I'll have to call the police."

The woman glanced around, then cringed. "You can't tell that I told you."

"Tell me what?"

"Jessica is out with her boyfriend. But she'll be back soon, I swear."

Chloe's mouth fell open. "Boyfriend?"

"Yeah, she met him just before we started taping."

"Then why is she doing this show?"

"Television exposure. She's hoping she'll get noticed by some Hollywood type." Kacey snorted. "Like that's going to happen. But I swear, she'll be back. She came back last night."

"She sneaks out every night?"

Kacey wasn't interested in telling any more. "Can I go back to sleep now?"

"Sure. And thanks."

Chloe left the room. In the kitchen, she started to pace. When the clock read five in the morning, Chloe decided she had no choice.

Slipping out into the dark, she crossed Julia's yard. She hurried through the lattice arch, momentarily surprised by how long the grass had gotten, then went inside her house, using the back door.

There wasn't a light on. Regardless, she could see enough to tell her that the house was a mess. It had been only four days since he moved in, but plates and glasses were scattered on the table as if their new Catch had eaten, then simply stood up and left. As best as she could tell, all the food was of the delivery sort. He hadn't cooked a single meal.

Through the darkened space, lit by moonlight, she made it to the guest bedroom, but it was empty. Retracing her steps, she found him in her bedroom, sound asleep.

She stopped in the doorway, the descending moon casting the room with bright silver light, highlighting the most gorgeous naked man she had ever seen in her life.

Trey Tanner, aka Sterling Prescott, lay sprawled on his stomach, stretched across the small bed at an angle, his large bare feet hanging off, without a stitch of clothing covering his amazing body.

And he *was* amazing.

Chloe stood, unable to move. He was beautiful. Hard carved, his hips narrow, his butt nicely shaped, the skin smooth and muscled. His shoulders were broad, his arms extending up, disappearing underneath the pillow. His mouth was slightly open, his dark hair falling forward in his face. It was hard to imagine that the always powerful man could look so vulnerable in sleep. And yet, despite that look of vulnerability, there was something about him that was still so arrogant and commanding. Dangerous.

Her pulse drummed inside her, pushing her on. She walked closer, her fingers itching to touch. But she wouldn't. She would not do that. And she would have left, she reasoned over the tingle racing through her body, if it hadn't been for the AWOL, already-has-a-boyfriend Rose who they needed to contend with.

Perhaps she should find a cover or an extra sheet.

"Chloe?"

His voice was groggy, sleep-filled, and surprisingly boyish in a gruff way.

Despite better instincts, she glanced back before she had found something to cover him with. Which was a mistake.

He pushed up onto his elbows as if he were pushing up a ton of bricks. With effort, he smiled. He looked exhausted and not a little worse for wear . . . and breathtakingly handsome. Despite the fact that he was half asleep, he was all heat and hard muscle. When his gaze met hers, his full lips spread like he was a devilish bad boy of the worst kind. It felt as if he touched her intimately, knowingly. Her heart tripped.

His eyes held hers, mesmerizing in the moonlight, distracting, seductive in their darkness. When his gaze lowered to her lips, she drew a ragged breath, a deep, pounding ache shuddering through her, pulsing between her thighs.

But when she ventured a step closer, the moonlight highlighting his strong face and body, she could see that his already rugged features were discolored by bruises on his arms, shoulders, and ribs. Scrapes raked across his torso, and his knuckles looked like they'd been through a meat grinder.

"What happened to you?" she gasped.

He rolled over and fell back on the mattress. Completely unfazed by his nakedness, he groaned.

Chloe wasn't as lucky. Her breath caught in her throat and her head swam—completely fazed. He was even more beautiful, if possible. His enormous strength rippled through his body. Powerful masculinity emanated from him like energy sizzling through a live wire.

"You look awful," she stammered.

"Thanks," he stated wryly. "You should see the other guy, though. He looks worse."

Worse?

"How did you get hurt? What happened? Were you in an accident? Were you hit by a car?" She hesitated, blinked, then added in disbelief, "Were you in a fight?"

He had the audacity to smile, though just a half smile, before he groaned with pain. "A little altercation. Nothing serious. Sometimes a man has to do what a man has to do."

"There is no excuse for fighting!"

He raised his head just barely, quirking a brow, and she wondered from his expression what had caused the altercation.

"Why were you fighting?"

Staring at her, he seemed to debate. Then he shrugged, even that causing a grimace of pain, before he fell back with a sigh of relief, one hand extended at his side, the other lying on his stomach.

"Nothing that you need to worry about."

"Tell me."

"Chloe," he all but groaned, his eyes closed, "leave it alone."

She thought. "Was it about the show?"

He grunted.

"It was! What did they say? They hate it. They said it's a flop."

"They did not."

"Then it was about the women. Oh, my gosh! It was about me! They said I was a hideous dog, didn't they?"

He raised his head with effort. "No one thinks you're a dog. So much not a dog that they wanted to get in your pants. Had to show them they weren't getting anywhere near you."

A start of surprise sizzled through her. "You got beat up defending me?" she squeaked.

"Forget it," he groaned, lying back, his hand running down his torso to rest just above his . . .

She could feel blood creep into her face. He truly was magnificent, big, and well proportioned, and she could see everything, including the light dusting of hair on his chest that narrowed into a slim path that trailed down his abdomen. He wore no shorts, or pants, or even the sheet.

He lay on the bed, his . . . private parts not so private. And impressively large—and suddenly getting larger.

Embarrassment rushed to the roots of her hair, and when she jerked her gaze up to his face, she realized belatedly that he was watching her.

"Oh . . . I . . . wasn't—"

"See, I told you no one thought you were a dog," he groused, though a maddening smile undermined his tone.

She snatched up the sheet that was falling onto the floor, and tossed it over him. But he wasn't interested in the linen. With predatory eyes gleaming, he pushed up from the bed until he stood, only a hint of grimace marking his face from the pain.

"What are you doing?" she asked nervously, taking a step back.

"Seems like it's only polite to show you just how desirable you are."

"No need, really."

He caught her easily, though she could hardly believe it when instead of kissing her as she thought he was about to do—as she had hoped—he swept her up over his shoulder like a sack of potatoes. He sucked in his breath at the contact, but that didn't stop him.

"Ahhh!" she cried as he twirled her around.

Yes, Chloe confirmed to herself, he was twirling her around. This man, this naked man, whose every movement was a study in discipline and control, was whirling her around like they were flirting in high school—that is, if you could forget the naked part.

"I'm not sure how this counts as proof of desirability." Not that that was the point. "Besides, you're hurt! Put me down!"

He did, but it all happened so fast that when he set her on her feet, she was light-headed and dizzy. To keep from falling, she had to grab his arm.

"If you insist," he stated boldly as he pulled her close.

Then he caught her off guard again and kissed her, his lips on hers in a way she could only call teasing and fun. He nipped and played, whispered things to her that made her laugh despite herself.

"Your lips are like strawberries."

She snorted and *mmm*ed at the same time.

"Your eyes are like big blue sapphires and your skin is like a bowl of fresh cream."

All sweet and romantic, but he was being playful, teasing and overly dramatic, making her laugh.

"Who knew you were a poet? Or did you read those in an old book?"

"Let's see," he said as if truly considering her question even as he nipped at her ear. "The last book I read was *CEOs, Corporate Culture, and American Commerce.*"

"A real page-turner."

"It had me turning the pages," he said, grazing his lips along her temple.

The sensation was wonderful and exquisite, his naked body enfolding her. His off-limits and very naked body, she reminded herself. She pushed away.

"Not so fast," he said, circling her waist, pulling her toward her tiny bed. Which seemed really wrong and really exciting all at the same time.

Never once in high school had she ever had the opportunity to sneak a boy into her room—not that she would have tried. But the possibility would have been nice. However, the fact remained that growing up, she'd never been kissed. Never had a boyfriend.

Kissing this man in this room filled her with both delicious yearning and poignant regret.

And still, though she was twenty-seven years old and her grandmother was no longer living, she had the fleeting thought that they'd get caught and there would be hell to pay.

"No!" she called out, jerking against him.

But she only managed to tangle their bodies together, causing them to lose their balance. She could feel his strength as he held on to her and tried to steady them at the same time. But there was nothing to grab on to. In a slow, inevitable motion, they tumbled down onto her tiny bed.

She landed next to him, each on their sides, lips almost touching. She was hardly aware that the wooden frame groaned in protest.

"Hell," he muttered, just before the whole bed crashed down to the floor like a cake going flat, the top of the mattress level with the frame.

Surprise froze them in place.

Then suddenly she started to laugh. The sound welled up and pushed through her like a tidal wave bursting to get out. She laughed and laughed until finally he started to laugh, too. But soon he was kissing her again, amusement trailing off into a sensual purr when he pulled her up and dragged her over his body.

They lay together, face-to-face, her chest pressed to his,

the hard contours of his body barely separated from her by her thin nightgown and robe.

He grimaced at the pain but his grip was firm and un-yielding.

"You're hurt," she accused.

"Not true. Just a little bruised." He nuzzled her cheek. "You smell nice."

She squirmed, perhaps not the best tactical plan given their proximity.

His deep, rumbling voice put any question to rest. "Care-ful, sweetheart," he whispered, threading his hands into her hair.

"Careful? You're telling me to be careful?"

"Are you always this prickly?"

He didn't let her answer. He rolled until she was on her back, her robe fluttering open, revealing her short night-gown. He wrapped her close in his arms, chest to chest, thigh laced with hard, steely thigh. Then he kissed her.

She wanted to be immune. She didn't like this stubborn attraction to a man who was playing some kind of dishon-est if not outright dangerous game. But heat was instanta-neous, burning and intense. She didn't know how to feel about herself or this purely sexual attraction to a man.

His fingers trailed down her throat, the tips pressing gently to the pulse in her neck. He arched back, his weight supported on his elbows. He looked at her, really looked, as if he had never seen another woman in his life. She felt as if she were the center of his world, the core.

The sensation was heady, nearly as heady as his touch trailing lower to her collarbone, his fingers drifting along one side. Shivers of longing shot through her when he touched the spaghetti strap of her gown. But he didn't push it away. He tugged at the open robe before his fingers trailed lower. When he reached her breast, she inhaled deeply.

He rolled to the side, his weight supported by his elbow. His intense gaze ran over her body, taking her in. She knew he wanted her. She could feel his naked desire against her hip. His expression, growing more intimate by the second, left her alternately unnerved and filled with a matching desire.

Pleasure surged when he ran the heel of his palm over her breast, not the nipple, but above, a teasing that made her body respond . . . demand . . . yearn for more. What little sense she had evaporated beneath his touch. And when his palm dipped low beneath her nightgown, finally cupping her breast, her eyes fluttered closed.

She had been waiting for this since the moment she walked into the conference room and found him. She had been waiting for his touch. Not just a kiss. Not just his arms wrapped around her, or even their bodies pressed together.

It was a coupling she sought, yearned for. Naked skin to naked skin. No barriers.

He bent his head to her mouth, his hand still on her flesh. With the tip of his tongue, he traced her lips, then nipped, just when his thumb found her nipple.

She opened her mouth on a gasp of sensation. She felt primal and hot. He took advantage, tasting her, touching her tongue to his. She didn't even try to resist. Her tongue sought his, her body arching to him.

His touch was knowledgeable and commanding as he slipped her robe free. Air hit skin, but she didn't have time to recover before his palm slid up under the hem of her nightgown, higher and higher, his touch searing.

He kissed her again, his need pressing against her in a slow, delicious rhythm as old as time.

"Chloe," he whispered, his voice like gravel.

He slid his hands down her back, beneath her panties, cupping her hips. When he pulled the thin material down her legs, she let him. When they caught on her foot, she kicked them off herself.

The bed was tiny, broken, and uncomfortable. But she didn't care. And when he flipped her onto her belly she only felt a sizzle of anticipation.

He lifted her hips until she was on her knees, his strength circling her from behind. The primal beat inside her pounded like an African drum, wild and uninhibited. And when he touched the juncture between her thighs, she could only spread her knees on the coverlet.

"Yes," he murmured against her ear, circling her secret folds.

She could feel her wetness, feel how her hips arched to him, and when he slid his finger inside her, she cried out with the sheer amazing joy of it.

He trailed his lips along the column of her neck. His tongue glided, his teeth nipped as his finger dipped into her, making her want until he slid a second inside.

She was tight, but she didn't want him to stop. She wanted more—she wanted what her body understood was promised. She moved against him, then she gasped when his thumb found the nub of her clitoris. With a satisfied rumble, he circled and teased as the intensity in her body mounted and grew. She squirmed helplessly, wanting, needing, until finally she cried out when her orgasm spasmed through her.

Chloe cried out, convulsing against his hand. It felt like fire burned along every nerve ending, as they collapsed together on the bed. He held her the entire time, holding her close. "Yes," he said again, cupping her as her body finally relaxed against him.

She lay there for long seconds, not wanting to move or

think or do anything more taxing than pull out a cigarette for a smoke. Not that she had ever smoked, she mused. But she felt alive with sensation and amazement at what she had just shared with this man, and everything seemed exciting and possible . . .

Her mind tripped on the thought. Everything seemed possible? With this man? Sterling Prescott? How could she even think that? She had conveniently forgotten that he was a predatory raider, all for an orgasm.

She tried to turn away.

"You're amazing," he said, nuzzling her cheek. "Filled with uninhibited passion. God, you're wild with it."

Wild with uninhibited passion. Her.

She groaned in dismay, her heartbeat speeding up again, only this time it had nothing to do with passion. If he had meant to compliment her, he might have tried commenting on her housework.

Mortified, ashamed, and embarrassingly weak with traitorous sexual satisfaction, she rolled off the bed.

"Chloe?"

"I have to go." With as much dignity as she could muster, she picked up her panties and robe. Unfortunately, she had to get down on her knees to find her slippers.

"There's no reason to be embarrassed," he said with deep kindness, making her blush even more.

"I'm not embarrassed," she swore. "I'm just . . ."

Just what?

"I'm just thinking . . . about business." That was it, and it was nearly true. She had come here about business.

"I don't want to talk about business. In fact, I don't want to talk."

He reached for her, but she leaped out of the way. "Sorry, we've got to talk."

"I'm not going to change your mind, am I?"

"Not a chance."

Yep, orgasm over, sense returned. An ironclad resolve kicked into gear *after* she needed it. She felt dismal with disappointment in herself. How did she keep falling for this guy?

With a groan, he fell back onto the sheets, his amazing and still-naked body threatening her resolve. "What business?" he asked.

She forced her gaze away from his torso and said, "I'm here because we have a problem with one of the women."

"What kind of a problem?" He rolled out of bed. He glanced her way, thought better of it, then pulled on a pair of pants, though not without a grimace.

"Jessica has a boyfriend. And she's missing."

The sound of a car pulling up outside in the early morning darkness caught their attention. They looked out the window and saw a late model Corvette coming to a halt in front of Julia's house next door. They could see someone lean across the seat, kiss the other person. Then the door opened and Jessica appeared. After a quick glance around, she waved to the driver, then ran into the backyard of the house where Chloe knew the back door was unlocked.

"She's sneaking out at night," he announced unnecessarily.

"What should we do about her?"

"Let's see how the next taping goes."

"Fine." She started to leave, then stopped. "Since clearly you don't know the first thing about taking care of the yard, I'll do it. But really, surely you can clean the house."

"Hey, I can do the yard."

She rolled her eyes.

"I can. And I will. And I'll clean the house, too. Now get out of here before I pull you back into that bed."

She squeaked, then dashed toward the door just as he

reached out. He caught her arm. But instead of pulling her back to him, he only looked at her.

"Are you afraid of me?" he asked.

The question surprised her. "Yes. Or no." She shook her head. She wasn't afraid of him. It was more that he worried her. She didn't know what he really wanted, what it was he was hoping to take. Or what she wanted to give him.

"Why are you really here?" she asked.

He looked at her long and hard, some sort of a battle going on inside of him. But in the end, he only smiled, that arrogantly sensual pull of lips that even the fresh cuts and bruises couldn't detract from. "The truth is, I've begun to wonder the same thing. I'm not sure anymore why I'm here. But when I come up with an answer, you'll be the first to know." He brushed his lips across her forehead, then he let her go. "The ladies will be up any minute. I suggest you get over there—unless you want to tell them you have an unfair advantage."

"I don't want an advantage!"

"I think we both know that I want you. And whether you like it or not, I plan to do everything in my power to win you over. Then I'm going to make love to you, the kind of slow sweet sex that we've been headed for since the night we met."

The promise sent a thrill of anticipation through her. But she wasn't about to lose her heart to this man. She was not going to let his playfulness or sexual promise fool her into believing he was anything other than what he was. Sterling Prescott, corporate raider, mercenary businessman. And she couldn't afford to believe that his strange, boyish antics here today or the way he had brought her body to life were anything other than an even more clever way to get what he wanted.

Truly, the man was more dangerous than she had thought.

thirteen

Sterling stepped out of the shower and grimaced. Forget his sore knuckles. After he had twirled Chloe around, his ribs hurt like hell.

Hell was right.

He still couldn't believe he had gotten into a fight like some unruly thug. Every time he turned around these days, he was doing something completely unlike him. All because of this town.

He shook his head. No, it wasn't the town. It was Chloe Sinclair. She had turned him into this, he thought unkindly. A man who went to bars with fish painted on them and got into fights defending her honor like he was a high school kid with an attitude.

But God, did she turn him on. He wanted her—he didn't deny that. But he wanted her in his bed only long enough to purge her from his mind. Then he'd be done with this show. Done with this town. And he'd head back to St. Louis, every trace of the strange dissatisfaction he felt with his life gone. Chloe finally forgotten.

Surely.

He rubbed the towel over his head as he walked out of the bathroom and about killed himself tripping over a pair of shoes. The place was a mess, just as Chloe had said. But he'd never had to clean in his life. He'd grown up in a house filled with servants, even when his family couldn't afford them. Clothes got cleaned, messes straightened, dishes done, yards . . . Hell, he'd never given a yard a thought.

Part of him, one he didn't recognize, knew that a woman like Chloe would be disgusted with him. What kind of a man didn't know how to clean up after himself?

He could all but hear her disdain.

He told himself that there was no reason to be embarrassed. But before he knew it, he had pulled on a pair of khaki pants, a shirt, and shoes and started cleaning the house. He picked up piles of dirty clothes and towels. He even considered fixing the bed in Chloe's bedroom. But that would have to wait. First he would attack the kitchen. Then, just as soon as there was enough sun, he would tackle the yard. He rubbed his hands together at the thought of that big red mower in the garage.

The kitchen wasn't nearly as easy as the rest of the house had been. After a grimace, and with no help for it, he dove into the project. He threw boxes of pizza away, shaking his head over the idea that he'd never had pizza in his life and now he had it nearly every night. The pizza place delivered.

Next he moved on to clearing the dishes out of the sink. He broke one cup, but that was it. Once the dishes were washed and put away, he wiped down every surface until they practically sparkled. Then he took the trash out. By the time he was finished, he strutted proudly all the way to the garage to find the lawn mower, feeling amazingly satisfied by the simple accomplishment.

In the driveway, he pulled up the single door, large hinges

creaking in protest. The garage was old, but immaculately kept. A lot like the house.

It didn't take more than a second to find the mower. It gleamed like a new toy. Sterling smiled like a kid at Christmas.

Pulling the machine out into the gravel drive, he took in the levers and pull cord. What had she said about the clutch?

He pushed the mower out to the side yard on the opposite side from Julia's house. If there was a learning curve involved, he wanted to learn out of sight.

Rolling his wrists, he reached out, held in the clutch, congratulated himself for remembering, then pulled the cord. It only took one yank for the machine to roar to life, the vibration shooting up his arm into his shoulders.

So far, so good. He was feeling pleased, and he estimated that he'd have the tiny yard done in no time. Maybe he'd even get the box spring and mattress fixed before he had to head next door for the day's taping, he thought, just as he let go of the clutch.

With a jerk, the mower took off, shooting grass out the side as it went. He had forgotten the grass catcher. But that was the least of his problems. He had a mower on the loose.

He caught up easily and grabbed the handle. He exerted sheer strength to bring the beast back in line. Then, finally, with sweat breaking out on his brow, he guided the machine up and down the side yard. After a few swipes, he moved on to the back. A professional couldn't have done better. When he was done, he relished the pride in something so . . . ordinary.

Then he grumbled. Mowing a yard was hardly an accomplishment. But he realized that it seemed like he had accomplished something more than simply cutting the grass—it was something deeper that he hadn't begun to grasp.

Pushing the mower around the house, sweat dripping down his back, he had just put it away when his cell phone rang. Tugging it off his belt, he answered.

"Hey, Sterling, it's Ben."

"I just mowed the lawn."

"What?"

"Nothing. What can I do for you?"

"I had a buddy of mine run a report on Albert Cummings and the rest of your e-mail friends. They all look harmless. But just to be on the safe side, I think you should keep a close eye on Chloe and the other girls."

But before Sterling could answer, he heard the scream.

"What the hell was that?" Ben demanded over the phone.

"It's Chloe."

Sterling slapped the phone shut and started to run.

Chloe had snuck back into bed, barely falling into a fitful sleep before a noise woke her.

She sat up on the mattress like a pop-up doll. Julia was still sound asleep. When Chloe heard the noise again, she groaned, got up, pulled on her robe and slippers.

The long hallway was lined with family portraits and original artwork that was worth a small fortune. The house was filled with opulence and luxury, Philippe Boudreaux having been a man who showed the world that he was worth a lot of money.

"*You are what people think you are,*" he had been fond of saying. And he had showed the world just how much he was worth in big, sweeping, extravagant strokes.

She moved quietly through the front foyer, finding nothing in the living room or dining room. Their makeshift stage was empty. But a halo of light seeped out from underneath the swinging door that led into the kitchen. One of the Roses must be up early.

But when she pushed open the door, a strange man was setting flowers on the kitchen table, making her scream.

"Oh, my word!" he cried with a start, nearly dropping the flowers. "I didn't hear you come in."

He was short with sandy blond hair receding at the temples. He wore an old-fashioned looking suit, but there wasn't a wrinkle or stain on it. His smile was kind, not threatening, and the flowers were stunning.

"Who are you?" she asked, trying to understand.

"Albert Cummings. I told you I was bringing you a surprise."

"I don't know any Albert Cummings."

"I e-mailed you. Didn't you get it?"

"No."

Chloe told herself not to panic, told herself that this man was simply foolish, not dangerous.

Footsteps came from every direction. Julia got there first, skidding to a halt in the doorway beside her. She gasped, then seemed confused.

"Who is he?" she asked.

Albert blushed. "Chloe's biggest fan. But I didn't mean to intrude. And I certainly never thought I'd have the opportunity to speak with such pretty ladies."

By then, every girl in the house had crowded into the kitchen, taking in the intruder like he was an exhibit at the zoo.

"What a thrill to meet each and every one of you. Though I have to admit, Chloe is my favorite." He then launched into a critique of each girl's performance on the opening show.

"So you're saying that you didn't like me at all?" Jo Beth queried, tapping one long painted fingernail to her cheek.

"I'm sorry, no," Albert confirmed with serious regret. "The word *bitch* comes to mind."

"But I am not a bitch," Jo Beth said with a pout. "Nina's the bitch!"

"I am not! I just speak my mind," Nina defended herself.

Leticia had concerns of her own. "Now tell me, what exactly was it that you didn't like about me?" she wanted to know.

"Ladies," Chloe interrupted. "I hardly think this is appropriate." She turned to the man. "While I appreciate the flowers, you really can't just come into our house."

"I know, and I apologize. I had intended to set them on the back porch, but the door was unlocked and I thought, What could it hurt to leave them on the kitchen table?"

He shrugged innocently just as the sweaty Catch vaulted through the back door. He stopped at the sight of the man.

"What the fuck?"

"Oh, dear," Albert stated. "I'm not sure explanations are going to work with this man." Then he smiled, waved and disappeared out the door.

Sterling and Ben stood in the kitchen of Chloe's small house. Sterling couldn't define what exactly he felt. His need to protect had grown fierce. He was responsible for these women, and he wouldn't allow them to be hurt. But it was the thought of someone hurting Chloe that made his skin go cold.

"Damn, I should have had security in the Roses' house all along. With the ratings we got, there are plenty of viewers, which means some are bound to be crazies."

"No one was hurt."

"Not this time." Sterling focused on his brother. "I want you to stay at the house."

"You want me to stay here?" He gestured to Chloe's home.

"No. I want you to stay at Julia's with the women. I don't want another intruder."

"Listen, I agree you need security. But I'm not your man. I'll find someone."

"I need someone now. Besides, you're on leave. If I've got it right, you're not working anywhere else."

Ben turned away.

"Please, Ben. The women know you. I've been winging it, thinking this was a slam dunk. But we're only at the beginning, and there is plenty I haven't given a thought to, like security. It's my responsibility to keep the women safe."

Whether Cummings was a true threat or not, Sterling didn't add what the sound of Chloe's scream had done to him. It had made his blood run cold. Sent a surge of strange emotion through him that he'd never experienced in his life. The closest he'd ever come to feeling something like that was the day he had learned that his father was running Prescott Media into the ground. In that instant, a surge went through him as he understood he would do whatever it took to save the company.

This was similar, but different. More intense, he had to admit, which was astounding in itself. He wanted to keep Chloe safe. He also realized the minute he heard Chloe scream that he wanted more from her than quick sex to purge her from his mind. He didn't know what exactly it would turn out to be. But sinking his flesh into hers wasn't going to make him forget her. He was sure of that now. She had seeped into his soul in a way that nothing else in his life ever had. He wanted her—that was nothing new. But first and foremost, he realized now, he wanted her safe.

"I need your help, Ben," he stated with more forthright need than he had ever used in his life.

His brother considered him, then he muttered an oath.

"All right. I'll do it. But if I'm the one who strangles Julia Boudreaux, it will be on your head."

Surprise straightened Sterling's spine. "You're interested in Julia?"

"Hell, no. I don't even like her. That's the problem. She's everything I don't like in a woman."

Sterling looked at him oddly. "It's hard, isn't it, when you have it bad."

Sterling returned to Julia's house after the police had departed.

"Ladies," Sterling announced when he walked through the back door, Ben coming up behind him.

Sterling took in the Roses who sat around the kitchen table, drinking coffee and eating yogurt. Chloe stopped in mid-bite of a chocolate-covered, custard-filled doughnut, her mouth open, her cheeks flaring with red as she undoubtedly remembered what had happened between them only a few hours ago.

At first she started to drop the doughnut to her plate, then suddenly she took a venomous bite.

It was all he could do not to walk over and slowly touch her lips, wipe away a smudge of custard. No, he had to get through *The Catch* with some semblance of impartiality. Then, after they were done, he would touch her, hold her, tell her all the things he wanted to share.

The other women were visibly surprised by his appearance. "Trey," Mindy said, sighing and looking at him with adoration glowing in her eyes. He'd been with enough women to know that she was sweet, kind, and falling hard for him. He felt a need to make sure he didn't hurt her.

"Mmm," Leticia cooed. "You were such a hero this morning. Big, fine, strapping hero."

Chloe took another bite of her doughnut.

"Not a hero," he corrected. Then he looked at each of the women. "We want to make sure something like what happened this morning doesn't happen again. To that end, you really have to keep this door locked."

Nodding in agreement, Chloe grumbled as if she resented him for being right.

"Second, my brother, Ben, is going to provide full-time security from now until the end of the show."

Ben grimaced.

Julia put her hands on her hips. "What do you mean, full-time security?"

"Ben is going to stay here at the house."

This time it was Julia who grimaced.

An hour later, after the girls had returned to their rooms to get ready for the day, Julia headed back to the kitchen. She and Chloe were going to have a planning session to ready the next episode, which they would tape that day. They had rerun the first episode to make sure they reached as much of an audience as possible. Tonight they would air show number two.

Ben stood in the foyer, talking to a man who was delivering a box of something. As soon as she appeared, Ben stopped speaking and watched every step she took. She could feel his eyes on her, appraising, running over her like he could see beneath her clothes.

She had told him that if he planned to stay there, he'd have to sleep on the sofa in the den, childishly thinking to make him as uncomfortable as possible. But it had seemed only fair since his mere existence did that to her.

Though if she was honest with herself, she couldn't put into words what really unsettled her about Ben. When she walked past him, he gave her the kind of smile that she rarely saw on a man's face—at least directed at her. Knowing, arrogant, and completely unintimidated. That was it. The man wasn't afraid of her, and her carefully aimed verbal jabs did nothing to make him lose his balance. In fact, it occurred to her that he was the first man she could remember who didn't even like her.

She continued on, then pushed through the swinging door and into the kitchen. Ben and the delivery guy followed her, though they didn't stop. They continued on into the utility room.

Julia was never more thankful than when Chloe walked into the kitchen.

"Chloe!" she enthused. "You look lovely!"

Chloe glanced down at her simple white blouse, brown plaid skirt, and plain pumps, then shot her an odd expression. "What's wrong now?"

"Nothing's wrong! Everything's great!"

"Lucky you," Chloe stated.

"What are you talking about? Are you upset about the intruder?"

"No, it's not the intruder. It's this idiotic show. Why won't he kick me off?"

Julia walked over and hooked her arm through her best friend's. "Because you are cute and wonderful and gorgeous now that you've stopped wearing those fake glasses. Besides, no doubt he has been swept away by your charm."

Chloe craned her neck to glance at her. "You've had too much caffeine. We both know that isn't the case. He should hate me by now. Just like I hate him. He's obnoxious, and arrogant, and—"

Ben and the man returned, the box gone, and Julia saw Chloe freeze.

"Where did you come from?" Chloe demanded.

"The utility room. I had new locks delivered that I'm going to install." Ben held up a dead bolt.

Chloe whirled to Julia and mouthed *Why didn't you tell me he was here?!*

"Don't worry about it, Chloe," Ben said. "Your secret's safe with me." He grinned like a mischievous bad boy.

"Me, worry?"

The other man chuckled. "I'm Sid, ma'am, and I've seen you on *The Catch*. You're great." He actually blushed.

Chloe thanked him, clearly self-conscious. Then she spun Julia around and dragged her toward the door.

"You know," Sid called out, stopping them. "If you really hate Trey so much and want to get kicked off the show, you're going about it the wrong way."

Chloe, Julia, and Ben looked at him in surprise.

"What do you mean?" Chloe asked.

Ben leaned back against the edge of the table, palming the dead bolt like a lover. "This should be good."

"You're being elusive, cool," Sid explained. "Unattainable."

"She's being a bitch," Julia countered.

Sid laughed. Chloe glared. "Whose side are you on?"

"Yours, sweetie. Always yours. And haven't you intentionally been a bitch?"

"Well, yes."

"But being elusive," Sid continued, "isn't going to do anything but get you rose after rose until you're the one with the bouquet. What man alive isn't intrigued by what he thinks he can't have?"

"That is so archaic!" Chloe declared.

"Good Lord," Julia mused, "have you been reading *The Rules*?"

"Call it what you want," the deliveryman said unapologetically. "But if you really want to get kicked off *The Catch*, you've got to change your tactics."

Chloe tapped her finger against her cheek, debating, then asked, "Like how?"

"Chloe! Don't listen to him."

Ben groaned.

Sid persisted. "Do you like a guy you barely know to get too serious too fast? Hell, do you deny that the worst thing a woman can do is have sex with a guy, then turn into a possessive, aren't-our-kids-going-to-be-beautiful clinging vine?"

Ben pushed away from the table. "Okay, Sid, time for you to go. We've got enough trouble around here without you giving anyone any ideas."

"You think I'm wrong?" Sid demanded of the group. "All I'm saying is that if you want off the show, you better think clingy instead of cool."

Julia couldn't believe what she was hearing. It was ridiculous. But when she turned around to tell Chloe that, her best friend had fled from the kitchen.

Julia turned on Sid. "Look what you've done!"

"I gave her a decent piece of advice given her goal." He raised his hands in surrender, then headed out the back door.

The minute he was gone, Julia's brow furrowed with concern. "She can't possibly take him seriously." She grimaced. "Can she?"

Ben shook his head. "Maybe not. But from the look on her face when she was dashing out the door, I'd bet money she's in her room right now trying to come up with a new plan of action for the next episode of *The Catch*."

Julia knew Chloe better than most anyone, and she hated to admit that she thought he was right.

To: Sterling Prescott <sterling@prescottmedia.com>
From: Serena Prescott <serena@prescottmedia.com>
Subject: Response requested

My dearest Sterling,

Please respond, as I have still not heard a word about what is going on. But I *am* well aware that you have missed yet another Sunday dinner. And this one I had felt certain would be attended not only by you, but by Ben as well.

Please update progress.

Yours,
Grandmère

p.s. I realize you don't want me to travel to Texas, but I've decided it is high time I made a visit to El Paso.

To: Ben Prescott <sc123@fastmail.com>
From: Sterling Prescott <sterling@prescottmedia.com>
Subject: Complication

Grandmère has gotten it in her head to visit. I think an e-mail from you could deter her.

To: Serena Prescott <serena@prescottmedia.com>
From: Ben Prescott <sc123@fastmail.com>
Subject: El Paso in October

Dear Grandmère,

I hear you are thinking of visiting the Sun City. I'm not sure that is such a good idea. Your eldest grandson is in the middle of a charade involving his identity. Your arrival could complicate things.

Love,
Ben

To: Betty Taylor <betty@prescottmedia.com>
From: Serena Prescott <serena@prescottmedia.com>
Subject: Flight

Dear Miss Taylor:

Is the company plane available for use?

Best regards,
Serena Prescott

fourteen

"What do you mean Grandmère is coming to town?" Sterling stared at Ben in disbelief. "You were supposed to deter her, not offer to pick her up at the airport."

Ben shrugged and took a bite of carrot, not looking particularly concerned. "Sorry. I tried to tell her this wasn't a great time for you, but she was adamant."

"And how do you expect me to explain this . . . this situation?"

"I was pretty much wondering the same thing. What are you going to tell her? The good news is that I gave her a heads-up about the fake identity."

"You what?"

"Yep, I mentioned it in e-mail. I told her that you weren't admitting that you were a Prescott." Ben's smile spread across his face like a half-moon of amusement.

"Why do I get the feeling that you're doing nothing to help me succeed?" Sterling demanded in exasperation.

Nodding unrepentantly, Ben said, "It's your job to make

this work, not mine. But enough about your problems. Let's talk about your request. I have some information on Chloe, as you asked."

Sterling knew he was racking sins up faster than a gambler in Las Vegas. Amazing how something that had seemed so simple in the beginning could spiral so quickly on him—and not in a good direction.

But as much as he now felt badly about spying on Chloe—no, delving into her past—he still felt a need to know. Especially after he had realized that he wanted more from her than a simple affair.

Hell, even he realized how bad that sounded. But old habits died hard.

He had started to wonder about her as a permanent person in his life. A mistress? The thought was repellent to him. But the idea of a wife made his mind cement against it.

He knew he had to pick the right woman to be his bride. Not only would she be the mother of his children, but she'd have to be the woman at his side as he ran Prescott Media. He needed a woman beyond reproach. He had always assumed his wife would be from one of the best families in St. Louis.

"What did you learn?" Sterling asked.

"Not much so far. Just that she lived with her grandmother since she was a kid. When Regina Sinclair died a year ago, she left Chloe the house."

"Why did you live with her grandmother and not her parents?"

"Don't know yet."

Sterling suddenly remembered the day she had said she wanted to spend more time with her father. Had the man just recently returned to her life, but then, given their need of the two houses, been driven off again?

Sterling didn't know. But regardless of the reason for her

father not being here, this was a situation he could rectify. And he felt a driving need to do something just for her.

"Find out where the father is. I want to surprise Chloe."

"For what?"

"The two final Roses introduce 'Trey' to their families. I'm going to make sure Chloe has a family here to include. I don't want her caught off guard and potentially embarrassed."

Ben shook his head. "You're smart and determined, I'll hand you that. Having her father show up on the last show is a nice touch that could help you win her over."

Win her over? Could he? he wondered suddenly.

For the first time in his life, Sterling felt the bite of regret. He wasn't a man to regret his actions. He did what he had to do. But it occurred to him that this time doing what he had to do might not be explanation enough for someone like Chloe Sinclair.

It was ludicrous, he thought with a curse, that he hadn't considered it before. Thrust into this world far removed from the power of Prescott Media, he felt like his eyes were being pried open, forcing him to see everything he did in a different light. He didn't like it at all. But that didn't help when with a grim start he realized that after this was done, he was afraid he'd need more forgiveness than approval.

Chloe felt exhaustion tick through her body. She now had a greater appreciation for actors who directed and starred in their own productions. While she might not be directing, she was producing and making sure all went smoothly.

She also missed her father. It was amazing to think how much the short time they had spent together had meant to her. She missed coming home and him asking about her day, how that eased the tension. She even missed his constant desire to fix things around the house. Did he miss her, too? Would he be glad to get back from Ruidoso when all this was over? Or would this give him the courage to return to a life on his own?

Chloe focused on the task at hand. The show. The Roses alone were enough to make her want to pull her hair out. But the behind-the-scenes machinations between the women was the icing on the cake of frustration. Regardless, she had to persevere. The whole thing would be over at the end of the following week.

Which is why when the Roses sat around the breakfast table, waiting for the day's taping to begin, alternately supporting one another and trying to find out how the other was planning to win Trey, Chloe didn't get up and go to the other room.

"I wonder what we're doing next," Mindy stated.

"I hear it's group dates," Jo Beth added.

Mindy groaned, and Chloe knew that she was thinking about how in a group, each of the women would be looking out for herself. Competition would be fierce.

What surprised Chloe about this was that while the women were in direct competition, they also seemed desperate to form bonds with one another, as if somehow the bond would keep them from being dragged too deep through the mud of competition. It also seemed like a way for each of them to get additional information that could help her get ahead in the quest to win the bachelor's heart.

"I'm so not good in a crowd," Mindy lamented.

Chloe believed her, having seen how awkward the nurse was in social settings. Chloe shuddered to think what it would be like in a hospital with her if she was that uncomfortable with syringes and heart monitors.

"Once I was applying for a flight attendant job with a major airline," Mindy continued. "We all sat around in a circle, and the interviewer would ask a question. She just put the questions out there, and she wouldn't call on us to respond. We had to jump in so she could see things like how assertive we were, how polite, how confident. Ugh. It was horrible because really, think about it . . . If you're too assertive, you're rude, but if you're not assertive enough, you're a wimp. So you have to time it just right. I was so unbelievably stressed that I was sweating, not to mention that not only do you have to get your answer in there in just the right way, you have to *come up* with an answer to put out there!"

"I'd hate that," Kacey conceded.

"I'd kick ass," Jo Beth preened, and no one there doubted that she would.

Leticia took a sip of her coffee. "What kind of questions did they ask?"

Mindy wrinkled her nose. "The woman asked about politics. And each of us had to tell our most embarrassing moment. But the worst question—at least the worst for me, because clearly I am a moron—was: Who, living or dead, do you admire the most?"

A traditional question, but all the women *mmm*ed and *ahhh*ed and considered their own answers.

Mindy chewed her lip as she remembered, then sighed dismally. "Most of the candidates came up with some of the most amazing responses. One lady said Jesus Christ. Jesus Christ! She was so impressive when she added that regardless of your religion, he's had an effect on just about every aspect of life around the world. Another said Hillary Clinton because she didn't let a twerp like Bill bring her down. Then this one guy, really cute and no doubt gay, said Cher because she didn't let *Sonny* bring her down. Everyone laughed, and I was burning up with mortification because I couldn't think of a single person living, dead, or even made up, whom I admired. How pathetic is that?!"

Mindy ran her finger along the rim of her coffee cup as if she wasn't going to go on.

"You can't leave us hanging!" Jo Beth exclaimed.

"What did you say?" Leticia prompted.

Closing her eyes for a second, Mindy sighed, then uttered two words. "Martha Washington."

"Martha Washington?" the group demanded.

"Who is Martha Washington?" Jo Beth wanted to know.

"Our first president's wife," Chloe supplied. "As in the guy who supposedly chopped down the cherry tree. The first George."

"Oh."

Everyone turned back to Mindy. "Why in the world did you say Martha Washington?" Kacey asked.

Mindy scrunched her hair in her hands. "I don't know. I was desperate, really desperate, and out of nowhere her name popped into my head. One minute I hadn't a clue who to say, then the next her name was just there."

"Oh, my gosh!" Leticia exclaimed.

"And you know the worst of it? When everyone else gave their answers, you could tell that the others in the group were busy composing their own responses, timing themselves, hardly giving a thought to what anyone else said. When I tossed out old Martha, everyone there, including the interviewer, stopped everything, turned to look at me, and asked, '*Why?*' "

By now every one of the Roses was leaning forward, staring at her, and wanting to know the exact same thing.

"What did you say?" Leticia demanded on a gasping laugh.

Mindy groaned her misery. "I said, '*Because she was so helpful to George.*' "

After a single, silent heartbeat, the group burst out laughing until even Mindy saw how ridiculous it was. Somehow the remembered mortification was mitigated and she felt very much a part of this group. She joined in and laughed.

"Okay, everyone," Chloe said, breaking into the fun. "We only have thirty minutes before we start taping. The crew will be here any second. So we'd better hurry."

"Come on, Mindy," Nina said with surprising kindness, "let's get ready for today's shoot. The other day I was thinking of a way that your hair would look awesome."

"Really?"

"Yeah, really."

Mindy beamed. "Thank you." She bit her lip. "It seems like Trey thinks I'm a dork. I would love for him to see me differently."

The Roses piled out of the kitchen just as Julia walked in. Chloe was the only one who stayed behind.

"Aren't they chipper this morning," Julia said.

Standing, Chloe came over to Julia, hugged her tight, then set her at arm's length.

"What's that about?" Julia asked.

"I haven't told you often enough how much I love your friendship."

"Great, what's happened now?"

"Nothing." Chloe studied her fingernails. "It's just that I realized that while we don't choose our families, we choose our friends. And I'm glad you chose me."

Then she headed upstairs to get ready with the rest of the Roses.

The group date consisted of a pool party in Julia's backyard swimming pool, which was built inside a huge glass atrium. It was a beautiful Indian summer day, a bright and sunny sixty-nine degrees. The station planned to shoot the episode in two parts to make it look like two separate parties. It wasn't the sort of big budget extravaganza that the major networks were able to stage for their bachelor-type shows. This was local television.

The cast grilled hot dogs, drank wine, and showed off lots of bare skin. The last thing Chloe wanted to do was get into a bathing suit. Though the others weren't having the same problem. That is, if tiny scraps of material could be considered bathing suits.

When Pete called action and started taping the party, Chloe stood on the sidelines. She debated her plan, but decided that: One, she wanted off the show, and Two, making herself look less than great on television wasn't such a bad idea, since she wasn't interested in attracting any more Albert Cummingses.

She decided plunging in was the best plan of action on all counts.

The second she stepped out of the shadows, it was as if there was some cosmic signal to the Catch, because he turned around and saw her despite the circle of women around him as he grilled hot dogs.

Chloe had the unexpected thought that while he clearly was a fish out of water in the regular pursuits of life, once he decided to do something, he actually did it quite well.

Which didn't endear him to her. Couldn't he do anything badly?

Chloe? he mouthed.

"Chloe?" Jo Beth blurted.

Chloe appeared poolside in a red, white, and blue one-piece bathing suit that had a flag skirt fluttering around her thighs. Chloe's suit used more fabric than all the other suits combined.

"You look . . . great," Mindy tried to enthuse.

Trey looked at her as if she had lost her mind.

And she did think of him as Trey—or rather, she forced herself to continue thinking of him as Trey so she wouldn't screw up on the show and call him Sterling.

"Hiya!" she called out with a wave.

Hiya?

No one ever would have accused her of being perky in the past, but she'd seen enough of it in these Roses to have learned a thing or two from some pros.

"Hi, hi, hi!" she added with a smile that made her cheeks hurt. "What do you think?" She twirled, the skirt swirling around her hips like she was a skater on ice.

"Wow," they said, their faces scrunched in false cheer.

"What are we having? Hot dogs! Yummy!" She marched right up to Trey and took his free hand. "You look yummy, too!"

Trey grimaced.

Perfect!

They taped for hours. They played water volleyball in the pool, all the women doing their best to keep their hair dry. Chloe dunked herself immediately and left her hair plastered to her head. She *oooed* and *gooed* over Trey in her flat hair and 1950s bathing suit, and by the time they were wrapping up the party segments, Trey looked like he didn't know what had hit him.

Finally, her plan was working. He'd seen the light that she was the plain-looking, too-sensible-for-fun sort of woman that she was. She would be ejected from the show before day's end, and she hadn't even had to lower herself and incorporate the more idiotic and certainly archaic aspects of Sid's suggestions. Being less elusive was good—she admitted that. But have sex, then act all clingy? Ha! She was bigger than that, smarter than that! She'd be leaving the rose ceremony without a rose and she hadn't even had to show much skin.

* * *

They had only an hour to tape the rose ceremony because Chloe had forgotten that after the pool party eight Roses would have to take baths, do their hair, and dress, seven of them hoping to receive one of the remaining six positions. But finally they were ready to begin.

The women wore formal eveningwear, this time compliments of Adriana's Accents. Jewels sparkled in the bright lights, makeup glittering on smiling faces.

Chloe wore a tweed skirt and blouse, just to be on the safe side.

Standing in a half circle, the Roses waited for Trey to appear. In real time, handing out the roses wouldn't take long. Later this afternoon, she, Julia, Pete, and Trey would edit the piece, drawing the moment out to create anticipation for the viewers. Plus they would add music, which would peak each time just before he offered a rose.

"Is everyone ready?" Pete called out. "Then . . . action."

Trey entered the room, causing each woman to sigh, including Chloe, even though she managed to swallow it back. He looked more dashing than she wanted him to.

He stopped next to the tray of yellow Texas roses. Then he looked at each of the women, smiling.

"This is the hardest part for me," he began, his deep timbered voice running through the room, along each woman's senses.

Chloe had the disconnected observation that this segment was going to make great television.

"But unfortunately," he continued, "I have only six roses left. I wish I could choose each and every one of you because I have enjoyed your company. But because that isn't possible, I must begin."

That seemed a little much, but still good TV.

"Mindy," he said first, "will you accept this rose?"

With a scrunch of shoulders and pert little nose, she hurried up to him and threw her arms around his shoulders. "Yes!"

The other girls waited nervously, looking at one another, then away.

Next came Nina. After that Leticia. A woman named Marnie, who had been in the background most of the time, strutted up and winked at him when he called her name, as if there had never been any doubt. Chloe fleetingly wondered what had gone on between the two of them that she hadn't seen.

Not that she cared. She didn't, she told herself firmly.

He moved on to Jo Beth. Then all too quickly, he had only one rose left.

He played it out beautifully, and part of Chloe thought how well the show was going. She also felt certain that the rose wouldn't be for her. She was relieved. Happy. Though a strange twist in her heart made her flinch.

And then he did the horribly impossible thing.

"Chloe."

Just that. Just her name.

He had picked her!

Her mood instantly plummeting like a ride on a roller coaster, it was all she could do not to launch herself at him and demand that he explain himself.

He couldn't choose her.

She should have run him off by now.

But all thoughts for her own dismal situation were lost when she realized that Kacey stood next to her, crying. Kacey was crushed, along with Jessica, who sat there fighting back tears. Which was crazy, since she had snuck out each night to meet her new boyfriend.

"Why, Trey?" Kacey choked out.

The girls who had been chosen were relieved that they weren't the ones kicked off the show. They'd made it through another cut.

Trey looked ill at ease in a way that Chloe never would have believed if she hadn't seen it firsthand. Plus, she felt horrible for Kacey. When he walked over to her, Chloe grabbed his arm.

"Pick Kacey instead of me," she implored him.

He looked down at her. Really looked. Then cupped her cheek, an intense emotion burning in his eyes, along with what she was sure was regret for hurting the other woman. "I wish I could."

Then he stepped away and went over to Kacey and said something that made her smile.

As much as Chloe didn't want to believe it, deep down, maybe, just maybe, there might be a bit of kindness in this coldly callous man.

fifteen

$\mathcal{D}$esperate times required desperate measures. And Chloe was desperate.

After two additional episodes of Roses doing their best to win the Catch and the Catch ultimately breaking more hearts, she was now one of only two women left in contention. Last night, on the Monday show, Trey had yet again given her another rose. She had become a finalist in a competition that she had no interest in winning, unlike the other finalist, Mindy, who wanted him so desperately that it was painful to watch. Chloe only had until Friday, when they would begin taping the final two episodes, to turn things around.

Sitting at the desk, her computer screen bright in the darkness, Chloe couldn't believe she had ever felt anything for a man who was really Sterling Prescott. She also couldn't believe that for even a second she might have thought he was kind.

She realized now that that was probably just what he wanted her to think—planning his seduction with the precision of a military sergeant. Or a corporate raider who wanted an even better price on a station that would fit nicely in his portfolio.

His reasons had come clear to her when she Googled his name and his company. What she learned had left her cold and stunned. In the last six months, he had purchased stations in Albuquerque and Tucson at rock-bottom prices. No wonder he knew so much about the demographics of the city, not to mention the region. She understood his plan now. He wanted to connect the three markets, which would give him an impressive toehold to use for national advertisers who wanted package rates for regional buys.

And he was playing this game to make sure he got what he wanted.

He was just the sort of man her grandmother had warned her about. His actions proved her grandmother's unforgiving dictates, and Chloe hated that most of all. She'd always held on to the hope that there was a man out there who wouldn't leave, who wouldn't cheat. Who wouldn't lie.

"Look what happened to your mother after your father left her. She died of a broken heart. Thank your lucky stars you were born plain-looking, Chloe love. Your gift is being smart and sensible. Don't ever let that desert you."

But Chloe hadn't been smart or sensible since the day Julia sent her that quiz. Everything had changed. Or was it simply that she had been living in a house of cards that had finally collapsed?

She pressed her eyes closed, hating those moments when determined happiness failed her. Those moments when she could see her mother, dancing, twirling, laughing in their small apartment in a bad part of town. She remembered her mother's beauty, the men who loved her, showered her with gifts. Then always left. Just like her father. But Chloe couldn't seem to find a way, or maybe it was the courage, to broach the subject with him and learn why he'd left. Would the why make a difference? Could she move on with her own life if she knew the answer?

Her palms were wet and clammy. She had to get off the show. She *needed* off the show.

She realized in some recess of her mind that if she forced the Catch to kick her off, then what she was really doing was maintaining control. He wasn't rejecting her, not really, and more important, he wasn't leaving her.

She wasn't her mother.

She shook the thought away and raised her chin. The fact was, she wasn't her mother no matter what. She needed off the show so she could devote her undivided attention to the task of figuring out how to fight Sterling Prescott. He was distracting her. He was luring her in to make her vulnerable, pliable. His tactics had been good, too good. Now it was time that she came up with a tactic of her own that would throw him off balance. Which brought her back to her original thought.

Desperate times required desperate measures.

Right or wrong, she couldn't forget Sid's advice. Sure, it was archaic and idiotic, but even she knew there was some truth to it. *"Hell, do you deny that the worst thing a woman can do is have sex with a guy, then turn into a possessive, aren't-our-kids-going-to-be-beautiful clinging vine?"*

Yep, it was time to sleep with the Catch.

An unwanted thrill raced through her body at the thought, but she quashed it ruthlessly. She also quashed the thought that she was going to an insane extreme that made little to no sense. She denied that what she really wanted was an excuse to finish off what they had started in the bathroom. That wasn't it, she promised herself firmly. It wouldn't be any sort of romantic night of passion. It was going to be meaningless, boring, nonimaginative sex. Then, as the pièce de résistance, she would act all clingy and in love afterward. *That* was sure to make Trey Tanner, aka Sterling Prescott, run for the hills.

Or more specifically, cause him to finally cut her from the show.

She felt her sense of control return, and her mood brightened until she was humming "Oh, What a Beautiful Morning." She refused to analyze her plan, refused to concede that the idea was neither smart nor sensible. It was simply needed. End of story.

It was the wee hours of the morning when she decided what had to be done. The moon was still high, the stars blazing in the dark sky. If she didn't get busy soon, everyone would be awake and it would be too late to take action. Since there were only two Roses left, everyone now had their own rooms—including Ben, who acted really strange around Julia. Not that Julia was acting normal. Chloe had never seen two people who disliked each other as much as Ben and Julia did. Well, perhaps she and the Catch might qualify.

The only snag in sneaking out might prove to be Ben. But when she crept past his room, he wasn't even there. In the kitchen, she found a note.

Girls, I've gone to the airport. I have a patrolman stationed out front if you need anything. Ben

She'd forgive him calling them girls since having him gone made things all the easier. At least a little easier. The patrolman was probably only marginally less alert than Ben, who had become obsessed with protecting them now that Albert Cummings had proved to be only the first of the crazed fans who were determined to sneak onto the set. And amazingly, the attention was mostly directed at her.

Who knew the plain-looking type would be in this year?

But Chloe wasn't about to let a little security keep her from her mission. She knew how to sneak through the back so that no one would be the wiser as she went in search of her prey. Oops, sorry, she meant *Trey*.

Wearing soft cotton pajama shorts and a matching cropped shirt underneath her robe, a pair of slippers, and her hair pulled back in a ponytail, she made her way out the back door and across the yard to her house. Under a dark, early morning sky, she knocked, but no one answered. When she turned the handle, it was unlocked.

"Ah, um, Trey," she called out. "Are you awake yet?"

Still nothing.

She debated, considered turning around and leaving when her bravado began to desert her. But she had a job to do. With a firm nod, she marched inside before the chicken in her could take control. She got all the way to the guest bedroom before she remembered that she shouldn't be barging in on any man.

For one thing, he could be with another woman.

For another, he could simply be asleep, and if he had anything in common with a professional killer, he might leap up and shoot her when she heard her enter.

Okay, so that was a stretch and completely unlike her to even think it, but the man really had her thinking and doing crazy things. Standing there determined to have sex with him being an example.

But heck, she was nothing if not focused on setting goals, developing a plan, then bringing it to fruition. Yet again, the good girl slipped away and the sinfully sassy side of herself that she had never known existed emerged. She wanted this. And for whatever reason, she was going to go through with it.

She came through the guest room doorway, but what she hadn't anticipated was that he'd be up, working at his computer, only a small lamp burning at his side. She stopped dead in her tracks as he turned in the wooden chair to face her. There wasn't an ounce of surprise on his face, as if he had been expecting her.

Unlike the last time she had arrived unannounced, this time he was dressed, his shirt untucked and hanging open. She could see the outline of his chest, the dusting of dark hair that disappeared beneath the waistband of his pants. She thought of the day she found him naked in bed, of the stunning beauty of his body, and a thrill of anticipation ran through her. Which probably wasn't the best thing to feel when this was supposed to be a job. Really. But as long as she did feel a tad warm—okay, so she was more than a tad warm for this guy—why not have a little fun in the process? Who knew when she'd have this kind of opportunity in the future?

A rush of hot, coursing power filled her.

She stared at his hand as he closed the screen of his notebook computer. Her senses flared when he stood and came around the desk, his height seeming to dwarf the guest bedroom with its decades-old oak furniture. Thoughts of having fun, being playful, or even merely getting the job done fled as something else pushed in. She was awed by the barely contained strength of him.

"Hey," she said softly.

His gaze swept over her. "Hello," he responded, running his broad hand down his chest as he stretched.

Then she just stood there, staring.

"Can I help you?" he asked, as always the perfect gentleman.

"Ah, well . . ."

She took a deep breath, remembered why she was there, remembered the night in the bathroom and what she had said that made things happen. "Kiss me," she whispered.

His hand stopped, splayed on his abdomen, only a barely perceptible flicker in his eyes showing that her words made him feel anything. Then he leaned back against the edge of the desk, crossed his arms, and chuckled.

"I wasn't trying to make you laugh."

"Then what were you trying to do?"

"Re-create the night at the hotel."

"Ah, yes. You said 'Kiss me' that night, too."

"Exactly. Which is exactly what got things started," she stated with modulated practicality.

" 'Things'?" His smile widened.

"You know. The near-sex things."

One slash of dark brow rose, his eyes glittering. "And now you've come looking for more."

His tone of voice didn't sound very promising. She hadn't given any thought to having to seduce him. She had assumed it would be easy, that all she'd have to do was say "Kiss me" and that would be that.

He seemed to consider, then said, "Come here."

Success, her mind cheered, followed quickly by sizzling electricity that swept through her at the low, deep command. She took a step toward him, her pulse leaping wildly. She crossed the room and didn't stop until she stood right in front of him. But he didn't reach out. He didn't touch her. He just studied her, some amusement dancing in his eyes.

"Well?" she demanded.

Wisps of her hair had come free from her ponytail. After a second, as if he wouldn't allow himself any more than this, he ran his fingers along the dark strands.

"That's it?" she managed with a deep shiver of feeling drifting low.

"I'm not sure that you really know what you want, Chloe. You come here asking me to kiss you. Over the last few weeks you've alternately tried to embarrass me, ignore me, and anger me, and now suddenly you want to seduce me? Why is that?"

Where were the men who never wanted to talk when you needed them? "So I have mood swings, sue me."

A smile crooked one side of his sensual mouth. "I think you're playing some sort of a game."

"And you're not?"

The words slipped out before she could think better of it.

His hand stilled, his expression growing grim. After a second, he nodded, though not necessarily in agreement. Then he continued, his fingers drifting from her hair to her collarbone beneath the thin cotton of her robe. Turning his hand over, he skimmed his knuckles ever so gently downward, stopping just above the swell of her breast. Then he dropped his hand away.

Her breath caught in disappointment. She could leave. She probably should. Instead she reached up and touched his face, her fingers tracing the contours.

This time he drew a deep breath, and when she pressed one fingertip to his lips, he opened and took it inside. The gentle sucking sent a thrill through her. Something so simple, but amazingly sensual, surprising her. Her breath winged out, and her body started to tremble in anticipation.

"It wasn't supposed to be like this," she whispered.

"Like what?"

"Romantic," she managed, before he gave in and leaned down. He didn't pull her close. But he did finally kiss her as she had asked.

Her fingers clutched the edges of his shirt. He coaxed her lips apart and she tasted him. Clean and fresh. And when she leaned into him, she felt his deep moan, but he still didn't pull her close. His fingers were curled around the edge of the desk, holding on.

"This isn't wise," he said against her open mouth. "Not now. Not while the show is still in progress." He sighed into her. "Though I haven't done a wise thing since you ran into me."

"You ran into me."

He laughed, and she could feel a notch of his ironclad control slip. Just a notch. Just barely. After a moment, he kissed her hairline, his lips drifting low until he nipped at her neck.

He leaned back and looked into her eyes. She saw a depth of feeling inside him—desire, yes, but it was more than that. She could see feelings of wonder and innocence, as well, that she would never have dreamed were possible in this man. He wanted to give in, but wouldn't.

"Why?" she whispered.

As if he understood her thoughts, he said, "You make me lose control."

Then he did what he said he wouldn't do. He reached out, circling her wrist with his strong hand, pulling her to him.

"Chloe," he murmured, pressing her against him. "God, I can't stay away."

She felt his desperation, felt the intensity shimmering through him. Almost savagely, he captured her mouth with his, seeking desperately, lips slanting, unleashing the strength of his need.

She inhaled deeply, and when she did, she felt his tongue, fleetingly, against her lips. The intimacy amazed her, as did the strange feeling that coursed through her body, making her want to press even closer.

The bathroom episode and even the television show were gone from her mind. Whatever her reasons for coming here, they were forgotten. Only this enigmatic man remained.

He widened the brace of his legs, wrapping his arms around her, and she clung to him. His heat drew her as his hands slid down her spine to cup her bottom, drawing her full against the hard planes of his body. She groaned into his mouth as he kissed her again coaxing, his need insistent against her.

She felt his breath brushing her ear. But his words caught her off guard.

"Why are you so determined that we make love?" he wanted to know.

Reality tried to intrude, making her remember why she was there. "Not make love. It's just sex," she stated with a primness that even she heard. "I can do *just sex*."

It blurted out of her, just like that, and she wasn't sure why.

He tilted his head and set her at arm's length. "Chloe? Are you a virgin?"

Her heart leaped and she unsuccessfully tried to pull away. "Maybe this isn't such a good idea, after all." She pushed at his chest to no avail.

"Chloe, talk to me."

"There's nothing to say. This was a mistake."

"How can you change your mind so quickly? One minute you walk in here trying to seduce me—"

She grimaced.

"—then the next you're trying to escape. All because I asked if you were a virgin. It's okay if you are."

Her shoulders came back. "I know it's okay! And for your information, I am not a virgin. I've had plenty of sex."

He looked at her as if he didn't believe her. And rightfully so. She might have had sex, but the allure of it eluded her. But she had thought the same thing about kissing until she met this man.

"But you didn't like it," he stated kindly, his hands still holding her shoulders.

She tried to glance away, but he cupped her cheek, forcing her to look at him.

"Okay, so it wasn't great," she admitted.

"I'm sorry. When was it?"

"My freshman year in college. The first and last time."

If he was surprised he didn't show it. He simply said, "That was a while ago."

"It's not a sin to abstain from sex, you know."

"You always get sarcastic when you're in uncertain waters."

"Yeah, right," she said, crossing her arms.

He smiled indulgently. "I love it when you prove my points for me." He pulled her back and wrapped her in his arms. "It was a bad experience, wasn't it?"

A frozen spot inside of her seemed to melt a bit at the heat coming from this man's body. It wasn't a sexual heat, just a warmth that she could lose herself in. Without warning, she started talking, saying things that she had never even shared with Julia or Kate. "Yes," she said, her arms folded between their bodies. "It was awful," she added softly.

He rubbed his hand down her back, then up again. "It won't always be awful," he promised.

She snorted. "So you say."

"I do."

She rolled her head until her brow pressed into his chest. "He said he wanted to show me his favorite place," she continued, closing her eyes. "We were hiking along the river. When we came to an empty stretch lined with cottonwood trees, he told me that it was his favorite spot. Then he kissed me and he sort of pushed me down."

The kindness in Sterling evaporated. She felt the tension in him. "He didn't do anything I didn't want him to do," she stated quickly, realizing what he must be thinking.

And he hadn't done anything she hadn't wanted him to do. The story unfolded from the locked place in her heart. The college guy hadn't done anything against her will. But she had always dreamed that when she made love for the first time, it would be romantic. It hadn't been.

In a voice that was void of emotion, Chloe found herself telling this man, the one who held her, all about it. From being pushed to the ground without a blanket and the gravel poking into her back as he had sex with her, to the next day and the day after that when he never called her again.

"I thought he was the one. When he told me he wanted to show me his special place, I was *hoping* that he was taking me there to make love to me. I was young and foolish and stupid to think that he was crazy about me."

"He was crazy," Sterling stated. "Crazy and an idiot and I wish I could get my hands on him."

His whole body hummed with tension, and the protective surge in him filled her with a sort of joy she hadn't experienced since she was in junior high and Julia had marched in and confronted her grandmother about the bedroom furniture.

"You deserved better than a bed of rocks on a river levee," he stated fiercely.

Before she could respond, he stood away from the desk and swept her up with ease, hooking his arm under her knees.

She grabbed on to his shoulders. "What are you doing?"

He didn't answer and her heart pounded wildly as he carried her to the bed. But he didn't lay her down. He sat on the edge with her in his lap. She could feel the ripple of muscle beneath the thin cotton of his shirt. He was like a cage of steel circling her, making her feel tiny and protected. She wanted to touch him, explore his body, but she held back. As if sensing her trepidation, he brought her hand up and placed it on his chest.

"I want you to touch me," he whispered against her ear.

A shiver raced through her, down her spine to the juncture between her legs. A blush seared her cheeks, and when she glanced at him, he was watching her.

"Go ahead," he said.

Biting her lip, she ran her hand between the edges of his open shirt, then she gasped when he arched back and ripped it off. The desk lamp cast a golden light on his bared chest. She did as he asked, reveling in the smooth tautness of his warm skin, his heart beating against her hand—strong and steady. Making her trust him. Making her want more.

"Kiss me," he said this time.

She realized that he was intentionally letting her be in control. He was revising her beliefs about sex. About love-making.

A thrill ran through her as this time she bent down and pressed her lips to his.

"Do you like that?" he murmured, his hands lightly holding her.

"Yes," she breathed.

She cupped his face, relishing the feel as she brushed her mouth over his. He groaned, but still didn't force her to go faster. He took what she gave at the pace she wanted to give it.

She pulled away slightly and he simply stroked her back, up and down, a slow glide of his palm over her robe.

They were locked in this small world of their own making. She felt safe and cared for.

"I'm going to kiss you now," he said.

He gave her a second to resist, then he gently pulled her head to his. The contact was light and brief, a fleeting touch, there and gone, then back again, a hint of what she knew he could give.

A moan escaped her, and she whispered, "More. Please."

He obliged. His mouth captured hers, a shudder running through his hard, chiseled body as his tongue gently traced the seam between her lips. No pressure, but making her want. She opened to him, and when he parted her robe and she felt his skin against her abdomen bared by her cropped top, her pulse leaped.

"Is this too fast?" he asked, his voice dark and deep.

"No." She meant it. And when his hand brushed up her body to cup one full breast, sensation shot along her skin. Her mouth fell open on a silent gasp when his thumb and forefinger gently pinched her nipple.

"This is what making love is about," he said to her. "Pleasure. Sensation. Two people connecting."

He lay back, pulling her with him. Then he rolled, coming over her, his weight supported on his elbows. He looked down into her eyes, then he kissed her.

"Chloe," he groaned into her mouth. "Chloe," he repeated, before lowering his head to nuzzle the taut bud of her breast that strained against her pajama top.

The touch sent her senses reeling, and she cried out, her back arching. "Mmm," she moaned.

His kisses turned to nips as he worked his way down her body, moving her clothes away. His teeth grazed the strip of skin that showed between her top and pajama shorts.

"I'm going to undress you," he explained patiently.

Again she didn't protest. As if she were a china doll, he tugged off her robe and top, the material binding her arms above her head. She could feel his admiring glance as he took in her breasts.

"I've touched you," he said with awe, "felt you pressed against my chest, but I haven't seen you. I've dreamed of witnessing what my hands have experienced. I've wanted to be able to take you in." Then he pulled the top free.

His reverence was amazing, and she trembled with desire when he pulled her pajama bottoms off, leaving her dressed in nothing more than her panties. She lay flat on her back while he lay to the side, propped up on his elbow, taking her in.

"So beautiful," he murmured.

He dipped his head and laved one nipple with his tongue. Her breath caught, and she felt his groan of satisfaction as the rose-colored tip pulled into a tight bud.

"You like that, don't you?" he asked.

"You know I do."

He chuckled, then he ran his tongue around first one nipple, then the other, his teeth grazing the tender flesh. Her breath grew shallow as he trailed his hand down her body, from the sensitive hollow between her breasts to the thin elastic of her bikini underwear. He didn't take them off, he only slipped inside, the tips of his fingers brushing the tight curls. Both of them were breathing rapidly as he brushed his hand back and forth.

"Chloe," he whispered, then trailed his lips down her burning skin, his hand sliding lower.

She trembled, wanting, needing, desire beating in her veins.

He felt her need, felt her seeking something she hadn't

experienced on a rocky levee by a river years ago. Sterling wanted to pummel any man who would be so thoughtless. But he couldn't think about that now. His only focus was Chloe and giving her the pleasure she deserved.

Her eyes widened, but she didn't stop him when he slipped off her panties.

"Pull up your knees," he commanded gently.

Shyly, nervously, she did as he asked.

"Spread them for me," he added.

She did that as well, though hesitantly. Then her eyes fluttered closed, her chest rising on a deep breath when he parted the curls, tracing the moist folds between her legs.

With her hands flung out to her sides, her fingers fisted in the bedspread. Then he brushed his lips over hers, his fingers circling her hot center.

He could feel the way her pulse leaped in her neck when he grazed his mouth along the slender column, then lower. And when he took one nipple deep in his mouth, he slipped his finger deep inside her sex. She gasped, her back arching at his touch. She shuddered with feeling.

His body leaped, making demands of its own, and it was all he could do to keep control of his throbbing erection. But he kept a fierce rein on himself.

With his thumb, he circled the secret spot, and he could feel her mounting sensation. He stroked her tender folds, long strokes, deep and slow, until her body began to move with him, low purring moans emanating from her.

Her mewling cries wound around him with the sharp bite of talons. Her mouth parted slightly when he stroked deep. He kissed her then, absorbing her cry. Then she finally gave in and clung to him.

She met his passion, thrilling him with her naïve desire. He brought her to a fevered pitch with his fingers, dipping and thrusting, taking her higher. He saw the minute her body exploded, sensation crystallizing inside her as she arched in silent, nearly torturous pleasure.

Release. The kind that went so deep that tension and the world around them washed away. As potent as a drug. Sterling knew.

With a wealth of emotion, he pulled her to him and wrapped her in his arms. He held her as tight as he had held anything in his life. Hard consuming sensation shivered through him. Both desire, but also a need to protect.

His body pulsed with need, a deep, powerful need that threatened to overwhelm them both. He wanted to sink his flesh in her. But he couldn't, not yet. Reality reared, and he realized he was going too fast. Passion and desire for this woman had pushed him to this point.

Since meeting her he had tried to purge himself of thoughts of her. He had lain in bed, his body hard with desire. But the only woman he wanted to be with was Chloe. He wanted to part her thighs, press at her opening until she pulled him to her, then slide slow and deep. He wanted to feel every inch of her satiny warmth wrap around him. He had nearly done just that seconds ago.

And that couldn't happen. Not yet. Not while she thought he was a man called Trey Tanner.

With ironclad willpower, he pulled back once her body's spiraling intensity had wound itself out. He rolled off the bed and reached for his shirt. Instantly she sat up in confusion.

"What about you?"

She surprised him, and his fingers stilled. "Me?"

"Yes, you," she said, jutting her chin forward in an expression of you-know-what-I-mean.

He nearly laughed out loud, but he couldn't for the sheer

amazement that rushed through him. Her innocent caring of him and his needs made his heart kick in his chest.

"I want you to have . . . you know . . . pleasure, too," she said.

With a gentleness he had never felt before, he came back to her. But when she reared up on her knees and would have wound her arms around his neck, he kissed her forehead, then held her away by her shoulders.

"Not tonight. Not yet."

She blinked.

"Now get dressed. You need to get back to Julia's house before anyone wakes up."

Slowly the passion drained from her face and something else seemed to sink in. He saw her glance around the room, see the clothes on the floor, see the two of them, their bodies, and this time color drained from her face.

But he was just as startled as she was. Days before, he had come to understand that he might need more forgiveness than approval from this woman once she found out who he really was. But for the first time since he started on this path, he wondered if he would get it once she learned what he had done.

He had no idea what she would do when she found out who he really was. A month ago he wouldn't have cared if someone forgave him or not. But now he cared. With this woman he cared.

Very carefully, as if he were afraid she would break— or that he would—he took her hand. For long seconds he didn't let go, only stared at her fingers, before he kissed each one.

"There are some things I need to work out," he said. "Then, if you'll still have me, I will come to you and never let you go again."

He could feel her confusion as he dressed her and gently pushed her out the door. "Go home, sweetheart."

Shutting it, he leaned back against the hard plank. He had to think.

"Damn," he whispered as he wondered how the hell he would tell her he wasn't the man she thought he was.

To: Ben Prescott <sc123@fastmail.com>
From: Jason Hughes <jhughes@HughesSecurity.com>
Subject: re: Question

Just finished up the Chloe Sinclair case for you. Turns out her mother died when she was seven years old, which explains why she went to live with her grandmother.

The death certificate on the mother lists the cause of death as multiple external lacerations and massive internal injuries caused by a high-speed motorcycle accident. No foul play, just damned bad luck.

Child Services was involved in the custody. The father wasn't around.

I'll send over the file so you can read it for yourself, but in a nutshell, you had a little girl whose father got her mother pregnant but never married her, then, topping it all off, the mother getting killed in an accident after the father left town.

I hope like hell whoever you're doing this for isn't asking about the family because he or she cares about social status crap. Chloe

Sinclair definitely isn't from the debutante crowd. But from everything I've learned, she is an honorable woman who has survived with a whole lot of class after a life of hard knocks.

If you have any questions after you get the file, let me know.

Jag

sixteen

$\mathcal{S}$he was falling in love with a man who was lying to her. The thought sent a shiver of foreboding through her. Surely it was something else that she felt.

Lust? Carnal attraction?

Something. Anything but love.

She couldn't afford to love the sort of man who was from a totally different world from her—who was everything she didn't respect.

But nothing else explained this inability to put him from her mind—the way, despite everything, he made her want him.

Racing down the hall from the guest bedroom, Chloe concentrated on putting one foot in front of the other without looking like she was panicking. It was her own house but she felt like an intruder as she scurried as quickly and as quietly as she could.

She was so consumed with her thoughts that she almost missed the noise coming from the kitchen. And just when the sound finally registered, she was already reaching out at the exact moment the door swung open.

She jumped and screamed, which caused another scream, high-pitched and refined, followed by a shuffle. Suddenly she was face-first into the wall, her hands outstretched on either side of her. Now she screamed in earnest.

She was barely aware of the cursing and banging, and then not aware at all that she was no longer being held against the wall.

"Chloe, it's me."

Sterling's voice.

Yes, Sterling. She could no longer think of him as Trey, the man who was playing a part, as if what happened in the guestroom had forced a seismic shift in her mind.

"It was Ben who grabbed you. He thought you were an intruder," he said.

She sagged against him, finding safety, the kind that she instinctively realized he provided—despite the weird game he was playing with her.

"It's okay," he murmured against her hair as he stroked her back. "No one's going to hurt you."

Then she felt him stiffen.

"Grandmère?" he asked, confused.

In some recess of her mind, Chloe finally registered the sound of a woman's heels on her hardwood floor.

"None other, my boy. Though I can tell you this wasn't the sort of welcome I was expecting."

Chloe pushed away, her normal good sense flooding back through her. Her eyes went wide.

"And who is this?" the older woman demanded.

She was every bit as intimidating as either one of what Chloe assumed were her grandsons, even though each of the men was over six feet tall and the woman couldn't have been more than a delicately boned five foot two. Just looking at her, Chloe knew this woman was a matriarch to a fine, old-moneyed family. The complete opposite of Chloe's own family. This woman and her family were from a world that Chloe knew nothing about.

Despite her age, the woman was also a beauty, with gray hair pulled up in a soft bun, rich chocolate brown eyes, and skin that was amazingly smooth.

Both men seemed to stand straighter.

"So," the woman intoned, dragging out the single syllable with the intimidation of a queen. "My grandsons," she added. "What have you gotten yourselves into now?"

Ben chuckled. "Not me, Grandmère."

Chloe noticed that Sterling implored the woman with his eyes. From the looks of her, Sterling Prescott's grandmother wouldn't take kindly to game playing of any sort. Especially the kind that involved lying.

Chloe had the fleeting thought to step forward and say, *You must be Trey's grandmother.* But everything had changed since she walked into the bedroom intent on seducing him. She was tired of playing games, too. But where to go from this difficult place?

"I'm Serena—"

Both Sterling and Ben made strange sounds in their chests.

Serena sniffed, gave Sterling a pointed look, then added, "Just call me Serena. And you are?"

"I'm Chloe Sinclair."

"Ah, yes. The woman on television who is making a fool of my grandson."

"Not really a fool," she responded with a wince.

The woman sniffed. "A fool, dear, and we both know it. I had Ben here provide me with a videotape." Then she actually chuckled. "There aren't many women who can make my grandson look anything less than powerful and commanding. But every now and again, I think, we all need to be brought down a peg or two."

Was this a compliment? Chloe didn't know.

"It was nice to meet you," Serena said, clearly dismissing her. "I noticed that you were on your way out when the altercation happened. Perhaps you should get yourself dressed."

"Grandmère," Sterling said sharply.

His grandmother looked at him imperiously while Chloe blushed a thousand shades of red.

"I've really got to go."

When Sterling tried to stop her, she dashed away into the kitchen, then out the back door. She needed space. She needed to find a way to breathe. And for reasons she didn't entirely understand, she realized that the more she tried to gain control, the more she lost it.

The Prescotts watched her go. As soon as the back door banged shut, Serena Prescott had to tip her head to look at her elder grandson. But tip she did and cast him a glaring eye. "I hear you've been calling yourself 'Trey,'" she said with an imperious tone.

This strong, forbidding man who intimidated most everyone he came in contact with grimaced. "I can explain."

"I suspect you will. But first I need to freshen up. Ben tried to put me in a hotel, but I insisted that I see you first. If you're staying here in this house, I see no reason why I can't stay with you. That is, unless you are making a habit of early morning tête-à-têtes with the woman who just dashed out the door."

"Grandmère," he stated firmly, "what I do with Chloe is none of your concern. I must respectfully ask you to stay out of it."

"Hmmm, talking back to me. She must mean more to you than I guessed."

She started walking down the hall as if she owned the place, stopping in front of Chloe's bedroom. She shuddered. "Good Lord, what happened to the bed?"

Not waiting for an answer, she disappeared into the bathroom off the hall. Ben didn't waste any time.

"What was I supposed to do?" he demanded in quiet tones. "You know how Grandmère is."

"I know. I know. I'm just thankful that Diana didn't decide to show up as well."

"Give her time."

"Great."

"Listen," Ben said, "I found out why Chloe lived with her grandmother."

Sterling focused intently.

"The mother, Nell Sinclair, was riding on the back of a Harley driven by some biker guy after Chloe's father moved out. Nell was twenty-six, wasn't wearing a helmet. Neither was he. They were traveling at a high rate of speed down Paisano, lost control, hit a tree, and were pronounced dead at the scene."

Sterling didn't let any of the surprise he felt show on his face. Instead his brain assimilated the information. He blocked from his mind how he felt about the idea of Chloe dealing with the sudden, unexpected loss of a parent. *That* he'd save for later, when he was alone, when he could take out and examine the pieces of emotion that only Chloe Sinclair had the ability to make him feel.

When Sterling didn't comment, Ben continued, running through the details from the Hughes Security file. About the mother and father, about Child Services placing the child with the grandmother.

Sterling's brows furrowed deeply. "So you're telling me Chloe's mother was an unwed parent."

"Yes," Ben said shortly.

Emotion tried to fight its way through his taut control. Sterling hated what he heard. He hated the knowledge that

Chloe's parents had never married, hated what, even in this day and age, that made her.

Was that why she was so reluctant to talk about her family? Why she kept personal information to herself?

But Sterling felt something else as well, yet another of the foreign emotions that he'd had since meeting Chloe. He felt a driving need to give her the family she had never had. He wanted to give her children; he wanted to give her himself—if she'd have him—offering her the one thing he had never been able to give anyone before.

It hit him so hard, his eyes narrowed against the tightening in his chest.

"Anything else?" he asked his brother, needing to be alone with his thoughts.

"There was a note in the file. When the responding officers got there, the mother was still alive. Apparently she said something like 'I didn't mean to leave.' Strange."

Sterling wondered if it wasn't strange at all, but rather the key to the woman who filled him as no other.

He started to turn away.

"Sterling," Ben said, stopping him.

"Yes? What is it?"

"Chloe might not be from our kind of family, but she is a wonderful woman regardless."

The words took him aback, and Sterling stared at his younger brother. After a long second he said, "If there's one thing in this world that I'm absolutely sure about, it's how truly wonderful she really is."

Chloe returned to Julia's house, hurrying along the walkway, half mortified, half amazed by how far she had gone with Sterling. As to being caught coming out of the bedroom by his grandmother, that deserved full-fledged embarrassment.

Even worse, Chloe hated to think about the introduction. The older woman had taken care not to use her grandson's name. Was the whole family in on it?

She slipped by Mindy's room, careful not to wake her. She wanted to talk to Julia, but when she went into the bedroom to find her friend, she wasn't there.

"Julia," she called, walking through the large expanse to the smaller connecting room. "Are you here?"

No one was there, and Chloe turned to leave. And as she did, she noticed the station's ledgers sitting on the desk.

Chloe couldn't believe it when she actually walked over and sat down. She told herself not to look. If she had questions, she just had to ask. But Julia had been acting too strange—one minute her old self, the next massively stressed—for everything to be on the verge of working out.

Telling herself that as the station manager she was doing nothing wrong, she opened the accounting ledger.

She went through the book once, then again. By the time she closed the black-bound tome, she could only stare blankly. The debt was far greater than Chloe had ever imagined.

Her mind was numb while she changed her clothes, pulling on faded jeans and a bulky sweatshirt, then went straight to her garage. It was the first time she had been alone in days, just her and this house that she loved, in the neighborhood that had been her refuge. But suddenly it wasn't any longer.

Yet again she wished she had the comfort of knowing her father was there. She loved Julia and Kate, but having family was different. Her father would listen to her, make her feel better.

Or was that just a dream, too?

She pressed her forehead against the garage door, relishing the metal warmed by the October West Texas sun. Breathing deep, she thought she could stay that way for a lifetime. Forget everything that was going on. Because the truth was, she was afraid she couldn't save the station after all.

Sure, ratings were good. Advertising dollars were pouring in. But what would they do next? How would they sustain this level of income after *The Catch* was over?

After going through the books, she felt very much like they were only putting a Band-Aid on the problem.

And then there were these feelings she had for Sterling. They left her aching and confused and scared that she was letting her guard down. The truth was, she still didn't know why he continued to pretend to be someone else.

That was when the real fear hit her, and she realized what had been lurking at the back of her mind since she had found the accounting ledgers.

Had Julia wanted to sell KTEX all along? Is that why she had gone to Prescott Media in the first place? But she didn't want anyone to know?

"Hello! Is that you, Chloe?"

Chloe jerked away from the garage door and saw Sterling's grandmother.

"Ah, hello," Chloe said.

"What a beautiful day it is. In St. Louis our weather is nice, but it can't compare with this."

Chloe stared at her.

The woman laughed and breathed deep like an aerobics instructor.

Chloe pulled open the garage door.

"What are you doing?" the woman asked, following her inside.

"I'm going to work in the garden."

"How wonderful. Do you mind if I join you? I can't tell you how long it's been since I've gotten down on my hands and knees and worked in the dirt."

"You garden?"

Serena laughed gaily. "Not so much anymore, I'll grant you that. But there was a day."

A bucket filled with tools and gardening gloves stood on the worktable. After searching out a second pair of gloves, Chloe handed them to Serena, then they headed to the backyard. All the while, the older woman didn't seem to so much as draw a breath through all her talking.

"Did . . . my grandson tell you that I'm from El Paso?"

He had. She remembered now. Though it seemed like ages ago when he had told her.

"Yes, born and raised," Serena added. A hint of a Hispanic accent mixed in with her perfectly refined Midwestern neutrality. "My maiden name was Cervantes. Serena Cervantes, from a long line of Cervanteses dating back for centuries."

No sooner had Chloe kneeled in the yard, than she sat back on her heels. "Then how did you end up in St. Louis?"

Serena sat down next to her on the grass, apparently not giving any thought to her fine slacks and silk blouse. "I met a handsome young soldier at Fort Bliss. My grandson's grandfather." She stared out through the trees that were still green, the mountains in the distance rising up in shades of purple. "I was working at my father's restaurant. It was love at first sight. I still remember that he ordered the combination plate. And when he finished, just so he could stay, he ordered another."

"Love at first bite."

Chloe couldn't believe she had said that. Serena looked at her, then stared to laugh. Then, amazingly, Chloe did, too.

"I guess that is true," Serena said. "After that, he came back for lunch every day he could leave the base. We were married within the year, and the minute he was discharged from the army, we traveled to his home in St. Louis."

"Is he still there now?"

"No, God rest his soul. But he's waiting for me in heaven."

"Looks to me he has a long time to wait."

Serena laughed. "I'm blessed with good health, even if I've got three grandchildren who want to give me a heart attack."

"But you love them."

Serena looked her directly in the eye. "With every ounce of my being."

Footsteps interrupted their ease.

"How are you two doing?"

They turned to find Sterling standing at the back door. "I'm getting to know your lovely young lady," Serena said.

Chloe blushed and started to correct her, but Serena cut her off. "I have an idea."

Sterling groaned.

"It's been a hundred years since I've had real Mexican food."

"Then we'll go have some."

Light sparkled in her eyes. "I have a better idea."

seventeen

Chloe realized quickly that what Serena Cervantes Prescott wanted, she got. And she wanted to prepare a feast.

They didn't have time for a feast, not really, but since the next show didn't tape until Friday, Chloe relented.

She couldn't believe it when she found herself wrist deep in masa. And if that didn't stretch the imagination, Sterling Prescott standing next to her was enough to make her believe she had to be dreaming.

"That's it," Serena instructed. "Spread the masa on the corn husk in a smooth layer, with more toward the top than the bottom of the husk."

The entire kitchen in Chloe's tiny house was filled with the signs of serious cooking. Serena wanted to relive her youth, and her memories were seasoned by food. When Serena had arrived, she had been beautifully regal, though reserved. Now, as if the preparation of food could change people, not only was Serena's expression relaxing, her elder grandson was changing before Chloe's eyes as well.

He was still the silently commanding sort. Not an ounce

of control left his chiseled frame. But there was an indulgent love, not the tough sort that he directed at Ben, that filled his eyes when he looked at his grandmother and softened him in a way that was compelling and not just a little overwhelming.

Chloe was intrigued by this man. She felt her heart pound with poignancy and yearning as she watched this family. The love they shared was visible. And while it was clear that Sterling was frustrated by his grandmother's arrival, he also felt a deep respect for her.

"So what else are you making?" he asked with a smile, kissing Serena on the forehead.

"What else are *we* making. We're starting with the tamales so we can get them out of the way. Then we'll move on to the enchiladas and chile rellenos. Your mother may not have taught any of her children about cooking, but it's time my grandchildren learned a thing about their heritage." Serena pronounced everything with a perfect Mexican accent. "After that, we'll move on to salpicón and refried beans and *mi padre*'s famous slaw."

"It sounds delicious," Chloe offered, meaning it.

"It is. Then tonight we will have all your Roses over and have a grand feast." She looked at her grandson. "Perhaps you should film that!"

"Are you trying to get on television, Grandmère?"

She smiled wickedly, but said, "Me, never."

Chloe was listening so intently that she wasn't watching what she was doing.

"That's one interesting tamale," Sterling said to her.

"Oh!"

Instead of moving on to the second tamale, she had added a second scoop to the first. It made her mouth dry just to think about taking a bite into the doubly thick corn masa.

Sterling came up beside her, his arm brushing against hers. He took the corn husk and dumped the masa mixed with broth and chile sauce back into the bowl. Then he guided her hands as they started over.

"You know how to make tamales?" she asked, a little rattled.

"No, but I'm getting pretty good at learning new tricks."

Needing to concentrate on anything but how this man made her feel, she turned her attention to Serena. "How many grandchildren did you say you have?" Chloe asked.

"Just the three. Which have proved more than enough, given that they are all a handful."

"There are the two men, but who else?"

"I have a granddaughter. Diana." Serena cast a baleful eye on her grandson. "She's been threatening to show up here herself."

Chloe heard Sterling's groan. But whatever concern she experienced disappeared the minute Serena left the room in search of Ben, who was next door. Sterling took a step so that he was behind her, then he got even more serious about tamales.

Her breath caught as his hand guided hers. Electricity sizzled through her when his chest touched her back, and every time he reached for something, their bodies came even closer together. The heat of him always surprised her. She told herself it was all the burners on the stove going. But she knew that it was him. He exuded a heat that she wanted to sink into.

"Now you're getting the hang of it," he said against her ear.

A shiver of delicious yearning ran down her spine, so delicious that she felt like a guilty teenager when the back door banged open again.

"The Catch looks caught," Serena announced with a laugh. "Enough with you two lovebirds."

Chloe ducked away. "Oh no, we aren't . . ." She felt flustered. "We are in the middle of a dating show or contest. And we can't be unfair to Mindy. She's a dream. Perfect Rose material."

Serena glanced back and forth between the two of them and didn't look like she believed Chloe for a second. Thankfully the woman only shrugged and commanded them to finish up with the tamales.

Every nerve tingled in Chloe's body as she scooped up the shredded, seasoned meat-filling and placed it on the now perfectly smooth masa. Serena didn't want any mistakes, and she came over and showed Chloe how to spread the filling along the center, then how to roll the corn husk and fold the bottom to create what was now recognizable as a tamale.

"*Perfecto!*" Serena exclaimed.

In short order they finished up the tamales, then moved on to a dish of succulent beef enchiladas with red sauce and chile rellenos that made Chloe's stomach grumble. And by the time the afternoon sun was fading in the sky, they had a feast that she thought she might be too exhausted to enjoy.

But it was food, after all, and the most heavenly of food available. Truly homemade Mexican food.

Shy sweet Mindy arrived with Julia and Ben. Even Kate and Jesse piled into the small house.

"I could smell the chile two doors down," Jesse enthused.

He was playing the best golf of his life, and Chloe had never seen two happier people. They talked and laughed, and Chloe wondered if she would ever have something like what they shared. When she glanced up, Sterling was studying her.

His gaze had that heated smolder to it. And then he smiled.

The entire table of people laughed at something Julia said. But neither Sterling nor Chloe heard what it was. He studied her with a sensuality that was matched only by the intensity in his eyes. Chloe sensed that things were coming to a head between them.

Everyone had a wonderful time. They ate lots of food and drank margaritas, and by the end, everyone had a rosy glow.

"Ben," Serena stated, "since you're the designated driver, I'm ready for you to take me to the hotel."

"I thought you were staying here," Sterling said.

She gave him a look, one delicate brow raised in amusement. "No, no, no. I just wanted to come here first to see what it is my boys were up to. Now I know." She practically snorted. "And now I'm ready to go to the hotel. It's been a long day and I'm exhausted."

When the group finally broke up, Chloe staying behind to clean up the mess, Sterling motioned for Ben to follow him into the living room.

"I'll just be a minute," Ben told their grandmother. "What is it?" he asked his brother.

Laughter from the kitchen floated out to them. Through the doorway, Sterling could see Serena and Chloe talking and laughing. Two realizations hit him at once.

More and more he understood that Chloe's view of men was skewed by her past. Beyond that, he finally understood why he had felt empty and restless. It hadn't been challenge that was missing from his life.

Sterling turned to his brother. "The deal's off."

"What?"

"The challenge, or whatever it was."

"But you're about to win—you'll save the station, and Chloe clearly has fallen for you. I'm on the verge of having to suck it up and return to St. Louis."

"I don't want Chloe that way. I want Chloe to know who I am, good or bad, and let her make the decision based on the truth, not based on this crazy challenge neither one of us ever should have agreed to." He hesitated. "And I don't want you returning to St. Louis unless you want to."

Ben's dark eyes widened with surprise. "What happened?"

"Chloe happened. Chloe made me realize what was wrong, why I got myself into this mess."

Ben cocked his head, waiting for the answer.

"She made me realize that there's more to life than work and winning and closing the best deals. And after learning about her past, I want to give her the family she never had. I can see now why she is trying to spend more time with her father. He's all she has. But now she has me, too. I can give her more family."

Ben clapped his hand on his brother's shoulder. "This is a brother who makes me proud," he said with great feeling.

Sterling glanced back at his grandmother and the woman he loved.

Yes, loved.

The sensation was powerful and amazing, nearly bringing him to his knees. He loved her and wanted her to marry him, despite whatever skewed feelings she might have toward men. He would change her mind. He would prove that he loved her.

But first he had to tell her who he really was.

He hated the thought that this might be the end, that she might never forgive him. But he had to do it. He had to have a chance to spend time with her as himself. One true moment. Whatever the consequences. He wanted her to see him, the real him. And when Ben and Serena finally walked out the door, Sterling couldn't help himself when he leaned down, cupped Chloe's chin, and kissed her. Softly. Just once. Then he kissed her long.

When he pulled back, her breath sighed out of her. "What was that for?"

"Have I told you how special I think you are?"

She pressed her hand to his forehead. "Are you getting sick?" She glanced after his grandmother and brother. "Maybe I should get them back here."

"I'm fine. And my grandmother can't fix what's really wrong."

Chloe laughed. "She seems like the type who could fix anything. She's lovely."

He nodded. "She is. She's always been strong and good."

"Is she your mother's or father's mother?"

"My father's. But that isn't what I want to talk about."

"No, I don't suspect it is," she replied with a smile, turning back to finish up the dishes.

Sterling wasn't a man to talk about himself. And certainly not to talk about anything personal. Most people were enthralled with their own stories. Which was fine by him. He listened and learned a lot, which put him at a distinct advantage when he was making deals. Deals that in the long run didn't matter.

He had learned that Chloe was one of those people, like him, who didn't talk about themselves. Now he had a better idea of why she didn't. A mother who never married, then was killed in an accident when Chloe was young. Leaving.

Unable to help himself, he wrapped his arms around this woman he loved and breathed in the scent of her. After the next few minutes, he wasn't sure what would happen. With most any other woman it wouldn't have mattered. But with

Chloe it was different. Which meant he had no choice. It was time.

He set her at arm's length. "Chloe, we need to talk."

"Trey, what is it?"

He looked her straight in the eye. "That. Trey."

She went very still. "What do you mean?"

"I'm not Trey Tanner."

He could hardly believe the way his heart beat nervously. But he wouldn't allow himself to go easier on what he had done.

"I've been lying to you since that first day in the conference room at KTEX."

He could tell he had surprised her, but he couldn't gauge how upset she was.

"This doesn't excuse my actions, but I want you to know that I never intended to lie, just as I never intended for it to get so out of control. Suddenly Julia was calling me Trey Tanner and you were saying all those horrible things about Sterling Prescott and Prescott Media that I . . . well . . ."

"You what?" she asked with an icy calmness that made his blood run cold.

"I lied," he stated clearly, knowing he couldn't whitewash it. "I am Sterling Prescott."

Then he did something else that wasn't like him. He waited for her to respond instead of demanding an answer.

She only stared at him, her blue eyes like chips of fury. He was stunned at the emotion he felt. He realized in that second that he couldn't afford to lose her.

"I'm sorry," he said sincerely. "I never meant for this to happen."

"Why are you telling me this now?" she asked with a cold cautiousness.

"Because I was tired of living this lie."

He laid it out for her, admitting his error, praying that she could find it in herself to forgive him. He remembered the unexpected thought he'd had days earlier that maybe he wouldn't be forgiven. Looking at her now, taking in her nearly black hair and bright blue eyes that burned with a piercing and incisive iciness, he felt a biting pain at the thought that he had been right.

And that was unacceptable. "Chloe—"

She cut him off. "Tell me this. Now that you've confessed, and as long as you're in the mood for a heart-to-heart, what do you really plan to do with KTEX?"

He stared at her forever, remembering his original plan. The three-jeweled trifecta that would be a gold mine of advertising revenue for Prescott Media. He had told his board of directors about it. He had a press release written and waiting to be sent out. He would fail at a goal he had established if he didn't swallow KTEX and combine it with the Tucson and Albuquerque stations. All because he had fallen in love with this woman.

"I will do whatever it takes to make things right for KTEX."

Her eyes narrowed. "You're not trying to ruin us?"

"Chloe, why would I ruin you?" He wanted to touch her, wanted to pull her close and have her say three simple words. *I forgive you.* But he understood there was nothing simple about it.

She inhaled sharply. "Swear that you'll make everything right."

"Chloe, you have my word."

Her irises dilated and her breathing grew agitated and shallow in her chest. And when she opened her mouth to speak, he couldn't imagine what she was about to say.

"I already know who you are."

A stunned moment of silence passed before his shoulders came back, his spine stiffening in surprise—and something else. "You know?" he demanded. "For how long?"

"Since we started taping the show. I called your office and I asked for Trey Tanner's secretary.

She explained the rest, and with each word she spoke, he grew angrier.

"You knew this whole time and didn't bother to tell me?"

Too late he realized his error. She exploded.

"You're mad at me?" she blurted out in disbelief. "You, who lied to me, are upset that I didn't come out and tell you that I knew all about your charade?"

"All right, I shouldn't have said that," he conceded gruffly.

"No, not good enough." She poked him in the chest with her finger. "I need a better apology than that." Another poke. "You need to *show* me how sorry you are. I want to see you beg and plead. I want to see you grovel!"

Only then did he realize that she was playing with him. The minute he did, she laughed out loud and launched herself into his arms so suddenly that he staggered back.

"I'm so happy!" she cried. "I'm so relieved!"

He felt the shift inside him, the joy, and his own relief. He could do nothing more than hold her tight, his face buried in her neck, inhaling her, assimilating that she was truly in his arms.

"Hey, you're about to squeeze me to death," she laughed.

Instantly he loosened his grip and set her down. He wanted to touch her, hold her, show her how much she meant to him. She must have seen something in his eyes, because all of a sudden she turned around and started to run.

Surprise held him frozen before he set off and chased after her.

She screamed in happiness as she careened down the hall. He caught her in the doorway of the guest bedroom.

They were both breathing hard, standing face-to-face, his arm braced above her head on the doorjamb. They stared at each other, waiting, anticipating. Then he gave in, his deep, guttural growl echoing against the walls.

"Chloe," he whispered raggedly.

They came together like two lost souls, their mouths slanting together, his groan reckless as he pulled her close. Their embrace was frantic, each surrendering, each forgetting everything else. He ran his hands down her body, cupping her hips, as if he couldn't quite believe she was really there. The freedom to touch her, now that she knew who he was, was nearly unbearably sweet.

They kissed frantically, neither able to get enough. The touch was like fire, burning and hot, a growl escaping him as his lips grazed back along her jaw, then lower.

He felt her shiver and sigh when he gently sucked the skin of her neck, a sensual dance of lips, the erotic nip of teeth. Then finally he returned to her mouth and kissed her.

She pressed against him, like she wanted to be consumed by his heat.

"Yes," he breathed, his arousal hard and insistent.

But just as quickly as it had started, it stopped. Chloe froze, startling him when she stepped back. She stared at him, and from the look on her face he was certain she would head for the door. But she surprised him when she reached up and started working the buttons of her shirt. One by one they gave way, her gaze never leaving his, until all her clothes were in a puddle around her ankles.

Humbled beyond imagining, Sterling felt young and exposed, though he was the one who still wore clothes. He almost hated the emotion. Hardly recognized it. But this woman had a way of making him accept things he wouldn't with anyone else.

Then she stepped forward and tugged at his shirt. In seconds it was gone and she took his breath away when she touched him, barely, softly, her finger circling his nipple. He closed his eyes, and he drew a deep shuddering breath. The power she had over him stunned and amazed him. His skin felt on fire when her finger drifted over to his other nipple, circling once, then finding the thin line of hair that trailed down, her hand stopping at the waist of his pants.

He coaxed her lips apart, tasting her. His mind flared and he groaned the second she reached for the clasp of his belt. She didn't tug for long before he kicked his pants away. Then he stood in front of her naked.

"You are beautiful," she whispered in awe.

His sex was hard and heavy with arousal, the muscles along his chest and abdomen quivering with his barely maintained control when she reached out and touched him, circling her fingers around the straining head. After a moment, he caught her wrist and pulled her back to him. His kiss became urgent, his palms caressing her bare skin, trailing down until he cupped her bottom, tucking his fingers into the notch between her thighs. He felt the way her body leaped, wanting, demanding more.

"Yes, Chloe." He nudged her knees apart with his own, his fingers brushing against the tight curls covering her sex.

She quivered and gasped. The sensation was intense, and he couldn't hold back the moan of satisfaction that started in his throat and only got deeper when she ran her palms up to his shoulders.

His erection throbbed, and he sucked in his breath as her fingers drifted lower along the trail of his chest hair, then even lower. With a groan, he took her hand, then wrapped it around his hard shaft.

She drew a shaky breath at the same time she seemed to find power in the clear control she had over his body. She stroked him with maddening slowness, her fingers tight as he groaned into her hair.

"God, yes," he whispered, his voice a rasp, his body thrusting into her grip.

But this wasn't how he wanted it to be. With the same furious control he had used to keep her distant, he took her hand away, then turned her around and guided them farther into the small room. When he brought her back up against his chest, they both faced a mirror over the dresser. Two strangers stared back. His warm hands drifted up against her bare skin, slipping higher and higher along her sides, then around her ribs until he cupped her full breasts, pressing the soft pertness high.

A sigh escaped her lips, and he felt her body tremble with need as his hard length pressed against her hips.

"Do you like this?" he whispered in her ear.

She trembled even more as he brushed the flats of his palms across her nipples.

"I think you do," he murmured.

She shivered when his hand drifted low down her belly, grazing over her abdomen, slipping between her legs, cupping her.

Her mouth opened on a silent cry.

"You're so soft," he said.

Running one hand down her back, he gently bent her over the wooden dresser top.

The sight of her brought heat flashing through him with raw intensity. He trailed his hand lower, cupping her bared bottom, then lower until he found the tight curls. He gently spread the folds, wet with need, then slid deep inside her in one erotic thrust.

He felt her body shudder and clench, and when she tried to stand, he gently pressed his hand to her back, keeping her there, his fingers sliding deeper. He stroked her, moving in a slow, steady rhythm that made her body pulse.

She began to move her hips, wanting more. Her breathing grew ragged, and Sterling couldn't believe the passion Chloe showed. It was like a burning that she gave in to, however reluctantly, that matched the burning that always surfaced inside him whenever he saw her. She was slick with desire, and his erection was nearly painful.

With tautly held control, he withdrew his fingers from her, then swept her into his arms. He kissed her again, as he set her on the bed, his lips traveling lower along her collarbone and then over the swell of her breast. Suckling and nipping, then the flick of his tongue, before continuing on, his kisses trailing over her abdomen.

Each of them was breathing hard. And she could no longer control the tremors that ran through her body as he pulled up her knees. His fingers scorched a path up from her ankle and along the inside of her thigh until they grazed the silken folds between her legs. He groaned when he felt her wetness. He circled, teasing but never entering, just grazing. He could feel when she gave herself over to sensation. But then he startled her when he pressed his tongue to the center of her being.

He felt her surprise and her resistance, but he circled his tongue, dipping, and she cried out in pleasure, her fingers tangling in his hair.

"Sterling," she cried out.

He went still at hearing his name on her lips, intense joy rippling through him. After a moment, he came over her.

Supporting his weight on his forearms, he framed her face with his hands. Their eyes met, locked.

"Love me," she demanded.

He looked at her forever, then said, "Not yet."

Her red mouth fell open. "Not yet?"

"Come over me."

She appeared confused, so he rolled, and in seconds she was on top of him. "Bring your knees up and straddle me."

She blinked. Tentatively she did as he asked, and her eyes went wide when she felt his hard flesh between her thighs.

"Oh," she breathed.

Sterling half chuckled, half groaned.

But Chloe barely heard over the rush of blood through her head as her heart raced with excitement. She felt nervous and insistent at the same time. But the desire for this man won out when his strong hands brushed up her sides, nudging her closer, then gently guided her down to his shaft.

When the folds of her flesh touched his slick hardness, her body quivered with need. But his sheer size concerned her.

With his hands instructing her, he moved her on him, slowly circling her hips, tantalizing her, until her head fell back and all concern evaporated. She only sought the pleasure he had given her before—though this time she sought something greater, something that pulled at her, something primal and innate. She yearned to feel him deep inside her.

Seeking, her body heated, she began to move without his guidance. She felt him suck in his breath when she tried to slide lower, taking more of him.

"God," he whispered on a strangled breath.

She moved again, but despite her body's insistent desire, she couldn't go farther.

Expelling his breath, he grabbed her hips and lifted her until they were nearly parted. But then he pulled her back down. Over and over again, barely a movement, slowly, deliciously, until she started moving again on her own. Moving and sliding, still seeking.

She looked down at this man, his jaw locked, his body hard and tense like stone.

Unable to help herself, she leaned down. And she pressed her lips to his. For one long, breathless moment, he wrapped her in his arms. Then without warning, he lifted her up and had her on her back, sinking into the bedspread.

He came over her, pinning her down. His eyes met hers, his elbows planted on either side of her, his hands framing her face.

"I'm going to make love to you, Chloe."

"I want you to," she whispered.

His gaze locked with hers, he came between her knees, lowering himself slowly, until the swollen tip of his manhood brushed against her. This time there was no thought that he was too large. She only wanted him.

Their bodies pressed together until there was nothing between them. Their eyes met and held. Sterling never looked away as he filled her as he had wanted, as he had dreamed about every second since the night he ran into her in the hotel parking lot.

She took him completely, raising her knees, inhaling a shuddering breath when he sank even deeper.

Then he began to move, slowly at first because she was so tight—so tight that it took every ounce of concentration not to thrust hard and be done with it. But then with a frustrated cry she moved against him. "Faster," she breathed.

Sensation shot through him as she arched her back, her eyes fluttering closed.

Almost reverently he laughed, then matched her thrusts, until they were both seeking. She clutched his shoulders, panting. He buried his face in her neck, calling out her name as he gave in to the primal need. He cupped her hips, pulling her body up to meet his bold, fevered thrusts until he felt her body tense, then quiver with sensation.

Only then did he give in, taking what his body wanted, needed. Taking his release in a moment of pure surrender. To her. To fate. To the fact that he had found the woman he was meant to be with. The woman he would make his wife.

They were meant to be together. Nothing, he told himself firmly, stood in their way any longer.

To: Ben Prescott <sc123@fastmail.com>
From: Sterling Prescott <sterling@prescottmedia.com>
Subject: The surprise

It took some doing, but I managed to find out from Chloe where her father is. I've contacted him, and he's on his way back to El Paso for the final show.

Also, thought you should know that I told Chloe who I was. Though, for now we aren't telling anyone else. For the show's sake, I will remain "Trey."

SHP

To: Sterling Prescott <sterling@prescottmedia.com>
From: Ben Prescott <sc123@fastmail.com>
Subject: Another surprise

I had an e-mail from Diana. She's heading to town and she's on the warpath. Sounds like the seller of her condo got tired of waiting for the money and accepted a contract from someone else.

Good luck. I think you're going to need it. . . .

Ben

To: Ben Prescott <sc123@fastmail.com>
From: Sterling Prescott <sterling@prescottmedia.com>
Subject: re: Another surprise

I can handle Diana.

To: Sterling Prescott <sterling@prescottmedia.com>
From: Ben Prescott <sc123@fastmail.com>
Subject: Diana

Tell me you're really not that naïve.

eighteen

*L*ove.

Sterling still found it hard to believe.

He stood in his makeshift office at KTEX and smiled. He shook his head in the pure joy at this unexpected turn in his life. He wanted to spend every second with Chloe. But first they had to finish *The Catch*. At the end of the week, they would begin taping and airing the grand finale, which they planned to show over two days. They were showing dinner with each of the finalists and their families on Friday, then the final rose ceremony on Saturday. Sterling was impatient to be done. He was ready to move on. He was ready to start a new life with Chloe.

On his way out of the office, he stopped in to see Julia. "I have a favor to ask," he stated without preamble.

Julia looked up from her paperwork and tapped her bright pink fingernails on the desk. "You? Asking? It must be important."

"It is. It's for Chloe. I have an idea for the final show."

"For the rose ceremony?"

"No, the first part. The dinner show."

"What do you need?"

Sterling told Julia his plan. And when he left her office, she stared after him, a tear of amazement in her eye.

Because of logistics and timing, the family segment would have to be taped entirely at Julia's house. There would be no ability to travel all over the city to go from one Rose's home to the next. Both Mindy and Chloe would have to bring their families to the Rose house. Sterling would meet them there.

Sterling couldn't believe how concerned he was over the family dinner show. Chloe looked nervous, which didn't help matters. Even after his confession and they had made love, she had begged him to let her off the show.

Which both of them knew was impossible.

But still, in a panic, she had blurted out, "I can't do a family show," confirming what he had suspected. She was worried about having no one there for her.

"It's going to be fine, I promise."

He had kissed her and added that there was no way he would let her go. As Trey, he wanted to win her. Then afterward, as Sterling, he planned to ask her to be his wife.

They just needed to get *The Catch* over with.

They started taping Friday morning.

"Hi, Trey," Mindy said when he entered the front door, the camera rolling. She looked as sweet as he knew her to be, and when he smiled at her and extended flowers, she all but melted in front of him.

"Trey, this is my mom, Elizabeth, and my dad, Bill."

Mindy had gotten used to the cameras, but her parents weren't. They glanced awkwardly between their daughter, the camera, and the Catch.

Sterling shook hands with both of her parents. "It's a

pleasure to meet you," he said, trying to put them at ease. "Your daughter is a wonderful woman."

With eyes wide with joy and pleasure, Mindy turned to two teenage boys. "And these are my brothers, Billy and Tom."

The teenagers shook his hand. "Cool," Billy said, glancing between Sterling and the camera. "Neat," the younger Tom added, smiling, his braces flashing in the lights.

Despite their *cool*s and *neat*s and obvious excitement to be on television, they were also protective of their sister.

"It's nice to meet you," Sterling said.

The family and the Catch moved to the dining room with the camera following. When they sat, Mindy shyly took Sterling's hand. He flinched, then cursed himself when she immediately dropped it and blushed.

He felt badly that he had embarrassed her. Hell, he felt badly that he wasn't going to choose her. Not because he had any desire for the nurse—he didn't—but because he didn't want to hurt her. Yet another new emotion Chloe had brought out in him. If he hadn't been so thrilled at finding his love, he would have been alarmed that he was going soft.

At noon, the meal was done and the crew was ready to move on.

"Chloe," Pete called out. "You're up."

Chloe jumped from her place in the dark recesses of the set. Her throat was tight at the memory of Mindy and her family, the concern they showed for their daughter and sister. The love that Mindy would have regardless of what happened on this show.

Determined not to be embarrassed by her own lack of family, she walked onto the set. But when she raised her chin, she had to blink back her tears as her heart swelled when she found Julia and Kate and even Jesse sitting around the table as the crew worked quickly to spread out a second meal.

She gasped and pressed her hands to her heart. "You guys!" she squealed excitedly.

"Get in here, sugar," Julia called out. "When it was a show with your family, who else did you think would be here?"

Kate came over to hug her. "We're your family, as you well know."

Tears tightened in Chloe's throat, then she thought she would outright cry when Julia leaned close and whispered, "As much as I hate to admit it, it was Trey's idea."

Chloe pushed back and looked at her.

"Yep, the guy's got it bad. He wants you like I've never seen a man want a woman. He's going to do whatever it takes to get you to accept his rose."

Chloe stared at her, hardly able to trust the joy she felt. Was it possible that even though he had lied about his identity, she could trust him? That he really never had any intention of hurting her?

"Come on, people," Pete called out. "We don't have all day. Take your places!"

Sterling appeared then, looking amazing and confident. She hurried across the dining room and threw her arms around his shoulders.

"Did we catch that on tape?" Pete called out. "That will be perfect for the opening."

"Got it, boss!" the cameraman replied.

Chloe hardly thought of the program. She was filled with nothing but excitement about how her life was changing.

"Thank you," she whispered.

"If you liked that surprise, just wait."

"What—"

"We're rolling, people!"

Sterling kissed her forehead, tucked her hand in the crook of his arm, then guided her into the dining room. Jesse stood, and the two men shook hands. The women said hello. But before anyone could say another word, the swinging door from the kitchen swung open.

"Hello, princess!"

Chloe whirled around. "Dad," she breathed. "You're here!"

"I'm family, aren't I?" he said, beaming.

"Yes!"

She raced over and hugged him. When she looked up, her gaze caught on Sterling. He looked happy and pleased for her. And she could only smile and mouth more thanks.

"Let's sit down," she said, noticing the extra chair for the first time.

But before they could move, someone else called out. "Richard! Richard, where are you?"

Her father blanched, then looked nervous.

When the door swung open again, a woman entered, walked up to Richard, preened for the camera, then said, "Silly, aren't you going to introduce me?"

"Bitsy, I told you to wait for me in the kitchen."

Bitsy?

Chloe couldn't imagine who this woman was. Though *woman* was being kind. *Teenager, schoolgirl, perky cheerleader* all seemed more appropriate. Bitsy was most any man's dream.

Blond, naturally, darn it all.

Tall, even without heels.

Thin, though with generous breasts that she was displaying prominently. It would only be fair if they were fake.

Chloe gaped, then turned to look at her father. "Yes, Dad, aren't you going to introduce us?"

"Ah, well, princess, this is Bitsy Young."

A more appropriate name, she couldn't imagine.

Chloe could only stare, not understanding what she felt.

"His girlfriend," Bitsy clarified, taking Richard's arm.

Whatever she was feeling just got worse.

"Isn't he a doll?" Bitsy cooed.

Richard blushed. Chloe's mouth closed, then opened again. Kate rushed over and took her by the arm. "It's nice to meet you, Bitsy. Isn't that right, Chloe?"

Chloe still only stared until Kate surreptitiously elbowed her in the ribs.

"Yes," she managed. "Isn't it time to eat?"

Chloe walked stiffly to the table, where another chair was hastily added. She hated that she was mad, but she was. She refused to consider why she felt so upset by this development.

At the table, with the camera rolling, conversation was strained. At least it was strained for everyone but Bitsy, who smiled and preened and plastered herself to Chloe's dad.

"So, where did you two meet?" Chloe asked, trying to find it in herself to be kind.

Her father looked like he didn't want to answer.

Bitsy wasn't as reluctant. "We met three months ago at the grocery store. You know, the one at the Crossroads. We've been dating ever since. In fact he just surprised me with the most romantic trip to Ruidoso."

No wonder he had been so eager to go.

"And what made you return?" Chloe asked.

"Well, your friend here," her dad said. "Trey. He said it was a surprise."

She turned a baleful eye on Sterling. She might have been thankful minutes ago, but her "thanks" quotient was suddenly running decidedly low. He had the good grace to grimace. "Surprise," he said, then added to Richard, "You didn't mention that you had your own surprise."

The meal was an eternity. But they somehow managed to muck through an hour's worth of eating and talking. Every word Chloe uttered was perfectly polite.

"Cut," Pete called out. "That was great! Tension, intrigue, the kind of family dynamic that contrasts beautifully with Mindy's happy, uncomplicated family. This is really fabulous, Chloe. Good job!"

Like she had planned it.

Richard stood. "Princess, I'll let you finish up here." He leaned down and kissed her on the cheek. "I hope I was okay . . . I didn't want to embarrass you."

She smiled wanly and watched him and Bitsy leave.

Silence reigned.

"Well," Julia said, "that was some woman."

"Woman?" Chloe bleated, then instantly cut herself off. She was mature and not about to make a scene.

"Chloe," Sterling said, commanding her attention. When she looked at him, he said, "I'm sorry. I didn't know. I wanted this to be perfect for you. I never meant to upset you."

"Upset?" she asked. "Me? I'm not upset," she lied. "I'm fine," she added. "I just need some fresh air."

She pushed up from the table and was out the back door before anyone could stop her. Afraid to go home and not wanting to go back inside, she decided to take a walk. Halfway down Julia's driveway, she stopped at the sight of an unfamiliar woman coming up the drive.

"Hello, there," the woman called out.

She was dressed impeccably, if outrageously. A bit like Julia, actually. Her hair was the same color as Sterling's and Ben's. She had the same eyes, even the same mouth.

"I'm Diana," the woman stated.

She was a tall woman, beautiful, with a smile that was both confident and knowing.

"You must be Chloe, from the show. I'm *Sterling*'s sister."

She emphasized her brother's name, and Chloe instantly realized that Diana knew of her brother's subterfuge.

"It's nice to meet you," Chloe responded. "Sterling mentioned he had a sister."

A flicker of surprise showed on the other woman's face before she recovered. "So you know. And I thought I was going to get a little revenge."

"Yes, I know. Actually, I've known for some time."

"Ah, well . . . Good. Glad to hear it. Though if it were me, I'd be furious about Sterling and Ben's bet. I guess you're just much nicer than me. Personally, I don't think I would ever speak to either of them again after what they've done."

It felt like the blood in her veins froze. "Bet? There was a bet?"

Instantly, Diana's eyes glittered and her smile turned wickedly triumphant. "You said you knew."

"That he's Sterling Prescott, yes."

"Oh, dear," Diana said, though she didn't bother to hide her smile. "I guess he didn't tell you everything, then." She started to step past her. "He doesn't know I'm in town yet, but Grandmère told me where I could find him. I'd better go in and say hello."

"Wait! Tell me what you're talking about."

"Shouldn't you ask Sterling about that?" Diana asked slyly.

"Please, just tell me."

"All right, if you insist." Clearly she was dying to spill what she knew. "Sterling made a bet that he could save this KTEX TV and win your heart or approval, or something.

Whatever, but Sterling had to do it without using his name or his money. The deal was if Sterling won, Ben would have to return to the family business in St. Louis. You can't imagine how hard we've been trying for years to get the black sheep to come home. The setup is inspired, actually. You knowing who Sterling is no doubt is a glitch. But I know my brother. One way or another, Sterling always gets what he wants."

Chloe stared, her mind reeling. Not only had Sterling lied to her, he had turned her into some sort of a bet. If the bet worked or not, didn't matter. She had been some man's pawn.

When Diana started to say something else, Chloe turned on her heel and headed down the drive. She needed to walk; she needed space to gather her thoughts.

She felt like she was breaking in two as the whole manipulative plan finally fell into place. No wonder she had never been able to understand why he had lied about who he was. It wasn't a simple misunderstanding, as he had claimed. It wasn't something he hadn't been able to control. He had controlled and manipulated the whole thing for a reason—a specific reason. She hadn't been wrong about Sterling Prescott after all. He was a callous, cutthroat corporate raider who would do whatever it took to get what he wanted. The fact that he had finally admitted who he was didn't take away the reality that he would make such a bet in the first place.

It was bad enough that she had fallen for a man's lie— she who had been on guard against them her whole life— but then to have forgiven him so quickly, so willingly, because he had made it sound so innocent, so unplanned. Forgiving him so easily made her doubt her judgment, and that was the hardest part of all.

Questions and doubts circled in her head as she strode

down Meadowlark Drive, the golf course stretching out beside her. If Sterling won her, if he gained whatever it was he actually wanted, would he tire of her just as that guy Sid had said? Could she ever let her guard down around him if he was the kind of man who would do something like this? Would she have to play games her whole life to keep him interested?

But more than that, what kind of a man did such a thing at all?

A deep, biting ache swept through her, followed quickly by a strange, foreign iciness that was oddly comforting. Sterling Prescott might think he had gotten away with turning her into a game. But he was wrong. He was about to learn that cutthroat corporate raiders couldn't act callously and get away with it. At least not with her.

nineteen

The next day, thirty minutes before they were scheduled to start filming the final installment of *The Catch,* Chloe was ready.

She had managed to avoid everyone since she had walked off the set yesterday. Given the need to prepare for the final show, it hadn't been too difficult to do. Just one word to Julia explaining that she had to be left alone to ready the grand finale kept everyone, including Sterling, at bay.

Today the ballroom set looked the same, only this time the crew had splurged and filled the space with dozens of yellow roses. The sheer draperies fluttered in a slight breeze caused not by the open window, but from a small wind machine just offstage. It was beautiful and romantic, and Mindy flitted around the room like a nervous princess in a gossamer gown that looked a lot like the draperies.

Now, with only minutes before they were scheduled to start taping the conclusion of *The Catch,* Chloe's pulse raced. It was time to act. She was nervous, but determined.

"Trey's here," Julia called out.

"Places, everyone," Pete added.

Chloe stood just off set, and she hated the way her breath caught at the sight of the man she had come to trust.

The minute he entered the ballroom, she saw that he looked around. She understood instinctively that he was looking for her.

"Trey," Pete said, "we're going to tape you and Mindy first."

Sterling hesitated before answering, but when he couldn't find her where she stood in the shadows, he turned to the director with his brow furrowed. "That will be fine."

Mindy was directed to a spot by the fireplace at the far end of the room. She looked timid but excited.

"Mindy, love," Pete said, "relax. It's just television."

Mindy nearly burst into tears of mounting stress before Julia rushed forward. "Don't cry. It's almost over and you look fabulous."

"Really?" the woman asked.

"Absolutely. You are going to wow the audience."

"What about Trey? Do you think he'll choose me?"

"Sweetie," Julia said, "you can't worry about that. You are stunningly beautiful and you're going to impress all of El Paso. Just think about that."

Mindy nodded and gathered herself. "I'm ready."

Music would be added in later. For now, Mindy stood there and raised her chin.

"Quiet on the set," Pete called out, then he motioned for their bachelor.

The French doors opened, the wind machine turned higher, and the Catch entered through a flutter of sheer curtains, like a god stepping out of the clouds. The sight seeped through Chloe, and she hated how everything had gone so wrong. Was she making a mistake? Her pulse beat in her ears, and the room felt like it spun around her.

Sterling stopped directly in front of Mindy, one single yellow rose blooming in a small crystal vase on the mantel between them. The shot was perfect. The Catch and the yellow rose of Texas.

"Mindy," he said, his deep voice filling the room, "you have amazed me during this time we've had to get to know each other."

Mindy softened at the words, the fear draining just a bit, and it was clear that she truly had blossomed into a beauty during the last two weeks. The audience would remember her sweetness. They would remember how she was kind even when the others were fighting.

"You are generous and funny," he added. "You care about so many things."

She relaxed even more, fear washing away as true hope started to build.

Sterling reached out and took her hand, and her lips parted as she inhaled deeply. Then he kissed her knuckles like some knight in shining armor.

But Chloe knew the truth. He wasn't a knight. There was no mistake.

He smiled at Mindy. "The man who wins your heart will be one very lucky man."

Mindy's breath caught. Chloe watched, mesmerized and aching, just as the audience would watch tonight, as understanding started to seep into the woman's blue eyes.

"But I'm not that man," he said gently. "I haven't caught your heart."

"But you ha—"

Sterling pressed his finger to her lips. "No, I haven't," he implored her.

Chloe knew that he didn't want Mindy to make a fool of herself. Those signs of true kindness in the man were hard to ignore. But today they didn't faze her.

"I have enjoyed our time together," he added. "And I know there is a very lucky man out there just waiting for you to find him."

By now, tears streamed down Mindy's cheeks. She stood there forever, as if she thought she needed to find a way to change his mind. But finally she must have realized it wasn't going to happen. She wiped the tears away, and as the genuinely nice person that she was, she reached up on tiptoes and kissed his cheek.

"I know who you really love," she said with heartbreaking sweetness. "And I understand."

This time Sterling was surprised, and his brow furrowed as he watched her exit the room. Every breath was held as the door clicked shut.

"Cut!" Pete called out. "That was great! Better than great! It was outstanding! Melodramatic and sappy! I love it!"

Voices rose through the room all at once.

"Great job," the director added. "Chloe, where are you? You're next! Trey, stay there. This time we're going to have the Rose enter the room. The audience will know that you're already there, and it will look idiotic if you make the same grand entrance twice." Pete rubbed his hands together. "This is going to be great!"

Julia squeezed her hand. "Are you okay, sugar?"

She nodded and found a smile for her friend. "I'm fine, really."

"Pete," Chloe called out. "I'm ready."

"Then action!"

Chloe pressed her eyes closed for one last second, then she turned the knob and entered through the same door through which Mindy had just fled.

Sterling saw her the minute she entered. She saw the heat

that flared in his eyes. But she just looked at him in return. She noticed the minute the heat turned to concern.

She walked up to him, stopping in the spot where earlier they had put a small X made from masking tape. Even upset and scared and hurting, she was a professional.

"Chloe," Sterling said.

She could feel a wealth of emotion in the single word, but she held firm against it.

He reached out and took her fingers. She felt the way she trembled, and knew he felt it, too. He wrapped her hand in his heat, as if to give her strength.

"We started this journey such a short time ago," he said, looking her directly in the eye. "And when we first met, I never would have believed that there was such a thing as love at first sight. But now, after having met you, I know it's true. It exists. Because I found it in you."

The words washed over her but she still held firm against them.

"Chloe?"

She blinked.

He looked at her intently. "Chloe?"

"I'm sorry, what did you say?"

Clearly not knowing what else to do, he reached over and took the rose from the vase. "Will you accept this rose?"

She stared at him forever. Her heart seemed to stop in her chest, blood rushing through her ears, and tears suddenly burned in her eyes.

With effort, she made herself pull her hand away. "No, I'm sorry. I can't accept the rose. You haven't captured my heart, and it would be unfair to lead you on any further."

She saw the surprise, then the hurt, in his eyes. She hated it. But he was the one who had turned her into a game.

Without another word, she turned and headed back to

the door. She felt the stunned silence in the room, the tension rushing all around them. She could feel Sterling's eyes boring into her back.

The minute the door shut behind her, Pete called cut.

"What the hell was that about?" the director shouted. "We are on a short deadline and you're playing games!"

"I'm not playing, Pete. I can't in good conscience accept his rose."

Julia rushed up. Sterling walked off the set and stood there, glowering and ominous.

Pete dragged his hand through his hair, not once, not twice, but over and over again until the thick strands stood up like a punk rocker's. "Why didn't anyone warn me about this? Now what are we going to do? We can't end the show with our Catch standing there looking like a discarded dork!"

Sterling Prescott's jaw cemented.

"Pete," Chloe cajoled. "No matter what he is, there's no denying that he looks like a very strong man. But we have a huge audience of women who will be thrilled that in the end a Rose stood up and said she didn't want this man. This really is a great, unique way to finish *The Catch*. Our ratings will be through the roof. In fact, I'm sure we'll double our revenue because it will be such a smash hit that viewers will be begging us to rerun all the episodes. And believe me, we need all the income we can get."

She sensed both Julia's and Sterling's burning stares, but she plunged ahead. "Have Trey say something about how finding the right woman is never easy. Then have him hold the rose as he exits through the French doors, the curtains fluttering, like he's a god returning to his lair. It will be perfect. Classic. And like I said, unique."

Pete grumbled. "I guess since it's the final show it could work."

"Of course it will. Now you better get on it if we're going to make our deadline."

Pete began calling out orders. Sterling barely listened. He watched as Chloe started to leave. She wanted away from him. He could sense it.

He stood there confused since he didn't have a clue about what had caused this change. And as much as he hardly recognized it, what she had done hurt. Not his pride. Rather something deeper.

Whatever it was, however, didn't matter, he told himself grimly. The least she could do was explain herself.

He took the steps that separated them and caught her arm. "Do you want to tell me what that was about?" he asked, his voice tight.

Something flared in her eyes and for half a second it looked like fear. Then she raised her chin.

"I said what I felt," she explained. "I don't want your rose. I don't want you."

A welcome coldness came over him. "That wasn't the case four days ago when we—"

He cut himself off. He wasn't a man for low blows. But he could tell she knew what he was talking about. She had all but begged him to make love to her. Reeled him in. Made him believe that she loved him as much as he loved her. However, if he thought she was embarrassed, he was mistaken.

"I might have wanted you," she said. "But that was before I learned how truly heartless you really are. Though that isn't true." She shook her head in surprise. "I knew it all along, said as much when you arrived at the station. But I let you fool me into believing that you weren't a cutthroat, prehistoric, noncaring warrior who made bets out of people's lives and emotions."

Her words turned the coldness into a bitter chill. "Bet?"

She pulled her arm away. "Don't play the innocent with me. Your sister told me all about the bet you made with Ben."

He felt like she had shot him straight between the eyes. "Damn Diana."

But he knew he had no one to blame but himself. He hadn't even thought to mention that part of the deal to Chloe. In fact, he hardly remembered it. To him, the bet had been about the work. But she couldn't possibly know that.

"Chloe, I'm sorry. I admit, I did things badly. This whole thing was a mistake."

She tried to turn away. But he wasn't about to give up. It was time to stop mincing words. He would lay it out straight. No games. "I love you, Chloe."

Her lips parted as she sucked in her breath, the blue of her eyes darkening. "You're just saying that because you want me to re-tape the episode so you won't look like a fool."

"I don't give a damn about *The Catch*. I love you as I have never loved a woman in my life. Any woman. Ever."

She looked trapped and cornered. The sight made him want to grab her in his arms and carry her to the nearest bed. He wanted to hold her, caress her, show her how much he cared for her. But sex wouldn't prove anything to this woman.

"I know what you're trying to do," she said. "You're on the verge of being embarrassed on TV, so you're taking drastic measures to win me back."

He snapped. "I'm not trying to win anything but your heart!" he bellowed, his voice echoing against the walls and ceiling. Then he forced himself to be calm. He realized that he had to finally, completely, open up to her.

"I wanted—no, *want*—you. I love you. I love that you fight for what you believe in—for the people you believe in. You don't put up with crap. And I love that when you saw me in that damned hotel bathroom, and had no idea who I was, you wanted me. Me, just me. Not Sterling Prescott—"

A gasp rustled through the room.

They turned to find the entire crew watching.

"He's Sterling Prescott?"

"The real Sterling Prescott of Prescott Media?"

"I thought he was Trey Tanner."

"Wow," Pete said. "Who knew we were filming a reality soap opera?" He turned to a stunned Julia. "Hey, what do you think? Could that work?"

Sterling muttered an oath, grabbed Chloe's hand, and pulled her down the hall to the kitchen.

"Upset that the cat's out of the bag?" she asked.

He raised a brow. "The smirk is beneath you."

Red seared her cheeks. "You bring out the worst in me—over and over again. You're the one who was found out for the liar that you are. Not me. I don't have to feel embarrassed."

"I don't give a rat's ass if the cat's out of the bag. Hell, I'm glad it's finally out there. I am Sterling Prescott," he shouted. "And I love Chloe Sinclair."

"Hush!"

"Why? I'm proud of who I am despite some idiotic actions on my part. But more than that, I want everyone to know how I feel about you. I don't give a damn if I look like a fool on TV. As to the bet, I told Ben the deal was off before I made love to you. I want you. I love you."

She stood there like she was breaking—and he could tell she still didn't understand.

He drew a deep breath, and plunged ahead. "I've given

up every one of my hopes and dreams to save Prescott Media."

Her brow furrowed.

"That's right. I didn't have any intention of joining the family business. When I started college, I was majoring in microbiology. I was going to do something great for the world. Something that wasn't about business or making money. But after my grandfather passed away, my grandmother came to me and explained the way it was. My father wasn't cut out to run the business, and she couldn't hold it together much longer."

It was completely against his nature to reveal so much. But for this woman he would do it. For this woman it felt amazing. Finally he got to share himself. He wasn't pretending anymore. And he realized in that second that he had been pretending for a lifetime. He had been who his family expected him to be, who he was raised to be. Regardless of what he really wanted. But no more.

"My mother and sister had no interest in anything but spending money, and if things had kept on as they were, there wouldn't be any money left to spend. My father spent most of his time building his toy soldiers. Letting others make decisions. No one was minding the store."

He knew he sounded like a pompous ass. Or worse, he felt like he was giving her a tale of woe. That wasn't his intent. "I switched majors. Got a business degree, then an MBA while Grandmère held things together. After that I came home and took over. I've done it without a single complaint or regret. That is until I met you. The minute I saw your face, saw the way you looked at me with innocence and longing, it was like I had stepped back in time to what my life could have been. A world where I could believe in true love. You gave me that. In a hotel bathroom in El Paso, Texas, you showed me what I was missing. Then during those first two weeks while we were putting the show together, for the first time in my life I experienced two people truly finding each other."

She bit her lip.

"Everything I felt for you had nothing to do with that bet," he repeated. "I sought you out. I wanted you for no other reason than when I'm with you, you make me feel alive." When he couldn't hold himself back any longer, he cupped her jaw with his hand, tilting her head back until she looked into his eyes. He had to force himself not to kiss her. "I love you, Chloe. I want you to be my wife. Say that you forgive me for being an ass."

She stared at him forever, tears burning in her eyes. Just when he was sure she would throw herself into his arms, she stepped away.

"I'm sorry, Sterling. This isn't a made for television movie. This is real life. Not everything is about happily ever after."

Then she ducked away from him, and walked out the door.

To: TheCatch@ktextv.com
From: MD20/20@sploto.com
Subject: Finale

Wow, man, I'm totally bummed. Trey, you should be totally embarrassed. But I bet you're really crushed. I know I would be if that hot babe Chloe dumped me. Hey, do you think you could give me her number?

Mad Dog

To: TheCatch@ktextv.com
From: theman@qakoo.com
Subject: The Catch

Dear Chloe:

Brava! Good job, saying no to that wretched man. You are far better than he deserves. Now you still owe me dinner. Let me know when is good for you.

Still your ardent admirer,
Albert Cummings

To: TheCatch@ktextv.com
From: Praying4U@nixpit.com
Subject: Sin

To Whom It May Concern:

As I said in my original e-mail, your show *The Catch* is an
abomination to the Lord. And now to leave the entire audience
who has watched your sins hanging? What is this? A completely
unsatisfying conclusion. I feel betrayed and used after the final
episode ran.

Disappointed,
Pastor Hartwell Lerner

To: TheCatch@ktextv.com
From: jbean@jbean.org (Jennie Bean)
Subject: Disappointed

Okay, not entirely. I still think Chloe is awesome! And great that she
didn't feel compelled to say yes to the Catch. But as a viewer, rather
than as a feminist, I feel majorly cheated. Is there going to be some
sort of follow-up so that we can see what the heck happened to
poor Trey?

Best,
Professor Jennie Bean

To: TheCatch@ktextv.com
From: mtaylor@nixpit.com
Subject: Say yes

Dear Chloe, All I can say is I'm in love. You are amazing and wonderful and the sexiest damn thing I have ever seen. How about dinner? Call me.

Mark Taylor
915-555-3654

To: TheCatch@ktextv.com
From: RaymondTarry@qakoo.com
Subject: Roses

Dear Chloe, I've sent roses and candy with my best regards. I hope you will enjoy them as much as I have enjoyed watching you on *The Catch.* If you'd ever consider dinner or even a cup of coffee, I would be honored to take you.

Sincerely,
Ray T.

twenty

KTEX TV headquarters was flooded with flowers and candy, balloon bouquets and cards, all delivered for Chloe. The station's e-mail system had gone down for three hours after being inundated with *I love Chloe* e-mails. Chloe was a hit, and nearly every man in West Texas swore he wanted to marry her.

Sterling felt frustration tick through him, frustration and that same need to protect. He doubted any of the e-mails were dangerous, but still. He put a call in to Ben, who assured him that he'd have security all over Chloe.

"For how long?" Ben asked.

"For as long as it takes for things to get back to normal."

"Whatever that is."

"Tell me about it. Just make sure we have someone watching her twenty-four/seven. I don't care what it costs."

"I'll take care of it."

That had been two days ago. Now Sterling paced the same damn makeshift office that had come to seem more comfortable to him than the plush penthouse suite he occupied at Prescott Media headquarters. Not that he had any reason to stay in El Paso. He couldn't even get Chloe to speak to him. And her friends weren't helping. She had locked herself away at Julia's, and between Kate, Julia, Julia's housekeeper, and the truckload of security he was paying for, everyone was keeping him the hell away from her.

"Fuck."

He flipped open his cell phone, raked his hand through his hair, then dialed the number he knew by heart. It was no surprise when the answering machine picked up.

With a curse, he left yet another message asking Chloe to call him back. He was surprised to find that he wasn't above groveling. Though he suspected that was because he knew he deserved to grovel. He had made the mess; Chloe hadn't. But he'd be damned if he was going to sit back and not fix things. That's what he did. He fixed things. Little did he know that his biggest challenge in his life would be to fix a mess he had caused.

He remembered her saying, *"Beg and plead. Grovel."* Hell, if groveling would get her back, then grovel he would.

Which was why he flipped the phone open again. The only problem was that in the thirty seconds between telling himself to grovel and the answering machine beeping, he'd forgotten. "Hell, Chloe, pick up the damn phone."

The jarring sound of a phone being yanked out of its holder and the answering machine squealing a surprised beat almost busted his eardrum.

"Don't you speak to me like that," Chloe belted nearly as loudly as the answering machine squeal. "You can't call up and swear and think you can get your way!"

"Finally. If I'd known that profanity would get you to answer, I would have done it sooner."

"That's why you called?" she demanded. "To chide me?"

Sterling mentally kicked himself, then sighed. "No, no! Don't hang up." He pressed his thumb and forefinger to the bridge of his nose. "Please." He felt the word as sincerely as he had ever felt anything, felt the vulnerable place inside him open up. "Just talk to me, Chloe."

"No," she stated stubbornly. "No more talking. There's nothing to talk about. I'm finished with you and *The Catch* and I'm going back to my old life. You should do the same. Go back to Prescott Media. Don't you have businesses to gobble up in other parts of the country? Aren't there some throats out there that need cutting? Aren't there any more *challenges* whose hearts need breaking?"

"Ah, Chloe. I swear I never meant to break your heart. I love you. And I called to tell you that you're wonderful and sexy and that I love you even if you hate me."

He heard her snort. "I am not sexy. I am smart and sensible and I'm not going to forget that ever again."

"Chloe—"

But she had already slammed the phone down so hard that what was left of his eardrum pleaded for mercy.

Suddenly even attempting to grovel lost its appeal.

Chloe banged down the phone and pushed away the half-eaten, sinfully decadent slice of velvet cake. She closed the top on the Fiddle Faddle, resealed the Oreo cookies, and decided it was time she stopped hiding away at Julia's. As she said to Sterling, it was time she got back to her old life—*sans* the sweets binge. She would put this chapter behind her. She refused to think about the pang in her heart when she thought about never seeing Sterling again.

She packed the few things she had brought with her to Julia's house. It really was time to go home. How she wished she had never laid eyes on that idiotic *Sexy!* quiz. But she'd just have to try even harder to return to who she was, get her life back in its perfect order. The thought of regaining control made her feel better already.

She left Julia's house, then walked across the backyard and through the lattice archway to her house. The minute she walked in the back door, she was struck by the sight of pans and dishes all over the kitchen.

"Dad?" she called out.

Music drifted in to her. Then she noticed a bottle of wine.

"Oh, my gosh!" she whispered. "My dad has a date! Here!"

Telling herself she was probably wrong, she walked into the living room. But she was just in time to see her father break free of a passionate embrace with Bitsy. Chloe felt like a parent walking in on a guilty child.

"Chloe!" he said, jerking up from the sofa.

Bitsy groaned and rolled her eyes, tucking her blouse back in place.

"What are you doing here?" Richard asked.

"It's my house," she squeaked as if she were the guilty party. And she wasn't the guilty one. Yet again she was feeling bad for things other people did! And she was tired of it!

"But you haven't been staying here, and now that Sterling moved out, I thought . . ."

"You thought you could . . . could . . . mess around with a . . . a . . . her?"

Every trace of awkwardness left her father, and he stood. "Bitsy, could you excuse us, please."

"Why?" Chloe demanded.

She felt like a third person watching herself act horribly. But still she couldn't stop it. "I'm not embarrassed to say what I have to say in front of her."

"You should be," her father stated.

Bitsy strolled past and smiled triumphantly. The minute the kitchen door shut behind her, Richard turned to Chloe.

"I'm not sure what has gotten into you—"

"What are you doing with her, Dad?"

Something inside her shifted and changed. She felt it. Felt a well of emotion rise up like it would strangle her. Since the day her mother rode away with the guy on the motorcycle, then never returned, Chloe had plastered a smile on her face, just as her grandmother had asked. She had been a good girl who made good grades and stayed out of trouble. She had bottled up every question she had in order to make sure that she didn't make people uncomfortable. Lovable Chloe. Isn't that who she had tried so hard to be?

But suddenly she couldn't hold emotion back anymore. She couldn't drum up smart or sensible to save her life.

"That isn't a woman in there," she stated, her voice barely steady. "That's a child. She's half your age if she's a day!"

"She is not a child. She is twenty-nine years old."

She made a production of choking, her eyes wide with disbelief. "Dad! She's only two years older than me! Your daughter!"

"Stop this. Stop it right now." His brow furrowed and he took her arms and actually gave her a slight shake. "I know I've never been a parent to you, and I have no right to act like one now. But I'm not going to sit by while you act this way. You're an adult, not a child. Stop acting like one."

Not even the bite of embarrassment could fight its way to the surface through the strange beating pain in her chest. "You've been dating her for months without even telling me."

"I told you, remember? The night that I took her to the Central."

"You said you were taking a friend! Even if I knew it was a date, you certainly didn't make it sound serious."

"So you'd feel better about it if I'd told you that I loved her?" he asked in a reasonable tone.

The words kicked at her chest. "No! I will never feel good about this."

"Chloe, stop it. Bitsy makes me happy. Can you understand that? Can you understand how that's all that matters? I've learned that life's too short to worry about age differences. Only God knows why, but she wants to be with me. And I want to be with her."

"What, so you can leave her just like you left my mother?"

The question hung in the air like an ugly surprise. Richard pressed his lips shut and stared at her. Chloe couldn't believe what she had just said.

Like a magician had snapped his fingers, she came out of that strange beating place and felt horrible. She was acting like an idiot. Worse, she was lashing out with meanness. But in the month since she let a stranger pull her into a hotel bathroom, her life had turned upside down, and she was struggling to find her way through this new world and back to her old one. The safe one. The one she recognized.

"That was unfair of me," she said, meaning it. "I'm sorry."

He nodded and found a tired smile for her. "I know you are. Since I've been here, I've seen firsthand how caring you are. And I understand now that you need control. Over the house, over the yard. Over me." His smile disappeared and he looked her in the eye. "But you're also so determined to be independent that you're unwilling to let people into your life."

"That's not true! I let you into my life!"

"Have you? You won't let me have any part in taking

care of the house. As you said the day I wanted to mow the lawn, I'm a guest here."

"But it's not because I don't want you in my life! I haven't wanted you to help because what if you over-exerted yourself and had another heart attack? I can't af-ford for you to leave me a second time!"

Chloe's breath caught in her throat. But she couldn't take the words back. The truth that she hadn't wanted to admit, not to Julia or to Kate and definitely not to her fa-ther, was that she lived with the fear that at any second he might have another heart attack, this time fatal, and they'd never have a chance to truly be father and daughter. They wouldn't have a chance to share their lives. She'd never learn who he really was.

Or why he had left.

Her father stared at her in surprise. "Is that what all of this is about?"

"I'm sorry," she said with a groan. "I'm not trying to make you feel vulnerable. But I worry—and I just thought that maybe before you got involved with someone else, we'd have a chance to get to know each other—that maybe I'd have you just to myself, at least for a little while." She wrinkled her nose at the sheer selfishness of her wish.

"Ah, Chloe," he said. "I don't feel vulnerable. Believe me, I feel fine. I'm eating healthy now. I'm walking every day. You have me for the rest of my life, or until you get tired of me—with or without a girlfriend. But I think this is deeper than you're admitting to me or even to yourself. Like I said, you need control over your life." Her father's voice filled with kindness and wisdom—like a true father's. "But now I realize that you won't let people in because you're afraid."

Her breath snagged.

"You're your mother's daughter," he said with heartfelt

emotion. "And she was your grandmother's daughter before that."

Pressure beat at the back of her eyes. "How does that have anything to do with me being independent?"

" 'Men lie, cheat, and leave.' "

Her mouth dropped open. "Where did you hear that?"

"From your mother, and your mother heard it from her mother. Words handed down like a legacy instead of china or a cherished piece of jewelry. But that legacy is untrue and damaging."

Heat burned her cheeks. "But you did leave her."

"No, I didn't. She pushed me away. Again and again."

She shook her head as if she could shake the words away. "But my mother was killed after *you* left. You know that."

"Technically, that's true. But the only reason I left was because she didn't want me." He closed his eyes, remembering. "Your mother was the most amazing woman I had ever met. I loved her for years. I tried to get her to marry me for as long as I knew her."

The words were as much of a surprise as they were something that fed her soul. Talking. About her parents. Hearing their story.

"Wild, beautiful, enticing Nell. God, she had a line of admirers. She loved men and they loved her. She gave them all up when she met me. She said we didn't need marriage. But after she got pregnant, I was convinced she'd finally say yes. Unfortunately that didn't happen. She became even more determined not to marry. She said that if she married me, I'd only get tired of her and leave. That's when she started to push me away. I hung on for years. I can't tell you the hoops I jumped through trying to convince her otherwise. But she never believed me. Finally I gave up trying."

Chloe's shoulders straightened in surprise—and recognition. Suddenly her mind whirled back; she was young. Her mother, stunningly vibrant, men falling all over themselves to please her. All until that last day when she left the house and never returned. Over the years, first her dad had left, then her mother had. All the leaving, combined with her grandmother's words seemed to have made up who she was.

Did that explain why she really couldn't forgive Sterling? Was she grasping at excuses to push him away to make sure he could never leave her? Had she become her mother after all?

Chloe's throat worked, and she pulled up the courage to ask the question that had plagued her for a lifetime. "If you loved her so much, why didn't you come for me after she died?"

"Oh, Chloe," he said, sighing her name. "I didn't know about the accident for months. My name wasn't on your birth certificate. The state didn't even know to notify me. It wasn't until later, after deciding that enough time had passed that I could try once again with Nell, that I learned she was gone. After that, I tracked down your grandmother to find you. But she said it was best for her to raise you. Hell, I was in my thirties, had a dead-end job. And I was reeling at the loss of your mother. On top of that, what did I know about kids? Nothing. At the time, your staying with Regina seemed like the best thing for everyone."

"Best for everyone, or just best for you?" she persisted.

He rubbed his hand over his face. "Believe it or not, it was best for you. I haven't had a decent job my entire adult life. Look at me. I'm closing in on sixty, but I have to live with my daughter because I can't afford a house of my own."

"You mean you'd leave if you could?"

"Not unless you want me to. It turns out the best thing

that ever happened to me was having that damned attack. It brought me back to you. Look at the wonderful woman you've grown up to be. I'm proud of you."

The words were like another gift.

"You're a generous, loving woman," he continued. "But you have to learn how to let people in. I'm older now—not wiser, granted—but I've been around enough to see that people do stupid things with the best intent."

"What do you mean?"

"Your grandmother loved you, I'm sure of it. And you have a much better life for having grown up with her instead of me, that's the truth. But Regina was overprotective. She didn't want your mother to get hurt, so she made sure Nell wasn't going to be taken in by some smooth talkin' man who would use her, then break her heart. 'Men lie, cheat, and leave.' It was Regina's mantra. I'm guessing that Regina told you the same thing, filled your head with the same fears. She didn't want you hurt, so she thought she could protect you from men who could hurt you. But Chloe, not all men are out to do you harm. Some men really can love. Regina never understood that. And while I believe she had the best intentions, she went about it the wrong way." His brow furrowed. "Hell, we all do stupid things. Like me not reaching out to you until I had a heart attack. But sometimes it takes something big to make us see the light. I got the hospital to call you because I was too damned afraid to call myself. And then once I was here, I didn't know what the hell to do, who to be. Your father? A friend? As I said, you have your life in perfect order. It was clear as soon as I got here that you didn't need me."

"But I do need you," she said, the words barely audible. "I still need you to be my dad."

"Then let me be. Let me tell you that life isn't as simple as men lie, cheat, and leave. Sometimes women won't let men into their lives. And sometimes grandmothers say the wrong things in hopes of keeping loved ones safe. But you are safe, Chloe. Physically, mentally, even monetarily, compared to most people. But no matter how hard you try to protect your heart, sometimes you just have to take a chance that maybe you won't get hurt. Have you ever taken a chance on anything in your life? The fact is, that's what living is about," he said with great passion. "There are no guarantees, just hope and blind faith that things will work out. But when you live like that, that's when you're really alive. Your mother would never take that chance. In order to feel like she was in control, she collected men and broke their hearts, and she rode around on motorcycles without helmets to feel like she was really daring and alive. Maybe she would have married me eventually, but we'll never know. I loved her. I wish every day that things had worked out differently. But they didn't. It's too late for me and your mother. But it's not too late for you and me to get to know each other."

Tears finally spilled over and after a second, she threw her arms around her father. "I'm sorry. I've been horrible."

He set her at arm's length. "You're not horrible, Chloe. You just need to stop working so hard to be sensible and smart, and take a chance for a change."

Sterling slammed out of his office. He strode down the hall and didn't even knock on Julia's door. He hadn't spoken to her since the final show.

"Well, well, if it isn't Mr. Prescott," she said, sitting back in her chair.

He shut the door behind him with a grimace. He'd never been much for apologizing, but for Chloe he'd do what it took. "I'm sorry about the misunderstanding."

"Misunderstanding? You lied to us."

"Let's call it a misunderstanding that spiraled out of control."

"That's easy for you to say. But how are any of us supposed to be able to believe you now? How can I know that you aren't lying about your intent regarding the station?"

"Am I saving it, or not?"

"That remains to be seen."

"How do you figure that?" he asked. "You have a record level of revenue coming in. You'll pay off your debt so you can hold on to the station. What more do you want?"

She stared at him forever, then sighed, seeming to deflate. "Do you really love Chloe?"

His brow furrowed. "Yes, I do."

"Give me your word."

His jaw ticked with frustration. Never before had anyone called him into question. But for Chloe . . . "I give you my word on the Prescott name."

She debated a second longer, then said, "The money we've brought in for *The Catch* isn't enough."

"What are you talking about?"

Julia closed her eyes for a second. "My father left more debt than anyone knows about."

It was all Sterling could do not to curse. He'd never tangled himself in the problems and issues of others. He came in, made the deals, then left. Since the day he ran into Chloe, truly, his life had changed in so many ways.

"What do you want me to do?" he asked, understanding that he had meant his promise to Chloe. He would do whatever it took to save her friends.

"I really don't know. I've been trying to make things work. Kate and Chloe have been with me forever. I can't let them down now." She bit her lip and looked worried. "But suddenly with Kate happy and in love, and if you can work things out with Chloe, then maybe I can finally admit that I'm in over my head."

He nodded. "Get me your books—all your books. I'll help you come up with a solution."

She looked at him. "Thank you," she said, meaning it.

"Thank Chloe."

And they both knew that he had told the truth. Had it not been for Chloe Sinclair, things would have been very different from the moment he walked through KTEX TV's doors.

They stared at each other, then she smiled. "If anyone could capture the big bad Sterling Prescott's heart, I'm not surprised it was our precious Chloe."

"Then call over to your house and tell that housekeeper of yours to let me in. I've got to see Chloe."

"I already called. Chloe left. She went home." Julia wrinkled her nose, considering him. "Go over there. And if she doesn't let you in, she keeps a key hidden by the back door under the big green flowerpot shaped like a frog."

He turned abruptly, but Julia stopped him. "If you are insincere—"

"I'll save your station, Julia."

"I'm not talking about me. I'm talking about my best friend. If I'm wrong about you and you hurt so much as a hair on Chloe's head, I will hunt you down and make you pay regardless of what you do to my station."

He looked at her closely before a smile pulled at his lips. "I have no doubt you'd do it, too. Good. Everyone deserves a friend like you."

Sterling careened down I-10 in the rented Taurus, flew up Country Club Road, and took a few more turns until he scrunched to a halt in Chloe's gravel drive. He marched to the back porch, found the green frog pot, then headed for the door.

Chloe stood in the kitchen, her father and Bitsy standing next to her. All three whirled around in surprise when the door banged open. Sterling was finished trying to do this the calm and reasonable way.

He walked straight up to Chloe. "Whoever said you were sensible and smart was delirious," he stated without preamble, his gaze boring into her. "You're not sensible! And you're not smart if you're going to keep me out of your life because you're afraid. As to your idiotic belief that you're not sexy, you're out of your mind. I'm paying a fortune to keep all your admirers away. If you'd ever go back to the station, you'd see that you've received enough candy, flowers, and proposals for every woman in the entire state of Texas. You're the sexiest woman I've ever met—so sexy you could make a celibate want to sin."

Chloe, Richard, and Bitsy blinked. But Sterling wasn't through with her yet. "I love you, Chloe, and I'm not going away," he added boldly. "It's time you realize that. It's time you stop punishing me, your dad, and every other man out there. Now what do you have to say to that?"

He stood there waiting, suddenly feeling like a schoolboy in a principal's office. Was he expelled or would he be given a second chance? When the heat of the moment faded away, he realized his heart was hammering and he felt exposed.

"I love you," he whispered, his voice a rough whisper. "Is it really so hard to forgive me?"

After a lifetime of going after what he wanted and getting it, he wanted to hear her say she would forgive him.

His heart twisted when she didn't.

"I've tried to go back," she said, her voice trembling.

His jaw ticked against the tightness and fear—yes, fear, he conceded—that he felt in his throat.

"But I can't," she added, her gaze meeting his.

"What do you mean?"

"I want to be smart, I want to be sensible. But it seems like no matter how hard I try, all I can think about is forgiving you." She shrugged guiltily. "I might have made a bigger deal out of the bet thing than it deserved, given that you'd already admitted who you were."

He sucked in a breath and he started to reach for her. She held out her hand to stop him.

"But—"

"No buts, Chloe."

"But that doesn't mean I could live with you."

Richard Maybry grumbled, and Chloe turned a frowning glare on him, which caused the man to implore her with a look before he guided Bitsy out of the kitchen.

"Sterling, I do forgive you, but that won't help us make a life together. You want everything your way. And I couldn't survive in St. Louis apart from my family. Without Kate and Julia. And I'm just getting to know my dad, and heck"—a tremulous smile tugged at her lips—"I've got to at least try to get to know Bitsy."

"Chloe—"

"Let me finish."

He had to force himself to keep his hands at his sides.

"Admit it, Sterling, could you survive without your family? Our families might be different, but mine means just as much to me as yours means to you. Could you live here?"

This was easy, and relief started to build. He was in familiar territory now. This he was prepared for, because no matter what, he was still a businessman who thought of every eventuality when he was executing a plan. And his plan was to do whatever it took to keep Chloe in his life.

"We'll compromise," he offered. "We'll divide our time between St. Louis and Texas. I can run Prescott Media from here part of the time. Besides, I plan to start delegating more. And you could work on special assignment for KTEX. You're a damn good producer."

Her lips parted in surprise. "The station is going to survive?"

"I promised you I would do whatever it took to make things right. Julia and I are going to come up with the solution. I didn't lie to you about that. I'll make that solution be whatever you and Julia want."

"You'd do that for us?"

"I'd do that for you."

"Oh, Sterling—"

He could see that she was excited, nearly afraid to hope. He was outlining a strategy that her smart and sensible head could get around.

"But there's one thing I won't compromise on," he added.

Instantly she grew wary.

Slowly a smile pulled at his mouth. "I have a challenge."

"Great. Don't you think you got into enough trouble with your last challenge?"

"This is a challenge for you."

Her eyes narrowed suspiciously.

"I challenge you to let go of your fears and believe that I will never lie to you again . . . and that I'll never leave you."

The words seemed to cause a tremor to race through her body. She closed her eyes, squeezing them shut as if she could block out demands she didn't know how to handle. But he wouldn't give up. He wouldn't be blocked out.

"Chloe, can you at least try to take a chance—take a chance on me?"

As soon as he said the words, her eyes popped open, a change coming over her like she had tasted bottled lightning. "Take a chance?"

"That's all I'm asking. Just give me a chance to prove that I won't leave you. And that I will never lie to you again."

"Oh, Sterling," she breathed. "That's right. I have to take a chance, some time, in some way."

"What are you saying?" His heart felt like it would burst as he tried to understand.

"I'm saying that I accept your challenge."

Then she was in his arms, holding on as if she'd never let go.

"I'm taking a chance on you, and on me," she whispered.

He lifted her up, burying his face in her neck as he felt the vise on his heart begin to loosen. "Marry me, Chloe," he stated gruffly. "Do me the honor of becoming my wife."

She lifted her face and laughed through the tears that streamed down her face. "Yes, I'll marry you. I want to be your wife." She ran her finger along his face, and for the first time he realized his cheeks were damp, too.

To: Bert Weber <bert@prescottmedia.com>
From: Sterling Prescott <sterling@prescottmedia.com>
Subject: Real estate transaction

Dear Bert:

Please send all documents relating to the purchase of the property at 45 Portland Court in the Central West End for my review.

Sincerely,
Sterling

Sterling Prescott
Chairman and CEO, Prescott Media

To: Kimberly Johnson <kimberly@prescottmedia.com>
From: Sterling Prescott <sterling@prescottmedia.com>
Subject: Money transfer

Dear Kim:

All the paperwork is now in order. Please make the money transfer into the KTEX TV account this afternoon in the amount per the agreement. If there are any questions, you can reach me on my cell phone.

Sincerely,
Sterling

Sterling Prescott
Chairman and CEO, Prescott Media

twenty-one

"**Y**ou're getting married!" Kate and Julia cheered.

"Can you believe it?" Chloe asked, her skin tingling with excitement.

"Of course we believe it!" Julia said. "We should have realized this was inevitable since the day you sat in Danny's Cuppa Joe and told us you nearly had sex with a stranger. You've been heading for the altar ever since without even knowing it!"

Kate sighed dreamily. Julia laughed wickedly.

For the first time in her life, Chloe was beyond happy. She was delirious with joy. She loved the feeling of letting go, loved the feeling she got when she looked at Sterling and allowed herself to believe that they were meant to be together.

It amazed her that just when she thought her life was falling apart, spinning irrevocably out of control, what she found was a new world—a new way of existing. Yes, she was beyond happy. She felt free and truly alive. But in all the excitement and turmoil, she realized there was something she had forgotten to tell Sterling.

Though first, she had to deal with something.

"I can't believe you're selling the station," Chloe said to Julia.

"It's amazing," Kate added.

Julia cringed. "Are you upset?"

"Absolutely not!" Kate promised.

"Of course not!" Chloe said. "But Sterling said he'd lend you the money you need to keep going. I don't want you doing anything you don't have to."

"KTEX will keep going better than ever with Sterling at the helm. But it's time I admit that I don't know the first thing about filling my father's shoes—heck, it turns out my father couldn't fill his own shoes, given the debt he left me in. But I can start fresh. I can sell, wipe the slate clean, and start over."

"Are you sure?"

Julia squeezed each of her friends' hands. "Very sure. I know you and Kate are secure at KTEX—that's all that matters."

"But what about you?"

A twinkle sparkled in Julia's eye. "I have an idea or two. You'll see."

A car pulled up into the driveway and the women peered out through Chloe's front window to see who had arrived. Her father and Bitsy had traveled back to Ruidoso. This time the couple had gone because Richard was helping Julia sell the mountain home. Chloe marveled at how thoroughly her friend was starting over.

Julia sucked in her breath. When Chloe and Kate peered closer, they saw that it was Ben Prescott who had pulled up. His grandmother and sister were with him.

"Great," Julia snapped.

"What?" Kate asked. "Are you still being weird around Ben?"

"I am not being weird around Ben."

Chloe snorted. Kate laughed.

"I'm not! I'm just concerned that Diana is going to cause more problems for you, sugar."

Chloe smiled fondly. "Don't worry about me and Diana."

Without warning, they had a big group hug, and Chloe marveled at the thought that they always had one another. When the phone rang, Chloe was reluctant to end the moment. But she'd been fielding newspaper reporters and television producers all morning. Everyone in the media wanted to get the scoop on the Catch.

Sterling was standing in the kitchen when he heard the phone ring. Amazing how his life had changed. Despite the late October date, he was hot, and he chugged a container of Gatorade. He was surprised when his grandmother, Ben, and Diana pushed through the back door.

"Good Lord," Serena said. "What have you been doing?"

Sterling beamed proudly. "Mowing the lawn."

Ben laughed. Diana stood still as stone in a cold way, but Sterling could tell she was nervous as hell. And rightly so.

"I'd tell you to go bathe," Serena stated, "but there's no time. I've learned what Diana did and I've told her she has no choice but to come here and face the repercussions."

Diana stood there, beautiful and proud. "I'm sorry, Sterling," she said.

He could see that she was. Worry marred her beautiful eyes, and despite the haughty way she held herself, he knew that she regretted what she had done.

It had always been that way with them as kids. Diana lashing out, frustrated, angry, then regretting her outburst afterward. He opened his arms to her.

At first she looked surprised, and why shouldn't she? He couldn't remember the last time he had given his sister a hug. But just as quickly she ran to him despite the fact that he had just spent the last hour dealing with the yard.

"I'm sorry," she whispered into his chest. "It just kind of spiraled out of control on me. One minute I was mad, the next I was on the plane, then after that I couldn't seem to stop myself."

He chuckled grimly. "I know how that goes."

"I didn't mean to ruin things for you. But I'll do whatever you want me to in order to make it right."

He set her away and reached over to a stack on the table. He extended a file.

"What's this?"

"Look inside."

When she did, her eyes went wide like a child's at Christmas. "It's the deed to my condo." Her arms dropped, her fingers clutching the file. "But I thought you were furious."

"I was. But I realized that I was furious at myself. I caused my problems. No one else. And had you not said something to Chloe and all that hadn't come out, who knew when it would have blown up in my face? And it would have blown up. Eventually she would have learned that I had made a bet regarding her. Now I know that. I also know that I can't keep acting like a father doling out allowances. I'm turning your trust fund over to you."

Serena went ramrod straight. Ben leaned back against the wall and raised a brow. "Aren't you full of surprises these days."

Sterling looked at his brother. "And I have another surprise. I realize that our bargain is already off—"

Ben's expression darkened. "But you're still going to badger me about returning to St. Louis anyway."

"No."

"You're not?"

"No. In fact, I don't think you should return to St. Louis."

This time Serena blurted out her shock. "What?"

"I don't want Ben to return, at least not yet." Sterling focused on his little brother. "You have some things to figure out. When you do, and if those answers point to leaving El Paso, then you are welcome at Prescott Media the minute you want a job. But I've seen how you love this city. I've seen how you are meant to be a cop. And I'm not going to be the person responsible for taking that away from you."

Their grandmother gave a sharp moan of distress.

Sterling didn't falter. "I'm here if you need help, Ben. In any way. We're all here if you need anything."

Sterling looked at Serena, imploring her with his eyes. A second passed before she sighed, her expression softening as she turned to her younger grandson. "Yes, we are all here if you need anything."

Ben straightened. "I hardly know what to say."

Sterling shook his head and smiled wryly. "We both know that you were never going to do anything other than what you wanted to do anyway."

A grin pulled at Ben's mouth. "True, but it's nice not to have you on my back." Then he grew serious. "Thank you."

"No, we all have someone else to thank."

They became aware of Chloe in the other room as she spoke on the phone, her voice raised, giving someone a blast of heated words.

"What do you mean Sterling Prescott was the most arrogant bachelor on reality TV? Of course he was arrogant. He deserves to be arrogant. And women agree. Our ratings with females in the eighteen-to-thirty-four demographic are through the roof. Women love him. They swoon over him. You'd be so lucky to have one fraction of his appeal! Now write that in your newspaper column!"

The phone banged down, and the Prescotts exchanged a glance. Chloe marched in, agitated. "I can't believe some people," she declared. "Maybe we should take out an ad. Maybe we should start a campaign. Or maybe I should just go on TV myself and tell El Paso how great you are and how much I regret not accepting your rose."

"You've been on the phone, talking about me, I take it," Sterling stated with a grin.

She stopped suddenly and looked at him. "Oh great, have I insulted you? You probably don't think you need a woman defending you. Well, let me tell you, Sterling Prescott—"

He cut her off when he laughed and pulled her to him, wrapping her against his chest. This was where he belonged. With this woman who had come into his life and made him start living.

"I'm not insulted." He breathed her in, not caring who was around. "You've given me the greatest gift. I always wondered what it would be like if you ever got it in your head to defend me."

Tilting her to him, he brushed his lips over hers. "Besides," he stated just as arrogantly as always, "all that matters is that in the end you accepted my rose."

The other Prescotts must have disappeared out the door, because when Chloe and Sterling finally broke their kiss they were alone.

Chloe laughed as Sterling backed her up across the floor until she bumped into the V formed by the kitchen counters. He pressed his hands to the tiled top, capturing her.

"You're being very, very bad," she said with a heartwarming and sexy smile.

"No, I'm being very, very good. I've been aching for you." He leaned down and pressed her body to his.

Fire shot through her, a fire and intensity that made her whole as she melted into his hard and hot body. When his hand found bare skin beneath her blouse, she shivered with sensation for one more second before she put her hand to his chest.

"Sterling?"

"Yes?" The word whispered against her ear as his mouth trailed against her skin.

"Stop—you're making me forget what I need to tell you."

"Tell me later."

She mentally shook herself. "No, no. This can't wait."

With great reluctance, he pulled away, though barely. "What is it?" he asked, his hands on her shoulders.

She looked him in the eye and relished all that she felt. "In all the mayhem, I forgot to mention something."

"What's that?" She saw the way his eyes narrowed with concern.

"I love you."

She said the words with a wealth of feeling, and he breathed in sharply when he pulled her back to him. "I know," he whispered raggedly. "God, I know."

But this time there was no arrogance. And as he held her tight, she could feel his deep sense of relief that they had finally found their way home.

*Turn the page for a sneak peek
at the next book in
Linda Francis Lee's Sexy series*

Simply Sexy

On sale November 2004

There were some men a smart girl just knew to steer clear of. Ben Prescott was one of them.

Julia had met him a month ago. He was Chloe's new brother-in-law, and Chloe wasn't lying when she said that Julia and Ben hadn't gotten along since the day they met. Which made Julia wonder about herself since she had knowingly invited the hard-chiseled, narrow-hipped, smooth-talkin' bad boy to stay with her.

Sitting in her father's study attempting to work, Julia was barely aware of the doorbell when it rang. It didn't occur to her to get up and answer. When it rang a second time, she called out.

"Zelda, sugar, can you get the door?"

But the minute the words were out of her mouth, she remembered. Three days ago she'd had to let the last of the Boudreaux staff go. And to make it worse, she'd had to say goodbye to the one person who had held on the longest, remained the truest, had been completely devoted by taking pay cut after pay cut. No one would have believed how much the housekeeper had meant to Julia. But given Philippe Boudreaux's revolving door policy regarding women, girlfriends, and dates since Julia's mother had died nearly two decades ago, Zelda had been like a sweet, wonderful great aunt of constancy.

But now Zelda was gone, yet another of the many changes that had occurred in Julia's life since her father's death.

She refused to think about the dwindling number of relatives she possessed or the fact that her pseudo-family of Kate and Chloe was marrying off faster than she could buy wedding gifts. She pushed away from the broad sprawling desk with its cavernous leg area where she used to curl up and sleep while she waited for her father to come home when she was a child.

Memories—the kind that filled the mind and made the heart twist and eyes burn. She missed her father, every single day. But just as she had said about Ben Prescott, she was no weak daisy either, and she wasn't about to let this setback in her life slow her down—much less ruin her.

Taking a deep breath, she dashed away the threat of tears. She took comfort in the knowledge that after selling KTEX TV, the house in the mountains, her father's assorted antique cars, all of his stocks and bonds, plus most of her jewelry, she'd been able to pay off her father's debt and had enough left over for one, maybe two months worth of bills. As much as she hated the thought, she knew she'd have to sell the house. But every realtor she spoke with told her that putting a house on the market just before the holidays was a sure fire way to announce desperation. And desperation meant lower offers. If she could hold out for a few more months, make it into spring, she was guaranteed a better price.

So she would wait. Which meant she had to find a way to make a living—and that meant she needed to prove she could create and produce content for KTEX.

She strode to the front door, wearing her favorite white wrap around blouse and bright green leopard print jeans. Her heels were high, her toe nails painted hot pink. A reminder of her once pampered rich girl's life. No more $500 pants for her.

Cocking her head, she waited a second as the thought sunk in.

"Nope," she said to herself, "still doesn't bother me."

Which was odd, since she thought she'd miss the money, miss owning the station. Miss her old life. But all she missed was her father.

She had left her long dark hair loose, hanging straight nearly to the small of her back. One day she'd have to cut it. She couldn't wear her hair long forever. But at twenty-seven, she wasn't yet ready to cut away her youth.

The doorbell rang a third time just as she pulled open the front door. Chloe and Sterling stood on the front steps. Sterling's strong jaw ticked with impatience, Chloe halted mid-search as she rummaged in her purse for a key. But it was Ben, as always, who commanded her attention.

He leaned against the red brick half wall that lined the three steps leading to the front door, looking like he didn't have a care in the world. He also seemed about as happy at this turn of events as she was.

His heated gaze slid over her, one dark brow rising in quiet assessment when he got a good look at her pants. As much as the man didn't like her, he looked like he wouldn't mind stripping the Escada leopard jeans off of her and slamming hard and deep.

A tingle of sensation raced through her at the thought. It had been way too long since she'd had sex.

"I thought you forgot we were coming," Chloe said, forcing a smile.

"Heavens no, sugar. Just forgot I no longer had anyone to answer the door," she answered with typical candor.

Sterling appeared a tad uncomfortable about that since he was the one who had bought the station from her. But Julia knew he had given her more than a fair price for KTEX, and had offered her a job to boot. He might be a cutthroat corporate raider, but when it came to Chloe, he turned into a knight in shining armor. Now Julia just needed to prove to everyone and herself that she deserved what had been offered. A job.

"Come in," she said, stepping aside.

Sterling reached down to pick up a thick canvas duffle bag.

"I can do that, Sterling," Ben stated through gritted teeth.

"Damn it, Ben, the doctor said you can't lift anything. That is unless you want to end up back in the hospital."

That shut the grumbler up.

Sterling and Chloe headed inside. Ben pushed away from the low wall and started to follow.

"I'm happy you're here," she said, trying to mean it.

There went that dark brow again, rising, the gesture appearing all the more sinister given the thin scar that slashed the brow in half. More than once since she'd met him, she had wondered how he hadn't lost an eye.

She pulled a beauty queen smile for him as he strode past her, his gait stiff, making her wonder how high up on the thigh he'd been hit. Lost in thoughts of thighs more than wounds, she stood there staring out into the front yard, not moving. She heard him grunt when he got inside, showing just how much of a rugged, unmannered heathen he truly was. She bet he was great in bed.

Damn.

She shook the image from her head and stared to turn away, but a utility truck parked across the street caught her attention. For a second she thought the driver was holding a camera.

"I can imagine how happy you are to see me," Ben said.

His voice was so close that she whirled around. He was right behind her.

"Oh," she squeaked.

She, Julia Boudreaux, tormentor of all deliciously bad men, squeaked. She couldn't believe it. She couldn't believe how Ben Prescott could turn her into someone she was not—a squeaking schoolgirl. And she wasn't, she told herself firmly. She ate men like him for breakfast, then spit them out in time for dinner.

But what really unsettled her was how he looked now that she was standing so close. Beneath the icy exterior was a man who was trying very hard to act like he wasn't hurt. Her heart kind of leaped with unaccustomed worry. Maybe she'd been a little hasty in offering him a place to stay. If he really wasn't okay, she didn't know the first thing about taking care of anyone, much less a man who had been shot.

Worse news, however, was something else she noticed. He smelled like a hot, sexy man. And she should know. She was an expert on hot, sexy men. But this was a specimen that her internal radar warned her against. Letting her guard down around this man spelled nothing but dark storms and turbulent seas. With her father's sudden death, and now her life turned upside down, she was managing, yes, but the last thing she needed was more bad weather.

"Do I make you nervous, cupcake?" he asked.

Cupcake, she mouthed silently with an incredulous shake of her head.

The corner of his mouth crooked up. On any other man it would have passed for a sign of amusement. But Ben Prescott didn't look amused.

Good.

"Nervous? Me?" she asked innocently. She bit her lip and looked at him through lowered lashes. "Not at all. Though I wonder if I make you nervous . . . beefcake."

That wiped the non-humorous grin off his too handsome face.

There, she felt better already. She had regained her footing.

"Shall we go inside?" she asked.

She didn't wait for an answer. She took one last glance across the street, found the utility man out of his truck fast at work with tools and wires, relieving her that it wasn't anything weird after all. Smiling, she swept past Ben like a queen at court. Or at least she tried. He caught her arm, grimaced when she jarred him, though he quickly pulled his features into a hard, implacable mask. God forbid this caveman show an ounce of pain.

"Just so we understand each other," he began, "I have no interest in staying with you, but I'm not going to be responsible for Sterling and Chloe canceling their honeymoon."

"Oh, darn," she pouted prettily. "I'm heartbroken. I thought you were about to rip off that leather jacket to reveal a tuxedo, whip out a bouquet of wild pink roses, and then propose." She stamped her foot. "Damn."

"Funny."

"Do you think?"

For reasons she couldn't imagine, his eyes suddenly sparked with humor. "What I think is that you're the only woman I know who'd rather have wild pink roses than the standard red."

"I'm anything but standard, beefcake, which you should know by now."

She flipped her hair over her shoulder, then leaned close and whispered, "If you don't want to play Wedding Proposal, maybe you'd rather play Doctor. Remember that little game we played a few weeks back? If you want, I can give you another exam."

She expected him to flinch, maybe even blush. Instead he tipped his head back and laughed. The sound was deep and rich and infectious, and she might have laughed along with him if she hadn't been so miffed that he was the only man she knew who never did anything that she expected.

Swallowing back annoyance, she headed toward the grand living room just beyond the wall of stained glass where Sterling and Chloe waited.

"Where should I put this?" Sterling asked.

"I have a guest room ready. The one down the hall with the door open. Thanks."

Sterling heaved the duffle over his shoulder as if it didn't weigh more than a feather and headed toward the east wing of the house.

Julia turned to Chloe. "I'm so excited about your trip. I can't wait to hear all about it when you get back."

"I'll keep in touch while we're gone."

"No keeping in touch! This is supposed to be just the two of you. Ben and I will be fine."

"Yeah, don't worry about us," Ben stated, though his voice had softened into a gruff kindness for his new sister-in-law. "You and Sterling need the time away."

"I'm not worried about you two—"

Julia and Ben snorted in unison.

"It's the new station manager I'm a little worried about."

"What's wrong with him?" Julia instantly wanted to know.

"Nothing, I'm sure. Sterling knows him, and thinks the world of him. But, well, KTEX has been my baby for so long . . ."

"And it's hard to let go," Julia finished for her. "Not to

worry, we both love KTEX. Between Kate and me, we'll keep an eye on him. You need to worry about making new babies."

Chloe flashed red. "Julia!"

"Oh, don't go all prude-girl on me, Miss I-better-seduce-Sterling-so-he'll-lose-interest-in-me."

The embarrassment on Chloe's face brightened even more. Ben actually chuckled.

"I've heard some pretty flimsy excuses in my day, but that one takes the cake." Julia laughed. "First Kate, going all sexy on us, then you. Thank God I don't have to turn into the complete opposite of who I am. I'm already sexy, sugar."

"Julia!"

Ben snorted again.

Julia smiled and winked.

Sterling reappeared. "Julia, I appreciate you doing this. I know my brother won't be any trouble."

"I'm standing right here," Ben stated from where he leaned one shoulder against the wall.

He was doing a lot of leaning, Julia noticed, looking ultra cool, like a living James Dean. And not the sausage guy.

"I know you're there, Ben, and I know you'll be the perfect gentleman."

This time it was Ben's strong jaw that ticked. Though when he spoke he plastered a smile on his face. "Me, cause problems for the lovely Julia?"

Sterling sighed. "Maybe we shouldn't—"

Julia leaped over to Ben and hooked her arm through his with exaggerated enthusiasm. "Look at us," she chimed.

Ben managed a grimace that passed for agreement.

"Like two peas in a pod," she drawled, "as happy as can be." Julia smiled at him like she'd found the Holy Grail.

"All right, all right," the older Prescott grumbled. "We're going. But I expect you to keep your promise, Ben."

The younger Prescott scowled.

"Just stay here until the end of the month," Sterling persisted. "Your apartment won't be ready until the first, and this way I don't have to worry about you."

Ben's jaw cemented. "I'm not your kid brother anymore, Sterling."

Sterling actually smiled at that. "Sure you are. You'll always be my kid brother. Consider this a wedding gift for Chloe and me."

"I already gave you china," he grumbled.

His smile widened. "I'd rather have your word."

"Hell."

Sterling took that for agreement, and he reached out and shook Ben's hand. "Thanks," Julia heard Sterling say softly.

Julia and Chloe hugged.

"Are you sure this is okay?" Chloe whispered.

"Absolutely. Don't you worry about a thing. Ben and I are going to be fine. Great. Better than great."

She hoped.

Chloe rolled her eyes, then added with a squeeze, "I love you."

"I love you, too. Now get out of here and go have an umbrella drink for me."

The door closed, leaving behind a startled silence. Ben and Julia stared at the suddenly empty entry hall.

"Well," Julia said.

"Yep," Ben added. Then he nodded. "I'll go and . . . unpack."

He really didn't seem like the go-to-his-room-and-unpack sort of guy. But the less time they spent around each other, the better.

"Great, I'll go to the kitchen and . . . do something."

She turned and headed away. She could feel his eyes on her back, the cool assessment. But she wasn't about to be intimidated. She walked away with the provocative swish of a Playboy bunny, certain she was turning his manly control to putty.

All she got for her efforts was deep rumble of laughter that didn't stop ringing in her ears, even after she had disappeared into the west wing of the house.

Determined to concentrate on work, Julia poured herself a Coke, then returned to her new office. Her goal was to have a television show of some sort developed by the time Chloe and Sterling returned in a month.

She was proud of the way she'd handled the sale of KTEX and paying off her father's debts. She had done it, and done it well. She could create a show, too. Surely.

A shiver of concern raced down her spine. What kind of new, fresh, interesting show could she create? It seemed like everything was done to death. The more she tried to think of something new, fresh, and different, her brain locked down a little more. By the time she finished her soda, she had gotten no farther along than scribbling a bunch of doodles on her note pad. She felt bored, antsy, and dying to get out of there.

She thought of a million things that needed to be done around the house. She even gave a thought to doing some laundry. But procrastination didn't accomplish anything.

Though surely she should check on Ben, she reasoned. That was it! What kind of a hostess was she if she didn't check on her guest? A wounded guest at that.

She bolted out of the study with its book-lined walls and Oriental rugs. She fled the west wing, leaving behind a living room, dining room, kitchen, utility area, and three-car garage, before she came into the high-ceiling entryway of marble and glass. A wall of stained glass separated the entry from the largest room in the house. Most of the time it was set up as another living room. But the furniture could be moved out, the carpets rolled up revealing a glistening hardwood floor, and suddenly they had a ballroom.

The house was U-shaped, the foyer and ballroom forming the base of the U. On the other side of the entrance stood the long hall that lead back to the many bedrooms and an informal den. Heading down the carpeted hall, she found the guestroom she had intended for Ben to use empty. Instead, Sterling had put his brother in the room that connected to hers. The set up had been intended as a mini-suite of sorts, two connected rooms that shared a bath. Definitely not the place she wanted Ben Prescott. But clearly Sterling wanted her to be close by the patient.

She felt a poignant tug that two brothers could have such a caring bond.

But the thought had barely flitted through her head when she tripped to a halt just outside the guestroom doorway. She could see Ben standing next to the bed, using an ironclad control to get his jacket off, then his shirt. The sight of his bare chest made her breath snag in her throat.

He was beautiful, like a statue, finely carved of smooth, bronzed skin over muscle. His shoulders were wide, his waist trim and washboard hard. Even after a week in the hospital, he was still amazing.

Gingerly, he lowered himself to sit on the edge of the bed as he tried to work off his pants. The grimace of pain brought her out of her reverie. Guilt pushed at sexual awareness.

Without a word or a knock, she opened the door wide like a grand dame entering stage right. "Why didn't you tell me you needed help?"

He jerked his head up. "Because I don't need any," he bit out. What little niceness he had shown earlier was gone completely. "Just get out."

"That tone might send some weak-spined individuals running for the hills, but you forget who you're talking to."

He actually groaned at this and hung his head. She had seen his brother do that a time or two when Chloe had done something particularly annoying.

"That's right. I'm Julia Boudreaux, a woman used to getting what she wants."

She went for his belt buckle.

He grabbed her hand.

The strength was solid, but surprising gentle considering he clearly didn't want her touching him.

"You're good at that, aren't you, cupcake?"

If he meant to embarrass her, he had the wrong girl.

"As a matter of fact, I am. And I will refrain from calling you beefcake again since it makes me cringe to think the word, much less say it. Now get your hands out of the way. You don't have anything I haven't seen before."

Though that wasn't altogether true since she really had felt an astounding . . . piece of steel . . . in his 501s the day she had done her best to shock him when she pretended to play Doctor. But she wasn't about to tell him that. She could just see the strut of arrogance that would cause.

His eyes narrowed and she was almost certain he growled.

"I can do it," he repeated.

"Sure, sure." She ignored him. "Let's start with your boots. We'll work up to the belt."

After a second, it was like he didn't have the energy left to fight and he fell back on the mattress, his boots still planted on the floor. She grabbed first one, tugged, ughed, then finally had to turn around and straddle his leg in order to remove it.

"Success!" she whelped, lurching forward in her stilettos when the boot came loose.

When she finally had both boots lined up against the wall, she was almost certain his face had broken out in a sweat.

Hmmm. Yet another bad sign. Nurse really didn't figure into her skill set.

"Let me get your jeans off."

"I can do the rest."

"Are you insane?"

He muttered. "I'll sleep in my pants."

She stepped back and smiled at him. "Isn't that sweet. Our hunky bad boy is shy."

"I'll show you shy."

It happened so fast that she barely had time to register what he was doing. By the time she had, she was lying flat on her back, Ben on top of her. She barely registered his grimace of pain for the feel of him pressed against her.

"Oh," she managed over the rapid beat of her heart.

She couldn't begin to explain what this man did to her. His body had an unerring ability to undo her.

He, on the other hand, was an entirely different story.

But right that second she wasn't thinking about personalities. She felt the hard press against her thigh and desire slid through her, making a very convincing case that there were times when personalities could or should be ignored. Just looking at Ben Prescott, she'd bet the house he could make her purr like a kitten. And maybe, she reasoned, having a tiny little taste of what he had to offer wouldn't be so bad . . .

In the game of love, being shy gets you nowhere. . .

Suddenly Sexy
The prequel to *Sinfully Sexy*
by Linda Francis Lee

Kate Bloom's ordered world is turned upside down when notorious bad boy and superstar athlete Jesse Chapman comes home. Seeing him again reminds Kate of all the reasons she harbored a Texas-sized crush on him back when they were kids. But she isn't a little girl anymore . . . and she's ready to show this hell-raising playboy just how sexy she can be.

After a reporter starts digging into his past, Jesse Chapman returns home looking for space. The last thing he needs is a distraction, but that's just what he gets when he sees his little Katie. Suddenly the girl next door is hot and sexy—and more than even this legendary ladies' man can handle.

Published by Ivy Books
Available wherever books are sold